主审 刘克东

北美文学史及经典作品选读
The History of Northern American Literature and Selected Classical Readings

主　编　蒙雪梅　张　扬
副主编　王　洋　王艳薇
　　　　张旭晶
参　编　杨宇慧　王　眺
　　　　许丽莹　李曼丽

哈尔滨工业大学出版社
HARBIN INSTITUTE OF TECHNOLOGY PRESS

内容简介

本书将"历史背景,文学史"和"文选"相结合,全书共分为 8 章,美国文学部分按照文学史的先后顺序分成 7 个不同的时期,加拿大文学一章。书中简明介绍了美加文学从起源到 20 世纪的历史文化背景、文学史特点,选择代表作家和经典作品。每章包括作家生平简介、作品介绍、注释、名词解释、思考题等。本书线索清晰,希望为学生搭建美加文学框架,引导学生阅读原著,感受美加文学的人文精神和丰富的思想内涵,帮助学生开扩国际视野。

本书既可作为我国高等院校使用的课程教材,也可供广大北美文学爱好者阅读。

图书在版编目(CIP)数据

北美文学史及经典作品选读. 英文/蒙雪梅,张扬主编. —哈尔滨:
哈尔滨工业大学出版社,2018.8
ISBN 978-7-5603-7542-7

Ⅰ.①北… Ⅱ.①蒙… ②张… Ⅲ.①英语-阅读教学-高等学校-教材 ②文学史-美国 ③文学史-加拿大 Ⅳ.①H319.37

中国版本图书馆 CIP 数据核字(2018)第 173985 号

策划编辑	常 雨	
责任编辑	李长波	
出版发行	哈尔滨工业大学出版社	
社 址	哈尔滨市南岗区复华四道街 10 号 邮编 150006	
传 真	0451-86414749	
网 址	http://hitpress.hit.edu.cn	
印 刷	哈尔滨市工大节能印刷厂	
开 本	787mm×960mm 1/16 印张 18.75 字数 384 千字	
版 次	2018 年 8 月第 1 版 2018 年 8 月第 1 次印刷	
书 号	ISBN 978-7-5603-7542-7	
定 价	38.00 元	

(如因印装质量问题影响阅读,我社负责调换)

前　言

近年来，我国学者对美国、加拿大文学（美加文学）的介绍和研究日益重视，根据 21 世纪大学英语发展要求，为适应不同层次学生的发展需求，哈尔滨工业大学开设了大学英语课程——"北美文学选读"。文学是对时代生活的审美表现，能够培养文学阅读、理解与鉴赏能力以及口头与书面表达等语言能力。加强对文学本质的意识，能够提高学生综合人文素质，增强对西方文学及文化的理解，适应新世纪人才培养的需要。

随着各大院校对英美文学的重视，学生和读者对出版的教材——《英美文学史与选读》提出了更高的要求和有益的建议。因此，我们推出了修订版。修订版既保留了原教材的优点，同时适当地修补了部分文学史、作品赏析和课后习题的内容。

本书共包括 8 章：各章按照文学史的时间顺序化分时期，简明地介绍各时期的历史背景和文学史特点，精选了每个时期的主要作家，并介绍作家在文学史中的地位、人生经历、创作经历和代表作品。入选作品着重其经典性，力求深入浅出、通俗易懂，为学生跨进美加文学殿堂提供快捷的通道，使其在较短的时间内了解美加文学的精华。阅读优秀的美加文学作品，可以感受到英语音乐性的语调和五光十色的语汇，回味其"弦外之音"。文学作品是对人生体验的文化表征。阅读文学作品，是了解西方文化的一条重要途径，可以接触到支撑表层文化的深层文化，即西方文化中根本性的思想观点、价值评判、西方社会经常使用的视角，以及对这些视角的批评。

本书是一本集历史、文本于一体的文学选读教材，为学生搭建了文学学习的框架。希望在培养学生欣赏美加文学的同时，让其领略美加文学的魅力，把握文化的精髓和人文精神的脉动，提高学生的英语认知水平和人文素养。

书中疏漏与不足之处恳请读者批评与指正，以便进一步修订与完善。

编　者
2018 年 5 月

Contents

Chapter 1	American Indian Lengend Literature	1
Chapter 2	The Literature of the Colonial and Puritan America	3
Unit 1	Anne Bradstreet	7
	To My Dear and Loving Husband	8
Unit 2	Philip Morin Freneau	8
	The Wild Honeysuckle	10
Chapter 3	The Literature of Reason and Revolution	11
Unit 1	Yankee Doodle	12
Unit 2	Benjamin Franklin	14
	The Autobiography	16
Unit 3	Katharine Lee Bates	23
	America the Beautiful	24
Chapter 4	American Romanticism and Transcendentalism	25
Unit 1	Washington Irving	29
	Rip Van Winkle	30
Unit 2	Ralph Waldo Emerson	36
	Nature	37
Unit 3	Henry David Thoreau	39
	Walden	40
Unit 4	Nathaniel Hawthorne	46
	The Scarlet Letter	48
Unit 5	Henry Wadsworth Longfellow	57
	A Psalm of Life	58
	The Tide Rises, the Tide Falls	60
	My Lost Youth	61
Unit 6	Walt Whitman	64
	Song of Myself	65
	City of Orgies	66
	O Captain! My Captain!	67
Unit 7	Emily Dickinson	69

		There Is Another Sky 70
		I'm Nobody! 71
Chapter 5	**American Realism and Naturalism** 72	
	Unit 1	Mark Twain 77
		The Million Pound Bank Note 79
	Unit 2	Henry James 102
		Daisy Miller 104
	Unit 3	O. Henry 116
		After Twenty Years 117
Chapter 6	**American Modernism Literature** 122	
	Unit 1	Robert Frost 128
		The Road Not Taken 129
		Stopping by Woods on a Snowy Evening 131
	Unit 2	Carl Sandburg 132
		Chicago 134
		Fog 136
	Unit 3	William Carlos Williams 136
		The Red Wheelbarrow 138
	Unit 4	Ezra Pound 138
		In a Station of the Metro 139
	Unit 5	Hart Crane 140
		To Brooklyn Bridge 141
	Unit 6	Edward Estlin Cummings 143
		L(a 144
	Unit 7	F. Scott Fitzgerald 145
		The Great Gatsby 147
	Unit 8	William Faulkner 162
		The Sound and the Fury 164
	Unit 9	Ernest Hemingway 166
		A Day's Wait 167
	Unit 10	Eugene O'Neill 172
		The Hairy Ape 173
Chapter 7	**American Literature Post-World War II** 184	
	Unit 1	John Cheever 191
		The Enormous Radio 192
	Unit 2	Arthur Miller 203
		Death of a Salesman 205

Unit 3	Robert Traill Spence Lowell	212
	Memories of West Street and Lepke	214
Unit 4	Jerome David Salinger	216
	The Catcher in the Rye	218
Unit 5	Kurt Vonnegut	227
	Slaughterhouse-Five	229
Unit 6	Joseph Heller	242
	Catch-22	244
Unit 7	John Ashbery	254
	Self-Portrait in a Convex Mirror	256
Unit 8	Bob Dylan	259
	Blowing in the Wind	261
Unit 9	John Denver	262
	Take Me Home, Country Road	262
Chapter 8	**Canadian Literature**	264
Unit 1	Red River Valley	267
Unit 2	Margaret Laurence	268
	The Loons	270
Unit 3	Alice Munro	284
	Runaway	285
References		290

Chapter 1

American Indian Lengend Literature

I. Historical Background

During the most recent of the Ice Ages, lasting from 30,000 to 10,000 years ago, an undersea ridge between Siberia and Alaska emerged from the sea, known as the Bering Land Bridge. When the melting ice submerged the bridge, about 10,000 years ago, the northeast Asians became isolated as the aboriginal Americans. They spread gradually eastwards along the edge of the Arctic Circle, eventually reaching Greenland. These hardiest of all human settlers survive today as the Eskimo.

1. The First American Farmers

The earliest civilization in America developed in the coastal regions of the Gulf of Mexico during 5000 – 2500 BC. Archaeology provides evidence of these various cultures, but the only ones known about in any great detail were those surviving when the Spaniards arrived—to marvel and destroy. These were the very ancient Maya, and the relatively upstart dominant cultures of the time, the Aztecs and the Incas.

2. Columbian Discovery

The arrival of Columbus in 1492 was a disaster for the original inhabitants of the American continent. Historians describe the previous American cultures as pre-Columbian culture. And the original people of the continent become known as Indians, simply because Columbus is under the illusion that he has reached the Indies.

II. Literary Background

The earliest works of Indian literature were orally transmitted. The Indians created their own oral literature in their struggle with the nature, mainly including folktales, songs, sacred stories, and narrative accounts of gods and heroes. In Native American cultures, poems, "songs" called by more people, were significant in transmission of tribal history, standards of ethical conduct, and religious beliefs. Their literature was collected and published in English and inspired the imagination of later writers.

The early Native American literary legend linked the native people with plants and animals, rivers and rocks, and all things believed significant in local life, which nurtured and explored a spiritual kinship between nature and the native people. Coyote, raven, fox, hawk, turtle, rabbit and other animal characters in the stories are considered to be their relatives. In the same way, oak, maple, pine, cedar, fir, corn, squash, berries and roots were viewed as relatives, too. The Animal People and Plant People participated in the building of a history before and after the arrival of humans.

Registering historic and geographical features of native societies include informal accounts of personal events and formally recited epics, which depict the creation of the world and other living things. Native American Indians' origin epics are the most distinctive, including *Earth Diver*, *Father Sky with Mother Earth*, *Emergence from an Underworld*, *Spider Weaving the World*, *Tricksters*, *Twins*, and *Dismemberment of a Giant*. In addition, repetition added an aesthetic value and a dramatic effect to the tale for it could help the listener to foretell what could happen to the hero.

Selected Reading

Love song[①]

I cannot bear it, I cannot bear it at all.
I cannot bear to be where I usually am.
She is yonder, she moves near me, she is dancing.
I cannot bear it
If I may not smell her breath, the fragrance of her.

Song of War

(Blackfeet)[②]
Old man on high[Sun]
Help me,
That I may be saved from my dream!
Give me a good day!
I prey you, pity me!

Spring Song

As me eyes search the prairie
I feel the summer in the spring

---

① Love song:选自居住在北美阿拉斯加的阿留申人的诗歌
② Blackfeet:黑脚族,历史上的印第安黑脚族以捕猎野牛为生,生活在现今美国蒙大拿以及加拿大阿尔伯塔。黑脚族视太阳为生命之神,是他们祈祷的对象。诗歌中对"怜悯"的祈求表达了对太阳的敬畏和依靠。诗歌中勇士因梦到即将到来的战斗而焦虑,因而祈求神灵的帮助

Chapter 2

The Literature of the Colonial and Puritan America

I. Historical Background

1. The Mayflower Voyage

In 1620, the famous "May Flower" left Plymouth and shipped 102 Puritans to Plymouth to seek fortune, to seek a paradise of their own. On 19 November, the Mayflower spotted land. Bradford signed the Mayflower Compact, which made rules on how they would live and treat each other.

Mayflower

Jon & Vangelis

The Sea like The Sea
The Wind like The Wind
The Stars in the Sky

In the wind—on the ship—a lullaby
We sailing pass the moment of time
We sailing' round the point
The kindly light The kindly light

We go sailing thru' the waters of the summers end
Long ago, search for land
Looking to and fro

> We searching in the day
> We searching in the night
> We looking everywhere for land a helping hand
> For there is hope if truth be there
> How much more will we share
> We pilgrims of the sea
> Looking for a home—
>
> Stars in The Sky
> Shining so bright
> Looking for light
> On this Earth
> On this Earth

2. The original 13 Colonies

The Thirteen Colonies were a group of British colonies on the east coast of North America founded in the 17th and 18th centuries that declared independence in 1776 and formed the United States of America. The non-separatist Puritans constituted a much larger group than the Pilgrims, and they established the Massachusetts Bay Colony in 1629 with 400 settlers.

3. American Puritanism

American Puritans regarded the reformation of the church under Elizabeth as incomplete, and called for further purification and simplicity to church services and the authority of the Bible. They regarded themselves as chosen people of God, who embraced hardships, industry and frugality. American Puritans not only favored a disciplined, hard, somber, ascetic and harsh life and also opposed arts and pleasure who suspected joy and laughter as symptoms of sin. American Puritanism just refers to the spirit and ideal of puritans who settled in the North American continent in the early part of the 17th century because of religious persecutions.

They came to the new continent with the dream that they would build the new land to an Eden on earth. They accepted the doctrine of predestination, original sin and total depravity, and limited atonement through a special infusion of grace from God. With time passing, it became a dominant factor in American life, shaping influences in American thought and American Literature.

Actually it is a code of values, a philosophy of life and a point of view in American

Chapter 2 The Literature of the Colonial and Puritan America

minds, also a two-faceted tradition of religious idealism and level-headed common sense. But in the grim struggle for survival after their arrival in America, they became more and more practical.

II. Literary Background

American literature is the written or literary works produced in the area of the United States and its preceding colonies. Before the founding of the United States, the British colonies on the eastern coast of the present-day United States were heavily influenced by English literature. However, unique American characteristics and the breadth of its production usually now cause it to be considered a separate path and tradition.

1. Beginning of American Literature

While the New England colonies have often been regarded as the centerpiece of early American literature, the first North American settlements had been founded elsewhere many years earlier. Many towns are older than Boston, such as Saint Augustine, Jamestown, Santa Fe, Albany, and New York.

English was not the only language in which early North American texts were written. The large initial immigration to Boston in the 1630s, the high articulation of Puritan cultural ideals, and the early establishment of a college and a printing press in Cambridge all gave New England a substantial edge. One such event is the conquering of New Amsterdam by the English in 1664, which was renamed New York. The first item printed in Pennsylvania was in German, and was the largest book printed in any of the colonies before the American Revolution.

The printing press was active in many areas, from Cambridge and Boston to New York, Philadelphia, and Annapolis. From 1696 to 1700, only about 250 separate items were issued in all these places combined. However, printing was established in the American colonies before it was allowed in most of England. In England restrictive laws had long confined printing to four locations: London, York, Oxford, and Cambridge. Because of this, the colonies ventured into the modern world earlier than their provincial English counterparts.

2. Colonial literature

Some of the earliest forms of American literature were pamphlets and writings extolling the benefits of the colonies to both a European and colonist audience. Captain John Smith could be considered the first American author with his works: *A True Relation of Virginia* (1608) and *The General Historie of Virginia, New England*, and *the*

Summer Isles (1624).

His reports of exploration were strongly shaped by a New World consciousness. In Jamestown, the first colony, he emerged as the leader, traded with Indians. His description of the new world stimulated colonial investment and lured settlers to the new world, among them the puritans who used his maps and surveys in seeking a New Jerusalem in America he had named "New England." He was once captured by Indians. His tale of capture and salvation has become one of the most potent of all American myths. He is the chief source of what we know about the Virginia Indians before they were conquered and all but destroyed by the White.

The religious disputes that prompted settlement in America were also topics of early writing. A journal written by John Winthrop discussed the religious foundations of the Massachusetts Bay Colony. Edward Winslow also recorded a diary of the first years after the Mayflower's arrival. Other religiously influenced writers included Increase Mather and William Bradford, author of the journal published as *a History of Plymouth Plantation*, 1620 – 47.

One of the most significant poets from this period was Anne Bradstreet (1612 – 1672). Her poems in *Tenth Muse Lately Sprung Up in America* (1650) reflected the con concerns of women who came to settle in the colonies, and in all her poems, however, she shows her strong belief in God. Some poetry also existed. Michael Wigglesworth wrote a best-selling poem, "The Day of Doom", describing the time of judgment. Nicholas Noyes was also known for his doggerel verse.

3. Characteristics of Colonial Literature

By far the most common form is the writing related to Biblical teachings, or sermons, that the church leaders wrote—the Puritan idealism and the literature served either God or colonial expansion or both.

Basis of American literature is the dream of building an Eden of Garden on earth. Early American literature was mainly optimistic because they believed that God sent them to the new continent to fulfill the sacred task so they would overcome all the difficulties they met at last. Another important form of writing from this period is the histories. These books, like Bradford's *History of Plymouth Plantation*, tell about the Puritans life.

People also wrote many poems, which were hidden and lost because people often considered poetry to be an inferior form of writing and not totally acceptable to Puritan thinking. The influence of Puritanism on American literature roughly are the spirit of optimism bustles out the pages of many writers, and symbolism as a technique has become a common practice in the writing of many American writers; simplicity had left an incredible imprint on American Writing.

Lots of American writers liked to employ symbolism in their works, typical way of Puritans who thought that all the simple objects existing in the world connoted deep meaning. Symbolism means using symbols in literary works. The symbol means something represents or stands for abstract deep meaning.

Style: simple, fresh and direct, tight and logic structure, precise and compact expression, avoidance of rhetorical decoration, adoption of homely imagery, simplicity of diction. The rhetoric is plain and honest.

Purpose: early American literature tends to be pragmatic and highly theoretical.

Form: diary, autobiography, sermon, letter.

Characteristics of works in colonial period Puritanism is to shape American life and literature as well as minds of Americans. The works is utilitarian, polemical, or didactic. In content, the literature of the colonial settlement served either God or colonial expansion both: their religions subject and imitation of English literature.

Unit 1 Anne Bradstreet (1612 – 1672)

Anne Bradstreet was the most prominent of early English poets of North America and first writer in England's North American colonies to be published. She was the first woman to be recognized as an accomplished New World Poet. Her volume of poetry *The Tenth Muse Lately Sprung Up* in America received considerable favorable attention when it was first published in London in 1650. Bradstreet's work has endured, and she is still considered to be one of the most important early American poets.

Brief Introduction

Anne Bradstreet is the first Puritan figure and notable for her large corpus of poetry, as well as personal writings published posthumously. She speaks to her husband, celebrating their unity and saying that there is no man in the world whose wife loves him more. If there was ever a wife more happy with her husband, the poet asks those women to compare themselves to her. She prizes her husband's love more than gold or the riches of the East. Rivers cannot quench her love and no love but his can ever satisfy her. There is no way she can ever repay him for his love. She believes they should love each other so much that when they die, their love will live on. As this poem shows, the style of poetry is passionate and unrestrained, full of human feelings, both the documentary characteristics of the American pioneering era, and there is no lack of rich poetry.

Selected Reading

To My Dear and Loving Husband

If ever two were one, then surely we.
If ever man were loved by wife, then thee;
If ever wife was happy in a man,
Compare with me ye women if you can.
I prize thy love more than whole mines of gold,
Or all the riches that the East doth hold.
My love is such that rivers cannot quench,
Nor ought but love from thee give recompense.
Thy love is such I can no way repay;
The heavens reward thee manifold, I pray.
Then while we live, in love let's so persever,
That when we live no more we may live ever.

Questions for Discussion

Make an Analysis of "To My Dear and Loving Husband".

Unit 2 Philip Morin Freneau (1752 – 1832)

Philip Morin Freneau was an American poet, essayist, and journalist. Remembered as the poet of the American Revolution and the father of American poetry, he was a transitional figure in American literature. He was born in New York and graduated from Princeton University who wrote lots of poems supporting American Revolution and human liberty. He was the most notable representative of dawning American nationalism in literature. His poems presented Romantic spirits but his form and taste were mainly influenced by Classicism. Most famous poems are *The Wild Honey Suckle* and *The Indian Burying Ground*. Freneau's major significance lies in his transitional role between neoclassicism and romanticism. As a brilliant satirist, he revealed his neoclassical bent by training in those poems that defended the Revolution and Jefferson's policy, or satirized the British and the Federalist. Freneau was at his best in his pre-romantic verses, many critics agree that he was romantic in essential spirit.

Freneau's poetry is also characterized by a profound patriotism and love for American rural scene, different from most of the major men of letters of the period who always set their eyes on the urban development. Literary historians and critics generally hold that American national poetry began with Freneau's verse, thus he has been entitled the "Father of American Poetry".

Brief Introduction

The poem was published in his Poems (1786) and was virtually unread in the time when he was living. Freneau expresses his keen awareness of the liveliness and transience of nature, celebrating the beauty of the frail forest flower, thus showing his deep love for nature. The poem was written in six-line iambic tetrameter stanzas rhymed on ababcc pattern, which is said to anticipate the 19th-century romantic use of simple nature imagery. It is considered one of Freneau's finest nature poems. Freneau deals with the themes of loveliness and the transience of life which is called the best American nature poem before Bryant's achievement in this field. The poet discovers the flower in an unfrequented spot and meditates on its beauty. In its retreat no foot shall crush it. Nature arrayed in white, "and sent soft waters murmuring by." It spends its days in repose, sad that Autumn shall destroy it. It was born of "morning suns and evening dews," and when it dies it is the same, thus losing nothing. Even though the poet does not say it, the reader is reminded of the fate of man.

Note: The name honeysuckle comes from the sweet nectar that the flower produces tointoxicate the greedy bee. Its powerful fragrance seduces the human senses as it pervades the air. The perfume of this passionate plant may turn a maiden's head, hence wildhoneysuckle is a symbol of inconstancy in love. 忍冬用产生的甘露迷醉贪婪的蜜蜂,由此而得名(忍冬英文一词是由"蜂蜜"和"吮吸"两词组成)。当它强烈的芬芳在空气中弥漫时,也陶醉了人的感官。充满激情的忍冬所散发的香气令少女却步回首,因此野生忍冬象征着爱情的反复无常。

Selected Reading

The Wild Honeysuckle

It is considered one of the author's finest nature poems.

Fair flower, that dost so comely grow,
Hid in this silent, dull retreat,
    Untouched thy honied blossoms blow,
    Unseen thy little branches greet:
        No roving foot shall crush thee here,
        No busy hand provoke a tear.

By Nature's self in white arrayed,
She bade thee shun the vulgar eye,
And planted here the guardian shade,
And sent soft waters murmuring by;
    Thus quietly thy summer goes,
    Thy days declining to repose.

Smit with those charms, that must decay,
I grieve to see your future doom;
They died—nor were those flowers more gay,
The flowers that did in Eden bloom;
    Unpitying frosts and Autumn's power
    Shall leave no vestige of this flower.

From morning suns and evening dews
At first thy little being came;
If nothing once, you nothing lose,
For when you die you are the same;
    The space between is but an hour,
    The frail duration of flower.

Questions for Discussion

Analyze and discuss the theme, rhyme scheme and some difficult dictions in "The Wild Honey Suckle".

Chapter 3

The Literature of Reason and Revolution

I. Historical Background

American War of Independence began as a war between the Kingdom of Great Britain and thirteen British colonies in North America. It was the culmination of the political American Revolution, whereby many of the colonists rejected the legitimacy of the Parliament of Great Britain to govern them without representation, claiming that this violated the Rights of Englishmen. The Americans responded in 1776 by formally declaring their independence as one new nation—the United States of America—claiming their own sovereignty and rejecting any allegiance to the British monarchy. The American Revolution was a colonial revolt that took place between 1765 and 1783. It was truly the first modern revolution and enjoyed widespread popular support and marked the first time in history that a people fought for their independence in the name of certain universal principles of human rights and civil liberties.

II. Literary Background

The revolutionary period is notable for the political writings of Benjamin Franklin and Thomas Paine. Thomas Jefferson's *United States Declaration of Independence* solidified his status as a key American writer. It was in the late 18th and early 19th centuries that the nation's first novels were published. An early example is William Hill Brown's *The Power of Sympathy* published in 1791. Brown's novel depicts a tragic love story between siblings who fall in love without knowing they are related.

(1) The Age of reason (1794–1796)

In the 18th century, people believed in man's own nature and the power of human reason. With Franklin as its spokesman, the 18th century America experienced an age of reason. During the revolution itself, poems and songs such as "Yankee Doodle" and

"Nathan Hale" were popular. Major satirists included John Trumbull and Francis Hopkinson. Philip Morin Freneau also wrote poems about the war's course.

Among the most renowned was the work *Common Sense* (1776) of Thomas Paine, spread quickly among literate colonists. It convinced many colonists, including George Washington and John Adams, to seek redress in political independence from the Kingdom of Great Britain, and argued strongly against any compromise short of independence. He also wrote *Crisis* and *The Age of Reason*. The pamphlets helped complete the debate that resulted in America's separation from England.

"*Those who expect to reap the blessings of freedom must undergo the fatigue of supporting it*". 想要收获自由之果的人,必须承受维护自由的劳苦。

"*Common sense will tell us, that the power which hath endeavoured to subdue us, is of all others, the most improper to defend us.*" 常识告诉我们,竭力征服我们的力量是最不适合保护我们的力量。

The most important document from this period was a single sheet of paper called *The Declaration of Independence*, mainly written by Thomas Jefferson and Benjamin Franklin. "We hold these truths to be self-evident, that *all men are created equal*, that they are endowed by their Creator with certain unalienable Rights, that among these are *Life, Liberty and the pursuit of Happiness.*" 我等之见解为,下述真理不证自明:凡人生而平等,秉造物者之赐,拥诸无可转让之权利,包含生命权、自由权与追寻幸福之权。

(2) **Early National Literature**

During the period of American Revolution War, American national literature came into being. The war helped the first important American prose writers and poets grow up both culturally and artistically and led to the independence of national literature. American people began to understand the meaning of being a real "American". The Federalist essays by Alexander Hamilton, James Madison, and John Jay presented a significant historical discussion of American government organization and republican values. Much of the early literature of the new nation struggled to find a uniquely American voice in existing literary genre, and was also reflected in novels.

Unit 1   Yankee Doodle

Brief Introduction

"Yankee Doodle" is a well-known American song, the early versions of which date to before the Seven Years' War and the American Revolution. It is often sung patriotically in the United States today and is the state anthem of Connecticut. The melody is thought to be much older than both the lyrics and the subject, going back to folk songs of Medieval Europe.

Traditions place its origin in a pre-Revolutionary War song originally sung by British military officers to mock the disheveled, disorganized colonial "Yankees" with whom they served in the French and Indian War. The British troops sang it to make fun of their stereotype of the American soldier as a Yankee simpleton who thought that he was stylish if he simply stuck a feather in his cap.

It was also popular among the Americans as a song of defiance. As per the American Library of Congress, the Americans added additional verses to the song, mocking the British troops and hailing the Commander of the Continental army George Washington. By 1781, *Yankee Doodle* had turned from being an insult to being a song of national pride.

Selected Reading

Yankee Doodle went to town riding on a pony,
Stuck a feather in his hat and called it macaroni.
Yankee Doodle keep it up, Yankee Doodle dandy!
Mind the music and the step and with the girls be handy.
Father and I went down to camp along with Captain Gooding.
There were all the men and boys as thick as hasty pudding.
Yankee Doodle keep it up, Yankee Koodle dandy!
Mind the music and the step and with the girls be handy.

And there was Captain Washington
Upon a slapping stallion.
Giving orders to his men I guess there were a million.
Yankee Doodle keep it up, Yankee Doodle dandy!
Mind the music and the step and with the girls be handy.
Yankee Doodle give a tune, it comes in mighty handy.
The enemy all runs away at Yankee Doodle dandy!
Yankee Doodle keep it up, Yankee Doodle dandy!
Mind the music and the step and with the girls be handy.

Unit 2　Benjamin Franklin (1706 – 1790)

Appreciation

***Benjamin Franklin's* 13 *Virtues*《本杰明-富兰克林的13项美德》**

1. Temperance 节制: Eat not to dullness and drink not to elevation.

2. Silence 沉默: Speak not but what may benefit others or yourself. Avoid trifling conversation.

3. Order 秩序: Let all your things have their places. Let each part of your business have its time.

4. Resolution 决心: Resolve to perform what you ought. Perform without fail what you resolve.

5. Frugality 节俭: Make no expense but to do good to others or yourself; i. e. Waste nothing.

6. Industry 勤奋: Lose no time. Be always employed in something useful. Cut off all unnecessary actions.

7. Sincerity 诚实: Use no hurtful deceit. Think innocently and justly; and, if you speak, speak accordingly.

8. Justice 正义: Wrong none, by doing injuries or omitting the benefits that are your duty.

9. Moderation 中庸: Avoid extremes. Forebear resenting injuries so much as you think they deserve.

10. Cleanliness 整洁: Tolerate no uncleanness in body, clothes or habitation.

11. Chastity 贞洁: Rarely use venery but for health or offspring; Never to dullness, weakness, or the injury of your own or another's peace or reputation.

12. Tranquility 冷静: Be not disturbed at trifles, or at accidents common or unavoidable.

13. Humility 谦逊: Imitate Jesus and Socrates.

Benjamin Franklin was one of the founding father of the United States of America and the most important American thinkers during the revolutionary period, who stood as the epitome of the Enlightenment and as the versatile embodiment of rational man.

Franklin was a printer, author, diplomat, philosopher, scientist, and a greatest statesman, who did the moat to make the United States a free and independent country. He exemplifies the Age of Enlightenment, whose image is an archetypal American success that has since become part of American popular culture. The Scottish philosopher David Hume called him America's "first great man of letters". Franklin was the embodiment of American dream. His major works: *The Autobiography*, *Poor Richard's Almanac* contains a large number of practical sayings about life. It was a particularly influential book in the early American literature.

Brief Introduction

Autobiography is a branch of literature which is an account of a person's life. The essential difference between a novel and autobiography is this: The novel "uses" real experience as the raw material for fiction by inventing plots and characters.

The autobiography is the simple yet fascinating record of a man rising to wealth and fame from a state of poverty and obscurity into which he was born, the faithful account of the colorful career of American's first self-made man. The style readily reveals that it is the pattern of Puritan simplicity, directness and concision. The American dream and sense of optimism are shown in Franklin's works. The wilderness filled the Puritans with the hope of restoring the Garden of Eden, and looked like the "Promised Land" with which God rewarded His chosen people. Thus for a long time the hope kept floating before the people, keeping them happy and optimistic about the future.

Part One portrays Franklin as a young man in Boston and Philadelphia. Part Two the controversial "art of virtue" section. Franklin recounts his youthful attempt to achieve "moral perfection." Part Three reveals how the adult Franklin uses his principles of conduct in order to perform his roles as a scientist, philanthropist and politician, partially due to his ability to self-promote.

The Autobiography simply presents with a more elegant and formally ordered version of the writer's experiences and memories, which is an embodiment of Puritanism and Enlightening spirits. It establishes in literary form the first example of the fulfillment of the American Dream and was one of the premier autobiographies in the English language and the prominent work that mythologizes a hero of the American Revolution, which tells us today what life was like in 18th century America and also a reflection of 18th century idealism.

Franklin's *Autobiography* has received widespread praise, both for its historical value as a record of an important early American and for its literary style, which is often considered the first American book to be taken seriously by Europeans as literature and towers over other autobiographies as Franklin towered over other men.

Selected Reading

The Autobiography①

TO HIS SON

Twyford②, at the Bishop of St. Asaph's, 1771

Dear Son③, I have ever had a pleasure in obtaining any little anecdotes of my ancestors. You may remember the enquiries I made among the remains of my relations④ when you were with me in England and the journey I undertook for that purpose. Imagining it may be equally agreeable to you to know the circumstances of my Life—many of which you are yet unacquainted with—and expecting a week's uninterrupted Leisure in my present country retirement, I sit down to write them for you. Besides, there are some other inducements that excite me to this undertaking. From the poverty and obscurity in which I was born and in which I passed my earliest years, I have raised myself to a state of affluence⑤ and some degree of celebrity in the world. As constant good fortune has accompanied me even to an advanced period of life, my posterity will perhaps be desirous of learning the means, which I employed, and which, thanks to Providence⑥, so well succeeded with me. They may also deem them fit to be imitated, should any of them find themselves in similar circumstances. That good fortune, when I reflected on it, which is frequently the case, has induced me sometimes to say that were it left to my choice, I should have no objection to go over the same life from its beginning to the end, only asking the advantage authors have of correcting in a second edition some faults of the first. So would I also wish to change some incidents of it for others more favorable.

---

① 选篇节自《自传》的第一部分,其一为该书的开场白,其二描述富兰克林离开哥哥初到费城时的情形。1723 年,17 岁的富兰克林两手空空、独自一人来到费城,这是他逐步走向成功的一个重要转折点

② Twyford: 伦敦西南约 50 英里(1 英里 = 1.609 344 千米)处的一个村落。富兰克林在此写作《自传》的第一部分

③ Dear Son: 指富兰克林的儿子威廉·富兰克林(1731 – 1813),当时任新泽西州州长。但在独立战争中威廉·富兰克林是忠于英国的保皇派

④ the remains of my relations: 仍然健在的亲属。1758 年,富兰克林曾携子访问祖先在英国的故乡

⑤ affluence: 富裕,充足

⑥ Providence: 上帝,神

Notwithstanding, if this condition were denied, I should still accept the offer. But as this repetition is not to be expected, that which resembles most living one's life over again, seems to be to recall all the circumstances of it; and, to render this remembrance more durable, to record them in writing. In thus employing myself I shall yield to the inclination so natural to old men of talking of themselves and their own actions, and I shall indulge it, without being tiresome to those who, from respect to my age, might conceive themselves obliged to listen to me, since they will be always free to read me or not. And lastly (I may as well confess it, as the denial of it would be believed by nobody) I shall perhaps not a little gratify my own vanity. Indeed, I never heard or saw the introductory words, "Without Vanity I may say," etc., but some vain thing immediately followed. Most people dislike vanity in others whatever share they have of it themselves, but I give it fair quarter① wherever I meet with it, being persuaded that it is often productive of good to the possessor and to others who are within his sphere of action. And therefore, in many cases it would not be altogether absurd if a man were to thank God for his vanity among the other comforts of life.

And now I speak of thanking God, I desire with all humility to acknowledge that I owe the mentioned happiness of my past life to his divine providence, which led me to the means I used and gave them success. My belief of this induces me to hope, though I must not presume, that the same goodness will still be exercised towards me in continuing that happiness or in enabling me to bear a fatal reverse, which I may experience as others have done—the complexion of my future fortune being known to him only, and in whose power it is to bless to us even our afflictions.

The Arrival in Philadelphia

[Following the altercation with his older brother to whom Franklin had been apprenticed (and whose oppressive treatment of Franklin, the latter says, gave him "that aversion to arbitrary power that has stuck to me through my whole life"), and after a brush with the law, the seventeen-year-old lad leaves Boston and comes to Philadelphia, the city whose first citizen he would eventually become.]

This might be one occasion of the differences we② began to have about this time. Though a brother, he considered himself as my master and me as his apprentice, and accordingly expected the same services from me as he would from another; while I thought he degraded me too much in some he required of

---

① but I give it fair quarter: 但我却公平地对待它
② we: 指富兰克林和他的哥哥。他当时给哥哥做学徒

me, who from a brother expected more indulgence. Our disputes were often brought before our father, and I fancy I was either generally in the right or else a better pleader, because the judgment was generally in my favor. But my brother was passionate and had often beaten me, which I took extremely a miss. I fancy his harsh and tyrannical treatment of me might be a means of impressing me with that aversion to arbitrary power that has stuck to me through my whole life. Thinking my apprenticeship very tedious, I was continually wishing for some opportunity of shortening it, which at length offered in a manner unexpected.

One of the pieces in our newspaper on some political point which I have now forgotten, gave offence to the Assembly①. He was taken up, censured, and imprisoned for a month by the Speaker's warrant, I suppose because he would not discover the author. I, too, was taken up and examined before the Council; but though I did not give them any satisfaction, they contented themselves with admonishing me and dismissed me, considering me, perhaps, as an apprentice who was bound to keep his master's secrets. During my brother's confinement, which I resented a good deal notwithstanding our private differences, I had the management of the paper, and I made bold to give our rulers some rubs in it, which my brother took very kindly, while others began to consider me in an unfavorable light as a young genius that had a turn for libelling and satire. My brother's discharge was accompanied with an order from the House (a very odd one) that "James Franklin should no longer print the paper called the *New England Courant.*" There was a consultation held in our printing house amongst his friends in this conjuncture. Some proposed to elude the order by changing the name of the paper; but my brother seeing inconveniences in that, it was finally concluded on as a better way to let it be printed for the future under the name of "Benjamin Franklin"; and to avoid the censure of the Assembly that might fall on him as still printing it by his apprentice, the contrivance was that my old indenture② should be returned to me with a full discharge on the back of it, to show in case of necessity; but to secure to him the benefit of my service, I should sign new indentures for the remainder of the term, which were to be kept private. A very flimsy③ scheme it was, but, however, it was immediately executed, and the paper went on accordingly under my name for several months. At length a fresh difference arising between my brother and me, I took upon me to assert my freedom, presuming that he would not venture to produce the new indentures. It was not fair in me to take this advantage, and this I

---

① the Assembly：马萨诸塞州议会的众议院
② indenture：师徒合同,定期服务契约
③ flimsy：不足以使人有信心的,薄弱的

therefore reckon one of the first errata① of my life. But the unfairness of it weighed little with me, when under the impressions of resentment for the blows his passion too often urged him to bestow upon me, though he was otherwise not an ill-natured man. Perhaps I was too saucy and provoking.

When he found I would leave him, he took care to prevent my getting employment in any other printing house of the town by going round and speaking to every master, who accordingly refused to give me work. I then thought of going to New York as the nearest place where there was a printer; and I was the rather inclined to leave Boston when I reflected that I had already made myself a little obnoxious② to the governing party; and from the arbitrary proceedings of the Assembly in my brother's case, it was likely I might if I stayed soon bring myself into scrapes, and further that my indiscreet disputations about religion began to make me pointed at with horror by good people as an infidel or atheist. I determined on the point, but my father now siding with my brother, I was sensible that if I attempted to go openly, means would be used to prevent me. My friend Collins therefore undertook to manage my flight. He agreed with the captain of a New York sloop for my passage, under pretence of my being a young man of his acquaintance that had had an intrigue with a girl of bad character, whose parents would compel me to marry her and therefore I could not appear or come away publicly. I sold some of my books to raise a little money, was taken on board the sloop privately, had a fair wind, and in three days found myself at New York, near three hundred miles from my home, at the age of seventeen, without the least recommendation to or knowledge of any person in the place, and with very little money in my pocket.

The inclination I had had for the sea was by this time done away, or I might now have gratified it. But having another profession and conceiving myself a pretty good workman, I offered my services to the printer of the place, old Mr. Wm. Bradford (who had been the first printer in Pennsylvania, but had removed thence in consequence of a quarrel with the Governor, Geo. Keith). He could give me no employment, having little to do and hands enough already. "But," says he, "my son at Philadelphia has lately lost his principal hand, Aquila Rose, by death. If you go thither I believe he may employ you."

Philadelphia was a hundred miles farther. I set out, however, in a boat for Amboy③, leaving my chest and things to follow me round by sea. In crossing the

---

① errata: erratum 复数形式,指书写或者印刷中的错误。此处,这一专业术语指人生中出现的失误
② obnoxious: 讨厌的,令人厌恶的
③ Amboy: 地名,位于新泽西州

bay we met with a squall that tore our rotten sails to pieces, prevented our getting into the kill, and drove us upon Long Island. In our way a drunken Dutchman, who was a passenger, too, fell overboard; when he was sinking, I reached through the water to his shock pate and drew him up so that we got him in again. His ducking sobered him a title, and he went to sleep, taking first out of his pocket a book which he desired I would dry for him. It proved to be my old favorite author Bunyan's *Pilgrim's Progress*[①] in Dutch, finely printed on good paper with copper cuts, a dress better than I had ever seen it wear in its own language. I have since found that it has been translated into most of the languages of Europe, and suppose it has been more generally read than any other book except, perhaps, the Bible. Honest John was the first that I know of who mixes narration and dialogue, a method of writing very engaging to the reader, who in the most interesting parts finds himself, as it were, admitted into the company and present at the conversation. Defoe has imitated him successfully in his *Robinson Crusoe*, in his *Moll Flanders*[②], and other pieces; and Richardson has done the same in his *Pamela*[③], etc.

On approaching the island, we found it was in a place where there could be no landing, there being a great surf on the stony beach. So we dropped anchor and swung out our cable towards the shore. Some people came down to the water edge and hallooed to us, as we did to them, but the wind was so high and the surf so loud that we could not understand each other. There were some canoes on the shore, and we made signs and called to them to fetch us, but they either did not comprehend us or thought it impracticable so they went off. Night approaching, we had no remedy but to have patience till the wind abated, and in the meantime the boatman and I concluded to sleep if we could, and so we crowded into the scuttle[④] with the Dutchman who was still wet, and the spray breaking over the head of our boat leaked through to us, so that we were soon almost as wet as he. In this manner we lay all night with very little rest; but the wind abating the next day, we made a shift to reach Amboy before night, having been thirty hours on the water without victuals or any drink but a bottle of filthy rum, the water we sailed on being salt.

In the evening I found myself very feverish and went to bed; but having read somewhere that cold water drank plentifully was good for a fever, I

---

① Bunyan's *Pilgrim's Progress*：英国作家约翰班扬(1628－1688)的小说《天路历程》

② *Moll Flanders*：笛福的小说《摩尔·弗兰德斯》

③ Richardson has done the same in his *Pamela*：指英国作家理查逊(Samuel Richardson, 1689－1761)以及他的书信体小说《帕美勒》

④ scuttle：小舱口,舷窗,船底孔洞

followed the prescription, sweat plentifully most of the night, my fever left me, and in the morning crossing the ferry, I proceeded on my journey on foot, having fifty miles to Burlington①, where I was told I should find boats that would carry me the rest of the way to Philadelphia.

It rained very hard all the day, I was thoroughly soaked and by noon a good deal tired, so I stopped at a poor inn, where I stayed all night, beginning now to wish I had never left home. I made so miserable a figure, too, that I found by the questions asked me I was suspected to be some runaway servant, and in danger of being taken up on that suspicion. However, I proceeded the next day, and got in the evening to an inn within eight or ten miles of Burlington, kept by one Dr. Brown②.

He entered into conversation with me while I took some refreshment and, finding I had read a little, became very sociable and friendly. Our acquaintance continued all the rest of his life. He had been, I imagine, an itinerant doctor, for there was no town in England or any country in Europe of which he could not give a very particular account. He had some letters and was ingenious, but he was an infidel and wickedly undertook some years after to travesty the Bible in doggerel verse as Cotton had done with Virgil③. By this means he set many of the facts in a very ridiculous light and might have done mischief with weak minds if his work had been published, but it never was. At his house I lay that night, and the next morning reached Burlington, but had the mortification to find that the regular boats were gone a little before and no other expected to go before Tuesday, this being Saturday. Wherefore④, I returned to an old woman in the town of whom I had bought some gingerbread⑤ to eat on the water and asked her advice; she invited me to lodge at her house till a passage by water should offer; and being tired with my foot travelling, I accepted the invitation. Understanding I was a printer, she would have had me remain in that town and follow my business, being ignorant of the stock necessary to begin with. She was very hospitable, gave me a dinner of ox cheek with great goodwill, accepting only of a pot of ale in return. And I thought myself fixed till Tuesday should

---

① Burlington：费城北面约18英里的一个城市，当时为新泽西州的州政府所在地

② Dr. Brown：（约1667－1737）旅馆的老板，也是当地有名的医生和无神论者

③ to travesty the Bible in doggerel verse as Cotton had done with Virgil：蹩脚地将《圣经》变为打油诗，就如同科顿拙劣地模仿维吉尔的作品那样。Cotton：即Charles Cotton（1630－1687），英国诗人，曾模仿维吉尔的《埃涅伊德》创作了诗作《斯卡龙尼德》。Virgil：古罗马诗人（前70－前19），主要作品为史诗《埃涅伊德》

④ wherefore：因此，所以

⑤ gingerbread：姜饼；华而不实的东西

come. However, walking in the evening by the side of the river, a boat came by, which I found was going towards Philadelphia with several people in her. They took me in, and as there was no wind, we rowed all the way; and about midnight, not having yet seen the city, some of the company were confident we must have passed it and would row no farther; the others knew not where we were, so we put towards the shore, got into a creek, landed near an old fence, with the rails of which we made a fire, the night being cold in October, and there we remained till daylight. Then one of the company knew the place to be Cooper's Creek, a little above Philadelphia, which we saw as soon as we got out of the creek, and arrived there about eight or nine o'clock, on the Sunday morning and landed at the Market Street wharf.

I have been the more particular in this description of my journey, and shall be so of my first entry into that city, that you may in your mind compare such unlikely beginnings with the figure I have since made there. I was in my working dress, my best clothes being to come round by sea. I was dirty from my journey; my pockets were stuffed out with shirts and stockings; I knew no soul, nor where to look for lodging. Fatigued with walking, rowing, and want of sleep, I was very hungry, and my whole stock of cash consisted of a Dutch dollar and about a shilling in copper coin, which I gave to the boatmen for my passage. At first they refused it on account of my having rowed, but I insisted on their taking it. A man is sometimes more generous when he has little money than when he has plenty, perhaps through fear of being thought to have but little. I walked towards the top of the street, gazing about till near Market Street, where I met a boy with bread. I have often made a meal of dry bread, and inquiring where he had bought it, I went immediately to the baker's he directed me to. I asked for biscuit, meaning such as we had in Boston, but that sort, it seems, was not made in Philadelphia. I then asked for a three penny loaf and was told they had none such. Not knowing the different prices nor the names of the different sorts of bread, I told him to give me three pennyworth of any sort. He gave me accordingly three great puffy rolls. I was surprised at the quantity but took it, and having no room in my pockets, walked off with a roll under each arm and eating the other. Thus I went up Market Street as far as Fourth Street, passing by the door of Mr. Read, my future wife's father, when she, standing at the door, saw me, and thought I made—as I certainly did—a most awkward, ridiculous appearance. Then I turned and went down Chestnut Street and part of Walnut Street, eating my roll all the way, and coming round, found myself again at Market Street wharf near the boat I came in, to which I went for a draught of the river water, and being filled with one of my rolls, gave the other two to a woman and her child that came down the river in the boat with us and were waiting to go farther. Thus refreshed, I walked again up the street, which by this time had many clean dressed people in it who were all walking the same way; I joined them, and thereby was led into the great meetinghouse of the Quakers① near the market. I sat down among them, and after looking round awhile and hearing nothing said, being very drowsy through labour and want of rest the preceding night, I fell fast asleep and continued so till the meeting broke up, when someone was kind enough to rouse me. This was therefore the first house I was in or slept in, in Philadelphia.

Questions for Discussion

1. Why did Franklin write his Autobiography?
2. What made Franklin decide to leave the brother to whom he had been apprenticed?
3. How did he arrive in Philadelphia?
4. What features do you find in the style of the above selection?
5. How would you describe Franklin's writing style?
6. What does the Autobiography tell us about the 18th century?

Unit 3 Katharine Lee Bates(1859 – 1929)

Katharine Lee Bates, a professor and a poet, she is remembered as the author of the words to the anthem "America the Beautiful". Bates originally wrote the words as a poem, "Pikes Peak" in 1895. Ward's music combined with the Bates poem was first published in 1910 and titled America the Beautiful. Her poem became the lyrics to the popular American ballad still enjoyed today.

Brief Introduction

"America the Beautiful" is an American patriotic song, which was inspired by the view from the top of Pikes Peak in Colorado. This version features all four verses and choruses, which are not frequently heard or sung, but they are pretty magnificent. In the summer of 1893, poet Katharine Lee Bates was teaching English at Colorado College in Colorado Springs, Colorado. Later she remembered:

---

① the Quakers：(基督教的一个教派)贵格会教徒。该教会由英国人乔治·福克斯(George Fox,1624 – 1690)创立,他主张将"内心之光",即灵感,置于圣经和教条之上,反对烦琐的、程式化的宗教仪式,因此受到宗教当局与政府的双重迫害

"One day some of the other teachers and I decided to go on a trip to 14,000 foot Pikes Peak. We hired a prairie wagon. Near the top we had to leave the wagon and go the rest of the way on mules. I was very tired. But when I saw the view, I felt great joy. All the wonder of America seemed displayed there, with the sea-like expanse." On the pinnacle of the mountain a poem started to come to her, and she wrote the words down upon returning to her hotel room. The song is one of the most popular of the many U.S. patriotic songs.

Selected Reading

America the Beautiful

O beautiful for spacious skies,
For amber waves of grain,
For purple mountain majesties
Above the fruited plain!
America! America!
God shed His grace on thee
And crown thy good with brotherhood
From sea to shining sea!

O beautiful for pilgrim feet,
Whose stern, impassioned stress
A thoroughfare for freedom beat
Across the wilderness!
America! America!
God mend thine every flaw,
Confirm thy soul in self-control,
Thy liberty in law!

O beautiful for heroes proved In liberating strife,
Who more than self their country loved
And mercy more than life!
America! America!
May God thy gold refine,
Till all success be nobleness,
And every gain divine!

O beautiful for patriot dream
That sees beyond the years
Thine alabaster cities gleam
Undimmed by human tears!
America! America!
God shed His grace on thee
And crown thy good with brotherhood
From sea to shining sea!

Terms

1. American Puritanism
2. Symbolism
3. American Dream

Chapter 4

American Romanticism and Transcendentalism

I. Historical Background

The victory of the American Revolution enabled to establish an independent nation, and introduced a new era. From 1789 to 1865, the United States gradually formed its national identity and established its political and legal institutions.

1. Independent Nation

In 1789, George Washington became the first President of the United States of America and united the two opposing political parties and strengthened the newly-established government. In the meantime, the French Revolution broke out, which gave the Americans more confidence to set up an independent, and democratic nation of their own. During Jefferson's presidency, agriculture was encouraged, land settlement was promoted and immigration was made easier, all of which strengthened the nation.

2. The Frontier of the American West

The American frontier comprises the geography, history, folklore, and cultural expression of life in the forward wave of American expansion that began with English colonial settlements in the early 17th century and ended with the admission of the last mainland territories as states in 1912. "Frontier" refers to a contrasting region at the edge of a European-American line of settlement. American historians cover multiple frontiers but the folklore is focused primarily on the conquest and settlement of Native American lands west of the Mississippi River, in what is now the Midwest, Texas, the Great Plains, the Rocky Mountains, the Southwest, and the West Coast. The nation witnessed an incredible expansion——the most influential westward expansion.

3. Louisiana Purchase

The nation witnessed an incredible expansion, among which the most influential one was westward expansion. In 1803, the United States bought a large track of land from France for $15,000,000, which comprised the western part of the Mississippi Valley, and forms the states of Louisiana, Arkansas, Missouri, Iowa and Nebraska and part of eight other states. It is known as the Louisiana Purchase. Subsequently, the Americans swallowed up Texas and then acquired California and New Mexico.

4. Gold Rush

The news of the discovery of gold in California in 1848 spread across America to Europe, and thousands of people joined in the search, which attracted many people to the West Coast, and caused a rapid push westward by pioneers. They pushed the frontier line of settlement by the Mississippi to the Great Plains and finally to the West Coast. The Gold Rush era in California lasted less than a decade. Prospectors had found more than $350 million worth of gold. The conquest of the new territories opened new horizons, but the country was also torn by the risk of internal division, which led to American Civil War.

5. Growth of Industrialization

When the United States began to change into an industrial and urban society, the principle of assembly-line mass production was established, and technology began to bring vast material benefits to the industrialized North. But the South remained agricultural. With an increasing number of farm laborers leaving the land to work in urban businesses and factories, cities grew bigger and bigger.

The United States became a new rising nation with rapid expansion. The economic boom brought with an overwhelming sense of optimism and hope among people. This mood and spirit, together with the traditional American cultural heritage—Puritanism, naturally brought out a romantic feeling. As time went by, this feeling, as a joint outcome of the foreign and domestic factors, developed itself into a national literary movement—Romanticism.

II. Literary Background

American Romanticism which is also called "American Renaissance", stretched from the end of the 18th century to the outbreak of the Civil War, which was crucial to the development of American literary traditions and the 55 years from 1810 to 1865 saw miraculous achievements in American literature.

In the new nation's search for a culturally independent identity, romanticism also helped build the bridge between the past and present, and between America and Europe. Romanticism and sentimentalism, as literary and cultural modes, have

Chapter 4 American Romanticism and Transcendentalism

persisted in American culture. The United States continues to be a Romantic culture whose fundamental values and symbols were shaped in the first half of the 19th century.

The Sketch Book written by Washington Irving marked the beginning of American Romanticism. Following the rise of romanticism, Transcendentalism, which appeared after 1830, marked the maturity of American Romanticism and the first renaissance in the American literary history. It was one of the most prolific literature periods and American literature became mature and grew into complexity and diversity.

1. Early Romanticism

As a result of the immense influence of European Romanticism, American writers gradually became aware of the need of paying attention to the creation of human spirit and Transcendentalism which aimed at pursuing freedom. Romantics emphasized freedom, individualism and intuition, believing that imagination and emotion were superior to rules and reason. The themes were a strong sense of optimism and a mood of "feeling good" of the whole country which focused on free expression of emotions, imaginative qualities such as picturesque, exotic, sensuous and supernatural and moralizing the wildness and American Puritanism. American Romanticism mostly contained Puritanism, Calvinistic view of original sin and gothic elements.

Although it was imitative—American romantic writing shared the general characteristics of European Romanticism. American romantic authors were responsive to the stimulus which American experience offered, whose subjects were the national ideals of individualism and democracy, history, and frontier life of the new nation.

Romanticism was spread to America in the early 19th century. Its manifestations varied yet romantics frequently shared certain general characteristics: moral enthusiasm, faith in the value of individualism and intuitive perception, and a presumption that the natural world was a source of goodness and man's societies a source of corruption. Romanticism influenced the major forms of American prose: transcendentalist writings, historical fiction and sentimental fiction.

2. Late Romanticism

Following the rise of Romanticism, Transcendentalism or Romantic Idealism emerged after 1830 when a little book entitled *Nature* by Ralph Waldo Emerson, was published in 1836. A totally new way of thinking began to exert its influence on the mind of man, which pushed American Romanticism into a new stage—American Transcendentalism, the summit of American Romanticism.

Transcendentalists placed emphasis on spirit or the supernatural, and stressed the importance of the individual. Men should trust and rely on themselves. They can make their own laws and live according to their own independent principles. The new world gives each the opportunity to become a completely free and independent individual. Transcendentalism disregards external authority, tradition and logical demonstration.

3. Representative Writers and Works

It was in the late 18th and early 19th centuries that the nation's first novels were published. With the War of 1812 and an increasing desire to produce unique American literature and culture, a number of key new literary figures emerged. The representatives are Washington Ivring who wrote *History of New York* and *The Sketch Book*, James Fenimore Cooper who wrote *The Last of the Mohicans* and *The Pilot* and Edgar Allan Poe who wrote *Tales of the Grotesque* and *Arabesque and Tales*. In 1836, Ralph Waldo Emerson started a movement known as Transcendentalism. Henry David Thoreau wrote *Walden*, urging resistance to the dictates of organized society.

(1) Romantic Novelists

The Scarlet Letter was Hawthorne's masterpiece, which is not only the representative of American Romantic novels but also the beginning of the American psychological novels. Melville was a major literary figure whose exploration of psychological and metaphysical theme foreshadowed 20th century literary concerns. *Moby-Dick* represented the bleak view of the world in which he lived. This book was a tragedy of man fighting against an indifferent universe.

The political conflict surrounding abolitionism inspired the writings of William Lloyd Garrison and Harriet Beecher Stowe in her world-famous *Uncle Tom's Cabin*.

(2) Poets

America's two greatest 19th century poets were Walt Whitman and Emily Dickinson.

Longfellow, one of New England poets and it was with him that American poetry began its emergence from the shadow of its British parentage. Longfellow and other poets constituted a group called the Fireside Poets, who earned this nickname because they frequently used the hearth as an image of comfort and unity, a place where families gathered to learn and tell stories. These tremendously popular poets also were widely read around the hearthside of 19th century American families.

By the end of the Civil War a new nation had been born, and it was to demand and receive a new literature more practical, earthier, and more honest in the age. The American dream had glowed with greatest intensity and American writers had created a great literary period by capturing on their pages the enthusiasm and the optimism of that dream. The Romanticism era in the United States was surpassed by the rise of Realism in the later 19th century.

Unit 1 Washington Irving (1783 – 1859)

Appreciation

Rip Van Winkle, however, was one of those happy mortals, of foolish, well-oiled dispositions, who take the world easy, eat white bread or brown, whichever can be got with least thought or trouble, and would rather starve on a penny than work for a pound. 然而,瑞普·凡·温克尔是那种有福分的人。他一副傻样,与世无争,接人待物从容快乐;他吃好吃差无所谓,只要得来全不费工夫。

Washington Irving was born on April 3, 1783 into a wealthy New York merchant family, the youngest son of the family with 11 children. He was so named after George Washington, quite out of his father's admiration to the first president of the country. Born with strong preference for literature, Irving read widely and wrote a lot of poems, essays, and plays at very early age.

His career as a writer started with writing for journals and newspapers, such as Morning Chronicle. *The Sketch Book*, a collection of essays, sketches and stories, including the immortal *Rip Van Winkle* and *The Legend of Sleepy Hollow*, established Irving's reputation at home and abroad and designated the beginning of American Romanticism.

Irving was the first American writer of imaginative literature to gain international fame. Irving, often considered the first writer to develop a unique American style, wrote humorous works in Salmagundi and the satire *A History of New York*, by Diedrich Knickerbocker (1809). Irving initiated the native American literature and introduced the familiar essay from Europe to America. His writings were often considered the earliest formal literary works of America and established the foundation for American literature. He is regarded as "father of American literature".

Brief Introduction

Rip Van Winkle is a fantasy tale about a man who somehow stepped outside the main stream of life. The hero, Rip Van Winkle, is a simple, good-natured, and henpecked man, living in an old Dutch village at the foot of the Kaatskiskill Mountains within the view of Hudson River. He does everything except take care of his own farm and family. He helps everyone except his wife and his own children. His wife keeps complaining about his carelessness and idleness. To escape his wife's harsh treatment, he often wanders in the mountains with his dog. One day, he happens to see a group of strange-looking people playing a game like bowling. Out of curiosity, Rip drinks some of their wine and falls asleep soon after. When he wakes up, he finds the group of people had disappeared and so has his dog. Quite to his surprise, his gun has already heavily rusted. Returning to his village, he finds it completely changed: his wife has gone, all of his contemporaries have passed away and strangers are everywhere. Fortunately, he gets reunited with his daughter, who reveals to him that his sleep on the mountain has lasted 20 years. Rip adjusts to his altered world and begins to live a pleasant life of leisure, which he expected all the time.

Selected Reading

Rip Van Winkle
(Selected)

Whoever has made a voyage up the Hudson must remember the Kaatskill mountains. They are a dismembered branch of the great Appalachian family, and are seen away to the west of the river, swelling up to a noble height, and lording it over the surrounding country. Every change of season, every change of weather, indeed, every hour of the day, produces some change in the magical hues and shapes of these mountains, and they are regarded by all the good wives, far and near, as perfect barometers. When the weather is fair and settled, they are clothed in blue and purple, and print their bold outlines on the clear evening sky, but, sometimes, when the rest of the landscape is cloudless, they will gather a hood of gray vapors about their summits, which, in the last rays of the setting sun, will glow and light up like a crown of glory.

In that same village, and in one of these very houses (which, to tell the precise truth, was sadly time-worn and weather-beaten), there lived, many years since, while the country was yet a province of Great Britain, a simple, good-natured fellow, of the name of Rip Van Winkle. He was a descendant of the Van Winkles who figured so gallantly in the chivalrous days of Peter Stuyvesant①, and accompanied him to the siege of Fort Christina②. He inherited, however, but little of the martial character of his ancestors. I have observed that he was a simple, good-natured man; he was, moreover, a kind neighbor, and an obedient, hen-pecked husband. Indeed, to the latter circumstance might be owing that meekness of spirit which gained him such universal popularity③; for those men are most apt to be obsequious and conciliating abroad, who are under the discipline of shrews at home. Their tempers, doubtless, are rendered pliant and malleable in the fiery furnace of domestic tribulation; and a curtain lecture④ is worth all the sermons in the world for teaching the virtues of patience and long-suffering. A termagant wife may, therefore, in some respects, be considered a tolerable blessing; and if so, Rip Van Winkle was thrice blessed.

Certain it is, that he was a great favorite among all the good wives of the village, who, as usual, with the amiable sex⑤, took his part in all family squabbles; and never failed, whenever they talked those matters over in their evening gossipings, to lay all the blame on Dame Van Winkle. The children of the village, too, would shout with joy whenever he approached. He assisted at their sports, made their playthings, taught them to fly kites and shoot marbles, and told them long stories of ghosts, witches, and Indians. Whenever he went dodging about the village, he was surrounded by a troop of them, hanging on his skirts, clambering on his back, and playing a thousand tricks on him with impunity; and not a dog would bark at him throughout the neighborhood.

The great error in Rip's composition was an insuperable aversion to all kinds of profitable labor. It could not be from the want of assiduity or

---

① Peter Stuyvesant: the Dutch governor of Manhattan Island. New York, in 1647

② Fort Christina: a fort captured by Dutchmen in 1665

③ to the latter circumstance might be owing that meekness of spirit which gained him such universal popularity: It is an inverted sentence. The normal order should be that meekness of spirit which gained him such universal popularity might be owing to the latter circumstance

④ curtain lecture: the private talk between husband and wife after the curtains are pulled round their bed

⑤ the amiable sex: the female sex

perseverance; for he would sit on a wet rock, with a rod as long and heavy as a Tartar①'s lance, and fish all day without a murmur, even though he should not be encouraged by a single nibble. He would carry a fowling-piece on his shoulder for hours together, trudging through woods and swamps, and up hill and down dale, to shoot a few squirrels or wild pigeons. He would never refuse to assist a neighbor even in the roughest toil, and was a foremost man at all country frolics for husking Indian corn, or building stone-fences; the women of the village, too, used to employ him to run their errands, and to do such little odd jobs as their less obliging husbands would not do for them. In a word Rip was ready to attend to anybody's business but his own; but as to doing family duty, and keeping his farm in order, he found it impossible.

In fact, he declared it was of no use to work on his farm; it was the most pestilent little piece of ground in the whole country; everything about it went wrong, and would go wrong, in spite of him. His fences were continually falling to pieces; his cow would either go astray, or get among the cabbages; weeds were sure to grow quicker in his fields than anywhere else; the rain always made a point of setting in just as he had some out-door work to do; so that though his patrimonial estate had dwindled away under his management, acre by acre, until there was little more left than a mere patch of Indian corn and potatoes, yet it was the worst conditioned farm in the neighborhood.

His children, too, were as ragged and wild as if they belonged to nobody. His son Rip, an urchin begotten in his own likeness, promised to inherit the habits, with the old clothes of his father. He was generally seen trooping like a colt at his mother's heels, equipped in a pair of his father's cast-off galligaskins②, which he had much ado to hold up with one hand, as a fine lady does her train in bad weather.

Rip Van Winkle, however, was one of those happy mortals, of foolish, well-oiled dispositions, who take the world easy, eat white bread or brown, whichever can be got with least thought or trouble, and would rather starve on a penny than work for a pound. If left to himself, he would have whistled life away in perfect contentment; but his wife kept continually dinning in his ears

---

① Tartar: member of a group of Central Asian peoples including Mongols and Turks
② galligaskins: loose riding breeches for men

about his idleness, his carelessness, and the ruin he was bringing on his family. Morning, noon, and night, her tongue was incessantly going, and everything he said or did was sure to produce a torrent of household eloquence. Rip had but one way of replying to all lectures of the kind, and that, by frequent use, had grown into a habit. He shrugged his shoulders, shook his head, cast up his eyes, but said nothing. This, however, always provoked a fresh volley from his wife; so that he was fain to draw off his forces, and take to the outside of the house— the only side which, in truth, belongs to a hen-pecked husband.

Rip's sole domestic adherent was his dog Wolf, who was as much hen-pecked as his master; for Dame Van Winkle regarded them as companions in idleness, and even looked upon Wolf with an evil eye, as the cause of his master's going so often astray. True it is, in all points of spirit befitting an honorable dog, he was as courageous an animal as ever scoured the woods; but what courage can withstand the ever-during and all-besetting terrors of a woman's tongue The moment Wolf entered the house his crest fell, his tail dropped to the ground, or curled between his legs, he sneaked about with a gallows air, casting many a sidelong glance at Dame Van Winkle, and at the least flourish of a broomstick or ladle, he would run to the door with yelping precipitation.

Times grew worse and worse with Rip Van Winkle as years of matrimony rolled on; a tart temper never mellows with age, and a sharp tongue is the only edged tool that grows keener with constant use. For a long while he used to console himself, when driven from home, by frequenting a kind of perpetual club of the sages, philosophers, and other idle personages of the village; which held its sessions on a bench before a small inn, designated by a rubicund portrait of His Majesty George the Third. Here they used to sit in the shade through a long lazy summer's day, talking listlessly over village gossip, or telling endless sleepy stories about nothing. But it would have been worth any statesman's money to have heard the profound discussions that sometimes took place, when by chance an old newspaper fell into their hands from some passing traveller. How solemnly they would listen to the contents, as drawled out by Derrick Van Bummel, the schoolmaster, a dapper learned little man, who was not to be daunted by the most gigantic word in the dictionary; and how sagely they would deliberate upon public events some months after they had taken place.

The opinions of this junto were completely controlled by Nicholas Vedder, a patriarch of the village, and landlord of the inn, at the door of which he took his seat from morning till night, just moving sufficiently to avoid the sun and keep in the shade of a large tree; so that the neighbors could tell the hour by his movements as accurately as by a sun-dial. It is true he was rarely heard to speak, but smoked his pipe incessantly. His adherents, however (for every great man has his adherents), perfectly understood him, and knew how to gather his opinions. When anything that was read or related displeased him, he was observed to smoke his pipe vehemently; and to send forth short, frequent and angry puffs; but when pleased, he would inhale the smoke slowly and tranquilly, and emit it in light and placid clouds; and sometimes, taking the pipe from his mouth, and letting the fragrant vapor curl about his nose, would gravely nod his head in token of perfect approbation.

From even this stronghold the unlucky Rip was at length routed by his termagant wife, who would suddenly break in upon the tranquility of the assemblage and call the members all to naught; nor was that august personage, Nicholas Vedder himself, sacred from the daring tongue of this terrible virago, who charged him outright with encouraging her husband in habits of idleness.

Poor Rip was at last reduced almost to despair; and his only alternative, to escape from the labor of the farm and clamor of his wife, was to take gun in hand and stroll away into the woods. Here he would sometimes seat himself at the foot of a tree, and share the contents of his wallet with Wolf, with whom he sympathized as a fellow-sufferer in persecution. "Poor Wolf," he would say, "the mistress leads thee a dog's life of it; but never mind, my lad, whilst I live thou shalt never want a friend to stand by thee!" Wolf would wag his tail, look wistfully in his master's face, and if dogs can feel pity I verily believe he reciprocated the sentiment with all his heart.

In a long ramble of the kind on a fine autumnal day, Rip had unconsciously scrambled to one of the highest parts of the Kaatskill Mountains. He was after his favorite sport of squirrels hooting, and the still solitudes had echoed and re-echoed with the reports of his gun. Panting and fatigued, he threw himself, late in the afternoon, on a green knoll, covered with mountain herbage, that crowned the brow of a precipice. From an opening between the trees he could overlook all the lower country for many a mile of rich woodland. He saw at a distance the lordly Hudson, far, far below him, moving on its silent but majestic course, with the reflection of a purple cloud, or the sail of a lagging bark, here and there sleeping on its glassy bosom, and at last losing itself in the blue highlands.

On the other side he looked down into a deep mountain glen, wild, lonely, and shagged, the bottom filled with fragments from the impending cliffs, and scarcely lighted by the reflected rays of the setting sun. For some time Rip lay musing on this scene; evening was gradually advancing; the mountains began to throw their long blue shadows over the valleys; he saw that it would be dark long before he could reach the village, and he heaved a heavy sigh when he thought of encountering the terrors of Dame Van Winkle.

As he was about to descend, he heard a voice from a distance, hallooing, "Rip Van Winkle! Rip Van Winkle!" He looked round, but could see nothing but a crow winging its solitary flight across the mountain. He thought his fancy must have deceived him, and turned again to descend, when he heard the same cry ring through the still evening air; "Rip Van Winkle! Rip Van Winkle!"—at the same time Wolf bristled up his back, and giving a low growl, skulked to his master's side, looking fearfully down into the glen. Rip now felt a vague apprehension stealing over him; he looked anxiously in the same direction, and perceived a strange figure slowly toiling up the rocks, and bending under the weight of something he carried on his back. He was surprised to see any human being in this lonely and unfrequented place; but supposing it to be some one of the neighborhood in need of his assistance, he hastened down to yield it.

Questions for Discussion

Rip Van Winkle has been seen as a symbol of several aspects of America. For example, the village itself symbolizes America—forever and rapidly changing. Then what do you think Rip and his wife symbolize respectively?

Unit 2 Ralph Waldo Emerson (1803 – 1882)

Appreciation

Philosophically considered, the universe is composed of Nature and the Soul.
从哲学角度来考虑,宇宙是由自然和灵魂组成的。

Ralph Waldo Emerson was widely known and admired as a poet, philosopher, public lecturer, and essayist of his day, whose essays were the most important works in English prose produced in the nineteenth century.

Emerson was born on May 25, 1803, in Boston. After his graduation from Harvard in 1821, he tried teaching in school for several years. He was licensed to preach in 1826 and became a minister of Boston's Second Church in 1829. He resigned his position two years later and went to Europe in 1832, where he met the prominent British Romanticists and learned from his English friends new ideas of German idealism and Transcendentalism. With people of like minds such as Thoreau he formed the Transcendentalist club to discuss matters of interest to the life of the nation and founded the Transcendentalist journal, *The Dial*, to explain their ideas.

In 1836, Emerson published his first book *Nature*, which is the fundamental document of his philosophy, and expresses his constant, deeply felt love for the natural scenes. In this book Emerson shows us that nature as the symbol of spirit serves man as the source of language and beauty and self-knowledge. In the years between 1837 – 1844 he published his most famous works *The American Scholar* (1837), *The Divinity School Address* (1838), and two volumes of *Essays* (first series, 1841; second series, 1844), which contained the influential pieces "Self-Reliance", "The Poet", "Friendship", and "The Oversoul".

Emerson's influence on American literature and culture cannot be overstated. He called on American writers to write about America in a peculiarly American way. His perception of humanity and nature as symbols of universal truth encouraged the development of the symbolist movement in American art and literature.

Brief Introduction

Considered the "gospel" of American Transcendentalism, *Nature* is a lyrical expression of the harmony Emerson felt between himself and nature. He believed that the individual soul can become the medium of the divine forces of Nature. In the "Introduction", Emerson pronounces the fundamental premise about Nature in Transcendentalism, that is, Nature is not simply the Not-Me but also the universal mind whose signs, or symbols, are visible for the individual to read, with eyes, heart and mind. The "Introduction" is followed by eight sections, each of which develops a general thesis: "Nature" "Commodity" "Beauty" "Language" "Discipline" "Idealism" "Spirit", and "Prospects".

Selected Reading

Nature

Introduction

Our age is retrospective. It builds the sepulchres① of the fathers. It writes biographies, histories, and criticism. The foregoing generations beheld God and nature face to face; we, through their eyes. Why should not we also enjoy an original relation to the universe Why should not we have a poetry and philosophy of insight and not of tradition, and a religion by revelation to us, and not the history of theirs Embosomed for a season in nature, whose floods of life stream around and through us, and invite us by the powers they supply, to action proportioned to nature, why should we grope among the dry bones of the past②, or put the living generation into masquerade out of its faded wardrobe The sun shines today also. There is more wool and flax in the fields. There are new lands, new men, new thoughts. Let us demand our own works and laws and worship.

Undoubtedly we have no questions to ask which are unanswerable. We must trust the perfection of the creation so far, as to believe that whatever curiosity the order of things has awakened in our minds, the order of things can satisfy. Every man's condition is a solution in hieroglyphic③ to those inquiries he would put. He acts it as life, before he apprehends it as truth. In like manner, nature is already, in its forms and tendencies, describing its own design. Let us

---

① sepulchre: 坟墓；圣体安置所

② why should we grope among the dry bones of the past: an echo of Ezekiel, where God tells Ezchiel to "Prophesy upon these bones, and say unto them, O ye dry bones, hear the word of the Lord." Emerson had left the ministry but was still writing as a prophet

③ hieroglyphic: 象形文字

interrogate the great apparition①, that shines so peacefully around us. Let us inquire, to what end is nature?

All science has one aim, namely, to find a theory of nature. We have theories of races and of functions, but scarcely yet a remote approach to an idea of creation. We are now so far from the road to truth, that religious teachers dispute and hate each other, and speculative men are esteemed unsound and frivolous②. But to a sound judgment, the most abstract truth is the most practical. Whenever a true theory appears, it will be its own evidence. Its test is, that it will explain all phenomena. Now many are thought not only unexplained but inexplicable③; as language, sleep, madness, dreams, beasts, sex.

Philosophically considered, the universe is composed of Nature and the Soul. Strictly speaking, therefore, all that is separate from us, all which Philosophy distinguishes as the NOT ME④, that is, both nature and art, all other men and my own body, must be ranked under this name, NATURE. In enumerating the values of nature and casting up their sum, I shall use the word in both senses;—in its common and in its philosophical import. In inquiries so general as our present one, the inaccuracy is not material; no confusion of thought will occur. Nature, in the common sense, refers to essences unchanged by man; space, the air, the river, the leaf. Art is applied to the mixture of his will with the same things, as in a house, a canal, a statue, a picture. But his operations taken together are so insignificant, a little chipping, baking, patching, and washing, that in an impression so grand as that of the world on the human mind, they do not vary the result.

Questions for Discussion

How does Emerson define Nature?

---

① apparition: 幽灵;鬼怪
② frivolous: 无聊的;轻佻的
③ inexplicable: 费解的;无法说明的
④ NOT ME: Emerson takes "not me" from Thomas Carlyle's *Sartor Resartus* (1833 – 1834), where it appears as a translation of the recent German philosophical term for everything but the self

Unit 3 Henry David Thoreau (1817 – 1862)

Appreciation

Walden 瓦尔登湖
Where I Lived, and What I Lived for 我的生活所在;我的生活追求

Henry David Thoreau was born in Concord, Massachusetts on July12, 1817. His father was a poor pencil-maker, while his mother was an aspiring woman who wanted her son to be well educated. He attended Concord Academy, learned surveying, and graduated from Harvard College in 1837. He never married, spending his time alone with nature. In his own time he was regarded as an eccentric and a loafer, but from time to time he would survey for farmers in the area. When Emerson moved to Concord, Thoreau was only seventeen. From 1841 to 1843 he lived with Emerson, who became his master, and who had a great influence on him. Actually Thoreau was Emerson's man of action. As an intimate of the members of the Transcendental Club, he worked with Emerson on *The Dial*, which was published to spread the transcendentalists' ideas. But they had different views on social reform and protest. Being more radical, Thoreau alienated himself from his master later on. He died on May 6, 1862.

As Emerson's disciple, Thoreau practiced the self-reflective and self-reliant Transcendentalism that Emerson preached. Today he is primarily remembered for two of his important works the book *Walden* (1854) and the essay *Civil Disobedience* (1849). He built himself a hut in the woods by Walden Pond, where he lived from July 4, 1845 to September 6, 1847, a period in which he wrote his most famous book *Walden*.

Brief Introduction

On July 4, 1845, Thoreau began his experiment in living alone in a hut by Walden Pond. There he deliberately lived a life of simplicity and independence, devoting his time to observations and reflections. The experiment he designed was to prove how far he could free himself from the hypocrisies and unnecessary complexities of a commercial society. Thoreau did not intend to live as a hermit, for he received visitors regularly, and returned their visits. For Thoreau, being close to nature means being closer to the divinity manifested as nature's signs.

Deceptively casual, *Walden* reads like a diary of a nature lover. It is a book of essays that explores subjects concerned with nature, with the meaning of life, and with morality. *Walden* is structured on the four seasons, beginning in summer and ending in spring. It is largely narrative—with reflective digressions. Thoreau's purposes of writing this book are to make his readers evaluate the way he lived and thought, to reveal the hidden spiritual possibilities in everyone's life, and to condemn the weakness and errors of society, such as the pursuit of material things.

Selected Reading

Walden

Chapter II—Where I Lived, and What I Lived for

At a certain season of our life we are accustomed to consider every spot as the possible site of a house. I have thus surveyed the country on every side within a dozen miles of where I live. In imagination I have bought all the farms in succession①, for all were to be bought, and I knew their price. I walked over each farmer's premises②, tasted his wild apples, discoursed on husbandry with him, took his farm at his price, at any price③, mortgaging it to him in my mind; even put a higher price on it—took everything but a deed of it④—took his word for his deed, for I dearly love to talk—cultivated it, and him⑤ too to some extent, I trust, and withdrew when I had enjoyed it long enough, leaving him to carry it on. This experience entitled me to be regarded as a sort of real-estate broker by my friends. Wherever I sat, there I might live, and the landscape radiated from me accordingly. What is a house but a sedes⑥, a seat—better if a country seat. I discovered many a site for a house not likely to be soon improved, which some might have thought too far from the village, but to my eyes the village was too far from it. Well, there I might live, I said; and there I did live, for an hour, a summer and a winter life; saw how I could let the years run off, buffet the winter through, and see the spring come in. The future

---

① in succession：按顺序。全句的意思是："在想象中,我已经依次买下了所有的农场"
② premises：房屋及其附属的土地。在现代英语中,该词用于这一意义时必须用复数
③ took his farm at his price, at any price：按他所开的价,不管他开什么价,买下他的农场
④ took everything but a deed of it：买下了所有东西,只是没有立契约
⑤ cultivated it, and him：耕耘了这片田地,也耕耘了他的心田
⑥ sedes：【拉丁文】座位

inhabitants of this region, wherever they may place their houses, may be sure that they have been anticipated. An afternoon sufficed to lay out the land into orchard, wood-lot, and pasture, and to decide what fine oaks or pines should be left to stand before the door, and whence each blasted tree could be seen to the best advantage; and then I let it lie, fallow, perchance, for a man is rich in proportion to the number of things which he can afford to let alone.

My imagination carried me so far that I even had the refusal of several farms—the refusal was all I wanted—but I never got my fingers burned by actual possession. The nearest that I came to actual possession was when I bought the Hollowell place①, and had begun to sort my seeds, and collected materials with which to make a wheelbarrow to carry it on or off with; but before the owner gave me a deed of it, his wife—every man has such a wife—changed her mind and wished to keep it, and he offered me ten dollars to release him. Now, to speak the truth, I had but ten cents in the world, and it surpassed my arithmetic to tell, if I was that man who had ten cents, or who had a farm, or ten dollars, or all together. However, I let him keep the ten dollars and the farm too, for I had carried it far enough; or rather, to be generous, I sold him the farm for just what I gave for it, and, as he was not a rich man, made him a present of ten dollars, and still had my ten cents, and seeds, and materials for a wheelbarrow left. I found thus that I had been a rich man without any damage to my poverty. But I retained the landscape, and I have since annually carried off what it yielded without a wheelbarrow. With respect to landscapes,

"I am monarch of all I *survey*,
My right there is none to dispute."

I have frequently seen a poet withdraw, having enjoyed the most valuable part of a farm, while the crusty farmer supposed that he had got a few wild apples only. Why, the owner does not know it for many years when a poet has put his farm in rhyme, the most admirable kind of invisible fence, has fairly impounded it, milked it, skimmed it, and got all the cream, and left the farmer only the skimmed milk.

The real attractions of the Hollowell farm, to me, were: its complete retirement, being, about two miles from the village, half a mile from the nearest neighbor, and separated from the highway by a broad field; its bounding on the

---

① Hollowell place: 康科德附近的一个老农场

river, which the owner said protected it by its fogs from frosts in the spring, though that was nothing to me; the gray color and ruinous state of the house and barn, and the dilapidated fences, which put such an interval between me and the last occupant; the hollow and lichen-covered apple trees, gnawed by rabbits, showing what kind of neighbors I should have; but above all, the recollection I had of it from my earliest voyages up the river, when the house was concealed behind a dense grove of red maples, through which I heard the house-dog bark. I was in haste to buy it, before the proprietor finished getting out some rocks, cutting down the hollow apple trees, and grubbing up some young birches which had sprung up in the pasture, or, in short, had made any more of his improvements. To enjoy these advantages I was ready to carry it on; like Atlas[①], to take the world on my shoulders,—I never heard what compensation he received for that—and do all those things which had no other motive or excuse but that I might pay for it and be unmolested in my possession of it; for I knew all the while that it would yield the most abundant crop of the kind I wanted, if I could only afford to let it alone. But it turned out as I have said.

All that I could say, then, with respect to farming on a large scale—I have always cultivated a garden—was, that I had had my seeds ready. Many think that seeds improve with age. I have no doubt that time discriminates between the good and the bad; and when at last I shall plant, I shall be less likely to be disappointed. But I would say to my fellows, once for all, as long as possible live free and uncommitted. It makes but little difference whether you are committed to a farm or the county jail.

Old Cato[②], whose "De Re Rustica" is my "Cultivator," says—and the only translation I have seen makes sheer nonsense of the passage—"When you think of getting a farm turn it thus in your mind, not to buy greedily; nor spare your pains to look at it, and do not think it enough to go round it once. The oftener you go there the more it will please you, if it is good." I think I shall not buy greedily, but go round and round it as long as I live, and be buried in it first, that it may please me the more at last.

The present was my next experiment of this kind, which I purpose to describe more at length, for convenience putting the experience of two years

---

① Atlas：阿特拉斯，希腊神话中的神，他将大地和天空扛在肩上

② Old Cato：大加图（Marcus Porcius Cato, 234－149 B. C.），罗马政治家、演说家、拉丁散文作家。*De Re Rustica*，又称 *De Agricultura*（160? B. C.）（《农书》），是他流传至今的唯一著作

into one. As I have said, I do not propose to write an ode to dejection, but to brag as lustily as chanticleer in the morning, standing on his roost, if only to wake my neighbors up.

When first I took up my abode in the woods, that is, began to spend my nights as well as days there, which, by accident, was on Independence Day, or the Fourth of July, 1845, my house was not finished for winter, but was merely a defence against the rain, without plastering or chimney, the walls being of rough, weather-stained boards, with wide chinks, which made it cool at night. The upright white hewn studs and freshly planed door and window casings gave it a clean and airy look, especially in the morning, when its timbers were saturated with dew, so that I fancied that by noon some sweet gum would exude from them. To my imagination it retained throughout the day more or less of this auroral character, reminding me of a certain house on a mountain which I had visited a year before. This was an airy and unplastered cabin, fit to entertain a travelling god, and where a goddess might trail her garments. The winds which passed over my dwelling were such as sweep over the ridges of mountains, bearing the broken strains, or celestial parts only, of terrestrial music. The morning wind forever blows, the poem of creation is uninterrupted; but few are the ears that hear it. Olympus[①] is but the outside of the earth everywhere.

The only house I had been the owner of before, if I except a boat, was a tent, which I used occasionally when making excursions in the summer, and this is still rolled up in my garret; but the boat, after passing from hand to hand, has gone down the stream of time. With this more substantial shelter about me, I had made some progress toward settling in the world. This frame, so slightly clad, was a sort of crystallization around me, and reacted on the builder. It was suggestive somewhat as a picture in outlines. I did not need to go outdoors to take the air, for the atmosphere within had lost none of its freshness. It was not so much within doors as behind a door where I sat, even in the rainiest weather. The Harivansa[②] says, "An abode without birds is like a meat without seasoning." Such was not my abode, for I found myself suddenly neighbor to the birds; not by having imprisoned one, but having caged myself near them. I was not only nearer to some of those which commonly frequent the garden and the orchard, but to those smaller and more thrilling songsters of the forest which

---

① Olympus：奥林波斯，希腊神话中诸神之家
② The Harivansa：哈利梵萨，印度 5 世纪的宗教史诗

never, or rarely, serenade a villager—the wood thrush, the veery, the scarlet tanager, the field sparrow, the whip-poor-will, and many others.

   I was seated by the shore of a small pond, about a mile and a half south of the village of Concord and somewhat higher than it, in the midst of an extensive wood between that town and Lincoln, and about two miles south of that our only field known to fame, Concord Battle Ground①; but I was so low in the woods that the opposite shore, half a mile off, like the rest, covered with wood, was my most distant horizon. For the first week, whenever I looked out on the pond it impressed me like a tarn high up on the side of a mountain, its bottom far above the surface of other lakes, and, as the sun arose, I saw it throwing off its nightly clothing of mist, and here and there, by degrees, its soft ripples or its smooth reflecting surface was revealed, while the mists, like ghosts, were stealthily withdrawing in every direction into the woods, as at the breaking up of some nocturnal conventicle. The very dew seemed to hang upon the trees later into the day than usual, as on the sides of mountains.

   This small lake was of most value as a neighbor in the intervals of a gentle rain-storm in August, when, both air and water being perfectly still, but the sky overcast, mid-afternoon had all the serenity of evening, and the wood thrush sang around, and was heard from shore to shore. A lake like this is never smoother than at such a time; and the clear portion of the air above it being, shallow and darkened by clouds, the water, full of light and reflections, becomes a lower heaven itself so much the more important. From a hill-top near by, where the wood had been recently cut off, there was a pleasing vista southward across the pond, through a wide indentation in the hills which form the shore there, where their opposite sides sloping toward each other suggested a stream flowing out in that direction through a wooded valley, but stream there was none. That way I looked between and over the near green hills to some distant and higher ones in the horizon, tinged with blue. Indeed, by standing on tiptoe I could catch a glimpse of some of the peaks of the still bluer and more distant mountain ranges in the northwest, those true-blue coins from heaven's own mint, and also of some portion of the village. But in other directions, even from this point, I could not see over or beyond the woods which surrounded me. It is well to have some water in your neighborhood, to give buoyancy to

---

   ① Concord Battle Ground：美国独立战争时期的著名战场(1775年4月19日)

and float the earth. One value even of the smallest well is, that when you look into it you see that earth is not continent but insular. This is as important as that it keeps butter cool. When I looked across the pond from this peak toward the Sudbury meadows, which in time of flood I distinguished elevated perhaps by a mirage in their seething valley, like a coin in a basin, all the earth beyond the pond appeared like a thin crust insulated and floated even by this small sheet of intervening water, and I was reminded that this on which I dwelt was but dry land.

Though the view from my door was still more contracted, I did not feel crowded or confined in the least. There was pasture enough for my imagination. The low shrub oak plateau to which the opposite shore arose stretched away toward the prairies of the West and the steppes of Tartary, affording ample room for all the roving families of men. "There are none happy in the world but beings who enjoy freely a vast horizon"—said Damodara①, when his herds required new and larger pastures.

Both place and time were changed, and I dwelt nearer to those parts of the universe and to those eras in history which had most attracted me. Where I lived was as far off as many a region viewed nightly by astronomers. We are wont to imagine rare and delectable places in some remote and more celestial corner of the system, behind the constellation of Cassiopeia's Chair②, far from noise and disturbance. I discovered that my house actually had its site in such a withdrawn, but forever new and unprofaned, part of the universe. If it were worth the while to settle in those parts near to the Pleiades or the Hyades, to Aldebaran③ or Altair, then I was really there, or at an equal remoteness from the life which I had left behind, dwindled and twinkling with as fine a ray to my nearest neighbor, and to be seen only in moonless nights by him. Such was that part of creation where I had squatted;

"There was a shepherd that did live,

And held his thoughts as high

As were the mounts whereon his flocks

Did hourly feed him by."

What should we think of the shepherd's life if his flocks always wandered to higher pastures than his thoughts?

---

① Damodara: 达摩达拉,《哈利梵萨》中的神
② Cassiopeia's Chair: 仙后座
③ the Pleiades or the Hyades, to Aldebaran: 昂星团,毕星团,毕宿五,牵牛星 – 星座星球名

Questions for Discussion

1. Is it significant that Thoreau mentioned the Fourth of July as the day on which he began to stay in the woods? Why?
2. Analyse "*Where I Lived and What I Lived For*".
3. "I went to the woods because I wished to live deliberately, to front only the essential facts of life, and see if I could not learn what it had to teach, and not, when I came to die, discover that I had not lived." what does it mean?

Unit 4 Nathaniel Hawthorne (1804 – 1864)

Appreciation

Had there been a Papist among the crowd of Puritans, he might have seen in this beautiful woman, so picturesque in her attire and mien, and with the infant at her bosom, an object to remind him of the image of Divine Maternity, which so many illustrious painters have vied with one another to represent; something which should remind him, indeed, but only by contrast, of that sacred image of sinless motherhood, whose infant was to redeem the world. Here, there was the taint of deepest sin in the most sacred quality of human life, working such effect, that the world was only the darker for this woman's beauty, and the more lost for the infant that she had borne.

如果在这一群清教徒之中有一个罗马天主教徒,他就会从这个服饰和神采如画、怀中紧抱婴儿的美妇身上,联想起众多杰出画家所竞先描绘的圣母的形象,诚然,他的这种联想只能在对比中才能产生,因为圣像中那圣洁清白的母性怀中的婴儿是献给世人来赎罪的。然而在她身上,世俗生活中最神圣的品德,却被最深重的罪孽所玷污了,其结果,只能使世界由于这妇人的美丽而更加晦暗,由于她生下的婴儿而愈发沉沦。

Hawthorne was born into a family with a long Puritan tradition, on July 4, 1804 in Salem (Massachusetts). His father, a sea captain, died when Hawthorne was four years old. Hawthorne was raised secluded from the world by his mother. Hawthorne was quiet by nature, and spent much time alone reading by himself in his childhood. After graduation from college in 1825, Hawthorne returned to his hometown and lived in seclusion for 12 years, reading widely and preparing for his literary career.

In 1837, his collection of short stories *Twice-Told Tales* gained the public attention. His most famous work *The Scarlet Letter* came out in the spring of 1850 and attained an immediate success, earning him considerable fame in both the United States and Great Britain. Soon he composed three important novels: *The House of the Seven Gables*, *The Blithedale Romance* and *The Marble Faun*.

Hawthorne has been considered to be the first greatest American fiction writer in the moralistic tradition. His Puritan family background exerted great influence on his imagination, giving him a dark vision of human nature. He was one of the first American writers to tell the dark truth of society, to explore the psychological conflicts and hidden motivations of his characters. Many of his stories feature moral allegories with a Puritan inspiration. Inherent evil and sin of humanity seem to be recurrent themes of his writing.

Brief Introduction

The story is set in the Puritan past of the 17th century. An ageing English scholar sends his beautiful wife Hester Prynne to make their new home in New England. When he comes over two years later he is surprised to see his wife on a pillory, wearing a scarlet letter "A" on her breast, holding her illegitimate daughter in her arms. Determined to find out who her lover is, the old scholar disguises himself as a physician and changes his name to Roger Chillingworth. Soon he becomes intimately acquainted with the much-admired brilliant young clergyman Arthur Dimmesdale and comes to know that the person who dishonored him is no other than Arthur. Tormenting himself ruthlessly for his sin and tortured by Chillingworth, Arthur Dimmesdale cuts himself off from the community and shrivels up spiritually as well as physically. When Hester learns of the suspicions and investigations of her husband, she and Dimmesdale decide to leave secretly for the Old World. On the very day before their departure, Dimmesdale preaches for the last time on the exact platform where Hester's adultery was made public. Seeing that Hester and Pearl are among the audience, Dimmesdale calls them to come up to the platform and tells the audience that he is the father of Pearl. Then he dies in Hester's arms. Chillingworth, who is unable to wreak his vengeance on Dimmesdale, soon dies, too. Hester disappears for a time. Years later, she is found living in her humble thatched cottage doing her best to alleviate the sorrows of the local people through her kind deeds. She still wears the letter "A" on her breast, which is no longer the sign of shame, but now an emblem of her tender mercy and kindness. Pearl, having received a large fortune from Chillingworth, marries into a noble family of Europe. As she contemplates her death, Hester hopes that the only inscription on her tombstone will be the scarlet letter "A."

Selected Reading

The Scarlet Letter

Chapter II—THE MARKET-PLACE

The grass-plot before the jail, in Prison Lane, on a certain summer morning, not less than two centuries ago, was occupied by a pretty large number of the inhabitants of Boston, all with their eyes intently fastened on the iron-clamped oaken door. Amongst any other population, or at a later period in the history of New England, the grim rigidity that petrified① the bearded physiognomies of these good people would have augured some awful business in hand. It could have betokened② nothing short of the anticipated execution of some rioted culprit③, on whom the sentence of a legal tribunal had but confirmed the verdict of public sentiment. But, in that early severity of the Puritan character, an inference of this kind could not so indubitably be drawn. It might be that a sluggish bondservant, or an undutiful child, whom his parents had given over to the civil authority, was to be corrected at the whipping-post. It might be that an Antinomian, a Quaker, or other heterodox④ religionist, was to be scourged out of the town, or an idle or vagrant Indian, whom the white man's firewater had made riotous about the streets, was to be driven with stripes into the shadow of the forest. It might be, too, that a witch, like old Mistress Hibbins, the bitter-tempered widow of the magistrate, was to die upon the gallows. In either case, there was very much the same solemnity of demeanor on the part of the spectators, as befitted a people among whom religion and law were almost identical, and in whose character both were so thoroughly interfused, that the mildest and severest acts of public discipline were alike made venerable and awful. Meagre, indeed, and cold, was the sympathy

---

① petrify: 使……石化;使……惊呆
② betoken: 预示;表示
③ culprit: 犯人,罪犯
④ heterodox: 异端的;非正统的

Chapter 4 American Romanticism and Transcendentalism

that a transgressor① might look for, from such bystanders, at the scaffold. On the other hand, a penalty which, in our days, would infer a degree of mocking infamy② and ridicule, might then be invested with almost as stern a dignity as the punishment of death itself.

It was a circumstance to be noted on the summer morning when our story begins its course, that the women, of whom there were several in the crowd, appeared to take a peculiar interest in whatever penal infliction might be expected to ensue. The age had not so much refinement, that any sense of impropriety restrained the wearers of petticoat③ and farthingale④ from stepping forth into the public ways, and wedging their not unsubstantial persons, if occasion were, into the throng nearest to the scaffold at an execution. Morally, as well as materially, there was a coarser fibre in those wives and maidens of old English birth and breeding than in their fair descendants, separated from them by a series of six or seven generations; for, throughout that chain of ancestry, every successive mother had transmitted to her child a fainter bloom, a more delicate and briefer beauty, and a slighter physical frame, if not character of less force and solidity than her own. The women who were now standing about the prison-door stood within less than half a century of the period when the man-like Elizabeth had been the not altogether unsuitable representative of the sex. They were her countrywomen; and the beef and ale of their native land, with a moral diet not a whit more refined, entered largely into their composition. The bright morning sun, therefore, shone on broad shoulders and well-developed busts, and on round and ruddy cheeks, that had ripened in the far-off island, and had hardly yet grown paler or thinner in the atmosphere of New England. There was, moreover, a boldness and rotundity⑤ of speech among these matrons⑥, as most of them seemed to be, that would startle us at the present day, whether in respect to its purport or its volume of tone.

"Goodwives," said a hard-featured dame of fifty, "I'll tell ye a piece of my

---

① transgressor: 违背者;罪人
② infamy: 声名狼藉;恶行
③ petticoat: 衬裙;裙子
④ farthingale: 用鲸骨圆环扩大的裙子
⑤ rotundity: 圆形物
⑥ matrons: 主妇

mind. It would be greatly for the public behoof① if we women, being of mature age and church-members in good repute, should have the handling of such malefactresses as this Hester Prynne. What think ye, gossips? If the hussy stood up for judgment before us five, that are now here in a knot together, would she come off with such a sentence as the worshipful magistrates have awarded? Marry, I trow not!"

"People say," said another, "that the Reverend Master Dimmesdale, her godly pastor, takes it very grievously to heart that such a scandal should have come upon his congregation."

"The magistrates are God-fearing gentlemen, but merciful overmuch—that is a truth," added a third autumnal matron. "At the very least, they should have put the brand of a hot iron on Hester Prynne's forehead. Madame Hester would have winced at that, I warrant me. But she—the naughty baggage—little will she care what they put upon the bodice of her gown Why, look you, she may cover it with a brooch, or such like. Heathenish adornment, and so walk the streets as brave as ever!"

"Ah, but," interposed, more softly, a young wife, holding a child by the hand, "let her cover the mark as she will, the pang② of it will be always in her heart."

"What do we talk of marks and brands, whether on the bodice of her gown or the flesh of her forehead?" cried another female, the ugliest as well as the most pitiless of these self-constituted judges. "This woman has brought shame upon us all, and ought to die. Is there not law for it? Truly there is, both in the Scripture and the statute-book. Then let the magistrates, who have made it of no effect, thank themselves if their own wives and daughters go astray!"

"Mercy on us, goodwife," exclaimed a man in the crowd, "is there no virtue in woman, save what springs from a wholesome fear of the gallows? That is the hardest word yet! Hush now, gossips! for the lock is turning in the prison-door, and here comes Mistress Prynne herself."

The door of the jail being flung open from within there appeared, in the first place, like a black shadow emerging into sunshine, the grim and gristly presence of the town-beadle, with a sword by his side, and his staff of office in his hand. This personage prefigured and represented in his aspect the whole dismal severity

---

① behoof：利益，好处
② pang：(肉体上)剧痛

of the Puritanic code of law, which it was his business to administer in its final and closest application to the offender. Stretching forth the official staff in his left hand, he laid his right upon the shoulder of a young woman, whom he thus drew forward, until, on the threshold of the prison-door, she repelled him, by an action marked with natural dignity and force of character, and stepped into the open air as if by her own free will. She bore in her arms a child, a baby of some three months old, who winked and turned aside its little face from the too vivid light of day; because its existence, heretofore, had brought it acquaintance only with the grey twilight of a dungeon, or other darksome apartment of the prison.

When the young woman—the mother of this child—stood fully revealed before the crowd, it seemed to be her first impulse to clasp the infant closely to her bosom; not so much by an impulse of motherly affection, as that she might thereby conceal a certain token, which was wrought or fastened into her dress. In a moment, however, wisely judging that one token of her shame would but poorly serve to hide another, she took the baby on her arm, and with a burning blush, and yet a haughty[①] smile, and a glance that would not be abashed[②], looked around at her townspeople and neighbours. On the breast of her gown, in fine red cloth, surrounded with an elaborate embroidery and fantastic flourishes of gold thread, appeared the letter A. It was so artistically done, and with so much fertility and gorgeous luxuriance of fancy, that it had all the effect of a last and fitting decoration to the apparel[③] which she wore, and which was of a splendor in accordance with the taste of the age, but greatly beyond what was allowed by the sumptuary[④] regulations of the colony.

The young woman was tall, with a figure of perfect elegance on a large scale. She had dark and abundant hair, so glossy that it threw off the sunshine with a gleam; and a face which, besides being beautiful from regularity of feature and richness of complexion, had the impressiveness belonging to a marked brow and deep black eyes. She was ladylike, too, after the manner of the feminine gentility of those days; characterised by a certain state and dignity,

---

① haughty: 傲慢的;自大的
② abashed: 不安的;窘迫的
③ apparel: 服装;衣
④ sumptuary: 禁止奢侈的

rather than by the delicate, evanescent①, and indescribable grace which is now recognised as its indication. And never had Hester Prynne appeared more ladylike, in the antique interpretation of the term, than as she issued from the prison. Those who had before known her, and had expected to behold her dimmed and obscured by a disastrous cloud, were astonished, and even startled, to perceive how her beauty shone out, and made a halo of the misfortune and ignominy in which she was enveloped. It may be true that, to a sensitive observer, there was something exquisitely painful in it. Her attire②, which indeed, she had wrought for the occasion in prison, and had modelled much after her own fancy, seemed to express the attitude of her spirit, the desperate recklessness of her mood, by its wild and picturesque peculiarity. But the point which drew all eyes, and, as it were, transfigured the wearer—so that both men and women who had been familiarly acquainted with Hester Prynne were now impressed as if they beheld her for the first time—was that SCARLET LETTER, so fantastically embroidered and illuminated upon her bosom. It had the effect of a spell, taking her out of the ordinary relations with humanity, and enclosing her in a sphere by herself.

"She hath good skill at her needle, that's certain," remarked one of her female spectators; "but did ever a woman, before this brazen hussy, contrive such a way of showing it? Why, gossips, what is it but to laugh in the faces of our godly magistrates, and make a pride out of what they, worthy gentlemen, meant for a punishment?"

"It were well," muttered the most iron-visaged of the old dames, "if we stripped Madame Hester's rich gown off her dainty③ shoulders; and as for the red letter which she hath stitched so curiously, I'll bestow a rag of mine own rheumatic flannel to make a fitter one!"

"Oh, peace, neighbours—peace!" whispered their youngest companion; "do not let her hear you! Not a stitch in that embroidered letter but she has felt it in her heart."

The grim beadle now made a gesture with his staff.

"Make way, good people—make way, in the King's name!" cried he. "Open a passage; and I promise ye, Mistress Prynne shall be set where man,

---

① evanescent：逐渐消失的；会凋零的
② attire：服装；盛装
③ dainty：讲究的；秀丽的

woman, and child may have a fair sight of her brave apparel from this time till an hour past meridian. A blessing on the righteous colony of the Massachusetts, where iniquity is dragged out into the sunshine! Come along, Madame Hester, and show your scarlet letter in the market-place!"

A lane was forthwith opened through the crowd of spectators. Preceded by the beadle, and attended by an irregular procession of stern-browed men and unkindly visaged women, Hester Prynne set forth towards the place appointed for her punishment. A crowd of eager and curious schoolboys, understanding little of the matter in hand, except that it gave them a half-holiday, ran before her progress, turning their heads continually to stare into her face and at the winking baby in her arms, and at the ignominious letter on her breast. It was no great distance, in those days, from the prison door to the market-place. Measured by the prisoner's experience, however, it might be reckoned a journey of some length; for haughty as her demeanor was, she perchance underwent an agony from every footstep of those that thronged to see her, as if her heart had been flung into the street for them all to spurn and trample upon. In our nature, however, there is a provision, alike marvellous and merciful, that the sufferer should never know the intensity of what he endures by its present torture, but chiefly by the pang that rankles after it. With almost a serene deportment, therefore, Hester Prynne passed through this portion of her ordeal, and came to a sort of scaffold, at the western extremity of the market-place. It stood nearly beneath the eaves of Boston's earliest church, and appeared to be a fixture there.

In fact, this scaffold constituted a portion of a penal machine, which now, for two or three generations past, has been merely historical and traditionary among us, but was held, in the old time, to be as effectual an agent, in the promotion of good citizenship, as ever was the guillotine[①] among the terrorists of France. It was, in short, the platform of the pillory[②]; and above it rose the framework of that instrument of discipline, so fashioned as to confine the human head in its tight grasp, and thus hold it up to the public gaze. The very ideal of ignominy was embodied and made manifest in this contrivance of wood and iron. There can be no outrage, methinks, against our common nature—

---

① guillotine：断头台
② pillory：示众；颈手枷

whatever be the delinquencies of the individual—no outrage more flagrant① than to forbid the culprit to hide his face for shame; as it was the essence of this punishment to do. In Hester Prynne's instance, however, as not unfrequently in other cases, her sentence bore that she should stand a certain time upon the platform, but without undergoing that gripe about the neck and confinement of the head, the proneness to which was the most devilish characteristic of this ugly engine. Knowing well her part, she ascended a flight of wooden steps, and was thus displayed to the surrounding multitude, at about the height of a man's shoulders above the street.

Had there been a Papist among the crowd of Puritans, he might have seen in this beautiful woman, so picturesque in her attire and mien, and with the infant at her bosom, an object to remind him of the image of Divine Maternity, which so many illustrious painters have vied with one another to represent; something which should remind him, indeed, but only by contrast, of that sacred image of sinless motherhood, whose infant was to redeem the world. Here, there was the taint of deepest sin in the most sacred quality of human life, working such effect, that the world was only the darker for this woman's beauty, and the more lost for the infant that she had borne.

The scene was not without a mixture of awe, such as must always invest the spectacle of guilt and shame in a fellow-creature, before society shall have grown corrupt enough to smile, instead of shuddering at it. The witnesses of Hester Prynne's disgrace had not yet passed beyond their simplicity. They were stern enough to look upon her death, had that been the sentence, without a murmur at its severity, but had none of the heartlessness of another social state, which would find only a theme for jest in an exhibition like the present. Even had there been a disposition to turn the matter into ridicule, it must have been repressed and overpowered by the solemn presence of men no less dignified than the governor, and several of his counsellors, a judge, a general, and the ministers of the town, all of whom sat or stood in a balcony of the meeting-house, looking down upon the platform. When such personages could constitute a part of the spectacle, without risking the majesty, or reverence of rank and office, it was safely to be inferred that the infliction of a legal sentence would have an earnest and effectual meaning. Accordingly, the crowd was sombre and

---

① flagrant：公然的；不能容忍的

grave. The unhappy culprit sustained herself as best a woman might, under the heavy weight of a thousand unrelenting eyes, all fastened upon her, and concentrated at her bosom. It was almost intolerable to be borne. Of an impulsive and passionate nature, she had fortified herself to encounter the stings and venomous stabs of public contumely, wreaking itself in every variety of insult; but there was a quality so much more terrible in the solemn mood of the popular mind, that she longed rather to behold all those rigid countenances contorted with scornful merriment, and herself the object. Had a roar of laughter burst from the multitude—each man, each woman, each little shrill-voiced child, contributing their individual parts—Hester Prynne might have repaid them all with a bitter and disdainful smile. But, under the leaden infliction which it was her doom to endure, she felt, at moments, as if she must needs shriek out with the full power of her lungs, and cast herself from the scaffold down upon the ground, or else go mad at once.

Yet there were intervals when the whole scene, in which she was the most conspicuous object, seemed to vanish from her eyes, or, at least, glimmered indistinctly before them, like a mass of imperfectly shaped and spectral images. Her mind, and especially her memory, was preternaturally active, and kept bringing up other scenes than this roughly hewn street of a little town, on the edge of the western wilderness: other faces than were lowering upon her from beneath the brims of those steeple-crowned hats. Reminiscences, the most trifling and immaterial, passages of infancy and school-days, sports, childish quarrels, and the little domestic traits of her maiden years, came swarming back upon her, intermingled with recollections of whatever was gravest in her subsequent life; one picture precisely as vivid as another; as if all were of similar importance, or all alike a play. Possibly, it was an instinctive device of her spirit to relieve itself by the exhibition of these phantasmagoric forms, from the cruel weight and hardness of the reality.

Be that as it might, the scaffold of the pillory was a point of view that revealed to Hester Prynne the entire track along which she had been treading, since her happy infancy. Standing on that miserable eminence①, she saw again her native village, in Old England, and her paternal home: a decayed house of grey stone, with a poverty-stricken aspect, but retaining a half obliterated shield

---

① eminence: 显赫；高处

of arms over the portal, in token of antique gentility. She saw her father's face, with its bold brow, and reverend white beard that flowed over the old-fashioned Elizabethan ruff; her mother's, too, with the look of heedful and anxious love which it always wore in her remembrance, and which, even since her death, had so often laid the impediment of a gentle remonstrance in her daughter's pathway. She saw her own face, glowing with girlish beauty, and illuminating all the interior of the dusky mirror in which she had been wont to gaze at it. There she beheld another countenance, of a man well stricken in years, a pale, thin, scholar-like visage, with eyes dim and bleared by the lamp-light that had served them to pore over many ponderous books. Yet those same bleared optics had a strange, penetrating power, when it was their owner's purpose to read the human soul. This figure of the study and the cloister, as Hester Prynne's womanly fancy failed not to recall, was slightly deformed, with the left shoulder a trifle higher than the right. Next rose before her in memory's picture-gallery, the intricate and narrow thoroughfares, the tall, grey houses, the huge cathedrals, and the public edifices, ancient in date and quaint in architecture, of a continental city; where new life had awaited her, still in connection with the misshapen scholar: a new life, but feeding itself on time-worn materials, like a tuft of① green moss on a crumbling wall. Lastly, in lieu of these shifting scenes, came back the rude market-place of the Puritan, settlement, with all the townspeople assembled, and levelling their stern regards at Hester Prynne—yes, at herself—who stood on the scaffold of the pillory, an infant on her arm, and the letter A, in scarlet, fantastically embroidered with gold thread, upon her bosom.

Could it be true She clutched the child so fiercely to her breast that it sent forth a cry; she turned her eyes downward at the scarlet letter, and even touched it with her finger, to assure herself that the infant and the shame were real. Yes these were her realities—all else had vanished!

Questions for Discussion

Different readers may put different interpretations on "the scarlet letter." What is your understanding?

---

① a tuft of: 一簇；一丛

Unit 5   Henry Wadsworth Longfellow (1807 – 1882)

Appreciation

Lives of great men all remind us   伟人的生平启示我们:
We can make our lives sublime   我们能够生活得高尚,
And, departing, leave behind us   而当告别人世的时候,
Footprints on the sands of time   留下脚印在时间的沙上

Longfellow was born into a well-to-do family in Portland, Maine, on February 27, 1807. He attended Bowdoin College in 1822, where he met Nathaniel Hawthorne as his fellow student. After he graduated in 1825, he went to Europe to study language. Four years later, he returned to the United States and then found a position as a professor at Harvard in 1837. He held this position until his retirement in 1854. The last twenty-eight years of his life were spent in writing, studying, and traveling.

Longfellow wrote poems on a wide range of subjects, contemporary and historical, and he used many different verse forms and meters with great technical skill. His early poems were mostly collected in *Voices of the Night* (1839), which was well accepted and assured him as a famous poet. "*A Psalm of Life*" was one of the best-known poems from this volume.

Longfellow enjoyed his popularity as a poet during his life time. His poetic works were regarded as the summit of the literary works of the 19th century. His poetry expresses a spirit of optimism and faith in the goodness of life which evokes immediate response in the emotions of his readers.

Brief Introduction

A Psalm of Life is one of the best-known poems of Longfellow. It has served as one of the most inspirational poems in literature since it was written. The poem strives to look at the human attitude toward life and death. The major theme is that living is not the only thing humans are put on earth for. While heaven may be the goal at the end of life, humans are also sent to earth to live productive and generous lives as well.

Selected Reading

A Psalm① of Life

Tell me not in mournful numbers②,
Life is but an empty dream!
For the soul is dead that slumbers③,
And things are not what they seem.

Life is real! Life is earnest!
And the grave is not its goal;
Dust thou art, to dust returnest④,
Was not spoken of the soul⑤.

Not enjoyment, and not sorrow,
Is our destin'd⑥ end or way;
But to act, that each tomorrow
Find us farther than today.

Art is long, and Time is fleeting⑦,
And our hearts, though stout⑧ and brave,
Still, like muffled drums⑨, are beating

---

① psalm：赞美诗,颂歌

② mournful numbers：伤感的诗句。numbers：韵文,诗

③ For the soul is dead that slumbers：= for the soul that slumbers is dead. slumber：睡眠；处于静止状态。此处可引申为"怠惰的"

④ Dust thou art, to dust returnest：thou（古英语）= you；art（古英语）= are；该句意思为：你本是尘土,必归于尘土。此为圣经《旧约:创世记》第 3 章第 19 节中耶和华对亚当说的话

⑤ Was not spoken of the soul：此句的主语为前一句,"你本是尘土,必归于尘土"指的并不是灵魂,而是肉体

⑥ destin'd：= destined,命中注定的

⑦ Art is long, and Time is fleeting：艺术长久,韶光飞逝。摘自古希腊希波克拉底的《格言集》

⑧ stout：坚定的

⑨ muffled drums：指鼓声沉闷。muffle 此处意为"用布将鼓包裹使其声音低沉"

Funeral marches① to the grave.

In the world's broad field of battle,
In the bivouac② of Life,
Be not like dumb, driven cattle③!
Be a hero in the strife④!

Thrust no Future, howe'er pleasant!
Let the dead Past bury its dead⑤!
Act,—act in the living Present!
Heart within, and God o'er head⑥!

Lives of great men all remind us
We can make our lives sublime⑦,
And, departing⑧, leave behind us
Footprints on the sands of time⑨;

Footprints⑩ that perhaps another,
Sailing o'er life's solemn main⑪,
A forlorn⑫ and shipwrecked⑬ brother,
Seeing, shall take heart again⑭.

---

① funeral marches：丧礼进行曲
② bivouac：露营地，与上一行中的"field of battle"相呼应
③ dumb, driven cattle：不会说话、任人驱使的牲畜
④ strife：斗争，竞争
⑤ Let the dead Past bury its dead：让失去的岁月将死者埋葬
⑥ Heart within, and God o'er head：心中充满勇气，相信苍天有上帝。heart：勇气
⑦ sublime：崇高的
⑧ departing：离开人世之时
⑨ the sands of time：此处的"沙"指古代计时用的沙漏中的沙粒。"时间的沙"指人类的历史。从下一诗节来看，"沙"还可指"人生的大海"岸边的滩，两个比喻遥相呼应
⑩ footprints：做该节第四行 seeing 的宾语
⑪ life's solemn main：人生庄严的大海。main 在诗中意为：海洋，沧海
⑫ forlorn：被遗弃的
⑬ shipwrecked：遭受船难的，(喻)遭受失败的
⑭ take heart again：重新鼓起勇气

Let us, then, be up and doing①,
With a heart for any face;
Still② achieving, still pursuing,
Learn to labor and to wait.

Questions for Discussion

> Discuss the theme of Psalm of Life.

The Tide Rises, the Tide Falls

Brief Introduction

"The Tide Rises, the Tide Falls" is a poem about cycles. "Life Goes On" would be a better title for "The Tide Rises, the Tide Falls," but the tides here are just a stand in for the natural world as we know it. The rising and falling of the tide is the speaker's way of describing the eternal cycles and rhythms of nature—of the rising and setting of the sun, of life and death, etc. While the natural world in this poem comes across almost like a machine (up and down, up and down, rise and fall, rise and fall), it's also kind of a strange force. The sea is almost like a monster, calling in the darkness, and then it uses those seemingly pure white hands to... erase the traveler's footprints, and symbolically his presence in life. This is definitely a natural world that you should be wary of.

Form and Meter: It is a rondeau that has no fixed meter for every, single line of the poem. Setting: It is a very dark poem, literally and thematically. The poem takes place at twilight, near the seashore.

Selected Reading

The tide rises, the tide falls,
The twilight darkens, the curfew calls;
Along the sea-sands damp and brown
The traveller hasten toward the town,
And the tide rises, the tide falls.

---

① up and doing: 活跃起来
② still: 此处相当于 always

Darkness settles on roofs and walls,
But the sea, the sea in the darkness calls;
The little waves, with their soft, white ands,
Efface the foot prints in the sands,
    And the tide rises, the tide falls.
The morning breaks, the steeds in their stalls
Stamp and neigh, as the hostler calls;
The day returns, but never more
Returns the traveller to the shore,
    And the tide rises, the tide falls.

Questions for Discussion

1. What's up with the title?
2. Discuss the themes of "The Tide Rises, The Tide Falls."
3. Make an analysis of "The Tide Rises, The Tide Falls".

My Lost Youth

Brief Introduction

"My Lost Youth" is a tribute to Longfellow's native town of Portland, Maine, which he never ceased to love, and whose beautiful surroundings and quiet, pure life he describes in this poem. "The sea-fight far away" is a reference to the War of 1812, which deeply impacted the author.

Selected Reading

Often I think of the beautiful town
    That is seated by the sea;
Often in thought go up and down
    The pleasant streets of that dear old town,
And my youth comes back to me.
    And a verse of a Lapland song
    Is haunting my memory still:

"A boy's will is the wind's will,
And the thoughts of youth are long, long thoughts."

I can see the shadowy lines of its trees,
    And catch, in sudden gleams,
The sheen of the far-surrounding seas,
And islands that were the Hesperides
    Of all my boyish dreams.
    And the burden of that old song,
    It murmurs and whispers still:
"A boy's will is the wind's will,
And the thoughts of youth are long, long thoughts."

I remember the black wharves and the ships,
    And the sea-tides tossing free;
And Spanish sailors with bearded lips,
And the beauty and mystery of the ships,
    And the magic of the sea.
And the voice of that wayward song
    Is singing and saying still:
"A boy's will is the wind's will,
And the thoughts of youth are long, long thoughts."

I remember the bulwarks by the shore,
    And the fort upon the hill;
The sunrise gun, with its hollow roar,
The drum-beat repeated o'er and o'er,
    And the bugle wild and shrill.
And the music of that old song
    Throbs in my memory still:
"A boy's will is the wind's will,
And the thoughts of youth are long, long thoughts."

I remember the sea-fight far away,
    How it thundered o'er the tide!
And the dead captains, as they lay

In their graves, o'erlooking the tranquil bay
    Where they in battle died.
And the sound of that mournful song
Goes through me with a thrill:
"A boy's will is the wind's will,
And the thoughts of youth are long, long thoughts."

I can see the breezy dome of groves,
    The shadows of Deering's Woods;
And the friendships old and the early loves
Come back with a Sabbath sound, as of doves
    In quiet neighborhoods.
    And the verse of that sweet old song,
It flutters and murmurs still:
"A boy's will is the wind's will,
And the thoughts of youth are long, long thoughts."

I remember the gleams and glooms that dart
    Across the school-boy's brain;
The song and the silence in the heart,
That in part are prophecies, and in part
    Are longings wild and vain.
    And the voice of that fitful song
Sings on, and is never still:
"A boy's will is the wind's will,
And the thoughts of youth are long, long thoughts."

There are things of which I may not speak;
    There are dreams that cannot die;
There are thoughts that make the strong heart weak,
And bring a pallor into the cheek,
    And a mist before the eye.
    And the words of that fatal song
Come over me like a chill:
"A boy's will is the wind's will,
And the thoughts of youth are long, long thoughts."

Strange to me now are the forms I meet
　　When I visit the dear old town;
But the native air is pure and sweet,
And the trees that o'er shadow each well-known street,

　　As they balance up and down,
　　Are singing the beautiful song,
　　Are sighing and whispering still:
"A boy's will is the wind's will,
And the thoughts of youth are long, long thoughts."

And Deering's Woods are fresh and fair,
　　And with joy that is almost pain
My heart goes back to wander there,
And among the dreams of the days that were,
　　I find my lost youth again.
　　And the strange and beautiful song,
　　The groves are repeating it still:
"A boy's will is the wind's will,
And the thoughts of youth are long, long thoughts."

Questions for Discussion:

Make an analysis of "My Lost Youth".

Unit 6　Walt Whitman (1819 – 1892)

Appreciation

　　I celebrate myself, and sing myself　我赞美我自己,歌唱我自己

　　Walt Whitman was born on Long Island, New York, into a Quaker family. His father was a carpenter and farmer. Whitman had very little education, but he taught himself by reading and writing and by learning from life. He left school at the age of eleven and became an office boy. Later on he changed several jobs, working as a shopkeeper, an apprentice to a printer and an editor of various newspapers. A variety of jobs and first-hand knowledge of life and people helped him a lot in his writing.

In 1848 Whitman began to write poetry. In 1855, he published his first edition of *Leaves of Grass*, which contains only 12 of his best poems. The collection was soon enlarged into 32 poems. In his life, he wrote over 400 poems. He continued expanding and revising it until his death in 1892. "*Song of Myself*" is considered the most significant poem of the volume.

Walt Whitman was one of the great innovators and pioneers in American poetry. His greatest contribution to American literature is the use of free verse, which has no regular meter, rhythm, or line length. He creates a rhythm that depends on natural speech rhythms. He is called "the father of free verse".

Brief Introduction

Walt Whitman's *Song of Myself* is the most famous of the twelve poems originally published in *Leaves of Grass*. In singing of himself, Whitman feels that he is singing of every other person too: every atom (even the smallest part) that belongs to Whitman is also true of the reader. He simply sings at his ease. Whitman reveals his desire to examine the individual, the communion between individuals, and the individual's place in the universe. The poem is at once a meditation on what it is to be human.

Selected Reading

Song of Myself

1

I celebrate myself, and sing myself,
And what I assume① you shall assume,
For every atom② belonging to me as good belongs to you.
I loafe③ and invite my soul,
I lean and loafe at my ease observing a spear of summer grass④.

---

① assume: 承认,接受
② atom: 原子。这里指构成人体的基本结构
③ loafe: 即 loaf,游荡、闲逛,此处意为"逍遥自在"
④ a spear of summer grass: 夏日的一片草叶。这是贯穿全诗始终的一个意象。spear:(草的)叶片,幼芽,幼苗

My tongue, every atom of my blood, form'd① from this soil, this air,
Born here of parents born here from parents the same, and their parents the same,
I, now thirty-seven years old in perfect health begin,
Hoping to cease not till death②,
Creeds and schools③ in abeyance④,
Retiring back a while⑤ sufficed at what they are⑥, but never forgotten,
I harbor for good or bad, I permit to speak at every hazard,
Nature without check with original energy⑦.

Questions for Discussion

What does the poet want to convey in "song of myself"?

City of Orgies
Brief Introduction

This "Calamus" poem, which acquired its present title in 1867, was originally called by its first line, "City of my walks and joys!," when published as number 18 in the "Calamus" series in 1860. The poem is characteristic of whiteman's structure of negation, and testifies to whiteman's interest in the city as subject of the poetry.

---

① form'd: formed
② Hoping to cease not till death: Hoping not to cease till death 愿永不停步,直到生命停息
③ creeds and schools: 各种信条和学说
④ in abeyance: 中止,暂搁
⑤ retiring back a while: (各种信条和学说)暂时隐退
⑥ sufficed at what they are: (我)满足于它们(指各种信条和学说)的现状
⑦ I harbor...at every hazard, Nature...original energy.: 该句中的 Nature 作为动词 harbor 和 permit 的宾语,这两行的语序应为 I harbor Nature for good or bad, I permit Nature to speak at every hazard, without check with original energy. 意思为:无论好坏,我无所畏惧地拥抱自然,让自然尽情地言说以展现其原始活力。harbor: 包含;怀有。at every hazard: 无论怎样

Selected Reading

> CITY of orgies, walks and joys,
> City whom that I have lived and sung in your midst will one day
>   make you illustrious,
> Not the pageants of you, not your shifting tableaus, your
>   spectacles, repay me,
> Not the interminable rows of your houses, nor the ships at the
>   wharves,
> Nor the processions in the streets, nor the bright windows,
>   with goods in them,
> Nor to converse with learn'd persons, or bear my share in the
>   soiree or feast;
> Not those, but as I pass O Manhattan, your frequent and swift
>   flash of eyes offering me love,
> Offering response to my own—these repay me,
> Lovers, continual lovers, only repay me.

Questions for Discussion

Make an analysis of "City of Orgies".

O Captain! My Captain!

Brief Introduction

"O Captain! My Captain!" is written in 1865 by Walt Whitman, about the death of American president Abraham Lincoln. It is an extended metaphor poem. It was published in the pamphlet Sequel to Drum-Taps which assembled 18 poems about the Civil War. The poem emphasizes or shows grief and sorrow. The fallen captain refers to Abraham Lincoln, captain of the ship that is the United States of America.

Two examples of alliteration are in line 10 "flag is flung", as well as in line 19 "safe and sound". The rhyme scheme is AABCDEFE, GGHIJEKE, and LLMNOEPE for each stanza. Repetition occurs many times in this poem, for example "O Captain!

My Captain", and "fallen cold and dead".

"O Captain! My Captain!" became one of Whitman's most famous poems, one that he would read at the end of his famous lecture about the Lincoln assassination. Whitman became so identified with the poem that late in life he remarked, "Damn My Captain... I'm almost sorry I ever wrote the poem."

Selected Reading

O Captain! my Captain! our fearful trip is done,
The ship has weather'd every rack, the prize we sought is won,
The port is near, the bells I hear, the people all exulting,
While follow eyes the steady keel, the vessel grim and daring;
  But O heart! heart! heart!
   O the bleeding drops of red,
    Where on the deck my Captain lies,
     Fallen cold and dead.

O Captain! my Captain! rise up and hear the bells;
Rise up—for you the flag is flung—for you the bugle trills,
For you bouquets and ribbon'd wreaths—for you the shores a-crowding,
For you they call, the swaying mass, their eager faces turning;
  Here Captain! dear father!
   This arm beneath your head!
    It is some dream that on the deck,
     You've fallen cold and dead.

My Captain does not answer, his lips are pale and still,
My father does not feel my arm, he has no pulse nor will,
The ship is anchor'd safe and sound, its voyage closed and done,
From fearful trip the victor ship comes in with object won;
  Exult O shores, and ring O bells!
   But I with mournful tread,
    Walk the deck my Captain lies,
     Fallen cold and dead.

Questions for Discussion

Make an analysis of "O Captain! My Captain!"

Unit 7 Emily Dickinson (1830 – 1886)

Emily Dickinson was an American poet. She was born in Amherst, Massachusetts, to a prominent family well known for their political and educational influence. Affected by an unhappy love affair with Reverend Charles Wadsworth, Dickinson became a total recluse. She dressed entirely in white and became known for her reluctance to greet guests or, later in life, to even leave her bedroom. Dickinson never married, and most friendships between her and others depended entirely upon letters and notes. Dickinson' poetry,1775 short poems in total, has a great impact upon the poetry of the early 20th century. Dickinson developed a style of clear, piercing imagery that was all her own, leaving the reader mixed with a sense of awe and wonder. Though her poetry was not truly appreciated in her lifetime, after her death, Dickinson has come to be regarded alongside Walt Whitman as one of the two great American poets of the nineteenth century.

Brief Introduction

This poem about finding a beautiful garden is one of Emily Dickinson's most well known poems. Its meaning is simplistic, literally. Dickinson wrote about a peaceful garden, where there were always warm sunshine, beautiful flowers and evergreen trees; a garden full of bliss.

Selected Reading

There Is Another Sky

There is another sky,
Ever serene① and fair,
And there is another sunshine,
Though it be darkness there;
Never mind faded forests, Austin,
Never mind silent fields—
Here is a little forest,
Whose leaf is ever green;
Here is a brighter garden,
Where not a frost has been;
In its unfading flowers
I hear the bright bee hum②:
Prithee③, my brother,
Into my garden come!

Questions for Discussion

Anolyze the peom "There is another sky".

Brief Introduction

I'm Nobody! published in 1891 in Poems, Series 2, is Dickinson's most popular and most defense of the kind of spiritual privacy she favored. "To be Nobody" is a luxury

---

① serene:祥和的;稳重的
② hum:(蜜蜂等)发嗡嗡声
③ Prithee:请

incomprehensible to a dreary somebody because they are too busy keeping their names in circulation, croaking like frogs in a swamp in the summertime. To be Somebody is not as fancy as it seems to be. Dickinson adopts the persona of a child who is open, naive, and innocent.

Selected Reading

I'm Nobody!

I'M Nobody! Who are you?
Are you—Nobody—too?
Then there's a pair of us!
Don't tell! They'd banish① us—you know!

How dreary②—to be—Somebody!
How public—like a Frog—
To tell your name—the livelong③ June—
To an admiring Bog④!

Questions for Discussion

1. What does "Somebody" and "Nobody" mean in the poem?
2. Why does the tone change in the second stanza?
3. Can you explain the image in the poem?

---

① banish:放逐,驱逐消除,排除
② dreary:沉寂的;阴沉的;令人厌烦的;枯燥的
③ livelong:漫长的,整个的
④ Bog:沼泽,泥塘

Chapter 5

American Realism and Naturalism

I. Historical Background

In the 1800 election, Jefferson, a scientist himself, supported expeditions to explore and map the new domain. Jefferson believed deeply in republicanism and argued it should be based on the independent yeoman farmer and planter; he distrusted cities, factories and banks.

1. Indian Removal

Indian removal was a policy of the United States government in the 19th century. In 1830, Congress passed the Indian Removal Act, which exchanged Native American tribal lands in the eastern states for lands west of the Mississippi River. Its goal was mainly to remove Native Americans from the American Southeast; they occupied land that settlers wanted. Thousands of deaths resulted from the relocations.

2. The Civil War

The central issue after 1848 was the expansion of slavery. The anti-slavery elements were a majority in the North, who declared that ownership of slaves was a sin and demanded its immediate abolition. Southern whites insisted that slavery was of economic, social, and cultural benefits to all whites.

The Civil War (1861–1865), largely a struggle of industry and capitalist democracy against agriculture and slavery, was a turning point in American history. In the end, the industrial North defeated the agrarian South and a new society came into being. Industry developed at an unprecedented rate.

Politically the Civil War affected both the social and the value system of the country. America had transformed into an industrialized and commercialized society. The war also brought some noticeable changes to the American economy, which stimulated technological development, and new methods of organization and management were tested to adapt to industrial modernization on a large scale.

Railroads were built, with which came vast commercial development and mobility. Many farmers, attracted by the prospect of factory work and higher pay, flocked to the industrial cities, causing an oversupply of labor. American cities expanded at an alarming rate. However, the wealth was more than ever in the possession of the few: bankers and industrialists. Business and financial tycoons were honored as national heroes and as models for the youth.

3. Social Problems

Problems of urbanization and industrialization appeared: poor and overcrowded housing, unsanitary conditions, low pay, difficult working conditions, and inadequate restraints on business. The gulf between the rich and the poor was widened and social contradictions were sharpened. The spread of industrialization inevitably created extremes of wealth and poverty. Slum areas appeared where crimes, murder, diseases, and violence found their way. For the countless ordinary people, life became a struggle for survival. As far as ideology was concerned, people were on a shaking ground. The harsh realities of life as well as the disillusion of heroism resulting from the dark memories of the Civil War had set the nation against the romance.

4. The West and the Gilded Age

The latter half of the 19th century was marked by the rapid development and settlement of the far West, first by wagon trains and riverboats and then aided by the completion of the transcontinental railroad. Large numbers of European immigrants (especially from Germany and Scandinavia) took up low-cost or free farms in the Prairie States. Mining for silver and copper opened up the Mountain West.

The United States Army fought frequent small-scale wars with Native Americans as settlers on their traditional lands. Gradually the US purchased the Native American tribal lands and extinguished their claims, forcing most tribes onto subsidized reservations. The Indian wars under the government of the United States have been more than 40 in number. They have cost the lives of about 19,000 white men, women and children, including those killed in individual combats, and the lives of about 30,000 Indians. The actual number of killed and wounded Indians must be very much higher than the given.... Fifty percent additional would be a safe estimate....

Toward the end of this century, the Westward Movement that had brought people constant hope for a better life half a century before was no longer inspiring since the frontier was about to close. Farmers were still going westward, but not much land was waiting to be cultivated. A sense of suffering, unhappiness, disillusionment and pessimism began to prevail. It was the beginning of what Mark Twain called "*The Gilded Age*," an age of extremes of decline and progress, of poverty and dazzling wealth, of gloom and buoyant hope. The term came into use in the 1920s and 1930s and was derived from writer Mark Twain's 1873 *The Gilded Age: A Tale of Today*, which satirized an era of serious social problems masked by a thin gold gilding. The early half of the Gilded Age roughly coincided with the middle portion of the Victorian era in Britain and the Belle époque in France.

II. Literary Background

1. American Realism

In American literature, "Realism" encompasses the period of time from the Civil War to the turn of the 20th century. American Realism, although influenced by English and European authors, was basically native. It first appeared in the United States in the literature of local color, a mixture of romantic plots and realistic descriptions of things immediately observable: the dialects, customs, sights, and sounds of regional America. But due to the influence of Civil War, the American society was in a turbulent situation. The writings about local life, critical realism and unveiling the dark side of the society were increased.

American Realism dominated the spirit of American literature, especially American fiction. Realism was characterized by a great interest in the realities of life. It aimed at the interpretation of the actualities of any aspect of life, free from subjective prejudice, idealism, or romantic color.

Realistic writers seek to portray American life as it really is, insisting that the ordinary and the local are most suitable for artistic representation. They select representative and ordinary characters from daily life, describe the setting in which these characters live in a faithful way, and try to avoid authorial intrusion into the judgment of either the characters or their behaviors.

(1) Regional and Local Color Writings

Regional and Local Color Writings are the Early Stage of Literary Realism, which are instances of realism in so far as they depict contemporary life, use the speech of the common people, and avoid fantastic plotlines. There are also often a romantic flavor in regional and local color writings as they receive influences from Washington Irving and the frontier tradition of tall tales. A regional work relies on the cultural, social and historical settings. If the setting is removed, the work is destroyed.

(2) Local colorism

American colorism was a unique variation of American literary realism, and reached its peak in the 1880s and began to decline by the turn of the century.

It depicts the characters from a specified setting of an era, which are marked by its customs, dialects, costumes, landscape, sounds of regional America or other peculiarities that have escaped standardizing cultural influence. Mark Twain represents the local colorists while Henry James represents the psychological realists who explore the psychology of their characters.

(3) Critical Realism

William Dean Howell, American writer and editor in chief of the *Atlantic Monthly*, encouraged a number of writers, including Mark Twain and Henry James. He also wrote many novels, such as *The Rise of Silas Lapham*, and books of literary criticism. Howells focused his discussion on the rising middle class and the way they lived.

(4) Psychological Realism

Henry James laid a great emphasis on the "inner world" of man. He tried to probe reaches of the psychological and moral nature of human beings. James believed that writers should not simply hold mirrors to the surface of social life; they should also use language to explore the innermost depth of the psychological and moral nature of human beings. He was a realist of the inner life. He was regarded as the forerunner of the Stream of Consciousness technique.

2. American Naturalism

After the Civil War, the rapid social changes caused by industrialization brought serious social problems. While the captains of industry piled up huge personal fortunes, the ordinary man became the victim of industrialization. Industrial proletariats were entirely at the mercy of external forces beyond their control, living a life of insecurity, suffering and violence. The harsh reality of the industrialization period changed man's understanding about himself and the world in which he lived in. Living in a cold, indifferent, and Godless world, man was completely thrown upon himself for survival.

In 1859, Charles Darwin's *The Origin of Species* was published. This book, together with Darwin's *Descent of Man* (1870) established a new theory of evolution which offered a great challenge to the old idea of man being created by God.

Naturalism was a literary movement of the late 19th century that yielded influence on the 20th. It was an extension of Realism, a reaction against the restrictions inherent in the realistic emphasis on the ordinary, insisted that the extraordinary is real, too.

Naturalism were strongly influenced by Darwin's theory of evolution, and adopted the more negative implication of the theory to account for the behavior of those characters conditioned by social and economic forces.

The writers sometimes labeled as "naturalists" attempted to achieve extreme objectivity and frankness, presenting characters of low social and economic classes who were dominated by their environment and heredity.

Representative Writers and Works

Frank Norris, Stephen Crane, Jack London and Theodore Dreiser are the representatives of Naturalism. Norris's *McTeague* is the manifesto of American naturalism. Crane's *Maggie: A Girl of the Streets*, is the first American naturalism work—designed, he wrote, "to show that environment is a tremendous thing in the world and frequently shapes lives regardless." Dreiser's *Sister Carrie* is the work in which naturalism attained maturity. Naturalisms also appear in the plays of Eufene O'Nell and the novels of James T. Farrell. Naturalisms reached its peak in the novels of Theodore Dreiser.

Features and Styles

They described in detail the lives of the downtrodden and of the abnormal by frankly treating human passion and sexuality to show the animalistic nature of human beings.

Characters in naturalistic works are frequently, ill-educated or lower-class characters whose lives are governed by the forces of heredity, environment, chance, instinct and passion. The term for this idea is "determinism".

The setting in those novels is frequently an urban one, as in Frank Norris's *McTeague*. The naturalist usually used carefully chosen surface detail to portray a gloomy and depressing setting. They emphasized that the universe is cold, indifferent and hostile to human desires, and also claimed that the works produced have tended to emphaszie either a biological determinism or a socio-economic determinism.

In theme, naturalists represent the life of the lower classes truthfully and break into such forbidden regions as violence, death and sex; in technique, their works exhibit honest skills and artistry. But they are evidently original and experimental in their perspective styles.

Open-ending leaves much room for readers to think by themselves.

Unit 1 Mark Twain (1835 – 1910)

Appreciation

You could not take up a newspaper, English, Scotch, or Irish, without finding in it one or more references to the "vest-pocket million-pounder" and his latest doings and saying. At first, in these mentions, I was at the bottom of the personal-gossip column; next, I was listed above the knights, next above the baronets, next above the barons, and so on, and so on, climbing steadily, as my notoriety augmented, until I reached the highest altitude possible, and there I remained, taking precedence of all dukes not royal, and of all ecclesiastics except the primate of all England. But mind, this was not fame; as yet I had achieved only notoriety. Then came the climaxing stroke—the accolade, so to speak—which in a single instant transmuted the perishable dross of notoriety into the enduring gold of fame. 说来也不足为奇;我已经成了这个世界大都会的显赫人物,我的思想何止是一星半点,简直是彻头彻尾地改造了。不管你翻开哪份报纸,无论是英格兰的,苏格兰的,还是爱尔兰的,你总会看到一两条有关"身藏百万英镑者"及其最新言行的消息。刚开始的时候,这些有关我的消息放在杂谈栏的尾巴上;接着我的位置就超过了各位爵士,后来盖过了二等男爵,再往后又凌驾于男爵之上了,如此这般,我的位置越升越高,名气也越来越响,直到无法再高的地方才停了下来。这时候,我已经居于皇室之下和众公爵之上;虽然比不上全英大主教,但足可俯瞰除他以外的一切神职人员。切记,直到这时,我还算不上有声望;只能说是有了名气。就在这时,高潮突起——就像封侯拜将一般——刹那间,我那过眼烟云似的名气化作了天长地久的黄金般的声望。

Mark Twain is the pen name of Samuel Langhorne Clemens. Born in Florida, Missouri, he moved with his family to the Mississippi River town of Hannibal when he was four. When his father died in 1847, Twain had to quit school to help support the family. He worked as a printer's apprentice, a travelling printer, a silver miner, a steamboat pilot on the Mississippi River, and a frontier journalist in Nevada and California. The early experiences, especially those on the steamboat, abundantly acquainted him with every possible type of human nature and a colorful language, providing him a wide knowledge of humanity.

Mark Twain is an outstanding humorist and satirist. He is the first American author to write great books using a genuinely colloquial and native American speech. He began his literary career by writing humorous sketches for newspapers. In 1865 a national magazine published his retelling of a tale he had heard from miners, "The Celebrated Jumping Frog of Calaveras County"《卡拉维拉斯县驰名的跳蛙》, which was an instant success. As a reporter for several newspapers, he traveled to Hawaii, Europe, and the Middle East. The book he wrote about his travels, *The Innocents Abroad*《傻子出国记》, made him famous. More books followed, including *Innocents Abroad*, *Roughing It*《艰苦岁月》, *The Gilded Age* (1873)《镀金时代》, *The Adventures of Tom Sawyer*, *Life on Mississippi* (1883)《密西西比河上的生活》, *Pudd'nhead Wilson*《傻瓜威尔逊》, *The Adventures of Huckleberry Finn* (1884)《哈克贝里·费恩历险记》, *The Man that Corrupted Hadleyburg*《败坏了哈德莱堡的人》, *What is Man?* (1906)《什么是人?》, *The Mysterious Stranger*《神秘来客》.

Characteristics of Mark Twain

His greatest achievement in literature is his use of the dialect and his portrayal of the local. He writes about his people and his own life. His works sum up the tradition of Western humor and frontier realism. Twain's literary style is that of a natural southern dialect intermingled with other dialects to represent the various attitudes of the Mississippian region; he does not intend to outrightly suggest Negro inferiority. Mark Twain definitely has a style of his own that depicts a realism in the novel about the society back in antebellum 内战期间的 America. Huckleberry is also a very important character to study to further contemplate Twain's literary style in that Huck is the main character and the voice through which Twain conveys the images of the South.

Brief Introduction

"The Million Pound Bank Note" (1893) is a short story by Mark Twain. It takes place in Victorian London, where two very rich, eccentric brothers give the penniless story protagonist, Henry Adams, one million pounds of money in the form of a single peerless bank note.

Henry is an American who is swept out to sea on a Saturday sail near San Francisco, and is picked up by a London—bound brig. Subsequently, he is given a million pound note by two old gentlemen who have a £20,000 bet on him. Henry would not be easily able to exchange that note in the bank without being questioned about how he had come to it, charged with theft and arrested. He would also not be able to spend it since no ordinary person would be able to change it. Henry realizes the danger of his inexplicable possession of the note while appearing as a pauper—eventually revealed as the subject of the bet—but his cunning lands him instant celebrity as the talk of the town. In the end, Gordon wins the bet between the two brothers.

Mark Twain published "The Million Pound Bank Note" towards the end of his writing career. Twain departed from his earlier work by setting "The Million Pound Bank Note" in London rather than in the United States. Twain still, however, highlights simplicity in his basic plotline, while focusing once more on his characters and their specific socioeconomic situation, social history and, in a larger sense, country of origin.

Selected Reading

The Million Pound Bank Note

Chapter 1

When I was twenty-seven years old, I was a mining-broker's clerk in San Francisco, and an expert in all the details of stock traffic. I was alone in the world, and had nothing to depend upon but my wits and a clean reputation; but these were setting my feet in the road to eventual fortune, and I was content with the prospect.

My time was my own after the afternoon board, Saturdays, and I was accustomed① to put it in on a little sail-boat on the bay. One day I ventured too far, and was carried out to sea. Just at nightfall, when hope was about gone, I was picked up by a small brig which was bound for London. It was a long and stormy voyage, and they made me work my passage without pay, as a common sailor. When I stepped ashore in London my clothes were ragged and shabby② and I had only a dollar in my pocket. This money fed and sheltered me twenty-four hours. During the next twenty-four I went without food and shelter.

About ten o'clock on the following morning, seedy and hungry, I was dragging myself along Portland Place, when a child that was passing, towed by a nurse-maid, tossed a luscious big pear-minus one bite-into the gutter. I stopped, of course, and fastened my desiring eye on that muddy treasure. My mouth watered for it, my stomach craved it, my whole being begged for it. But every time I made a move to get it some passing eye detected my purpose, and of course I straightened up then, and looked indifferent, and pretended that I

---

① accustomed:通常的,习惯的,按照风俗习惯的
② shabby:破旧的,褴褛的

hadn't been thinking about the pear at all. This same thing kept happening and happening, and I couldn't get the pear. I was just getting desperate enough to brave all the shame, and to seize it, when a window behind me was raised, and a gentleman spoke out of it, saying:

"Step in here, please."

I was admitted by a gorgeous① flunkey②, and shown into a sumptuous③ room where a couple of elderly gentlemen were sitting. They sent away the servant, and made me sit down. They had just finished their breakfast, and the sight of the remains of it almost overpowered me. I could hardly keep my wits④ together in the presence of that food, but as I was not asked to sample it, I had to bear my trouble as best I could.

Now, something had been happening there a little before, which I did not know anything about until a good many days afterwards, but I will tell you about it now. Those two old brothers had been having a pretty hot argument a couple of days before, and had ended by agreeing to decide it by a bet, which is the English way of settling everything.

You will remember that the Bank of England once issued⑤ two notes of a million pounds each, to be used for a special purpose connected with some public transaction⑥ with a foreign country. For some reason or other only one of these had been used and canceled; the other still lay in the vaults⑦ of the Bank. Well, the brothers, chatting along, happened to get to wondering what might be the fate of a perfectly honest and intelligent stranger who should be turned adrift⑧ in London without a friend, and with no money but that million-pound bank-note, and no way to account for⑨ his being in possession⑩ of it. Brother A

---

① gorgeous:华丽的,灿烂的
② flunkey:穿制服的仆役,谄媚者
③ sumptuous:豪华的
④ keep my wits:才智
⑤ issue:发行
⑥ transaction:交易
⑦ vault:金库
⑧ adrift:落难
⑨ account for:证明
⑩ possession:拥有,占有,所有

said he would starve to death; Brother B said he wouldn't. Brother A said he couldn't offer it at a bank or anywhere else, because he would be arrested on the spot. So they went on disputing till Brother B said he would bet twenty thousand pounds that the man would live thirty days, anyway, on that million, and keep out of jail, too. Brother A took him up. Brother B went down to the Bank and bought that note. Just like an Englishman, you see; pluck to the backbone. Then he dictated a letter, which one of his clerks wrote out in a beautiful round hand, and then the two brothers sat at the window a whole day watching for the right man to give it to.

They saw many honest faces go by that were not intelligent enough; many that were intelligent, but not honest enough; many that were both, but the possessors[①] were not poor enough, or, if poor enough, were not strangers. There was always a defect, until I came along; but they agreed that I filled the bill all around; so they elected me unanimously, and there I was now waiting to know why I was called in. They began to ask me questions about myself, and pretty soon they had my story. Finally they told me I would answer their purpose. I said I was sincerely glad, and asked what it was. Then one of them handed me an envelope, and said I would find the explanation inside. I was going to open it, but he said no; take it to my lodgings[②], and look it over carefully, and not be hasty[③] or rash[④]. I was puzzled, and wanted to discuss the matter a little further, but they didn't; so I took my leave, feeling hurt and insulted to be made the butt of what was apparently some kind of a practical joke, and yet obliged to put up with it, not being in circumstances to resent affronts from rich and strong folk.

I would have picked up the pear now and eaten it before all the world, but it was gone; so I had lost that by this unlucky business, and the thought of it did not soften my feeling towards those men. As soon as I was out of sight of that house I opened my envelope, and saw that it contained money! My opinion of those people changed, I can tell you! I lost not a moment, but shoved note and money into my vest pocket, and broke for the nearest cheap eating house. Well,

---

① possessors:所有者,所有者的
② lodgings:住处
③ hasty:草率
④ rash:慌张

how I did eat! When at last I couldn't hold any more, I took out my money and unfolded it, took one glimpse and nearly fainted. Five millions of dollars! Why, it made my head swim.

I must have sat there stunned and blinking at the note as much as a minute before I came rightly to myself again. The first thing I noticed, then, was the landlord. His eye was on the note, and he was petrified①. He was worshiping②, with all his body and soul, but he looked as if he couldn't stir hand or foot. I took my cue③, in a moment, and did the only rational④ thing there was to do. I reached the note towards him, and said, carelessly:

"Give me the change, please."

Then he was restored to his normal condition, and made a thousand apologies for not being able to break the bill, and I couldn't get him to touch it. He wanted to look at it, and keep on looking at it; he couldn't seem to get enough of it to quench the thirst of his eye, but he shrank from touching it as if it had been something too sacred for poor common clay to handle. I said:

"I am sorry if it is an inconvenience, but I must insist. Please change it; I haven't anything else."

But he said that wasn't any matter; he was quite willing to let the trifle stand over till another time. I said I might not be in his neighborhood again for a good while; but he said it was of no consequence, he could wait, and, moreover, I could have anything I wanted, any time I chose, and let the account run as long as I pleased. He said he hoped he wasn't afraid to trust as rich a gentleman as I was, merely because I was of a merry disposition⑤, and chose to play larks on the public in the matter of dress. By this time another customer was entering, and the landlord hinted to me to put the monster out of sight; then he bowed me all the way to the door, and I started straight for that house and those brothers, to correct the mistake which had been made before the police should hunt me up, and help me do it. I was pretty nervous; in fact, pretty badly frightened, though, of course, I was no way in fault; but I knew

---

① petrify:石化,吓呆
② worship:祷告
③ cue:暗示,提示
④ rational:理性的,合理的,推理的
⑤ disposition:聪明的,伶俐的,有才智的

men well enough to know that when they find they've given a tramp a million-pound bill when they thought it was a one-pounder, they are in a frantic rage against him instead of quarreling with their own near—sightedness, as they ought. As I approached the house my excitement began to abate, for all was quiet there, which made me feel pretty sure the blunder was not discovered yet. I rang. The same servant appeared. I asked for those gentlemen.

"They are gone." This in the lofty, cold way of that fellow's tribe.

"Gone? Gone where?"

"On a journey."

"But whereabouts?"

"To the Continent, I think."

"The Continent?"

"Yes, sir."

"Which way-by what route?"

"I can't say, sir."

"When will they be back?"

"In a month, they said."

"A month! Oh, this is awful! Give me some sort of idea of how to get a word to them. It's of the last importance."

"I can't, indeed. I've no idea where they've gone, sir."

"Then I must see some member of the family."

"Family's away, too; been abroad months—in Egypt and India, I think."

"Man, there's been an immense① mistake made. They'll be back before night. Will you tell them I've been here, and that I will keep coming till It's all made right, and they needn't be afraid?"

"I'll tell them, if they come back, but I am not expecting them. They said you would be here in an hour to make inquiries, but I must tell you It's all right, they'll be here on time and expect you."

So I had to give it up and go away. What a riddle it all was! I was like to lose my mind. They would be here "on time." What could that mean Oh, the letter would explain, maybe. I had forgotten the letter; I got it out and read it. This is what it said:

---

① immense: 极广大的，无边的

"You are an intelligent① and honest man, as one may see by your face. We conceive② you to be poor and a stranger. Enclosed you will find a sum of money. It is lent to you for thirty days, without interest. Report at this house at the end of that time. I have a bet on you. If I win it you shall have any situation that is in my gift—any, that is, that you shall be able to prove yourself familiar with and competent to fill."

No signature, no address, no date.

Well, here was a coil to be in! You are posted on what had preceded③ all this, but I was not. It was just a deep, dark puzzle to me. I hadn't the least idea what the game was, nor whether harm was meant me or a kindness. I went into a park, and sat down to try to think it out, and to consider what I had best do.

At the end of an hour my reasonings had crystallized into this verdict.

Maybe those men mean me well, maybe they mean me ill; no way to decide that—let it go. They've got a game, or a scheme, or an experiment, of some kind on hand; no way to determine what it is—let it go. There's a bet on me; no way to find out what it is—let it go. That disposes of the indeterminable quantities; the remainder of the matter is tangible④, solid, and may be classed and labeled with certainty. If I ask the Bank of England to place this bill to the credit of the man it belongs to, they'll do it, for they know him, although I don't; but they will ask me how I came in possession of it, and if I tell the truth, they'll put me in the asylum, naturally, and a lie will land me in jail. The same result would follow if I tried to bank the bill anywhere or to borrow money on it. I have got to carry this immense burden around until those men come back, whether I want to or not. It is useless to me, as useless as a handful of ashes, and yet I must take care of it, and watch over it, while I beg my living. I couldn't give it away, if I should try, for neither honest citizen nor highwayman would accept it or meddle with it for anything. Those brothers are safe. Even if I lose their bill, or burn it, they are still safe, because they can stop payment, and the Bank will make them whole; but meantime I've got to do a

---

① intelligent:聪明的,伶俐的,有才智的
② conceive:构思,以为,持有
③ precede:领先(于),在……之前,先于
④ tangible:切实的

month's suffering without wages or profit—unless I help win that bet, whatever it may be, and get that situation that I am promised. I should like to get that; men of their sort have situations in their gift that are worth having.

I got to thinking a good deal about that situation. My hopes began to rise high. Without doubt the salary would be large. It would begin in a month; after that I should be all right. Pretty soon I was feeling first-rate. By this time I was tramping the streets again. The sight of a tailor-shop gave me a sharp longing to shed my rags, and to clothe myself decently once more. Could I afford it No; I had nothing in the world but a million pounds. So I forced myself to go on by. But soon I was drifting back again. The temptation persecuted① me cruelly. I must have passed that shop back and forth six times during that manful struggle. At last I gave in; I had to. I asked if they had a misfit suit that had been thrown on their hands. The fellow I spoke to nodded his head towards another fellow, and gave me no answer. I went to the indicated fellow, and he indicated② another fellow with his head, and no words. I went to him, and he said:

"Tend to you presently."

I waited till he was done with what he was at, then he took me into a back room, and overhauled③ a pile of rejected④ suits, and selected the rattiest⑤ one for me. I put it on. It didn't fit, and wasn't in any way attractive, but it was new, and I was anxious to have it; so I didn't find any fault, but said, with some diffidence:

"It would be an accommodation⑥ to me if you could wait some days for the money. I haven't any small change about me."

The fellow worked up a most sarcastic⑦ expression of countenance⑧ and said:

"Oh, you haven't Well, of course, I didn't expect it. I'd only expect

---

① persecute:迫害,烦扰
② indicate:指出,显示,象征,预示,需要,简要地说
③ overhaul:检查,翻出
④ reject:拒绝,抵制,否决
⑤ rattiest:破烂的
⑥ accommodation:住处,膳宿
⑦ sarcastic:讽刺的
⑧ countenance:刻薄至极面容,脸色,支持,赞助

gentlemen like you to carry large change."

I was nettled, and said:

"My friend, you shouldn't judge a stranger always by the clothes he wears. I am quite able to pay for this suit; I simply didn't wish to put you to the trouble of changing a large note."

He modified[①] his style a little at that, and said, though still with something of an air:

"I didn't mean any particular harm, but as long as rebukes[②] are going, I might say it wasn't quite your affair to jump to the conclusion that we couldn't change any note that you might happen to be carrying around. On the contrary, we can."

I handed the note to him, and said:

"Oh, very well; I apologize."

He received it with a smile, one of those large smiles which goes all around over, and has folds in it, and wrinkles, and spirals 螺旋形的, and looks like the place where you have thrown a brick in a pond; and then in the act of his taking a glimpse of the bill this smile froze solid, and turned yellow, and looked like those wavy, wormy spreads of lava which you find hardened on little levels on the side of Vesuvius[③]. I never before saw a smile caught like that, and perpetuated[④]. The man stood there holding the bill, and looking like that, and the proprietor[⑤] hustled up[⑥] to see what was the matter, and said, briskly[⑦]:

"Well, what's up what's the trouble what's wanting?"

I said: "There isn't any trouble. I'm waiting for my change."

"Come, come; get him his change, Tod; get him his change."

Tod retorted: "Get him his change! It's easy to say, sir; but look at the bill yourself."

---

① modify:改进的，修正的
② rebukes:指责，谴责，非难
③ Vesuvius:维苏威火山[意大利西南部]（欧洲大陆唯一的活火山）
④ perpetuate:使永存，使不朽
⑤ proprietor:所有者，经营者
⑥ hustle up:催促
⑦ briskly:活泼地，精神勃勃地

The proprietor took a look, gave a low, eloquent① whistle, then made a dive for the pile of rejected clothing, and began to snatch it this way and that, talking all the time excitedly, and as if to himself:

"Sell an eccentric② millionaire such an unspeakable suit as that! Tod's a fool—a born fool. Always doing something like this. Drives every millionaire away from this place, because he can't tell a millionaire from a tramp③, and never could. Ah, here's the thing I am after. Please get those things off, sir, and throw them in the fire. Do me the favor to put on this shirt and this suit; It's just the thing, the very thing—plain, rich, modest, and just ducally④, nobby⑤; made to order for a foreign prince—you may know him, sir, his Serene Highness the Hospodar of Halifax; had to leave it with us and take a mourning-suit because his mother was going to die—which she didn't. But That's all right; we can't always have things the way we—that is, the way they—there! trousers all right, they fit you to a charm, sir; now the waistcoat; aha, right again! now the coat-Lord! look at that, now! Perfect—the whole thing! I never saw such a triumph in all my experience."

Chapter 2

I expressed my satisfaction.

"Quite right, sir, quite right; it'll do for a makeshift, I'm bound⑥ to say. But wait till you see what We'll get up for you on your own measure. Come, Tod, book and pen; get at it. Length of leg, 32"—and so on. Before I could get in a word he had measured me, and was giving orders for dress-suits, morning suits, shirts, and all sorts of things. When I got a chance I said:

"But, my dear sir, I can't give these orders, unless you can wait indefinitely⑦ or change the bill."

"Indefinitely! It's a weak word, sir, a weak word. Eternally—That's the

---

① eloquent：雄辩的，有口才的，动人的
② eccentric：非同寻常的
③ tramp：流浪汉
④ ducally：公爵的
⑤ nobby：王公贵族的气派
⑥ bound：我敢保证，我敢肯定
⑦ indefinitely：不确定地

word, sir. Tod, rush these things through, and send them to the gentleman's address without any waste of time. Let the minor customers wait. Set down the gentleman's address and—"

"I'm changing my quarters. I will drop in and leave the new address."

"Quite right, sir, quite right. One moment—let me show you out, sir. There—good day, sir, good day."

Well, don't you see what was bound to happen I drifted naturally into buying whatever I wanted, and asking for change. Within a week I was sumptuously① equipped with all needful comforts and luxuries②, and was housed in an expensive private hotel in Hanover Square. I took my dinners here, but for breakfast I stuck by Harris's humble feeding house, where I had got my first meal on my million-pound bill. I was the making of Harris. The fact had gone all abroad that the foreign crank who carried million-pound bills in his vest pocket was the patron saint of the place. That was enough. From being a poor, struggling, little hand-to-mouth enterprise, it had become celebrated, and overcrowded with customers. Harris was so grateful that he forced loans upon me, and would not be denied; and so, pauper as I was, I had money to spend, and was living like the rich and the great. I judged that there was going to be a crash by and by, but I was in now and must swim across or drown. You see there was just that element of impending③ disaster to give a serious side, a sober side, yes, a tragic side, to a state of things which would otherwise have been purely ridiculous④. In the night, in the dark, the tragedy part was always to the front, and always warning, always threatening; and so I moaned 唉声叹气 and tossed⑤, and sleep was hard to find. But in the cheerful daylight the tragedy element faded out and disappeared, and I walked on air, and was happy to giddiness⑥, to intoxication⑦, you may say.

---

① sumptuously:奢侈地,豪华地
② luxury:奢华
③ impend:进行威胁,即将发生
④ ridiculous:荒谬的,可笑的
⑤ toss:辗转反侧,投掷
⑥ giddiness:眼花,轻率
⑦ intoxication:陶醉

And it was natural; for I had become one of the notorieties① of the metropolis② of the world, and it turned my head, not just a little, but a good deal. You could not take up a newspaper, English, Scotch, or Irish, without finding in it one or more references to the "vest-pocket million-pounder" and his latest doings and saying. At first, in these mentions, I was at the bottom of the personal-gossip column; next, I was listed above the knights, next above the baronets, next above the barons, and so on, and so on, climbing steadily, as my notoriety augmented, until I reached the highest altitude possible, and there I remained, taking precedence of all dukes not royal, and of all ecclesiastics except the primate of all England. But mind, this was not fame; as yet I had achieved only notoriety. Then came the climaxing stroke—the accolade③, so to speak—which in a single instant transmuted④ the perishable⑤ dross of notoriety into the enduring gold of fame: Punch⑥ caricatured⑦ me! Yes, I was a made man now; my place was established. I might be joked about still, but reverently⑧, not hilariously⑨, not rudely; I could be smiled at, but not laughed at. The time for that had gone by. Punch pictured me all a flutter⑩ with rags, dickering⑪ with a beef-eater for the Tower of London. Well, you can imagine how it was with a young fellow who had never been taken notice of before, and now all of a sudden couldn't say a thing that wasn't taken up and repeated everywhere; couldn't stir abroad without constantly overhearing the remark flying from lip to lip, "There he goes; That's him!" couldn't take his breakfast without a crowd to look on; couldn't appear in an opera box without

① notoriety:恶名，丑名，声名狼藉,远扬的名声
② metropolis:首都，主要都市,都会，大主教教区，大城市
③ accolade:赞美,骑士爵位的授予,连谱号
④ transmute:改变
⑤ perishable:容易腐烂的
⑥ Punch:《笨拙》画刊潘趣(英国木偶戏 Punch and Judy 中的主角)
⑦ caricature:画成漫画讽刺
⑧ reverently:虔诚地
⑨ hilariously:欢闹
⑩ flutter:摆动，鼓翼，烦扰，飘动，悸动，乱跳，烦扰;拍(翅)，使焦急
⑪ dicker:还价

concentrating there the fire of a thousand lorgnettes①. Why, I just swam② in glory all day long—that is the amount of it.

You know, I even kept my old suit of rags, and every now and then appeared in them, so as to have the old pleasure of buying trifles, and being insulted③, and then shooting the scoffer④ dead with the million-pound bill. But I couldn't keep that up. The illustrated papers made the outfit⑤ so familiar that when I went out in it I was at once recognized and followed by a crowd, and if I attempted a purchase⑥ the man would offer me his whole shop on credit before I could pull my note on him.

About the tenth day of my fame I went to fulfil my duty to my flag by paying my respects to the American minister. He received me with the enthusiasm proper in my case, upbraided me for being so tardy in my duty, and said that there was only one way to get his forgiveness, and that was to take the seat at his dinner-party that night made vacant by the illness of one of his guests. I said I would, and we got to talking. It turned out that he and my father had been schoolmates in boyhood, Yale students together later, and always warm friends up to my father's death. So then he required me to put in at his house all the odd time I might have to spare, and I was very willing, of course.

In fact, I was more than willing; I was glad. When the crash should come, he might somehow be able to save me from total destruction; I didn't know how, but he might think of a way, maybe. I couldn't venture to unbosom⑦ myself to him at this late date, a thing which I would have been quick to do in the beginning of this awful career of mine in London. No, I couldn't venture it now; I was in too deep; that is, too deep for me to be risking revelations⑧ to so new a friend, though not clear beyond my depth, as I looked at it. Because, you see, with all my borrowing, I was carefully keeping within my means—I

---

① lorgnette:望远镜
② swam:使浮起
③ insult:侮辱,凌辱
④ scoffer:嘲笑者
⑤ outfit:配备,装备
⑥ purchase:买,购买
⑦ unbosom:吐露心事,剖明心迹
⑧ revelations:启示者,揭发者

mean within my salary. Of course, I couldn't know what my salary was going to be, but I had a good enough basis for an estimate in the fact, that if I won the bet I was to have choice of any situation in that rich old gentleman's gift provided I was competent—and I should certainly prove competent; I hadn't any doubt about that. And as to the bet, I wasn't worrying about that; I had always been lucky. Now my estimate of the salary was six hundred to a thousand a year; say, six hundred for the first year, and so on up year by year, till I struck the upper figure by proved merit. At present I was only in debt for my first year's salary. Everybody had been trying to lend me money, but I had fought off the most of them on one pretext or another; so this indebtedness represented only £300 borrowed money, the other £300 represented my keep and my purchases. I believed my second year's salary would carry me through the rest of the month if I went on being cautious and economical, and I intended to look sharply out for that. My month ended, my employer back from his journey, I should be all right once more, for I should at once divide the two years' salary among my creditors by assignment, and get right down to my work.

It was a lovely dinner-party of fourteen. The Duke and Duchess of Shoreditch, and their daughter the Lady Anne-Grace-Eleanor-Celeste-and-so-forth-and-so-forth-de-Bohun, the Earl and Countess of Newgate, Viscount Cheapside, Lord and Lady Blatherskite, some untitled people of both sexes, the minister and his wife and daughter, and his daughter's visiting friend, an English girl of twenty-two, named Portia Langham, whom I fell in love with in two minutes, and she with me—I could see it without glasses. There was still another guest, an American—but I am a little ahead of my story. While the people were still in the drawing-room, whetting① up for dinner, and coldly inspecting the late comers, the servant announced:

"Mr. Lloyd Hastings."

The moment the usual civilities② were over, Hastings caught sight of me, and came straight with cordially③ outstretched hand; then stopped short when

---

① whetting:刺激,促进(食欲、好奇心等)
② civility:礼貌,端庄
③ cordially:诚恳地,诚实地,诚挚地

about to shake, and said, with an embarrassed① look:

"I beg your pardon, sir, I thought I knew you."

"Why, you do know me, old fellow."

"No. Are you the—the—"

"Vest-pocket monster I am, indeed. don't be afraid to call me by my nickname; I'm used to it."

"Well, well, well, this is a surprise. Once or twice I've seen your own name coupled with the nickname②, but it never occurred to me that you could be the Henry Adams referred to. Why, it isn't six months since you were clerking away for Blake Hopkins in Frisco on a salary, and sitting up nights on an extra allowance③ helping me arrange and verify the Gould and Curry Extension papers and statistics. The idea of your being in London, and a vast millionaire, and a colossal④ celebrity! Why, It's the Arabian Nights come again. Man, I can't take it in at all; can't realize it; give me time to settle the whirl⑤, in my head."

"The fact is, Lloyd, you are no worse off than I am. I can't realize it myself."

"Dear me, it is stunning, now isn't it Why, It's just three months today since we went to the Miners' restaurant—"

"No; the What Cheer."

"Right, it was the What Cheer; went there at two in the morning, and had a chop and coffee after a hard six-hours grind over those Extension papers, and I tried to persuade you to come to London with me, and offered to get leave of absence for you and pay all your expenses, and give you something over if I succeeded in making the sale; and you would not listen to me, said I wouldn't succeed, and you couldn't afford to lose the run of business and be no end of time getting the hang of things again when you got back home. And yet here you are. How odd it all is! How did you happen to come, and whatever did give you this incredible start?"

① embarrass:尴尬的,局促不安的,难堪的
② nickname:外号
③ allowance:津贴,补助
④ colossal:巨大的,庞大的
⑤ whirl:旋转,一连串快速的活动

"Oh, just an accident. It's a long story—a romance, a body may say. I'll tell you all about it, but not now."

"When?"

"The end of this month."

"That's more than a fortnight yet. It's too much of a strain on a person's curiosity. Make it a week."

"I can't. you'll know why, by and by. But how's the trade getting along?"

His cheerfulness vanished like a breath, and he said with a sigh:

"You were a true prophet, Hal, a true prophet. I wish I hadn't come. I don't want to talk about it."

"But you must. You must come and stop with me tonight, when we leave here, and tell me all about it."

"Oh, may I Are you in earnest" and the water showed in his eyes.

"Yes; I want to hear the whole story, every word."

"I'm so grateful! Just to find a human interest once more, in some voice and in some eye, in me and affairs of mine, after what I've been through here—lord! I could go down on my knees for it!"

He gripped my hand hard, and braced up, and was all right and lively after that for the dinner—which didn't come off. No; the usual thing happened, the thing that is always happening under that vicious and aggravating① English system—the matter of precedence couldn't be settled, and so there was no dinner. Englishmen always eat dinner before they go out to dinner, because they know the risks they are running; but nobody ever warns the stranger, and so he walks placidly into trap. Of course, nobody was hurt this time, because we had all been to dinner, none of us being novices② excepting Hastings, and he having been informed by the minister at the time that he invited him that in deference to the English custom he had not provided any dinner. Everybody took a lady and processioned down to the dining-room, because it is usual to go through the motions; but there the dispute began. The Duke of Shoreditch wanted to take precedence③, and sit at the head of the table, holding that he outranked a

---

① aggravate:加重(病情、负担、罪行、危机等的),更恶化,恼怒
② novices:新手,初学者
③ precedence:优先,居先

minister who represented merely a nation and not a monarch①; but I stood for my rights, and refused to yield. In the gossip column I ranked all dukes not royal, and said so, and claimed precedence of this one. It couldn't be settled, of course, struggle as we might and did, he finally (and injudiciously②) trying to play birth and antiquity③, and I "seeing" his Conqueror and "raising" him with Adam, whose direct posterity④ I was, as shown by my name, while he was of a collateral branch, as shown by his, and by his recent Norman origin; so we all processioned⑤ back to the drawing-room again and had a perpendicular⑥ lunch-plate of sardines and a strawberry, and you group yourself and stand up and eat it. Here the religion of precedence is not so strenuous⑦; the two persons of highest rank chuck up a shilling, the one that wins has first go at his strawberry, and the loser gets the shilling. The next two chuck up, then the next two, and so on. After refreshment⑧, tables were brought, and we all played cribbage 纸牌玩法之一, sixpence a game. The English never play any game for amusement. If they can't make something or lose something—they don't care which—they won't play.

We had a lovely time; certainly two of us had, Miss Langham and I. I was so bewitch⑨ with her that I couldn't count my hands if they went above a double sequence; and when I struck home I never discovered it, and started up the outside row again, and would have lost the game every time, only the girl did the same, she being in just my condition, you see; and consequently neither of us ever got out, or cared to wonder why we didn't; we only just knew we were happy, and didn't wish to know anything else, and didn't want to be interrupted. And I told her—I did, indeed—told her I loved her; and she—well, she blushed till her hair turned red, but she liked it; she said she did. Oh, there

---

① monarch:君主
② injudiciously:判断不当地；欠考虑地
③ antiquity:古代，古老，古代的遗物
④ posterity:子孙，后裔
⑤ procession:行列，队伍
⑥ perpendicular:垂直的，正交的
⑦ strenuous:奋发的，使劲的，紧张的，热烈的，艰辛发奋的
⑧ refreshment:点心，饮料，精力恢复，爽快
⑨ bewitch:施魔法于，蛊惑，迷人

was never such an evening! Every time I pegged① I put on a postscript②; every time she pegged she acknowledged receipt of it, counting the hands the same. Why, I couldn't even say "Two for his heels" without adding, "My, how sweet you do look!" and she would say, "Fifteen two, fifteen four, fifteen six, and a pair are eight, and eight are sixteen—do you think so" peeping out aslant from under her lashes, you know, so sweet and cunning. Oh, it was just too—too!

Well, I was perfectly honest and square with her; told her I hadn't a cent in the world but just the million-pound note she'd heard so much talk about, and it didn't belong to me, and that started her curiosity; and then I talked low, and told her the whole history right from the start, and it nearly killed her laughing. What in the nation she could find to laugh about I couldn't see, but there it was; every half-minute some new detail would fetch her, and I would have to stop as much as a minute and a half to give her a chance to settle down again. Why, she laughed herself lame—she did, indeed; I never saw anything like it. I mean I never saw a painful story—a story of a person's troubles and worries and fears-produce just that kind of effect before. So I loved her all the more, seeing she could be so cheerful when there wasn't anything to be cheerful about; for I might soon need that kind of wife, you know, the way things looked. Of course, I told her we should have to wait a couple of years, till I could catch up on my salary; but she didn't mind that, only she hoped I would be as careful as possible in the matter of expenses, and not let them run the least risk of trenching on our third year's pay. Then she began to get a little worried, and wondered if we were making any mistake, and starting the salary on a higher figure for the first year than I would get. This was good sense, and it made me feel a little less confident than I had been feeling before; but it gave me a good business idea, and I brought it frankly out.

"Portia, dear, would you mind going with me that day, when I confront those old gentlemen?"

She shrank a little, but said:

"N—o; if my being with you would help hearten you. But—would it be quite proper, do you think?"

---

① peg:钉，栓，桩，销子，借口钉木钉，固定，限制，坚持不懈地工作
② postscript:附言，后记

"No, I don't know that it would—in fact, I'm afraid it wouldn't; but, you see, there's so much dependent upon it that—"

"Then I'll go anyway, proper or improper," she said, with a beautiful and generous enthusiasm. "Oh, I shall be so happy to think I'm helping!"

"Helping, dear Why, you'll be doing it all. you're so beautiful and so lovely and so winning, that with you there I can pile our salary up till I break those good old fellows, and they'll never have the heart to struggle."

Sho! you should have seen the rich blood mount, and her happy eyes shine!

"You wicked flatterer[①]! There isn't a word of truth in what you say, but still I'll go with you. Maybe it will teach you not to expect other people to look with your eyes."

Were my doubts dissipated[②] Was my confidence restored You may judge by this fact: privately I raised my salary to twelve hundred the first year on the spot. But I didn't tell her; I saved it for a surprise.

All the way home I was in the clouds, Hastings talking, I not hearing a word. When he and I entered my parlor, he brought me to myself with his fervent appreciations of my manifold comforts and luxuries.

"Let me just stand here a little and look my fill. Dear me! It's a palace—It's just a palace! And in it everything a body could desire, including cosy[③] coal fire and supper standing ready. Henry, it doesn't merely make me realize how rich you are; it makes me realize, to the bone, to the marrow[④], how poor I am—how poor I am, and how miserable, how defeated, routed, annihilated!"

Plague take it! this language gave me the cold shudders. It scared me broad awake, and made me comprehend that I was standing on a half inch crust, with a crater[⑤] underneath[⑥]. I didn't know I had been dreaming—that is, I hadn't been allowing myself to know it for a while back; but now—oh, dear! Deep in debt, not a cent in the world, a lovely girl's happiness or woe in my hands, and nothing in front of me but a salary which might never—oh, would never—

---

① flatterer:奉承者
② dissipated:驱散，(使)(云、雾、疑虑等)消散，浪费(金钱或时间)
③ cosy:舒适的，安逸的
④ marrow:髓，骨髓，精华，活力，[苏格兰]配偶
⑤ crater:弹坑
⑥ underneath:在下面

materialize! Oh, oh, oh! I am ruined past hope! nothing can save me!

"Henry, the mere unconsidered drippings of your daily income would—"

"Oh, my daily income! Here, down with this hot Scotch, and cheer up your soul. Here's with you! Or, no—you're hungry; sit down and—"

"Not a bite for me; I'm past it. I can't eat, these days; but I'll drink with you till I drop. Come!"

"Barrel for barrel, I'm with you! Ready Here we go! Now, then, Lloyd, unreel your story while I brew."

"Unreel it? What, again?"

"Again? What do you mean by that?"

"Why, I mean do you want to hear it over again?"

"Do I want to hear it over again? This is a puzzler. Wait; don't take any more of that liquid. You don't need it."

"Look here, Henry, you alarm me. Didn't I tell you the whole story on the way here?"

"You?"

"Yes, I."

"I'll be hanged if I heard a word of it."

"Henry, this is a serious thing. It troubles me. What did you take up yonder at the minister's?"

Chapter 3

Then it all flashed on me, and I owned up like a man.

"I took the dearest girl in this world—prisoner!"

So then he came with a rush, and we shook, and shook, and shook till our hands ached; and he didn't blame me for not having heard a word of a story which had lasted while we walked three miles. He just sat down then, like the patient, good fellow he was, and told it all over again. Synopsized[①], it amounted to this: He had come to England with what he thought was a grand opportunity; he had an "option" to sell the Gould and Curry Extension for the "locators" of it, and keep all he could get over a million dollars. He had worked hard, had pulled every wire he knew of, had left no honest expedient untried, had spent nearly all the money he had in the world, had not been able to get a

---

① Synopsize: 做……的提要，写……的梗概，概述……的大意

solitary capitalist to listen to him, and his option would run out at the end of the month. In a word, he was ruined. Then he jumped up and cried out:

"Henry, you can save me! You can save me, and you're the only man in the universe that can. Will you do it Won't you do it?"

"Tell me how. Speak out, my boy."

"Give me a million and my passage home for my 'option'! don't, don't refuse!"

I was in a kind of agony. I was right on the point of coming out with the words, "Lloyd, I'm a pauper myself – absolutely penniless, and in debt!" But a white-hot idea came flaming through my head, and I gripped my jaws together, and calmed myself down till I was as cold as a capitalist. Then I said, in a commercial and self-possessed way:

"I will save you, Lloyd—"

"Then I'm already saved! God be merciful to you forever! If ever I—"

"Let me finish, Lloyd. I will save you, but not in that way; for that would not be fair to you, after your hard work, and the risks you've run. I don't need to buy mines; I can keep my capital moving, in a commercial center like London, without that; It's what I'm at, all the time; but here is what I'll do. I know all about that mine, of course; I know its immense value, and can swear to it if anybody wishes it. You shall sell out inside of the fortnight for three millions cash, using my name freely, and We'll divide, share and share alike."

Do you know, he would have danced the furniture to kindling-wood in his insane joy, and broken everything on the place, if I hadn't tripped him up and tied him.

Then he lay there, perfectly happy, saying:

"I may use your name! Your name—think of it! Man, they'll flock in droves, these rich Londoners; they'll fight for that stock! I'm a made man, I'm a made man forever, and I'll never forget you as long as I live!"

In less than twenty-four hours London was abuzz! I hadn't anything to do, day after day, but sit at home, and say to all comers:

"Yes; I told him to refer to me. I know the man, and I know the mine. His character is above reproach, and the mine is worth far more than he asks for it."

Meantime I spent all my evenings at the minister's with Portia. I didn't say a word to her about the mine; I saved it for a surprise. We talked salary; never anything but salary and love; sometimes love, sometimes salary, sometimes love and salary together. And my! the interest the minister's wife and daughter took in our little affair, and the endless ingenuities they invented to save us from interruption[①], and to keep the minister in the dark and unsuspicious[②]—well, it was just lovely of them!

When the month was up at last, I had a million dollars to my credit in the London and County Bank, and Hastings was fixed in the same way. Dressed at my level best, I drove by the house in Portland Place, judged by the look of things that my birds were home again, went on towards the minister's and got my precious, and we started back, talking salary with all our might. She was so excited and anxious that it made her just intolerably beautiful. I said:

"Dearie, the way you're looking It's a crime to strike for a salary a single penny under three thousand a year."

"Henry, Henry, you'll ruin us!"

"don't you be afraid. Just keep up those looks, and trust to me. It'll all come out right."

So, as it turned out, I had to keep bolstering up her courage all the way. She kept pleading with me, and saying:

"Oh, please remember that if we ask for too much we may get no salary at all; and then what will become of us, with no way in the world to earn our living?"

We were ushered in by that same servant, and there they were, the two old gentlemen. Of course, they were surprised to see that wonderful creature with me, but I said:

"It's all right, gentlemen; she is my future stay and helpmate."

And I introduced them to her, and called them by name. It didn't surprise them; they knew I would know enough to consult the directory. They seated us, and were very polite to me, and very solicitous to relieve her from embarrassment, and put her as much at her ease as they could. Then I said:

"Gentlemen, I am ready to report."

---

① interruption:中断,打断

② unsuspicious:不怀疑的,无猜疑的

"We are glad to hear it," said my man, "for now we can decide the bet which my brother Abel and I made. If you have won for me, you shall have any situation in my gift. Have you the million-pound note?"

"Here it is, sir," and I handed it to him.

"I've won!" he shouted, and slapped Abel on the back. "Now what do you say, brother?"

"I say he did survive, and I've lost twenty thousand pounds. I never would have believed it."

"I've a further report to make," I said, "and a pretty long one. I want you to let me come soon, and detail my whole month's history; and I promise you It's worth hearing. Meantime, take a look at that."

"What, man! Certificate of deposit for £200,000. Is it yours?"

"Mine. I earned it by thirty days' judicious use of that little loan you let me have. And the only use I made of it was to buy trifles and offer the bill in change."

"Come, this is astonishing! It's incredible, man!"

"Never mind, I'll prove it. don't take my word unsupported."

But now Portia's turn was come to be surprised. Her eyes were spread wide, and she said:

"Henry, is that really your money Have you been fibbing to me?"

"I have, indeed, dearie. But you'll forgive me, I know."

She put up an arch pout, and said:

"don't you be so sure. You are a naughty thing to deceive me so!"

"Oh, you'll get over it, sweetheart, you'll get over it; it was only fun, you know. Come, let's be going."

"But wait, wait! The situation, you know. I want to give you the situation," said my man.

"Well," I said, "I'm just as grateful as I can be, but really I don't want one."

"But you can have the very choicest one in my gift."

"Thanks again, with all my heart; but I don't even want that one."

"Henry, I'm ashamed of you. You don't half thank the good gentleman. May I do it for you?"

"Indeed, you shall, dear, if you can improve it. Let us see you try."

She walked to my man, got up in his lap, put her arm round his neck, and kissed him right on the mouth. Then the two old gentlemen shouted with laughter, but I was dumfounded, just petrified, as you may say. Portia said:

"Papa, he has said you haven't a situation in his gift that he'd take; and I feel just as hurt as—"

"My darling, is that your papa?"

"Yes; he's my step-papa, and the dearest one that ever was. You understand now, don't you, why I was able to laugh when you told me at the minister's, not knowing my relationships, what trouble and worry papa's and Uncle Abel's scheme was giving you?"

Of course, I spoke right up now, without any fooling, and went straight to the point.

"Oh, my dearest dear sir, I want to take back what I said. You have got a situation open that I want."

"Name it."

"Son-in-law."

"Well, well, well! But you know, if you haven't ever served in that capacity, you, of course, can't furnish recommendations of a sort to satisfy the conditions of the contract, and so—"

"Try me—oh, do, I beg of you! Only just try me thirty or forty years, and if—"

"Oh, well, all right; It's but a little thing to ask, take her along."

Happy, we two There are not words enough in the unabridged to describe it. And when London got the whole history, a day or two later, of my month's adventures with that bank-note, and how they ended, did London talk, and have a good time Yes.

My Portia's papa took that friendly and hospitable bill back to the Bank of England and cashed it; then the Bank canceled it and made him a present of it, and he gave it to us at our wedding, and it has always hung in its frame in the sacredest[①] place in our home ever since. For it gave me my Portia. But for it I could not have remained in London, would not have appeared at the minister's, never should have met her. And so I always say, "Yes, It's a million-pounder,

---

① sacredness:牺牲,献身,祭品,供奉

as you see; but it never made but one purchase in its life, and then got the article for only about a tenth part of its value."

Questions for Discussion

1. What do you think will happen to Henry at the beginning of the story?
2. Will the bank-note help him or get him into trouble? Give a possible development to the story.
3. Mark Twain was famous for his humorous and ironic words. How did Mark Twain achieve humor/Irony?

Unit 2 Henry James (1843 – 1916)

Appreciation

There are, indeed, many hotels, for the entertainment of tourists is the business of the place, which, as many travelers will remember, is seated upon the edge of a remarkably blue lake—a lake that it behooves every tourist to visit. The shore of the lake presents an unbroken array of establishments of this order, of every category, from the "grand hotel" of the newest fashion, with a chalk-white front, a hundred balconies, and a dozen flags flying from its roof, to the little Swiss pension of an elder day, with its name inscribed in German—looking lettering upon a pink or yellow wall and an awkward summerhouse in the angle of the garden. 许多旅行者一定会记得,小镇坐落在一片蓝得出奇的湖畔。此湖风光绮丽,是每位游客的必游之地。岸边整整齐齐地排列着一长串这样的旅馆,从最新样式的"大饭店"到小巧玲珑、古色古香的瑞士膳宿公寓,真可谓五花八门,应有尽有。"大饭店"都有一道白色的正门、无数个阳台和十来面在屋顶上迎风招展的彩旗。至于膳宿公寓,它的名字往往用德文模样的字体刻在一堵粉色或黄色的墙上,而且花园一角还会安上一座蹩脚的凉亭。

Henry James was born in New York City, son of a wealthy amateur philosopher. He was educated by private tutors until 1855; the family spent most of the years 1855—60 traveling in Europe, where Henry continued his education, then settled in Newport, R. I. where he apparently suffered an unspecified injury in a stable fire. He attended Harvard Law School, and then withdrew to devote himself to writing.

In 1876 he settled in England, where he would spend most of the rest of his life, chiefly in London and in Rye, Sussex; he never married but he was a sociable man, often in the company of other writers such as Edith Wharton. He traveled frequently on the Continent, and published several notable travel books between 1875 and 1909.

His first novels—of the so-called international period, dealing as they do with interactions between Americans and Europeans—include *The American*, *The Europeans*, *Daisy Miller*, and *The Portrait of a Lady*《贵妇的画像》. The works of his second period stressed psychological and social relationships and include *Washington Square*, *The Bostonians*, *What Maisie Knew*, and *The Sacred Fount*.

During the 1890s he also wrote plays but he never found much success in the theater. He continued his examination of intricate psychological realities in the works of his final period that include his three masterworks, The *Wings of the Dove*, The *Ambassadors*, and *The Golden Bowl*. His intricate and complex sentence structure and delicately nuanced perceptions have never appealed to all readers but ultimately they became the models for one "school" of modern fiction and James has become recognized as one of the supreme writers of all time. His novel was Novel of manners 世态小说.

Henry James was a master of psychological realism, novelist of psychological analysis, and pioneer of American Stream of Consciousness 心理现实主义的大师,心理分析小说家,意识流文学先驱.

His writing features

1. Point of View

In his whole writing career James was concerned with "point of view" which is in the center of his aesthetic of the novel. James discovered the trick of making his characters reveal themselves with minimal intervention of the author. He used a particular method of telling the story, that is, illumination of the situation and characters through one or several minds. This method he termed "point of view".

2. Psychological analysis

James, by emphasizing the inner awareness and inward movements of his characters in face of outside occurrences rather than merely delineating their environment in any detail, became probably the first of the modern psychological analysts in the novel and anticipated in his works the modern stream-of-consciousness technique so widely employed in the first decades of this century. Henry James has extensively used the "stream of consciousness" method in his fictional writing.

3. International theme

It refers to the moral and psychological complications when the American innocence encountered the European sophistication; the cultural conflict between Europe and America. The typical Americans in James' novels: fresh, enthusiastic, eager to learn, and basically, novels "good", showing disregard for the conventions, and standing for morality. The Europeans in James, novels: highly cultivated, elegant in manners, but sophisticated, standing for manners.

Brief Introduction

Daisy Miller, an 1878 novella by Henry James, portrays the courtship of the beautiful American girl Daisy Miller by Winterbourne, a more sophisticated compatriot of hers. His pursuit of her is hampered by her own flirtatiousness, which is frowned upon by the other expatriates they meet in Switzerland and Italy.

This novel serves as both a psychological description of the mind of a young woman, and an analysis of the traditional views of a society where she is a clear outsider. Henry James uses Daisy's story to discuss what he thinks Europeans and Americans believe about each other, and more generally the prejudices common in any culture. In a letter James said that Daisy is the victim of a "social rumpus" that goes on either over her head or beneath her notice.

The names of the characters are also symbolic. Daisy is a flower in full bloom, without inhibitions and in the springtime of her life. Daisy contrasts sharply with Winterbourne, who is more ambivalent and unwilling to commit to any relationship. Flowers die in winter and this is precisely what happens to Daisy, after catching the Roman Fever or, to put it more bluntly, the attention of foreign men. As an objective analogue to this psychological reality, Daisy catches the very real Roman fever, the malaria that was endemic to many Roman neighborhoods in the 19th century.

Selected Reading

Daisy Miller

PART I

At the little town of Vevey①, in Switzerland, there is a particularly comfortable hotel. There are, indeed, many hotels, for the entertainment of

---

① Vevey: [地名] [瑞士] 沃韦

tourists is the business of the place, which, as many travelers will remember, is seated upon the edge of a remarkably blue lake—a lake that it behooves① every tourist to visit. The shore of the lake presents an unbroken array of establishments of this order, of every category, from the "grand hotel" of the newest fashion, with a chalk—white front, a hundred balconies, and a dozen flags flying from its roof, to the little Swiss pension of an elder day, with its name inscribed in German—looking lettering upon a pink or yellow wall and an awkward summerhouse in the angle of the garden. One of the hotels at Vevey, however, is famous, even classical, being distinguished from many of its upstart neighbors by an air both of luxury and of maturity②. In this region, in the month of June, American travelers are extremely numerous; it may be said, indeed, that Vevey assumes at this period some of the characteristics of an American watering place. There are sights and sounds which evoke a vision, an echo, of Newport and Saratoga③. There is a flitting④ hither and thither⑤ of "stylish" young girls, a rustling of muslin⑥ flounces⑦, a rattle⑧ of dance music in the morning hours, a sound of high-pitched voices at all times. You receive an impression of these things at the excellent inn of the "Trois Couronnes"⑨ and are transported in fancy to the Ocean House or to Congress⑩ Hall. But at the "Trois Couronnes," it must be added, there are other features that are much at variance⑪ with these suggestions: neat German waiters, who look like secretaries of legation; Russian princesses sitting in the garden; little Polish boys walking about held by the hand, with their governors; a view of the sunny

---

① behoove：适宜
② maturity：成熟，完备
③ Saratoga：萨拉托加（美国纽约州东部一村落，附近有温泉疗养地）
④ flit：掠过，迁徙，迅速飞过，（鸟，蝙蝠等）飞来飞去
⑤ hither and thither：到处
⑥ muslin：一种薄细的棉布平纹细布
⑦ flounce：衣裙上的荷边装饰
⑧ rattle：沙沙的响声
⑨ Trois Couronnes：the Hotel of Trois Couronnes，三冠大饭店
⑩ the house of Congres：国会大厦
⑪ variance：不一致，变化，变异，变迁，分歧，不和

crest① of the Dentdu Midi② and the picturesque③ towers of the Castle of Chillon④.

I hardly know whether it was the analogies or the differences that were uppermost⑤ in the mind of a young American, who, two or three years ago, sat in the garden of the "Trois Couronnes," looking about him, rather idly, at some of the graceful objects I have mentioned. It was a beautiful summer morning, and in whatever fashion the young American looked at things, they must have seemed to him charming. He had come from Geneva⑥ the day before by the little steamer, to see his aunt, who was staying at the hotel—Geneva having been for a long time his place of residence. Bu his aunt had a headache—his aunt had almost always a headache—and now she was shut up in her room, smelling camphor⑦, so that he was at liberty to wander about. He was some seven-and-twenty years of age; when his friends spoke of him, they usually said that he was at Geneva "studying." When his enemies spoke of him, they said—but, after all, he had no enemies; he was an extremely amiable fellow, and universally liked. What I should say is, simply, that when certain persons spoke of him they affirmed that the reason of his spending so much time at Geneva was that he was extremely devoted to a lady who lived there—a foreign lady—a person older than himself. Very few Americans—indeed, I think none—had ever seen this lady, about whom there were some singular stories. But Winterbourne had an old attachment for the little metropolis⑧ of Calvinism⑨; he had been put to school there as a boy, and he had afterward gone to college there—circumstances which had led to his forming a great many youthful friendships. Many of these he had kept, and they were a source of great satisfaction to him.

After knocking at his aunt's door and learning that she was indisposed, he

---

① crest：顶部，顶峰
② the Dentdu Midi：南峭峰
③ picturesque：（景色等）如画的，美丽的
④ the Castle of Chillon：希永古堡
⑤ uppermost：至上的，最高的，最主要的；在最上，最初，首先
⑥ Geneva：日内瓦城(瑞士西南部城市)
⑦ camphor：樟脑油
⑧ metropolis：首都，主要都市，都会，大主教教区，大城市
⑨ Calvinism：加尔文教派，加尔文主义

had taken a walk about the town, and then he had come in to his breakfast. He had now finished his breakfast; but he was drinking a small cup of coffee, which had been served to him on a little table in the garden by one of the waiters who looked like an attach. At last he finished his coffee and lit a cigarette. Presently a small boy came walking along the path—an urchin① of nine or ten. The child, who was diminutive② for his years, had an aged expression of countenance③ a pale complexion, and sharp little features. He was dressed in knickerbockers④, with red stockings, which displayed his poor little spindle-shanks⑤; he also wore a brilliant red cravat⑥. He carried in his hand a long alpenstock, the sharp point of which he thrust into everything that he approached—the flowerbeds, the garden benches, the trains of the ladies' dresses. In front of Winterbourne he paused, looking at him with a pair of bright, penetrating little eyes.

"Will you give me a lump of sugar" he asked in a sharp, hard little voice— a voice immature and yet, somehow, not young.

Winterbourne glanced at the small table near him, on which his coffee service rested, and saw that several morsels of sugar remained. "Yes, you may take one," he answered; "but I don't think sugar is good for little boys."

This little boy stepped forward and carefully selected three of the coveted⑦ fragments, two of which he buried in the pocket of his knickerbockers, depositing the other as promptly in another place. He poked his alpenstock⑧ lance-fashion⑨ into Winterbourne's bench and tried to crack the lump of sugar with his teeth.

"Oh, blazesn⑩? It's har—r—d!" he exclaimed, pronouncing the adjective

---

① urchin:顽童
② diminutive:小的,指小的,小型的
③ countenance:面容,脸色
④ knickerbockers:灯笼裤
⑤ spindle-shanks:细长腿,细长腿的人
⑥ cravat:领结,领巾,围巾,三角绷带
⑦ covet:垂涎,觊觎
⑧ alpenstock:登山杖
⑨ lance-fashion:标枪,长矛,矛状器具,捕鲸枪,铁头登山杖
⑩ blaze:火焰,光辉,情感爆发,燃烧,照耀,激发

in a peculiar manner. Winterbourne had immediately perceived[①] that he might have the honor of claiming him as a fellow countryman.

"Take care you don't hurt your teeth," he said, paternally[②].

"I haven't got any teeth to hurt. They have all come out. I have only got seven teeth. My mother counted them last night, and one came out right afterward. She said she'd slap me if any more came out. I can't help it. It's this old Europe. It's the climate that makes them come out. In America they didn't come out. It's these hotels."

Winterbourne was much amused. "If you eat three lumps of sugar, your mother will certainly slap you," he said.

"She's got to give me some candy, then," rejoined his young interlocutor. "I can't get any candy here—any American candy. American candy's the best candy."

"And are American little boys the best little boys" asked Winterbourne.

"I don't know. I'm an American boy," said the child.

"I see you are one of the best!" laughed Winterbourne.

"Are you an American man?" pursued this vivacious infant. And then, on Winterbourne's affirmative reply—"American men are the best," he declared.

His companion thanked him for the compliment, and the child, who had now got astride of his alpenstock, stood looking about him, while he attacked a second lump of sugar. Winterbourne wondered if he himself had been like this in his infancy, for he had been brought to Europe at about this age.

"Here comes my sister!" cried the child in a moment. "She's an American girl."

Winterbourne looked along the path and saw a beautiful young lady advancing. "American girls are the best girls," he said cheerfully to his young companion.

"My sister ain't the best!" the child declared. "She's always blowing at me."

"I imagine that is your fault, not hers," said Winterbourne. The young lady meanwhile had drawn near. She was dressed in white muslin, with a hundred

---

① perceive: 察觉,感知,感到,认识到
② paternally: 父亲一般地

frills① and flounces②, and knots of pale-colored ribbon. She was bareheaded, but she balanced in her hand a large parasol③, with a deep border of embroidery④ and she was strikingly, admirably pretty. "How pretty they are!" thought Winterbourne, straightening himself in his seat, as if he were prepared to rise.

The young lady paused in front of his bench, near the parapet of the garden, which overlooked the lake. The little boy had now converted his alpenstock into a vaulting pole, by the aid of which he was springing about in the gravel and kicking it up not a little.

"Randolph," said the young lady, "what ARE you doing?"

"I'm going up the Alps," replied Randolph. "This is the way!" And he gave another little jump, scattering the pebbles⑤ about Winterbourne's ears.

"That's the way they come down," said Winterbourne.

"He's an American man!" cried Randolph, in his little hard voice.

The young lady gave no heed to this announcement, but looked straight at her brother. "Well, I guess you had better be quiet," she simply observed.

It seemed to Winterbourne that he had been in a manner presented. He got up and stepped slowly toward the young girl, throwing away his cigarette. "This little boy and I have made acquaintance," he said, with great civility. In Geneva, as he had been perfectly aware, a young man was not at liberty to speak to a young unmarried lady except under certain rarely occurring conditions; but here at Vevey, what conditions could be better than these—a pretty American girl coming and standing in front of you in a garden. This pretty American girl, however, on hearing Winterbourne's observation, simply glanced at him; she then turned her head and looked over the parapet, at the lake and the opposite mountains. He wondered whether he had gone too far, but he decided that he must advance farther, rather than retreat. While he was thinking of something else to say, the young lady turned to the little boy again.

"I should like to know where you got that pole," she said.

---

① frill：装饰
② flounce：衣裙上的荷边装饰
③ parasol：（女用）阳伞
④ embroidery：刺绣品，粉饰，刺绣，装饰
⑤ pebble：小圆石，小鹅卵石

"I bought it," responded Randolph.

"You don't mean to say you're going to take it to Italy?"

"Yes, I am going to take it to Italy," the child declared.

The young girl glanced over the front of her dress and smoothed out a knot or two of ribbon. Then she rested her eyes upon the prospect again.

"Well, I guess you had better leave it somewhere," she said after a moment.

"Are you going to Italy?" Winterbourne inquired in a tone of great respect.

The young lady glanced at him again. "Yes, sir," she replied. And she said nothing more.

"Are you—a—going over the Simplon?" Winterbourne pursued, a little embarrassed①.

"I don't know," she said. "I suppose It's some mountain. Randolph, what mountain are we going over?"

"Going where?" the child demanded.

"To Italy," Winterbourne explained.

"I don't know," said Randolph. "I don't want to go to Italy. I want to go to America."

"Oh, Italy is a beautiful place!" rejoined the young man.

"Can you get candy there?" Randolph loudly inquired.

"I hope not," said his sister. "I guess you have had enough candy, and mother thinks so too."

"I haven't had any for ever so long—for a hundred weeks!" cried the boy, still jumping about.

The young lady inspected her flounces and smoothed her ribbons again; and Winterbourne presently risked an observation upon the beauty of the view. He was ceasing to be embarrassed, for he had begun to perceive that she was not in the least embarrassed herself. There had not been the slightest alteration in her charming② complexion③; she was evidently neither offended nor flattered④. If she looked another way when he spoke to her, and seemed not particularly to hear him, this was simply her habit, her manner. Yet, as he talked a little more

---

① embarrassed：尴尬的，局促不安的，难堪的
② charming：迷人的，娇媚的
③ complexion：面色，肤色
④ flatter：奉承，阿谀

and pointed out some of the objects of interest in the view, with which she appeared quite unacquainted, she gradually gave him more of the benefit of her glance; and then he saw that this glance was perfectly direct and unshrinking. It was not, however, what would have been called an immodest glance, for the young girl's eyes were singularly honest and fresh. They were wonderfully pretty eyes; and, indeed, Winterbourne had not seen for a long time anything prettier than his fair countrywoman's various features—her complexion, her nose, her ears, her teeth. He had a great relish for feminine[①] beauty; he was addicted to observing and analyzing it; and as regards this young lady's face he made several observations. It was not at all insipid[②], but it was not exactly expressive; and though it was eminently[③] delicate[④] Winterbourne mentally accused it—very forgivingly—of a want of finish. He thought it very possible that Master Randolph's sister was a coquette[⑤]; he was sure she had a spirit of her own; but in her bright, sweet, superficial[⑥] little visage there was no mockery, no irony. Before long it became obvious that she was much disposed toward conversation. She told him that they were going to Rome for the winter—she and her mother and Randolph. She asked him if he was a "real American"; she shouldn't have taken him for one; he seemed more like a German—this was said after a little hesitation—especially when he spoke. Winterbourne, laughing, answered that he had met Germans who spoke like Americans, but that he had not, so far as he remembered, met an American who spoke like a German. Then he asked her if she should not be more comfortable in sitting upon the bench which he had just quitted. She answered that she liked standing up and walking about; but she presently sat down. She told him she was from New York State—"if you know where that is." Winterbourne learned more about her by catching hold of her small, slippery brother and making him stand a few minutes by his side.

"Tell me your name, my boy," he said.

"Randolph C. Miller," said the boy sharply. "And I'll tell you her name";

---

① feminine: 妇女(似)的，娇柔的，阴性的，女性的
② insipid: 没有味道的，平淡的
③ eminently: 不寻常地
④ delicate: 精巧的，精致的
⑤ coquette: 卖弄风情的女子
⑥ superficial: 表面性的事物，浅薄

and he leveled his alpenstock at his sister.

"You had better wait till you are asked!" said this young lady calmly.

"I should like very much to know your name," said Winterbourne.

"Her name is Daisy Miller!" cried the child. "But that isn't her real name; that isn't her name on her cards."

"It's a pity you haven't got one of my cards!" said Miss Miller.

"Her real name is Annie P. Miller," the boy went on.

"Ask him HIS name," said his sister, indicating Winterbourne.

But on this point Randolph seemed perfectly indifferent①; he continued to supply information with regard to his own family. "My father's name is Ezra B. Miller," he announced. "My father ain't in Europe; my father's in a better place than Europe."

Winterbourne imagined for a moment that this was the manner in which the child had been taught to intimate that Mr. Miller had been removed to the sphere of celestial② reward. But Randolph immediately added, "My father's in Schenectady③. He's got a big business. My father's rich, you bet!"

"Well!" ejaculated④ Miss Miller, lowering her parasol and looking at the embroidered border. Winterbourne presently released the child, who departed, dragging his alpenstock along the path.

"He doesn't like Europe," said the young girl. "He wants to go back."

"To Schenectady, you mean?"

"Yes; he wants to go right home. He hasn't got any boys here. There is one boy here, but he always goes round with a teacher; they won't let him play."

"And your brother hasn't any teacher?" Winterbourne inquired.

"Mother thought of getting him one, to travel round with us. There was a lady told her of a very good teacher; an American lady—perhaps you know her—Mrs. Sanders. I think she came from Boston. She told her of this teacher, and we thought of getting him to travel round with us. But Randolph said he

---

① indifferent：无关紧要的
② celestial：天上的
③ Schenectady：[地名][美国]斯克内克塔迪，美国纽约州东部城市，在奥尔巴尼西北20千米，莫霍克河畔，建于17世纪60年代，河港和铁路交通中心，以电气机械、电子机械、化学等工业为著名，有联合大学(创于1795年)、杰克逊植物园、斯克内克塔迪博物馆等
④ ejaculate：突然说出，射出

didn't want a teacher traveling round with us. He said he wouldn't have lessons when he was in the cars. And we ARE in the cars about half the time. There was an English lady we met in the cars—I think her name was Miss Featherstone; perhaps you know her. She wanted to know why I didn't give Randolph lessons—give him 'instruction,' she called it. I guess he could give me more instruction than I could give him. He's very smart."

"Yes," said Winterbourne; "he seems very smart."

"Mother's going to get a teacher for him as soon as we get to Italy. Can you get good teachers in Italy?"

"Very good, I should think," said Winterbourne.

"Or else she's going to find some school. He ought to learn some more. He's only nine. He's going to college." And in this way Miss Miller continued to converse upon the affairs of her family and upon other topics. She sat there with her extremely pretty hands, ornamented① with very brilliant rings, folded in her lap, and with her pretty eyes now resting upon those of Winterbourne, now wandering over the garden, the people who passed by, and the beautiful view. She talked to Winterbourne as if she had known him a long time. He found it very pleasant. It was many years since he had heard a young girl talk so much. It might have been said of this unknown young lady, who had come and sat down beside him upon a bench that she chattered. She was very quiet; she sat in a charming, tranquil attitude; but her lips and her eyes were constantly moving. She had a soft, slender, agreeable voice, and her tone was decidedly sociable. She gave Winterbourne a history of her movements and intentions and those of her mother and brother, in Europe, and enumerated, in particular, the various hotels at which they had stopped.

"That English lady in the cars," she said—"Miss Featherstone—asked me if we didn't all live in hotels in America. I told her I had never been in so many hotels in my life as since I came to Europe. I have never seen so many—It's nothing but hotels." But Miss Miller did not make this remark with a querulous accent; she appeared to be in the best humor with everything. She declared that the hotels were very good, when once you got used to their ways, and that Europe was perfectly sweet. She was not disappointed—not a bit. Perhaps it was

---

① ornament: 装饰，修饰 with

because she had heard so much about it before. She had ever so many intimate① friends that had been there ever so many times. And then she had had ever so many dresses and things from Paris. Whenever she put on a Paris dress she felt as if she were in Europe.

"It was a kind of a wishing cap," said Winterbourne.

"Yes," said Miss Miller without examining this analogy; "it always made me wish I was here. But I needn't have done that for dresses. I am sure they send all the pretty ones to America; you see the most frightful things here. The only thing I don't like," she proceeded, "is the society. There isn't any society; or, if there is, I don't know where it keeps itself. Do you I suppose there is some society somewhere, but I haven't seen anything of it. I'm very fond of society, and I have always had a great deal of it. I don't mean only in Schenectady, but in New York. I used to go to New York every winter. In New York I had lots of society. Last winter I had seventeen dinners given me; and three of them were by gentlemen," added Daisy Miller. "I have more friends in New York than in Schenectady—more gentleman friends; and more young lady friends too," she resumed in a moment. She paused again for an instant; she was looking at Winterbourne with all her prettiness in her lively eyes and in her light, slightly monotonous smile. "I have always had," she said, "a great deal of gentlemen's society."

Poor Winterbourne was amused, perplexed②, and decidedly charmed. He had never yet heard a young girl express herself in just this fashion; never, at least, save in cases where to say such things seemed a kind of demonstrative③ evidence of a certain laxity of deportment. And yet was he to accuse④ Miss Daisy Miller of actual or potential⑤, inconduite⑥, as they said at Geneva He felt that he had lived at Geneva so long that he had lost a good deal; he had become dishabituated to the American tone. Never, indeed, since he had grown old

---

① intimate:亲密的
② perplex:困惑
③ emonstrative:说明的,(语法)指示的
④ accuse:控告,谴责,非难
⑤ potential:潜在的,可能的
⑥ inconduite:不愿服从的,不遵从的

enough to appreciate things, had he encountered[①] a young American girl of so pronounced a type as this. Certainly she was very charming, but how deucedly[②] sociable[③]! Was she simply a pretty girl from New York State Were they all like that, the pretty girls who had a good deal of gentlemen's society Or was she also a designing, an audacious, an unscrupulous[④] young person Winterbourne had lost his instinct in this matter, and his reason could not help him. Miss Daisy Miller looked extremely innocent[⑤]. Some people had told him that, after all, American girls were exceedingly innocent; and others had told him that, after all, they were not. He was inclined to think Miss Daisy Miller was a flirt[⑥]—a pretty American flirt. He had never, as yet, had any relations with young ladies of this category. He had known, here in Europe, two or three women—persons older than Miss Daisy Miller, and provided, for respectability's sake, with husbands—who were great coquettes—dangerous, terrible women, with whom one's relations were liable to take a serious turn. But this young girl was not a coquette in that sense; she was very unsophisticated[⑦]; she was only a pretty American flirt. Winterbourne was almost grateful for having found the formula[⑧] that applied to Miss Daisy Miller. He leaned back in his seat; he remarked to himself that she had the most charming nose he had ever seen; he wondered what were the regular conditions and limitations of one's intercourse[⑨] with a pretty American flirt. It presently became apparent that he was on the way to learn.

Questions for Discussion

Make an analysis of the major characters in *Daisy Miller*.

① encounter:遭遇,遇到,相遇
② deucedly:非常,过度
③ sociable:好交际的,友善的
④ unscrupulous:肆无忌惮的,无道德的,不谨慎的
⑤ innocent:清白的,无罪的,天真的,无知的
⑥ flirt:卖弄风情的人,调情的人
⑦ unsophisticate:不懂世故的,单纯的,纯洁的
⑧ formula:公式,规则,客套语
⑨ intercourse:交往,交流

Unit 3   O. Henry (1862 – 1910)

Appreciation

I'm just waiting for a friend. It's an appointment made twenty years ago. 我只是在这儿等一位朋友罢了。

The next morning I was to start for the West to make my fortune. Well, we agreed that night that we would meet here again exactly twenty years from that date and time, no matter what our conditions might be or from what distance we might have to come. 这是20年前定下的一个约会。当时,我正准备第二天早上就动身到西部去谋生。那天夜晚临分手的时候,我们俩约定:20年后的同一日期、同一时间,我们俩将来到这里再次相会。

O. Henry is the pseudonym of William Sydney Porter, one of the most prestigious short story writers in the world. He produced trademark tales of varied characters and ironic plot twists which have been widely acclaimed as "O. Henry Ending". To a large extent he had a great impact on the American short story genre.

He was born on 11 September, 1862 in Greensboro, North Carolina. From his mother he inherited writing and drawing talents. From his aunt he learned much about writing and literature. At the same time, he was an avid reader especially of the English classics. At the age of fifteen, he became locally famed for telling stories and drawing caricatures when he was a drugstore apprentice. Later he took up to about ten jobs, for example, licensed pharmacist, ranch cowboy, colonist, bank teller and so on. Unfortunately the charge of embezzlement led to his 3-year prison term since 1898. Just during the confinement he began his short story career with the name of O. Henry. Once set free, he lived in New York City where he produced an amazing number of stories in a short time. In addition, quite a few of his works were just set in N. Y. City. The author had no intention to cover up his love of the city. He once said he "would like to live a lifetime in each street in New York. Every house has a drama in it."

As one of the most prolific writers in the history of American literature, he composed 10 collections and about 400 short stories. Among the universal classics are *Whistling Dick's Christmas Stocking* (1899, his first story), *The Duplicity of Hargraves*. *Cabbages and Kings*《白菜与国王》, *The Cop and the Anthem*《警察与赞美诗》, *The Gift of Magi*《麦琪的礼物》, *The Last Leave*, *Heart of the West*, *The Gentle Grafter*,

The Ransom of Red Chief, *Let Me Feel Your Pulse*, etc.

The legendary life experiences inspired and enriched the writing of O. Henry. In return, he projected his profound humanist concern onto his works which speak highly of the encyclopedia of American life. As a master of literary depiction, he told everyday tales, tragic or romantic, of ordinary characters with vivid imagination, witty puns, great humor, and polished irony. His works are characterized by the down-on-his-luck hero, the small-detail-revealing-all style and above all the jaw-dropping ending. The surprise ending is identified with his name O. Henry

Afflicted with heavy drinking and financial burden, William Sidney Porter died of cirrhosis 硬化 of liver, complications of diabetes 糖尿病, and an enlarged heart in New York City on 5 June, 1910. The O. Henry Museum was set up in Austen, Texas, to collect, preserve and interpret artifacts and archival materials relatied to him for literary, educational, and historical purposes. In addition, the O. Henry Festival was founded in 1985 to honor his life every April. Besides, the O. Henry Award, named after him, is bestowed annually onto the most notable short stories in U.S.

Selected Reading

After Twenty Years

The policeman on the beat① moved up the avenue impressively. The impressiveness was habitual② and not for show, for spectators were few. The time was barely 10 o'clock at night, but chilly gusts of wind with a taste of rain in them had well nigh③ depeopled④ the streets.

Trying doors as he went, twirling his club⑤ with many intricate⑥ and artful movements, turning now and then to cast his watchful eye adown the pacific

---

① beat:(警察的)辖区,巡逻区
② habitual:惯常的
③ nigh:接近,几乎,差不多
④ depeople:减少人口
⑤ twirling his club：旋转棍棒
⑥ intricate：复杂精细的

thoroughfare, the officer, with his stalwart① form and slight swagger② made a fine picture of a guardian of the peace. The vicinity③; was one that kept early hours. Now and then you might see the lights of a cigar store or of an all-night lunch counter; but the majority of the doors belonged to business places that had long since been closed.

When about midway of a certain block the policeman suddenly slowed his walk. In the doorway of a darkened hardware store a man leaned, with an unlighted cigar in his mouth. As the policeman walked up to him the man spoke up quickly.

"It's all right, officer," he said, reassuringly④ "I'm just waiting for a friend. It's an appointment made twenty years ago. Sounds a little funny to you, doesn't it? Well, I'll explain if you'd like to make certain It's all straight. About that long ago there used to be a restaurant where this store stands—'Big Joe' Brady's restaurant."

"Until five years ago," said the policeman. "It was torn down then."

The man in the doorway struck a match and lit his cigar. The light showed a pale, square-jawed face with keen eyes, and a little white scar⑤ near his right eyebrow. His scarf pin⑥ was a large diamond, oddly set.

"Twenty years ago to-night," said the man, "I dined here at 'Big Joe' Brady's with Jimmy Wells, my best chum⑦ and the finest chap⑧ in the world. He and I were raised here in New York, just like two brothers, together. I was eighteen and Jimmy was twenty. The next morning I was to start for the West to make my fortune. You couldn't have dragged Jimmy out of New York; he thought it was the only place on earth. Well, we agreed that night that we would meet here again exactly twenty years from that date and time, no matter what our conditions might be or from what distance we might have to come. We

---

① stalwart:强健的,坚定的
② swagger:昂首阔步
③ vicinity:附近地区
④ reassuringly:令人安心的
⑤ scar:伤疤
⑥ scarf pin:领带针,围巾夹
⑦ chum:密友
⑧ chap:小伙子,小家伙

figured that in twenty years each of us ought to have our destiny worked out and our fortunes made, whatever they were going to be."

"It sounds pretty interesting," said the policeman. "Rather a long time between meets, though, it seems to me. Haven't you heard from your friend since you left?"

"Well, yes, for a time we corresponded①," said the other. "But after a year or two we lost track of each other. You see, the West is a pretty big proposition②, and I kept hustling③ around over it pretty lively. But I know Jimmy will meet me here if he's alive, for he always was the truest, stanchest④ old chap in the world. He'll never forget. I came a thousand miles to stand in this door to-night, and It's worth it if my old partner turns up."

The waiting man pulled out a handsome watch, the lids of it set with small diamonds.

"Three minutes to ten," he announced. "It was exactly ten o'clock when we parted here at the restaurant door."

"Did pretty well out West, didn't you?" asked the policeman.

"You bet! I hope Jimmy has done half as well. He was a kind of plodder⑤, though, good fellow as he was. I've had to compete with some of the sharpest wits going to get my pile. A man gets in a groove⑥ in New York. It takes the West to put a razor-edge on him."

The policeman twirled his club and took a step or two.

"I'll be on my way. Hope your friend comes around all right. Going to call time on him sharp?"

"I should say not!" said the other. "I'll give him half an hour at least. If Jimmy is alive on earth he'll be here by that time. So long, officer."

"Good-night, sir," said the policeman, passing on along his beat, trying doors as he went.

---

① correspond：通信
② proposition：(难办或诱人的)事情，任务
③ hustling：快走，熙攘
④ stanchest：最坚定可靠的
⑤ plodder：慢条斯理的人
⑥ groove：沟槽

There was now a fine, cold drizzle① falling, and the wind had risen from its uncertain puffs into a steady blow. The few foot passengers astir② in that quarter hurried dismally and silently along with coat collars turned high and pocketed hands. And in the door of the hardware store the man who had come a thousand miles to fill an appointment, uncertain almost to absurdity③, with the friend of his youth, smoked his cigar and waited.

About twenty minutes he waited, and then a tall man in a long overcoat, with collar turned up to his ears, hurried across from the opposite side of the street. He went directly to the waiting man.

"Is that you, Bob" he asked, doubtfully.

"Is that you, Jimmy Wells" cried the man in the door.

"Bless my heart!" exclaimed the new arrival, grasping both the other's hands with his own. "It's Bob, sure as fate. I was certain I'd find you here if you were still in existence. Well, well, well! —twenty years is a long time. The old gone, Bob; I wish it had lasted, so we could have had another dinner there. How has the West treated you, old man?"

"Bully④; it has given me everything I asked it for. you've changed lots, Jimmy. I never thought you were so tall by two or three inches."

"Oh, I grew a bit after I was twenty."

"Doing well in New York, Jimmy?"

"Moderately. I have a position in one of the city departments. Come on, Bob; We'll go around to a place I know of, and have a good long talk about old times."

The two men started up the street, arm in arm. The man from the West, his egotism⑤ enlarged by success, was beginning to outline the history of his career. The other, submerged in his overcoat, listened with interest.

At the corner stood a drug store, brilliant with electric lights. When they came into this glare each of them turned simultaneously⑥ to gaze upon the

---

① drizzle:蒙蒙细雨,毛毛雨
② astir:活动的, 骚动的
③ absurdity:荒谬的行为;荒诞
④ Bully:一流的,特好的
⑤ egotism:自尊自大
⑥ simultaneously:同步地

other's face.

The man from the West stopped suddenly and released his arm.

"you're not Jimmy Wells," he snapped. "Twenty years is a long time, but not long enough to change a man's nose from a Roman to a pug."

"It sometimes changes a good man into a bad one," said the tall man, "you've been under arrest for ten minutes, "Silky" Bob. Chicago thinks you may have dropped over our way and wires us she wants to have a chat with you. Going quietly, are you? That's sensible. Now, before we go on to the station here's a note I was asked to hand you. You may read it here at the window. It's from Patrolman Wells."

The man from the West unfolded the little piece of paper handed him. His hand was steady when he began to read, but it trembled a little by the time he had finished. The note was rather short.

"Bob: I was at the appointed place on time. When you struck the match to light your cigar I saw it was the face of the man wanted in Chicago. Somehow I couldn't do it myself, so I went around and got a plain clothes man to do the job. JIMMY."

Questions for Discussion

1. If you were Jimmy, would you make the same choice? Why or why not?
2. Use your imagination and write a short story with the beginning "It has been twenty years since...."

Terms:
1. American Realism
2. American Naturalism
3. O. Henry endings
4. Pun

Chapter 6

American Modernism Literature

I. Historical Background

1. World War I

In WWI, President Woodrow Wilson took full control of foreign policy, declaring neutrality but warning Germany that resumption of unrestricted submarine warfare against American ships supplying goods to Allied nations would mean war. Germany decided to take the risk and try to win by cutting off supplies to Britain through the sinking of ships such as the RMS Lusitania; the U. S. declared war in April 1917 mainly from the threat. American money, food, and munitions arrived quickly, but troops had to be drafted and trained; by summer 1918 American soldiers under General John J. Pershing arrived at the rate of 10,000 a day. The result was Allied victory in November 1918.

In the early 20th century, the United States became a world power, fighting in WWI and WWII, and became a "modern" nation. Urbanization and industrialization had altered national demographics of the 1920s, After WWI, there appeared an economic boom called the Roaring Twenties when people became richer and a bust called The Great Depression ended with WWII. However, the economic crisis in America at the beginning of the 1930s left a mark in the literary creations of this period.

2. Politics and Economical Background

The United States' participation in the war marked a crucial stage in the nation's evolution to a world power. Since the war was not fought on the American soil, by the second decade of the 20th century, the United States had become the most powerful industrialized nation in the world, outstripping Britain and Germany in terms of industrial production. There was an economic boom and a deceptive affluence after the war. American entered the era of big industry and big technology, a mechanized age that deprived individuals of their sense of identity.

3. Cultural and Social Background

Along with the changes in the material landscape came the changes in the non-material system of belief and behavior. The war destroyed not only the lives of many promising young men, but also the early innocent beliefs of a whole generation, casting them into an age of disorientation, alienation and dissent.

Consumerism reached its peak when America witnessed an unparalleled economic boom. The prosperity brought about dramatic changes in people's lives while in the pursuit of pleasure and fun, responsibility for one's own actions tended to be ignored. Some Americans seemed so prepared to embrace the change that they were willing to discard traditional customs or values.

The War fundamentally transformed the outlook of many Americans. As the war scare and enthusiasm dissipated, some of those who had fought the war "to make the world safe for democracy" soon perceived themselves to have been deceived and were disappointed. Old moral values broke down. Young people wore bobbed hair and short skirts. Women took to drinking and smoking. The War, to a larger extent, deprived many Americans of provincialism, and intensified their pessimism.

4. The Roaring Twenties (the Jazz Age)

The Roaring Twenties is a term sometimes used to refer to the 1920s, characterizing the decade's distinctive cultural edge in most of the major cities of the "west" for a period of economic prosperity. French speakers dubbed it the "Crazy Years", emphasizing the era's social, artistic, and cultural dynamism. "Normalcy" returned to politics in the wake of hyper-emotional patriotism during WWI, jazz music blossomed, the flapper redefined modern womanhood, and Art peaked.

Economically, the era saw the large-scale diffusion and use of automobiles, telephones, motion pictures, and electricity, proliferated "modernity" to a large part of the population unprecedented industrial growth, accelerated consumer demand and aspirations, and significant changes in lifestyle and culture. The media focused on celebrities, especially sports heroes and movie stars, as cities rooted for their home team and filled the new palatial cinemas and gigantic stadiums. In most major countries women were voting for the first time. By the middle of the decade, prosperity was widespread, with the second half of the decade later becoming known as the "Golden Twenties".

The spirit of the Roaring Twenties was marked by a general feeling of discontinuity associated with modernity and a break with traditions. Everything seemed to be feasible through modern technology. Formal decorative frills were shed in favor of practicality in both daily life and architecture. Jazz and dancing rose in popularity, the period is also often referred to as the Jazz Age.

5. Great Depression

To many Americans, the 1930s was a dark decade. The Wall Street crash of 1929 suddenly ended the prosperity in the previous decade, marking the beginning of the Great Depression. Factories slowed down their production and more workers were laid off. All the contradictions inherent in free capitalist system were intensified. By 1933, America was ready to collapse. F. D Roosevelt launched a famous program named the New Deal, taking a series of positive measures: social security, welfare, unemployment insurance and acts securing job opportunities in public sectors—to restore people's confidence and make the nation recover.

II. Literary Background

The era following WWI gave rise to modernism, which is a complex and diverse international movement in all creative arts: painting, novel, poem and play, which provided the greatest renaissance of the 20th century. American modernism is an artistic and cultural movement in the United States starting at the turn of the 20th century with its core period between the wars and continuing into the 21st century.

1. American Modernism

Modernism is a general term which is applied to the wide range of experimental and avant-garde trends in the literature of the early 20th century, including Imagism, the Stream of Consciousness, Symbolism, Surrealism, Cubism, Expressionism, Futurism, Dadaism, and Constructivism. Modernism takes the irrational philosophy and the theory of psycho-analysis as its theoretical base. The modernist writers are mainly concerned with the inner being of an individual. As a result, modernism casts away almost all the traditional elements in literature such as story, plot, character, etc. The works are often labeled as anti-novel, anti-poetry and anti-drama.

American modernism is a trend of thought that affirms the power of human beings to create, improve, and reshape their environment, with the aid of scientific knowledge, technology and practical experimentation, and is thus in its essence both progressive and optimistic.

Many modernistic writers believed that the previously sustaining structures of human life. The subject matter of a modernistic writing often became the work itself since the writer was obsessed with the interrelationship between literature and life. A modernistic writing seemed "to begin arbitrarily, to advance without explanation, and to end without resolution, consisting of vivid segments juxtaposed without cushioning or integrating transitions." Fragments and fragmentation dominated human experience as well as artistic writing. No matter what modernistic techniques were employed, the search for meaning—the meaning of life, the meaning of literature—remained the ultimate purpose of many modernistic writers.

2. The Lost Generation

The most recognizable "modernist" figures in fiction are "the Lost Generation", which refers to the disillusioned intellectuals and artists of the years following WWI, who rebelled against former ideals and values but could replace them only by despair or a cynical hedonism. The remark of Gertrude Stein, "You are all a lost generation," addressed to Hemingway, was used as a Preface to the latter's novel *The Sun Also Rises*, which brilliantly describes those expatriates who had cut themselves off from their past in America in order to create new types of writing.

The Lost Generation was a society where individual thought and expression were crushed. These intellectuals were especially "disillusioned by their war experiences and alienated by what they perceived as the crassness of American culture and its puritanical repressions", living in European cities such as London and Paris, standing aside and writing about what they saw—the failure of the American society. They believed that the American bourgeois society was hypocritical, vulgar and crude, concerning only with making money.

American writers expressed disillusionment following WWI. The stories and novels of F. Scott Fitzgerald capture the mood of the 1920s, and John Dos Passos wrote about the war. Ernest Hemingway became notable for *The Sun Also Rises* and *A Farewell to Arms*; in 1954, he won the Nobel Prize in Literature.

3. Southern literature

Traditionally, the study of southern literature has emphasized a common Southern history, the significance of family, a sense of community and one's role within it, a sense of justice, the region's dominant religion (Christianity—see Protestantism), and the burdens/rewards religion often brings, issues of racial tension, land and the promise it brings, a sense of social class and place, and the use of the Southern dialect.

The Southern Renaissance

In the 1920s and 1930s, a renaissance in Southern literature began with the appearance of writers such as William Faulkner, Katherine Anne Porter, Caroline Gordon, Allen Tate, Thomas Wolfe, Robert Penn Warren, and Tennessee Williams. Because of the distance the Southern Renaissance authors had from the American Civil War and slavery, they were more objective in their writings about the South.

William Faulkner who won the Nobel Prize in Literature in 1949 was known for his epic portrayal of the tragic conflict between the old and the new South. Most of his works are set in the American south, with his emphasis on the southern subjects and consciousness. His masterpiece is *The Sound and the Fury*. Writers like Faulkner, also brought new techniques such as stream of consciousness and complex narrative techniques to their writings. For instance, his novel *As I Lay Dying* is told by changing narrators ranging from the deceased Addie to her young son.

The late 1930s also saw the publication of one of the best-known Southern novels, *Gone with the Wind* by Margaret Mitchell. The novel, published in 1936, quickly became a bestseller. It won the 1937 Pulitzer Prize, and in 1939 an equally famous movie of the novel premiered. Mitchell's novel consolidated white supremacist Lost Cause ideologies to construct a bucolic plantation South in which slavery was a benign, or even benevolent, institution. She presents white southerners as victims of a rapacious Northern industrial capitalism and depicts black southerners as either lazy, stupid, and over sexualized, or as docile, childlike, and resolutely loyal to their white masters. Southern literature has always drawn audiences outside the South and outside the United States, and *Gone with the Wind* has continued to popularize harmful stereotypes of southern history and culture for audiences around the world.

4. Poetry

Led by the American poet Ezra Pound, Imagist Movement is a poetic movement that flourished in the U.S and England during 1909 – 1917. Pound endorsed three main principles as guidelines for Imagism, including direct treatment of poetic subjects, elimination of merely ornamental of superfluous words, and rhythmical composition should be composed with the phrasing of music, not a metronome. The primary Imagist objective is to stick closely to the object or experience being described.

An outstanding representative of Imagist poems is Ezra Pound's two-line poem, *In a Station of the Metro*. Other well-known Imagist poems include William Carlos Williams' *The Red Wheelbarrow*, Amy Lowell's *Wind and Silver*, Hilda Doolitde's *Oread*, T. E. American Poetry began to utter the voice of its own in the mid-19th century.

He influenced many other poets, notably T. S. Eliot (1888 – 1965), another expatriate. Eliot wrote spare, cerebral poetry, carried by a dense structure of symbols. In "The Waste Land", he embodied a jaundiced vision of post-World War I society in fragmented, haunted images. Like Pound's, Eliot's poetry could be highly allusive, and some editions of "The Waste Land" come with footnotes supplied by the poet. In 1948, Eliot won the Nobel Prize in Literature. T. S Eliot led an intellectual reaction against the 19th century romantic. And as his following group Fugitive Group focus of the study of literary criticism and initiated the movement of New Criticism.

Other well-known Imagist poems include William Carlos Williams' "The Red Wheelbarrow", Amy Lowell's "Wind and Silver", Hilda Doolitde's "Oread, T. E".

5. The rise of American drama

American drama attained international status only in the 1920s and 1930s, with the works of Eugene O'Neill, who won four Pulitzer Prizes and the Nobel Prize.

The years between the World Wars were years of extremes. Eugene O'Neill's plays were the high point for serious dramatic plays leading up to the outbreak of war in Europe. *Beyond the Horizon* (1920), for which he won his first Pulitzer Prize; he later won Pulitzers for *Anna Christie* (1922) and *Strange Interlude* (1928) as well as the Nobel Prize in Literature. Alfred Lunt and Lynn Fontanne remained a popular acting couple in the 1930s.

6. American Realism—Depression-era Literature

In the 1930s of the Great Depression, American realism appeared in American literary history. Whether it was a cultural portrayal, or a scenic view of downtown New York City, these images and works of literature, music and painting depicted a contemporary view of what was happening; an attempt at defining what was real.

In Steinbeck's words, for the first time in American literature, ideas were used as weapons protecting or being turned against individuals. John Steinbeck wrote about the lives of poor farmers. A sympathetic depiction of two migrant workers in *Of Mice and Men* won him immediate success. The publication of *The Grapes of Wrath* ranked him among the greatest writers, which is about the migration of the Joad family to California during the economic depression of Depression era.

Literature of this period struggled to understand the new and diverse responses to the advent of modernity. Some writers celebrated the changes; others lamented the loss of old ways of being. Some imagined future utopias; others searched for new forms to speak of the new realities.

Unit 1　Robert Frost (1874 – 1963)

Appreciation

> Two roads diverged in a yellow wood,　　黄色的树林里分出两条路，
> And sorry I could not travel both　　　　可惜我不能同时去涉足，
> I took the one less traveled by,　　　　　而我选择了人迹更少的一条，
> And that has made all the difference.　　从此决定了我一生的道路。

Robert Lee Frost, an American poet, is highly regarded for his realistic depictions of rural life and his command of American colloquial speech. His work frequently employed settings from rural life in New England in the early twentieth century, using them to examine complex social and philosophical themes. As one of the most popular and critically respected American poets of his generation, Frost was honored frequently during his lifetime, receiving four Pulitzer Prizes for Poetry. In 1961, at the inauguration of John F. Kennedy, he became the first poet to read a poem *The Gift Outright* at a presidential inauguration.

Robert Frost was born in San Francisco and spent his early childhood there. His first professional poem, *My Butterfly* was published on November 8, 1894, in the New York newspaper *The Independent*.

Farm and farming activities became a focus in Frost's poems but his ways of expressing them were varied so as not to make them dull. He wrote excellent sonnets, heroic couplets, and blank verse poems, and he was an expert at using meter and rhythm in such a way that traditional rhythmical patterns no longer seemed monotonous.

What made Frost's poems valuable in modern times was their profound simplicity and dynamic views of daily life. In describing landscape and everyday events in New England Frost managed to probe into the depths of life and Nature. Lyric poems such as *Mending Wall*, *The Road Not Taken*, *Stopping by Woods on a Snowy Evening*, and *Death of the Hired Man* were counted among Frost's best-known poems.

Brief Introduction

The Road Not Taken is published in 1916 in the collection *Mountain Interval*. It is the first poem in the volume.

The Road Not Taken is a narrative poem consisting of four stanzas of iambic tetrameter (though it is hypermetric by one beat—there are nine syllables per line instead of the strict eight required for tetrameter) and is one of Frost's most popular works. It has been commonly studied in high school literature classes and can often relate to the reader's life as in making difficult decisions. The lines "I took the one less traveled by, and that has made all the difference." are often cited as emblematic of America's individualist spirit of adventure, in a reading that assumes they are to be taken literally. This is doubtful: whatever difference the choice might have made, it was not made on the basis of a discerned difference between the two paths that opened up before the traveller. The speaker admits in the second and third stanzas that both paths may be equally worn and equally leaf-covered, and it is only in his future recollection that he will call one of the two roads, the one he took, "less traveled by."

Selected Reading

The Road Not Taken

Two roads diverged① in a yellow wood,
And sorry I could not travel both
And be one traveler, long I stood②
And looked down③ one as far as I could
To where it bent④ in the undergrowth⑤;

Then took the other, as just as fair⑥,
And having perhaps the better claim⑦,
Because it was grassy and wanted wear⑧;

---

① diverge: (道路、路线等)分叉,叉开
② long I stood: 伫立长久,表明叙事人犹疑不决
③ down: down the road
④ bend: 弯曲,拐弯
⑤ undergrowth: 树林里的矮小灌木丛
⑥ Then took the other, as just as fair: Then I took the other road, which seems as proper and as beautiful. 意思是:我选了同样不错的另一条路
⑦ the better claim: 更大的吸引力
⑧ want wear: 缺少磨损,即因行人稀少而鲜有足迹

Though as for that the passing there[①]
Had worn them really about the same[②],

And both that morning equally lay
In leaves no step had trodden black[③].
Oh, I kept the first for another day!
Yet knowing how way leads on to way[④],
I doubted if I should ever come back.

I shall be telling this with a sigh[⑤]
Somewhere ages and ages hence[⑥]:
Two roads diverged in a wood, and I—
I took the one less traveled by,
And that has made all the difference[⑦].

Questions for Discussion

What is the theme of *The Road Not Taken* How does symbolism in the poem help express the theme?

Brief Introduction

Stopping by Woods on a Snowy Evening is a lyric poem in iambic tetrameter quatrain. It is about a weary journeyer stopping by the woods to contemplate over death on the "darkest evening of the year." Through the analogy between the traveler's actions in the poem and a person's journey through life, the poet reveals that in the

---

① the passing there: 指来往于小路的行人对小路的踩踏
② Had worn them really about the same: 给两条不同的小路留下的是同等的痕迹
③ had trodden black: 被踩脏; black: 指被踩的落叶会变成黑色
④ Yet knowing how way leads on to way: 然而我知道,路总是一条接着一条,很难折回
⑤ I shall be telling this with a sigh: 我将会叹息着讲述这件事。这是因为叙事人也许在多年之后对未选之路感到遗憾
⑥ ages and ages hence: 很久很久以后
⑦ that has made all the difference: 而一切都因此而截然不同

hard struggle of life people may feel tired and desire to have a momentary relief from the obligations of life. The journeyer's complex feelings for death are summarized in three simple words: "lovely, dark, deep."

Selected Reading

Stopping by Woods[①] on a Snowy Evening

Whose woods these are I think I know.
His house is in the village though[②];
He will not see me stopping here
To watch his woods fill up with snow[③].

My little horse must think it queer[④]
To stop without a farmhouse near
Between the woods and frozen lake
The darkest evening of the year[⑤].
He gives his harness bells a shake[⑥]
To ask[⑦] if there is some mistake.
The only other sound's the sweep
Of easy wind[⑧] and downy flake[⑨].

---

① woods：在弗罗斯特的许多抒情诗中，woods 树林是常见的意象，常象征着死亡和毁灭

② Whose woods these are I think I know. His house is in the village though：树林的主人住在林外的村镇里。诗人远离林主和村镇所代表的人的世界，来到林中

③ snow：在弗罗斯特的抒情诗中，雪也是常见的意象，象征高洁单纯。woods fill up with snow 是代表着自然美的意象

④ My little horse must think it queer：诗人想象马对主人为什么停在没有农庄的林边感到奇怪，实际是在探讨自己雪夜林边停下的动机

⑤ The darkest evening of the year：一年中最黑暗的夜晚。不仅写实，也象征人的心境

⑥ He gives his harness bells a shake：小马轻摇它脖颈上的佩铃

⑦ to ask：小马被人格化了

⑧ easy wind：微风

⑨ downy flake：雪绒花

The woods are lovely, dark and deep①.
But I have promises② to keep,
And miles to go before I sleep③,
And miles to go before I sleep.

Questions for Discussion

What is the theme of *Stopping by Woods on a Snowy Evening* How does symbolism in the poem help express the theme?

Unit 2　Carl Sandburg (1878 – 1967)

  Carl Sandburg was an American writer and editor, best known for his poetry. He won three Pulitzer Prizes, two for his poetry and another for a biography of Abraham Lincoln. H. L. Mencken called Carl Sandburg "indubitably an American in every pulse-beat."

  Carl Sandburg was born in Galesburg, Illinois, on January 6, 1878. His parents, August and Clara Johnson, had emigrated to America from the north of Sweden. After encountering several August Johnsons in his job for the railroad, the Sandburg's father renamed the family. The Sandburgs were very poor; Carl left school at the age of thirteen to work odd jobs, from laying bricks to dishwashing, to help support his family. At seventeen, he traveled west to Kansas as a hobo. He then served eight months in Puerto Rico during the Spanish-American war. While serving, Sandburg met a student at Lombard College, the small school located in Sandburg's hometown. The young man convinced Sandburg to enroll in Lombard after his return from the war.

  The Sandburgs soon moved to Chicago, where Carl became an editorial writer for

---

  ① The woods are lovely, dark and deep: 该句与第一节中白雪覆盖的树林形成对照, 从更深的层面展现树林美丽, 但神秘莫测, 具有一种难以抗拒的诱惑力, 使人流连忘返, 象征渴求最后安息的愿望

  ② promises: 可理解为个人承诺或使命, 也可理解为社会责任

  ③ And miles to go before I sleep: 结尾两句重复, 耐人寻味, 既写实又具有象征含义。睡前有一段很长的路程要走, 同时蕴含"安息前还有漫长的人生路"之意

the Chicago Daily News. Harriet Monroe had just started Poetry: A Magazine of Verse, and began publishing Sandburg's poems, encouraging him to continue writing in the free-verse, Whitman-like style he had cultivated in college. Monroe liked the poems' homely speech, which distinguished Sandburg from his predecessors. It was during this period that Sandburg was recognized as a member of the Chicago literary renaissance, which included Ben Hecht, Theodore Dreiser, Sherwood Anderson, and Edgar Lee Masters. He established his reputation with *Chicago Poems* (1916), and then "Cornhuskers" (1918), for which he received the Pulitzer Prize in 1919. Soon after the publication of these volumes Sandburg wrote "Smoke and Steel" (1920), his first prolonged attempt to find beauty in modern industrialism. With these three volumes, Sandburg became known for his free verse poems that portrayed industrial America.

During his lifetime, Sandburg was widely regarded as "a major figure in contemporary literature", especially for volumes of his collected verse, including. He enjoyed "unrivaled appeal as a poet in his day, perhaps because the breadth of his experiences connected him with so many strands of American life", and at his death in 1967, President Lyndon B. Johnson observed that "Carl Sandburg was more than the voice of America, more than the poet of its strength and genius. He was America."

Brief Introduction

Much of Carl Sandburg's poetry, such as "Chicago", focused on Chicago, Illinois, where he spent time as a reporter for the Chicago Daily News and the Day Book. His most famous description of the city is as "Hog Butcher for the World/Tool Maker, Stacker of Wheat/Player with Railroads and the Nation's Freight Handler,/Stormy, Husky, Brawling, City of the Big Shoulders."

"Chicago" is a poem about the U.S. city of Chicago. It was republished in 1916 in Sandburg's first mainstream collection of poems, also titled *Chicago Poems*.

The Chicago Poems, and its follow-up volumes of verse, "Cornhuskers" (1918) and "Smoke and Steel" (1920) represent Sandburg's attempts to found an American version of social realism, writing expansive verse in praise of American agriculture and industry. All of these tendencies are manifest in "Chicago" itself. Then, as now, the city of Chicago was a hub of commodities trading, and a key financial center for agricultural markets. The city was also a center of the meat-packing industry, and an important railroad hub; these industries are also mentioned in the poem.

Chicago Poems established Sandburg as a major figure in contemporary literature.

Sandburg has described the poem as a chant of defiance by Chicago... its defiance of New York, Boston, Philadelphia, London, Paris, Berlin and Rome. The poem sort of says "Maybe we ain't got culture, but we're eatin' regular." One of Chicago's many nicknames, "City of the Big Shoulders," is taken from the poem's fifth line.

Selected Reading

Chicago

Hog Butcher for the World,
Tool Maker, Stacker of Wheat,
Player with Railroads and the Nation's Freight Handler;
Stormy, husky, brawling,
City of the Big Shoulders:

They tell me you are wicked and I believe them, for I
have seen your painted women under the gas lamps
luring the farm boys.
And they tell me you are crooked and I answer: Yes, it
is true I have seen the gunman kill and go free to
kill again.
And they tell me you are brutal and my reply is: On the
faces of women and children I have seen the marks
of wanton hunger.
And having answered so I turn once more to those who
sneer at this my city, and I give them back the sneer
and say to them:
Come and show me another city with lifted head singing
so proud to be alive and coarse and strong and cunning.
Flinging magnetic curses amid the toil of piling job on
job, here is a tall bold slugger set vivid against the
little soft cities;

Fierce as a dog with tongue lapping for action, cunning
as a savage pitted against the wilderness,

Bareheaded,
Shoveling,
Wrecking,
Planning,
Building, breaking, rebuilding,
Under the smoke, dust all over his mouth, laughing with
white teeth,
Under the terrible burden of destiny laughing as a young
man laughs,
Laughing even as an ignorant fighter laughs who has
never lost a battle,
Bragging and laughing that under his wrist is the pulse,
and under his ribs the heart of the people,

Laughing!

Laughing the stormy, husky, brawling laughter of
Youth, half-naked, sweating, proud to be Hog
Butcher, Tool Maker, Stacker of Wheat, Player with
Railroads and Freight Handler to the Nation.

Questions for Discussion

What Is the Main Idea in Carl Sandburg's Poem "Chicago"?

Brief Introduction

"Fog" is probably Carl Sandburg's best-known poem and has been a popular choice for study since it was first published in Sandburg's first mainstream collection of poems, Chicago Poems in 1916. Sandburg has described the genesis of the poem. Sandburg was inspired to write it one day whilst out walking near Chicago's Grant Park. At a time when he was carrying a book of Japanese Haiku, he went to interview a juvenile court judge, and he had cut through Grant Park and saw the fog over Chicago harbor. He had certainly seen many fogs before, but this time he had to wait forty minutes for the judge, and he only had a piece of newsprint handy, so he decided to create an "American Haiku".

He had with him a book of Japanese haiku, the short 17-syllable poems that capture essences of the natural world. He was on his way to meet someone and had some spare time, so he wrote "Fog" and developed what is essentially a haiku into something more.

Carl Sandburg wrote a great deal of poetry throughout his busy life and was also well known as a collector of American folk songs. He wrote a biography of Abraham Lincoln that is still a popular read today.

"Fog" is a poem that reflects Sandburg's interest in the natural world and beautifully captures a moment or two when the fog came moving in over the harbor waters, a powerful image given life through a metaphorical cat.

Selected Reading

Fog

**The fog comes
on little cat feet.**

**It sits looking
over the harbor and city
on silent haunches,
and then moves on.**

Questions for Discussion

1. What Is the Meaning of "Fog" by Carl Sandburg?
2. Make an analysis of the poem "Fog".

Unit 3　William Carlos Williams(1883 – 1963)

William Carlos Williams was an American poet closely associated with modernism and imagism. In addition to his writing, Williams had a long career as a physician practicing both pediatrics and general medicine. He began writing poetry while a student at Horace Mann High School, at which time he made the decision to become both a writer and a doctor. He received his MD from the University of Pennsylvania, where he met and befriended Ezra Pound, who became a great influence on his writing, and in 1913 arranged for the London publication of Williams's second collection, *The Tempers*. Returning to Rutherford, where he sustained his medical practice throughout his life, Williams began publishing in small magazines and embarked on a prolific career as a poet, novelist, essayist, and playwright.

Following Pound, he was one of the principal poets of the Imagist movement, though as time went on, he began to increasingly disagree with the values put forth in the work of Pound and especially Eliot, who he felt were too attached to European culture and traditions. Continuing to experiment with new techniques of meter and lineation, Williams sought to invent an entirely fresh—and singularly American—poetic, whose subject matter was centered on the everyday circumstances of life and the lives of common people.

His influence as a poet spread slowly during the 1920s and 1930s, overshadowed, he felt, by the immense popularity of Eliot's "The Waste Land"; however, his work received increasing attention in the 1950s and 1960s as younger poets, including Allen Ginsberg and the Beats, were impressed by the accessibility of his language and his openness as a mentor. His major works include *Kora in Hell* (1920); *Spring and All* (1923); *Pictures from Brueghel* and *Other Poems* (1962), which was awarded the Pulitzer Prize; the five-volume epic *Paterson* (1963, 1992); and *Imaginations* (1970).

His most anthologized poem is "*The Red Wheelbarrow*", an example of the Imagist movement's style and principles.

Brief Introduction

"The Red Wheelbarrow" is a poem by American modernist poet and physician William Carlos Williams (1883 – 1963). The poem was originally published without a title and was designated as "XXII" as the twenty-second work in Williams' 1923 book Spring and All, a hybrid collection which incorporated alternating selections of free verse poetry and prose. It is one of Williams' most frequently anthologized poems, and is considered a prime example of early twentieth-century Imagism.

Selected Reading

The Red Wheelbarrow

so much depends
upon

a red wheel
barrow

glazed with rain
water

beside the white
chickens.

Questions for Discussion

1. What three items are mentioned in the poem?
2. Why might the objects in the poem be very important? Explain.
3. What is the theme of the poem?
4. What elements of Imagism does this poem exhibit?

Unit 4 Ezra Pound (1885 – 1972)

Ezra Weston Loomis Pound was an American expatriate poet and critic, a forerunner or founder of American modern poetry, and one of the most controversial figures in the 20th century American literature. His contribution to poetry began with his promotion of Imagism. His best-known works include *Ripostes* (1912), *Hugh Selwyn Mauberley* (1920) and his unfinished 120-section epic, *The Cantos* (1917 – 1969).

Pound was born in Hailey, Idaho and brought up in Pennsylvania. In high school, the study of Latin inspired him to be a poet. In 1908 Pound left for Europe and settled in London where he quickly involved himself in a literary circle, through which he was in contact with men like T. E. Hulme and William Butler Yeats. Later, Pound became the leader of the "Imagist" movement and began to revolutionize poetry. Upset by WW I and disgusted by the spiritual disillusionment he perceived, Pound moved from London to Paris in 1920. There he joined the group of the Lost Generation.

Despite the fact that he was politically controversial and notorious for what he did during the war, Pound's literary talents are self-evident. His poetic works include twelve volumes of verse which were later collected and published in *Collected Poems of Ezra Pound* (1982). Of all Pound's poems before *The Cantos*, the best two were two translations: *The Seafarer* and *Cathay*. The latter was adapted from the American scholar Ernest Fenollosa's attempts to translate classical Chinese poetry through knowledge of the Chinese ideograms, which was positive proof of the great influence of ancient Chinese culture upon Pound. The best poem Pound ever wrote was *Hugh Selwyn Mauberly* (1920), which, in some way, deplored the Western civilization in the Great War and its aftermath. *The Cantos* written in sections between 1915 and 1945 is generally considered to be Pound's major work.

Brief Introduction

In a Station of the Metro is a classic Imagist poem, presenting a quick, sharp image of people seen in the darkness of the Paris subway (the Metro). One day in 1913, the poet was struck by the beautiful faces of some women and children against the wet and dark background in a Paris subway station. His effort to express this experience ended in a 130-odd-line poem which the poet tore into pieces since he was not satisfied with it. A year later, the poet presented a two-line poem as we see here today.

Selected Reading

In a Station of the Metro

The apparition① of these faces in the crowd;
Petals on a wet, black bough②.

---

① apparition: 幽灵,幻影
② Petals on a wet, black bough: 湿漉漉黑色枝条上的众多花瓣

Questions for Discussion

1. In what way does this poem reflect imagist poetry?
2. How many images are there in this poem? What are they?
3. How do you appreciate the poem?

Unit 5 Hart Crane (1889 – 1932)

Hart Crane is considered a pivotal even prophetic figure in American literature; he is often cast as a Romantic in the decades of high Modernism. According to Harold Bloom, "like a new Byron or Shelley, Crane was a pilgrim of the Absolute. His quest was for agonistic supremacy, against Eliot, in order to join Whitman, Dickinson, Melville in the American Pantheon." Crane's version of American Romanticism extended back through Walt Whitman to Ralph Waldo Emerson, and in his most ambitious work, *The Bridge*, he sought nothing less than an expression of the American experience in its entirety. As Allen Tate wrote in Essays of Four Decades, "Crane was one of those men whom every age seems to select as the spokesman of its spiritual life; they give the age away."

In 1926, while Crane worked on *The Bridge*, his verse collection White Buildings was published. This work earned him substantial respect as an imposing stylist, one whose lyricism and imagery recalled the French Romantics Baudelaire and Rimbaud. But it prompted speculation that Crane was an imprecise and confused artist, one who sometimes settled for sound instead of sense. Edmund Wilson, for instance, wrote in New Republic that "though Crane can sometimes move us, the emotion is oddly vague." For Wilson, whose essay was later reprinted in *The Shores of Light*, Crane possessed "a style that is strikingly original—almost something like a great style, if there could be such a thing as a great style which was ... not ... applied to any subject at all."

Brief Introduction

"To Brooklyn Bridge" is the short lyrical ode to the Brooklyn Bridge and New York City which opens the sequence and serves as an introduction (and New York City's urban landscape remains a dominant presence throughout the book). After beginning with this ode, "Ave Maria" begins the first longer sequence labeled Roman numeral I which describes Columbus' eastward return from his accidental voyage to the Americas. The title of the piece is based upon the fact that Columbus attributed his crew's survival across the Atlantic Ocean to "the intercession of the Virgin Mary." The second major section of the poem, "Powhatan's Daughter," is divided into five parts, and one well-known part, entitled "The River," follows a group of vagabonds, in the 20th century, who are traveling west through America via train. In "The River," Crane incorporates advertisements and references Minstrel shows. He claimed in a letter that "the rhythm is jazz." The section also includes the story of Pocahontas and a section on the fictional character Rip Van Winkle.

Other major sections of the poem include "Cape Hatteras" (the longest individual section of the poem), "Quaker Hill," "The Tunnel," and "Atlantis," the rapturous final section that returns the poem's focus back to the Brooklyn Bridge, and which was actually the first part of the overall poem finished despite its reservation for the end.

Selected Reading

To Brooklyn Bridge

How many dawns, chill from his rippling rest
The seagull's wings shall dip and pivot him,
Shedding white rings of tumult, building high
Over the chained bay waters Liberty—

Then, with inviolate curve, forsake our eyes
As apparitional as sails that cross
Some page of figures to be filed away;
—Till elevators drop us from our day . . .

I think of cinemas, panoramic sleights
With multitudes bent toward some flashing scene
Never disclosed, but hastened to again,
Foretold to other eyes on the same screen;

And Thee, across the harbor, silver-paced
As though the sun took step of thee, yet left
Some motion ever unspent in thy stride,—

Implicitly thy freedom staying thee!

Out of some subway scuttle, cell or loft
A bedlamite speeds to thy parapets,
Tilting there momently, shrill shirt ballooning,
A jest falls from the speechless caravan.

Down Wall, from girder into street noon leaks,
A rip-tooth of the sky's acetylene;
All afternoon the cloud-flown derricks turn . . .
Thy cables breathe the North Atlantic still.

And obscure as that heaven of the Jews,
Thy guerdon . . . Accolade thou dost bestow
Of anonymity time cannot raise:
Vibrant reprieve and pardon thou dost show.

O harp and altar, of the fury fused,
(How could mere toil align thy choiring strings!)
Terrific threshold of the prophet's pledge,
Prayer of pariah, and the lover's cry,—

Again the traffic lights that skim thy swift
Unfractioned idiom, immaculate sigh of stars,
Beading thy path—condense eternity:
And we have seen night lifted in thine arms.

Under thy shadow by the piers I waited;
Only in darkness is thy shadow clear.
The City's fiery parcels all undone,
Already snow submerges an iron year . . .

O Sleepless as the river under thee,
Vaulting the sea, the prairies' dreaming sod,
Unto us lowliest sometime sweep, descend
And of the curveship lend a myth to God.

Questions for Discussion

Make an analysis of "To Brooklyn Bridge".

Unit 6　Edward Estlin Cummings (1894 – 1962)

Edward Estlin(E. E.) Cummings was born on October 14, 1894, in Cambridge, Massachusetts to Edward Cummings and the former Rebecca Haswell Clarke, a well-known Unitarian couple in the city. Edward Estlin Cummings, often styled as e e cummings, as he sometimes signed his name, was an American poet, painter, essayist, author, and playwright.

Cummings was politically neutral much of his life until the rise of the Cold War when he became a Republican in political orientation and a supporter of Joseph McCarthy during the height of the Cold War. He died in the 1960s after briefly teaching at Harvard University in the 1950s having lived nearly seventy years.

He wrote approximately 2,900 poems, two autobiographical novels, four plays, and several essays. He is associated with the modernist free-form poetry associated with much poetry in the 20th century. Much of his poetry is written with a original syntax and largely inclining toward an extended use of lower case typography for poetic expression.

His use of lower case syntax extended to the rendering even of personal pronouns such as "I" to the lower case "i" as may be found in the phrase "i shall go".

As well as being influenced by notable modernists, including Gertrude Stein and Ezra Pound, Cummings in his early work drew upon the imagist experiments of Amy Lowell. Many of his poems are sonnets, albeit often with a modern twist. He occasionally used the blues form and acrostics.

Cummings' poetry often deals with themes of love and nature, as well as the relationship of the individual to the masses and to the world. His poems are also often rife with satire. Later, his visits to Paris exposed him to Dada and Surrealism, which he reflected in his work. He began to rely on symbolism and allegory, where he once had used simile and metaphor. In his later work, he rarely used comparisons that required objects that were not previously mentioned in the poem, choosing to use a symbol instead. His later poetry is "frequently more lucid, more moving, and more profound than his earlier." Cummings also liked to incorporate imagery of nature and death into much of his poetry.

While his poetic forms and themes share an affinity with the Romantic tradition, Cummings' work universally shows a particular idiosyncrasy of syntax, or way of arranging individual words into larger phrases and sentences. Many of his most striking poems do not involve any typographical or punctuation innovations at all, but purely syntactic ones.

Brief Introduction

E. E. Cummings is an American poet who is famous for his fantastic poems. L(a, one of his representative works, the first poem in his 1958 collection 95 Poems, is a unique visual poem that shows Cummings' feeling of loneliness and takes readers into a sentimental scene. A great many researches have been done on this poem focusing on the morphology, visual effects, tonality and Cummings' inner world. However, a comprehensive literature review of this poem has hardly been made.

"l(a" is arranged vertically in groups of one to five letters. When the text is laid out horizontally, it either reads as l(a leaf falls) oneliness—in other words, a leaf falls inserted between the first two letters of loneliness—or l(a le af fa ll s) one l iness, with a le af fa ll s between a l and one.

Cummings biographer Richard S. Kennedy calls the poem "the most delicately beautiful literary construct that Cummings ever created".

Selected Reading

<pre>
            L(a

            l(a

            le

            af

            fa

            ll

            s)
            one
            l

            iness
</pre>

Questions for Discussion

Make an Analysis of E. E. Cummings poem "l(a".

Unit 7　F. Scott Fitzgerald (1896–1940)

Appreciation

　　Gatsby believed in the green light, the orgastic future that year by year recedes before us. It eluded us then, but that's no matter—tomorrow we will run faster, stretch out our arms farther.... And one fine morning—盖茨比信奉这盏绿灯,这个一年年在我们眼前渐渐远去的极乐的未来。它从前逃脱了我们的追求,不过那没关系——明天我们跑得更快一点,把胳臂伸得更远一点……总有一天……

　　So we beat on, boats against the current, borne back ceaselessly into the past. 于是我们奋力向前划,逆流向上的小舟,不停地倒退,进入过去。

　　Francis Scott Key Fitzgerald was an American author of novels and short stories, whose works are the paradigm writings of the Jazz Age. He is widely regarded as one of the greatest American writers of the 20th century and is considered a member of the "Lost Generation" of the 1920s. His most famous novel "*The Great Gatsby*" has been the basis for numerous films of the same name, spanning nearly 90 years; 1926, 1949, 1974, 2000, and an upcoming 2013 adaption.

　　F. Scott Fitzgerald was born on September 26, 1896 into a middle-class family in St. Paul, Minnesota. He had an expensive education, first in private schools, and then at Princeton. In 1917 he left Princeton without graduating and decided to fight as a soldier in the WW I. During his fifteen-month service he met Zelda Sayre in much the same way as Gatsby meets Daisy. Zelda was the daughter of a prominent judge, a beautiful, light-hearted society girl. She told Fitzgerald that she liked him but that she was too expensive for him. Fitzgerald went back to his father's home. Six months later he surfaced again with the news that his first novel *This Side of Paradise* had been accepted and promised to sell well. In the spring of 1920, *This Side of Paradise* was published and won immediate success. Fitzgerald was made rich enough to marry Zelda. He and Zelda frequently went abroad and lived a luxurious life.

To support their extravagant life, Fitzgerald wrote at a rapid speed and made a fabulous amount of money, which went as soon as it came. In 1925, he published *The Great Gatsby*. His finest novel, *The Great Gatsby* (1925), shattered the "American dream" that so many people craved. Although it is generally regarded as his masterpiece, it didn't sell well. then he wrote one more important novel, *Tender is the Night*, which is almost a confessional story of his life with Zelda. In the 1930s Fitzgerald's reputation declined; his wealth fell; his health failed and Zelda suffered from mental illness. He plunged himself into alcoholism. Loneliness, combined with alcoholism, ruined him, and he died in 1940 of a heart attack without finishing his last novel *The Last Tycoon*, which many critics believe is the most mature of all his novels. After his death, his friend Edmund Wilson chose *The Crack-up* as the title for the posthumous edition of essays, letters, and notes.

Fitzgerald also wrote many short stories that treat themes of youth and promise along, whose fiction reveals the hollowness of the American worship of riches and American dream of a new world. He dealt with the double theme of love and money, and believed that the fascination for wealth corrupted American values and led one to existential emptiness. His writing style is simple, graceful, precise and polished. He excelled in creating literary metaphors. His works not only reflected, but also helped to influence the prevailing mood of the time.

Brief Introduction

The Great Gatsby is a novel that is set against the ending of the war. A masterpiece in American literature, *The Great Gatsby* evokes a haunting mood of a glamorous, wild time that seemingly will never come again. Besides, the loss of an ideal and the disillusionment that comes with the failure are exploited fully in the personal tragedy of a young man whose "incorruptible dream" is "smashed into pieces by the relentless reality." Gatsby is a mythical figure whose intensity of dream partakes of a state of mind that embodies America itself; Gatsby is the last of the romantic heroes, whose energy and sense of commitment take him in search of his personal grail; Gatsby's failure magnifies to a great extent the end of the American Dream. However, the affirmation of hope and expectation is self-asserted in Fitzgerald's artistic manipulation of the central symbol in the novel, the green light.

Selected Reading

The Great Gatsby

Chapter 9

After two years I[①] remember the rest of that day, and that night and the next day, only as an endless drill of police and photographers and newspaper men in and out of Gatsby's front door. A rope stretched across the main gate and a policeman by it kept out the curious, but little boys soon discovered that they could enter through my yard and there were always a few of them clustered open-mouthed about the pool.

Someone with a positive manner, perhaps a detective, used the expression "mad man" as he bent over Wilson's[②] body that afternoon, and the adventitious authority of his voice set the key for the newspaper reports next morning.

Most of those reports were a nightmare—grotesque, circumstantial, eager and untrue. When Michaelis's[③] testimony at the inquest brought to light Wilson's suspicions of his wife I thought the whole tale would shortly be served up in racy pasquinade—but Catherine[④], who might have said anything, didn't say a word. She showed a surprising amount of character about it too—looked at the coroner with determined eyes under that corrected brow of hers and swore that her sister had never seen Gatsby, that her sister was completely happy with her husband, that her sister had been into no mischief whatever. She convinced herself of it and cried into her handkerchief as if the very suggestion was more than she could endure. So Wilson was reduced to a man "deranged by grief" in order that the case might remain in its simplest form. And it rested there.

But all this part of it seemed remote and unessential. I found myself on

---

① I: 故事叙述人尼克(Nick Carraway)

② Wilson: (George B. Wilson) 威尔逊是汤姆情妇的丈夫。黛西驾车时将他妻子撞死。他误认为是盖茨比将他妻子撞死,在枪杀盖茨比后自杀

③ Michaelis: 咖啡店店主,汽车肇事时他在现场,但连汽车的颜色都没看清(第七章)

④ Catherine: 车祸受害者(Myrtle)的妹妹(第二章)

Gatsby's side, and alone. From the moment I telephoned news of the catastrophe to West Egg village①, every surmise about him, and every practical question, was referred to me. At first I was surprised and confused; then, as he lay in his house and didn't move or breathe or speak hour upon hour it grew upon me that I was responsible, because no one else was interested—interested, I mean, with that intense personal interest to which every one has some vague right at the end.

I called up Daisy② half an hour after we found him, called her instinctively and without hesitation. But she and Tom③ had gone away early that afternoon, and taken baggage with them.

"Left no address?"

"No."

"Say when they'd be back?"

"No."

"Any idea where they are How I could reach them?"

"I don't know. Can't say."

I wanted to get somebody for him. I wanted to go into the room where he lay and reassure him: "I'll get somebody for you, Gatsby. Don't worry. Just trust me and I'll get somebody for you—"

Meyer Wolfshiem's④ name wasn't in the phone book. The butler gave me his office address on Broadway and I called Information, but by the time I had the number it was long after five and no one answered the phone.

"Will you ring again?"

"I've rung them three times."

"It's very important."

"Sorry. I'm afraid no one's there."

I went back to the drawing room and thought for an instant that they were chance visitors, all these official people who suddenly filled it. But as they drew back the sheet and looked at Gatsby with unmoved eyes, his protest continued in my brain.

---

① West Egg Village：西卵镇。主人公盖茨比(Jay Gatzby)和故事叙述者尼克居住的地方
② Daisy：(Daisy Buchanan) 黛西,曾经是盖茨比的情人,后嫁给汤姆
③ Tom：(Tom Buchanan) 汤姆
④ Meyer Wolfsheim：非法操纵比赛的赌徒,盖茨比做非法生意的伙伴

"Look here, old sport, you've got to get somebody for me. You've got to try hard. I can't go through this alone."

Some one started to ask me questions but I broke away and going upstairs looked hastily through the unlocked parts of his desk—he'd never told me definitely that his parents were dead. But there was nothing—only the picture of Dan Cody①, a token of forgotten violence staring down from the wall.

Next morning I sent the butler to New York with a letter to Wolfshiem which asked for information and urged him to come out on the next train. That request seemed superfluous when I wrote it. I was sure he'd start when he saw the newspapers, just as I was sure there'd be a wire from Daisy before noon—but neither a wire nor Mr. Wolfshiem arrived, no one arrived except more police and photographers and newspaper men.

When the butler brought back Wolfshiem's answer I began to have a feeling of defiance, of scornful solidarity between Gatsby and me against them all.

Dear Mr. Carraway,

This has been one of the most terrible shocks of my life to me I hardly can believe it that it is true at all. Such a mad act as that man did should make us all think. I cannot come down now as I am tied up in some very important business and cannot get mixed up in this thing now. If there is anything I can do a little later let me know in a letter by Edgar. I hardly know where I am when I hear about a thing like this and am completely knocked down and out.

Yours truly,
MEYER WOLFSHIEM

and then hasty addenda beneath:
Let me know about the funeral etc. do not know his family at all.

When the phone rang that afternoon and Long Distance said Chicago was calling I thought this would be Daisy at last. But the connection came through as a man's voice, very thin and far away.

---

① Dan Cody：曾在西部内华达州开银矿发迹,盖茨比年轻时遇到他并为他工作(第6章)

"This is Slagle① speaking...."

"Yes" The name was unfamiliar.

"Hell of a note, isn't it? Get my wire?"

"There haven't been any wires."

"Young Parke'②s in trouble," he said rapidly. "They picked him up③ when he handed the bonds over the counter. They got a circular from New York giving 'em the numbers just five minutes before. What d'you know about that, hey? You never can tell in these hick towns—"

"Hello!" I interrupted breathlessly. "Look here—this isn't Mr. Gatsby. Mr. Gatsby's dead."

There was a long silence on the other end of the wire, followed by an exclamation... then a quick squawk as the connection was broken.

I think it was on the third day that a telegram signed Henry C. Gatz arrived from a town in Minnesota. It said only that the sender was leaving immediately and to postpone the funeral until he came.

It was Gatsby's father, a solemn old man very helpless and dismayed, bundled up in a long cheap ulster against the warm September day. His eyes leaked continuously with excitement and when I took the bag and umbrella from his hands he began to pull so incessantly at his sparse grey beard that I had difficulty in getting off his coat. He was on the point of collapse so I took him into the music room and made him sit down while I sent for something to eat. But he wouldn't eat and the glass of milk spilled from his trembling hand.

"I saw it in the Chicago newspaper," he said. "It was all in the Chicago newspaper. I started right away."

"I didn't know how to reach you."

His eyes, seeing nothing, moved ceaselessly about the room.

"It was a mad man," he said. "He must have been mad."

"Wouldn't you like some coffee" I urged him.

"I don't want anything. I'm all right now, Mr.—"

"Carraway."

"Well, I'm all right now. Where have they got Jimmy?"

---

① Slagle：盖茨比做非法生意的伙伴
② Parke：盖茨比做非法生意的伙伴
③ They picked him up：他们把他逮捕了,这证实了盖茨比参与了非法生意

I took him into the drawing-room, where his son lay, and left him there.

Some little boys had come up on the steps and were looking into the hall; when I told them who had arrived they went reluctantly away.

After a little while Mr. Gatz opened the door and came out, his mouth ajar, his face flushed slightly, his eyes leaking isolated and unpunctual tears. He had reached an age where death no longer has the quality of ghastly surprise, and when he looked around him now for the first time and saw the height and splendor of the hall and the great rooms opening out from it into other rooms his grief began to be mixed with an awed pride. I helped him to a bedroom upstairs; while he took off his coat and vest I told him that all arrangements had been deferred until he came.

"I didn't know what you'd want, Mr. Gatsby—"

"Gatz is my name."

"—Mr. Gatz. I thought you might want to take the body west."

He shook his head.

"Jimmy always liked it better down East. He rose up to his position in the East. Were you a friend of my boy's, Mr.—?"

"We were close friends."

"He had a big future before him, you know. He was only a young man but he had a lot of brain power here."

He touched his head impressively and I nodded.

"If he'd of lived he'd of been a great man[①]. A man like James J. Hill[②]. He'd of helped build up the country."

"That's true," I said, uncomfortably.

He fumbled at the embroidered coverlet, trying to take it from the bed, and lay down stiffly—was instantly asleep.

That night an obviously frightened person called up and demanded to know who I was before he would give his name.

"This is Mr. Carraway," I said.

"Oh—" He sounded relieved. "This is Klipspringer[③]."

I was relieved too for that seemed to promise another friend at Gatsby's

---

① If he'd of lived, he'd of been a great man.: If he'd lived, he'd have been a great man
② James J. Hill: 詹姆斯·J. 希尔(1838—1916),美国金融家和铁路建筑家
③ Klipspringer: 一个经常寄宿在盖茨比家的人(第四章)

grave. I didn't want it to be in the papers and draw a sightseeing crowd so I'd been calling up a few people myself.

They were hard to find.

"The funeral's tomorrow," I said. "Three o'clock, here at the house. I wish you'd tell anybody who'd be interested."

"Oh, I will," he broke out hastily. "Of course I'm not likely to see anybody, but if I do."

His tone made me suspicious.

"Of course you'll be there yourself."

"Well, I'll certainly try. What I called up about is—"

"Wait a minute," I interrupted. "How about saying you'll come?"

"Well, the fact is—the truth of the matter is that I'm staying with some people up here in Greenwich① and they rather expect me to be with them tomorrow. In fact there's a sort of picnic or something.

Of course I'll do my very best to get away."

I ejaculated an unrestrained "Huh!" and he must have heard me for he went on nervously:

"What I called up about was a pair of shoes I left there. I wonder if it'd be too much trouble to have the butler send them on. You see they're tennis shoes and I'm sort of helpless without them. My address is care of B. F.—"

I didn't hear the rest of the name because I hung up the receiver.

After that I felt a certain shame for Gatsby—one gentleman to whom I telephoned implied that he had got what he deserved. However, that was my fault, for he was one of those who used to sneer most bitterly at Gatsby on the courage of Gatsby's liquor and I should have known better than to call him.

The morning of the funeral I went up to New York to see Meyer Wolfshiem; I couldn't seem to reach him any other way. The door that I pushed open on the advice of an elevator boy was marked "The Swastika Holding Company" and at first there didn't seem to be any one inside.

But when I'd shouted "Hello" several times in vain an argument broke out behind a partition and presently a lovely Jewess appeared at an interior door and scrutinized me with black hostile eyes.

---

① Greenwich：格林尼治，美国康涅狄格州西南部城镇

※ Chapter 6 American Modernism Literature ※

"Nobody's in," she said. "Mr. Wolfshiem's gone to Chicago."

The first part of this was obviously untrue for someone had begun to whistle "The Rosary," tunelessly, inside.

"Please say that Mr. Carraway wants to see him."

"I can't get him back from Chicago, can I?"

At this moment a voice, unmistakably Wolfshiem's called "Stella!" from the other side of the door.

"Leave your name on the desk," she said quickly. "I'll give it to him when he gets back."

"But I know he's there."

She took a step toward me and began to slide her hands indignantly up and down her hips.

"You young men think you can force your way in here any time," she scolded. "We're getting sickantired① of it. When I say he's in Chicago, he's in ChiCAgo."

I mentioned Gatsby.

"Oh—h!" She looked at me over again. "Will you just—what was your name?"

She vanished. In a moment Meyer Wolfshiem stood solemnly in the doorway, holding out both hands. He drew me into his office, remarking in a reverent voice that it was a sad time for all of us, and offered me a cigar.

"My memory goes back to when I first met him," he said. "A young major just out of the army and covered over with medals he got in the war. He was so hard up he had to keep on wearing his uniform because he couldn't buy some regular clothes. First time I saw him was when he come② into Winebrenner's poolroom at Forty-third Street and asked for a job. He hadn't eat anything③ for a couple of days. 'Come on have some lunch with me,' I sid④. He ate more than four dollars' worth of food in half an hour."

"Did you start him in business?" I inquired.

"Start him! I made him."

---

① sickantired: sick and tired
② he come: he came
③ He hadn't eat anything: he hadn't eaten anything
④ I sid: I said

"Oh."

"I raised him up out of nothing, right out of the gutter. I saw right away he was a fine appearing, gentlemanly young man, and when he told me he was an Oggsford① I knew I could use him good. I got him to join up in the American Legion② and he used to stand high there. Right off he did some work for a client of mine up to Albany. We were so thick like that in everything—" He held up two bulbous fingers—"always together."

I wondered if this partnership had included the World's Series transaction③ in 1919.

"Now he's dead," I said after a moment. "You were his closest friend, so I know you'll want to come to his funeral this afternoon."

"I'd like to come."

"Well, come then."

The hair in his nostrils quivered slightly and as he shook his head his eyes filled with tears.

"I can't do it—I can't get mixed up in it," he said.

"There's nothing to get mixed up in. It's all over now."

"When a man gets killed I never like to get mixed up in it in any way. I keep out. When I was a young man it was different—if a friend of mine died, no matter how, I stuck with them to the end. You may think that's sentimental but I mean it—to the bitter end."

I saw that for some reason of his own he was determined not to come, so I stood up.

"Are you a college man?" he inquired suddenly.

For a moment I thought he was going to suggest a "gonnegtion④" but he only nodded and shook my hand.

"Let us learn to show our friendship for a man when he is alive and not after he is dead," he suggested. "After that my own rule is to let everything alone."

When I left his office the sky had turned dark and I got back to West Egg in

---

① Oggsford: Oxford
② American Legion: 美国军团(美国退伍军人组织)
③ World's Series transaction: World Series: 世界系列赛(美国棒球系列比赛); transaction: 这里指操纵比赛的非法交易
④ gonnegtion: connection

a drizzle. After changing my clothes I went next door and found Mr. Gatz walking up and down excitedly in the hall. His pride in his son and in his son's possessions was continually increasing and now he had something to show me.

"Jimmy sent me this picture." He took out his wallet with trembling fingers. "Look there."

It was a photograph of the house, cracked in the corners and dirty with many hands. He pointed out every detail to me eagerly. "Look there!" and then sought admiration from my eyes. He had shown it so often that I think it was more real to him now than the house itself.

"Jimmy sent it to me. I think it's a very pretty picture. It shows up well."

"Very well. Had you seen him lately?"

"He come out to see me two years ago and bought me the house I live in now. Of course we was broke up when he run off① from home but I see now there was a reason for it. He knew he had a big future in front of him. And ever since he made a success he was very generous with me."

He seemed reluctant to put away the picture, held it for another minute, lingeringly, before my eyes. Then he returned the wallet and pulled from his pocket a ragged old copy of a book called "Hopalong Cassidy."

"Look here, this is a book he had when he was a boy. It just shows you."

He opened it at the back cover and turned it around for me to see.

On the last fly—leaf was printed the word SCHEDULE, and the date September 12th, 1906. And underneath:

Rise from bed	6.00	A.M.
Dumbbell exercise and wall-scaling	6.15–6.30	...
Study electricity, etc	7.15–8.15	...
Work	8.30–4.30	P.M.
Baseball and sports	4.30–5.00	...
Practice elocution, poise and how to attain it	5.00–6.00	...
Study needed inventions	7.00–9.00	...

GENERAL RESOLVES

---

① we was broke up when he run off: we broke up when he ran off

No wasting time at Shafters or a name, indecipherable
No more smokeing or chewing
Bath every other day
Read one improving book or magazine per week
Save $5.00 crossed out $3.00 per week
Be better to parents

"I come across this book① by accident," said the old man. "It just shows you, don't it?"②

"It just shows you."

"Jimmy was bound to get ahead. He always had some resolves like this or something. Do you notice what he's got about improving his mind He was always great for that. He told me I et like a hog③ once and I beat him for it."

He was reluctant to close the book, reading each item aloud and then looking eagerly at me. I think he rather expected me to copy down the list for my own use.

A little before three the Lutheran minister arrived from Flushing and I began to look involuntarily out the windows for other cars. So did Gatsby's father. And as the time passed and the servants came in and stood waiting in the hall, his eyes began to blink anxiously and he spoke of the rain in a worried uncertain way. The minister glanced several times at his watch so I took him aside and asked him to wait for half an hour. But it wasn't any use. Nobody came.

About five o'clock our procession of three cars reached the cemetery and stopped in a thick drizzle beside the gate—first motor hearse, horribly black and wet, then Mr. Gatz and the minister and I in the limousine, and, a little later, four or five servants and the postman from West Egg in Gatsby's station wagon, all wet to the skin. As we started through the gate into the cemetery I heard a car stop and then the sound of someone splashing after us over the soggy ground. I looked around. It was the man with owl-eyed glasses④ whom I had

---

① I come across this book: I came across this book
② It just shows you, don't it: It just shows you, doesn't it?
③ I et like a hog: I ate like a hog
④ the man with owl-eye glasses: 盖茨比宴会上的客人(第三章)。小说中有一些非常独特的眼睛形象,如眼镜广告牌上巨大的埃克尔伯格医生(Dr. Eckleburg)的眼睛透过黄色眼镜注视灰暗的世界。这些眼睛形象使读者联想到盖茨比对世界的错误看法,他完全被虚幻的理想蒙住了视线,看不清真实的世界,而与此形成对照的是黛西夫妇,他们的眼睛却只能看见物质的世界。他们各自的视线都是扭曲的

found marvelling over Gatsby's books in the library one night three months before.

I'd never seen him since then. I don't know how he knew about the funeral or even his name. The rain poured down his thick glasses and he took them off and wiped them to see the protecting canvas unrolled from Gatsby's grave.

I tried to think about Gatsby then for a moment but he was already too far away and I could only remember, without resentment, that Daisy hadn't sent a message or a flower. Dimly I heard someone murmur "Blessed are the dead that the rain falls on," and then the owl-eyed man said "Amen to that," in a brave voice.

We straggled down quickly through the rain to the cars. Owl-Eyes spoke to me by the gate.

"I couldn't get to the house," he remarked.

"Neither could anybody else."

"Go on!" He started. "Why, my God! they used to go there by the hundreds."

He took off his glasses and wiped them again outside and in.

"The poor son-of-a-bitch," he said.

One of my most vivid memories is of coming back west from prep school and later from college at Christmas time. Those who went farther than Chicago would gather in the old dim Union Station at six o'clock of a December evening with a few Chicago friends already caught up into their own holiday gayeties to bid them a hasty goodbye. I remember the fur coats of the girls returning from Miss This or That's and the chatter of frozen breath and the hands waving overhead as we caught sight of old acquaintances and the matchings of invitations:

"Are you going to the Ordways' the Herseys' the Schultzes'" and the long green tickets clasped tight in our gloved hands.

And last the murky yellow cars of the Chicago, Milwaukee and St. Paul Railroad looking cheerful as Christmas itself on the tracks beside the gate.

When we pulled out into the winter night and the real snow, our snow, began to stretch out beside us and twinkle against the windows, and the dim lights of small Wisconsin stations moved by, a sharp wild brace came suddenly into the air. We drew in deep breaths of it as we walked back from dinner through the cold vestibules, unutterably aware of our identity with this country for one strange hour before we melted indistinguishably into it again.

That's my middle west—not the wheat or the prairies or the lost Swede towns but the thrilling, returning trains of my youth and the street lamps and sleigh bells in the frosty dark and the shadows of holly wreaths thrown by lighted windows on the snow. I am part of that, a little solemn with the feel of those long winters, a little complacent from growing up in the Carraway house in a city where dwellings are still called through decades by a family's name. I see now that this has been a story of the West, after all—Tom and Gatsby, Daisy and Jordan① and I, were all Westerners, and perhaps we possessed some deficiency in common which made us subtly unadaptable to Eastern life.

Even when the East excited me most, even when I was most keenly aware of its superiority to the bored, sprawling, swollen towns beyond the Ohio②, with their interminable inquisitions which spared only the children and the very old—even then it had always for me a quality of distortion. West Egg especially still figures in my more fantastic dreams. I see it as a night scene by El Greco③: a hundred houses, at once conventional and grotesque, crouching under a sullen, overhanging sky and a lustreless moon. In the foreground four solemn men in dress suits are walking along the sidewalk with a stretcher on which lies a drunken woman in a white evening dress. Her hand, which dangles over the side, sparkles cold with jewels. Gravely the men turn in at a house—the wrong house. But no one knows the woman's name, and no one cares.

After Gatsby's death the East was haunted for me like that, distorted beyond my eyes' power of correction. So when the blue smoke of brittle leaves was in the air and the wind blew the wet laundry stiff on the line I decided to come back home.

There was one thing to be done before I left, an awkward, unpleasant thing that perhaps had better have been let alone. But I wanted to leave things in order and not just trust that obliging and indifferent sea to sweep my refuse away. I saw Jordan Baker and talked over and around what had happened to us together and what had happened afterward to me, and she lay perfectly still listening in a big chair.

She was dressed to play golf and I remember thinking she looked like a good illustration, her chin raised a little, jauntily, her hair the color of an autumn leaf, her face the same brown tint as the fingerless glove on her knee. When I had finished she told me without comment that she was engaged to another man. I doubted that though there were several she could have married at a nod

---

① Jordan: Jordan Baker 乔丹, 高尔夫球运动员, 曾与尼克有恋爱关系(第一章)

② the Ohio: the Ohio River, 美国中东部主要河流

③ a night scene by El Greco: El Greco (1541-1614), 西班牙画家。这里尼克以画中变形了的景物暗喻东部地区的扭曲生活方式

of her head but I pretended to be surprised. For just a minute I wondered if I wasn't making a mistake, then I thought it all over again quickly and got up to say goodbye.

"Nevertheless you did throw me over," said Jordan suddenly. "You threw me over on the telephone. I don't give a damn about you now but it was a new experience for me and I felt a little dizzy for a while."

We shook hands.

"Oh, and do you remember—" she added, "—a conversation we had once about driving a car?"

"Why—not exactly."

"You said a bad driver was only safe until she met another bad driver? Well, I met another bad driver, didn't I I mean it was careless of me to make such a wrong guess. I thought you were rather an honest, straightforward person. I thought it was your secret pride."

"I'm thirty," I said. "I'm five years too old to lie to myself and call it honor."

She didn't answer. Angry, and half in love with her, and tremendously sorry, I turned away.

One afternoon late in October I saw Tom Buchanan. He was walking ahead of me along Fifth Avenue in his alert, aggressive way, his hands out a little from his body as if to fight off interference, his head moving sharply here and there, adapting itself to his restless eyes. Just as I slowed up to avoid overtaking him he stopped and began frowning into the windows of a jewelry store. Suddenly he saw me and walked back holding out his hand.

"What's the matter, Nick? Do you object to shaking hands with me?"

"Yes. You know what I think of you."

"You're crazy, Nick," he said quickly. "Crazy as hell. I don't know what's the matter with you."

"Tom," I inquired, "what did you say to Wilson that afternoon?"

He stared at me without a word and I knew I had guessed right about those missing hours. I started to turn away but he took a step after me and grabbed my arm.

"I told him the truth," he said. "He came to the door while we were getting ready to leave and when I sent down word that we weren't in he tried to force his way upstairs. He was crazy enough to kill me if I hadn't told him who owned the car. His hand was on a revolver in his pocket every minute he was in the house—" He broke off defiantly.

"What if I did tell him That fellow had it coming to him. He threw dust into your eyes just like he did in Daisy's but he was a tough one. He ran over Myrtle like you'd run over a dog and never even stopped his car."

There was nothing I could say, except the one unutterable fact that it wasn't true.

"And if you think I didn't have my share of suffering—look here, when I went to give up that flat and saw that damn box of dog biscuits sitting there on the sideboard I sat down and cried like a baby. By God it was awful—"

I couldn't forgive him or like him but I saw that what he had done was, to him, entirely justified. It was all very careless and confused.

They were careless people, Tom and Daisy—they smashed up things and creatures and then retreated back into their money or their vast carelessness or whatever it was that kept them together, and let other people clean up the mess they had made...

I shook hands with him; it seemed silly not to, for I felt suddenly as though I were talking to a child. Then he went into the jewelry store to buy a pearl necklace—or perhaps only a pair of cuff buttons—rid of my provincial squeamishness forever.

Gatsby's house was still empty when I left—the grass on his lawn had grown as long as mine. One of the taxi drivers in the village never took a fare past the entrance gate without stopping for a minute and pointing inside; perhaps it was he who drove Daisy and Gatsby over to East Egg① the night of the accident and perhaps he had made a story about it all his own. I didn't want to hear it and I avoided him when I got off the train.

I spent my Saturday nights in New York because those gleaming, dazzling parties of his were with me so vividly that I could still hear the music and the laughter faint and incessant from his garden and the cars going up and down his drive. One night I did hear a material car② there and saw its lights stop at his front steps. But I didn't investigate. Probably it was some final guest who had been away at the ends of the earth and didn't know that the party was over.

On the last night, with my trunk packed and my car sold to the grocer, I went over and looked at that huge incoherent failure of a house once more. On the white steps an obscene word, scrawled by some boy with a piece of brick, stood out clearly in the moonlight and I erased it, drawing my shoe raspingly along the stone. Then I wandered down to the beach and sprawled out on the sand.

Most of the big shore places were closed now and there were hardly any

---

① East Egg: 东卵镇，黛西夫妇居住的富人区
② a material car: 真实的而不是幻觉中的汽车

lights except the shadowy, moving glow of a ferryboat across the Sound①.

And as the moon rose higher the inessential houses began to melt away until gradually I became aware of the old island② here that flowered once for Dutch sailors' eyes—a fresh, green breast of the new world.

Its vanished trees, the trees that had made way for Gatsby's house, had once pandered in whispers to the last and greatest of all human dreams; for a transitory enchanted moment man must have held his breath in the presence of this continent, compelled into an aesthetic contemplation he neither understood nor desired, face to face for the last time in history with something commensurate to his capacity for wonder.

And as I sat there brooding on the old, unknown world, I thought of Gatsby's wonder when he first picked out the green light③ at the end of Daisy's dock④. He had come a long way to this blue lawn and his dream must have seemed so close that he could hardly fail to grasp it. He did not know that it was already behind him, somewhere back in that vast obscurity beyond the city, where the dark fields of the republic rolled on under the night.

Gatsby believed in the green light, the orgastic future that year by year recedes before us. It eluded us then, but that's no matter—tomorrow we will run faster, stretch out our arms farther... And one fine morning—

So we beat on, boats against the current, borne back ceaselessly into the past.

Questions for Discussion

1. Do you think Gatsby deserves to be called "the great"? Why?
2. How does Gatsby as well as F. Scott Fitzgerald himself, depict the disillusionment with "the American Dreamland illustrate the paradox of it"?

---

① the Sound: Long Island Sound, 长岛海峡
② the old island: Long Island
③ green light: 绿色在英语里象征青春和生命。西方文化传统中光明与黑暗往往有不同的象征意义：如，善与恶、愚昧与知识等。书中多次提到盖茨比对绿色光明的向往（第一章），他以为黛西就是他向往的光明
④ Daisy's dock: 这里既指黛西住所外码头上的指示灯（其实应该是红色的），又指盖茨比心中理想的停泊港湾

Unit 8　William Faulkner（1897 – 1962）

Appreciation

　　Through the fence, between the curling flower spaces, I could see them hitting. They were coming toward where the flag was and I went along the fence. Luster was hunting in the grass by the flower tree. They took the flag out, and they were hitting. Then they put the flag back and they went to the table, and he hit and the other hit. Then they went on, and I went along the fence. Luster came away from the flower tree and we went along the fence and they stopped and we stopped and I looked through the fence while Luster was hunting in the grass. 透过栅栏,穿过攀绕的花枝的空当,我看见他们在打球。他们朝插着小旗的地方走过来,我顺着栅栏朝前走。勒斯特在那棵开花的树旁草地里找东西。他们把小旗拔出来,打球了。接着他们又把小旗插回去,来到高地上,这人打了一下,另外那人也打了一下。他们接着朝前走,我也顺着栅栏朝前走。勒斯特离开了那棵开花的树,我们沿着栅栏一起走,这时候他们站住了,我们也站住了。我透过栅栏张望,勒斯特在草丛里找东西。

　　William Cuthbert Faulkner is recognized as one of America's greatest novelists, short story writers of the 20th century, and Nobel Prize laureate from Oxford, Mississippi. Faulkner worked in a variety of media; he wrote novels, short stories, a play, poems, essays and screenplays during his career. He is primarily known and acclaimed for his novels and short stories, many of which are set in the fictional Yoknapatawpha County, a setting Faulkner created based on Lafayette County, where he spent most of his life.

　　William Faulkner was born in an old and distinguished family in New Albany, Mississippi. He showed signs of artistic talent from a young age, but became bored with his classes and never finished high school. At the outbreak of WW I, Faulkner enlisted in the Canadian Air Force. However, he never saw battle action. Faulkner's first book, *The Marble Faun*(1924), a collection of pastoral poems. From 1929, Faulkner began his series of baroque, brooding novels set in the mythical Yoknapatawpha County (based on Lafayette County, Mississippi), peopling it with his own ancestors, native Americans, Blacks, shadowy backwoods hermits, and loutish poor Whites. Faulkner died of a heart attack in his home, Rowan Oak, in Oxford, Mississippi, on July 6, 1962.

　　Faulkner's reputation as one of the greatest novelists of the 20th century is largely due to his highly experimental style. Faulkner was a pioneer in literary modernism, dramatically diverging from the forms and structures traditionally used in novels before his time. Faulkner often employs stream of consciousness narrative, dumps any notion of chronological order, uses multiple narrators, shifts between the present and past tense, and tends toward impossibly long and complex sentences. Not surprisingly, these stylistic innovations make some of Faulkner's novels incredibly challenging to the reader. However, these bold innovations paved the way for countless future writers to continue to experiment with the possibilities of the English language. Two of his works, *A Fable* (1954) and his last novel *The Reivers* (1962), won the Pulitzer Prize for Fiction. In 1998, the Modern Library ranked his 1929 novel *The Sound and the Fury* sixth on its list of the 100 best English-language novels of the 20th century; also on the list were *As I Lay Dying* and *Light in August*. *Absalom, Absalom!* is often included on similar lists.

Brief Introduction

The Sound and the Fury was Faulkner's fourth novel, published in 1929. It employs a number of narrative styles, including the technique known as stream of consciousness. The novel is set in the fictional Yoknapatawpha County, which centers on the Compson family, former Southern aristocrats who are struggling to deal with the dissolution of their family and its reputation. Over the course of the thirty years or so related in the novel, the family falls into financial ruin, loses its religious faith and the respect of the town of Jefferson, and many of them die tragically. The novel is separated into four distinct sections. The first, April 7, 1928, is written from the perspective of Benjamin "Benjy" Compson, a 33-year-old man with severe mental handicaps. Benjy's section is characterized by a highly disjointed narrative style with frequent chronological leaps. The second section, June 2, 1910, focuses on Quentin Compson, Benjy's older brother, and the events leading up to his suicide. In the third section, April 6, 1928, Faulkner writes from the point of view of Jason, Quentin's cynical younger brother. In the fourth and final section, set a day after the first, on April 8, 1928, Faulkner introduces a third person omniscient point of view. The last section primarily focuses on Dilsey, one of the Compson's black servants. Jason is also a focus in the section, but Faulkner presents glimpses of the thoughts and deeds of everyone in the family.

No doubt that *The Sound and the Fury* is a representative masterpiece of stream of consciousness. The novel's appreciation has in large part been due to the technique of its construction: Faulkner's ability to recreate the thought patterns of the human mind, even the disabled one (the stream of consciousness of two brothers, especially the bold exploration of the inner world of an idiot). In this sense, it was an essential development in the stream-of-consciousness narrative technique, fulfilling the need of describing particular characters—the characters in the first three parts are unhealthy mentally: Benjy is an idiot; Quentin has decided to commit suicide on June 2. It is no wonder that he is disorder mentally, his mental state is extremely delirious; Jason is also abnormal, and he is a monomania.

Selected Reading

The Sound and the Fury

(Selected from the first section: April 7, 1928)

Through the fence, between the curling flower spaces, I[①] could see them hitting. They were coming toward where the flag was and I went along the fence. Luster was hunting in the grass by the flower tree. They took the flag out, and they were hitting. Then they put the flag back and they went to the table[②], and he hit and the other hit. Then they went on, and I went along the fence. Luster[③] came away from the flower tree and we went along the fence and they stopped and we stopped and I looked through the fence while Luster was hunting in the grass.

"Here, caddie[④]." He hit. They went away across the pasture. I held to the fence and watched them going away.

"Listen at you, now." Luster said. "Ain't you something, thirty-three years old, going on that way. After I done went all the way to town to buy you that cake. Hush up that moaning. Ain't you going to help me find that quarter so I can go to the show tonight."

They were hitting little, across the pasture. I went back along the fence to where the flag was. It flapped on the bright grass and the trees.

"Come on." Luster said. "We done looked there. They ain't no more coming right now. Ley's[⑤] go down to the branch and find that quarter before them niggers finds it."

It was red, flapping on the pasture. Then there was a bird slanting and tilting on it. Luster threw. The flag flapped on the bright grass and the trees. I held to the fence.

---

① I: 班吉,班吉明·康普生(Benjy, Benjaming Compson)。一个白痴,从小受姐姐凯蒂的保护。凯蒂出走之后,他也失去了依靠

② table: 指高尔夫球的发球处

③ Luster: 勒斯特,黑佣人迪尔西(Dilsey)的小外孙

④ caddie: 该词本应译为"受佣替人背高尔夫球棒的人,球童"。但此词在文中与班吉姐姐的名字凯蒂(Caddy)同音,所以班吉每次听见别人叫"球童",便会想起心爱的姐姐,哼叫起来

⑤ Ley's: Let's

"Shut up that moaning." Luster said. "I can't make them come if they ain't coming, can I. If you don't hush up, mammy① ain't going to have no birthday for you. If you don't hush, you know what I going to do. I going to eat that cake all up. Eat them candles, too. Eat all them thirty three candles. Come on, let's go down to the branch. I got to find my quarter. Maybe we can find one of they balls. Here. Here they is. Way over yonder. See." He came to the fence and pointed his arm. "See them. They ain't coming back here no more. Come on."

We went along the fence and came to the garden fence, where our shadows were. My shadow was higher than Luster's on the fence. We came to the broken place and went through it.

"Wait a minute." Luster said. "You snagged on that nail again②. Can't you never crawl through here without snagging on that nail."

Caddy uncaught me and we crawled through. Uncle Maury said to not let anybody see us, so we better stoop over, Caddy said. Stoop over, Benjy. Like this, see. We stooped over and crossed the garden, where the flowers rasped and rattled against us. The ground was hard. We climbed the fence, where the pigs were grunting and snuffing. I expect they're sorry because one of them got killed today, Caddy said. The ground was hard, churned and knotted. Keep your hands in your pockets, Caddy said. Or they'll get froze. You don't want your hands froze on Christmas, do you.

"It's too cold out there." Versh said.③"You don't want to go outdoors."
"What is it now." Mother said.
"He want to go out doors." Versh said.
"Let him go." Uncle Maury said.
"It's too cold." Mother said. "He'd better stay in. Benjamin. Stop that,

---

① mammy：康普生家的黑女佣迪尔西，勒斯特(Luster)的外祖母

② You snagged on that nail again.：你又挂在钉子上了。班吉的衣服被钩住，使他脑子里浮现出另一次他的衣服在栅栏缺口处被钩住的情景。那是在 1900 年圣诞节前两天(12 月 23 日)，当时，凯蒂带着他穿过栅栏去完成毛莱舅舅(Uncle Maury)交给他们的一个任务——送情书去给隔壁的帕特生太太(Mrs Patterson)

③ "It's too cold out there." Versh said.：此段内容发生在同一天的较早时间里，在康普生家。威尔许(Versh)是康普生家的黑小厮，迪尔西的大儿子。前后有三个黑小厮服侍过班吉。1905 年前是威尔许，1905 年以后是 T. P. (迪尔西的小儿子)，"当前"(1928 年)则是勒斯特。福克纳用不同的黑小厮来标明不同的时序

now."

"It wont hurt him." Uncle Maury said.

"You, Benjamin." Mother said. "If you don't be good, you'll have to go to the kitchen."

"Mammy say keep him out the kitchen today." Versh said. "She say she got all that cooking to get done."

"Let him go, Caroline①." Uncle Maury said. "You'll worry yourself sick over him."

"I know it." Mother said. "It's a judgment on me. I sometimes wonder."

"I know, I know." Uncle Maury said. "You must keep your strength up. I'll make you a toddy."

"It just upsets me that much more." Mother said. "Don't you know it does."

"You'll feel better." Uncle Maury said. "Wrap him up good, boy, and take him out for a while."

Questions for Discussion

1. Why Faulkner used an idiot's narration to open the novel?
2. How does the selected reading reflect Faulkner's stream of consciousness?

Unit 9　Ernest Hemingway (1899 – 1961)

Appreciation

People are not born to be defeated, the man can be destroyed but not defeated.
人不是生来就被打败的,人可以毁灭,但不可以被打败。

Ernest Miller Hemingway was an American author and journalist. His economical and understated style had a strong influence on 20th century fiction, while his life of adventure and his public image influenced later generations. Hemingway produced most of his work between the mid-1920s and the mid-1950s, and won the Nobel Prize in Literature in 1954 for his powerful, style-forming mastery of the art of narration. He published 7 novels, 6 short story collections, and two non-fiction works. 3 novels, 4

---

① Caroline：卡罗琳(Mrs. Caroline Compson)

collections of short stories, and 3 non-fiction works were published posthumously. Many of these are considered classics of American literature.

Hemingway was born into a well-to-do family in Illinois and was raised in Oak Park, Illinois. After high school he reported for a few months for *The Kansas City Star*, before leaving for the Italian front to enlist with the WW I ambulance drivers. In 1918, he was seriously wounded and returned home. His wartime experiences formed the basis for his novel *A Farewell to Arms*. In 1922, he married and moved to Paris, where he worked as a foreign correspondent, and fell under the influence of the modernist writers and artists of the 1920s "Lost Generation" expatriate community as Gertrude Stein, T. S. Eliot, James Joyce, Sherwood Anderson, and Ezra Pound. *The Sun Also Rises*, Hemingway's first novel, was published in 1926. After his 1927 divorce, Hemingway married and divorced again after he returned from the Spanish Civil War where he had been a journalist, and after which he wrote *For Whom the Bell Tolls*. His third marriage in 1940 ended when he met his fourth wife in London during WW II. Shortly after the publication of his masterpiece *The Old Man and the Sea* in 1952, Hemingway went on safari to Africa, where he was almost killed in two successive plane crashes that left him in pain or ill health for much of the rest of his life. Hemingway shot himself on July 2, 1961, for the sake of extreme depression and anxiety.

He is known for his writing styles, Hemingway heroes and Hemingway themes. The term was popularized by Ernest Hemingway who used it as one of two contrasting epigraphs for his novel, *The Sun Also Rises*. The typical Hemingway hero enjoys the pleasure of life in the face of ruin and death, who acts with grace under pressure, and maintains courage and dignity in the face of despair, disaster and defeat.

Brief Introduction

Ernest Hemingway's story is about an incident that happens between a father and his son. The small boy's misunderstanding of the difference in measuring temperature on a Fahrenheit and a Celsius Scale causes him to believe that he is drying of a high fever. However, the father doesn't realize it until very late that day...

Selected Reading

A Day's Wait

He came into the room to shut the windows while we were still in bed and I saw he looked ill. He was shivering, his face was white, and he walked slowly as though it ached to move.

"What's the matter, Schatz?"

"I've got a headache."

"You better go back to bed."

"No, I'm all right."

"You go to bed. I'll see you when I'm dressed."

But when I came downstairs he was dressed, sitting by the fire, looking a very sick and miserable boy of nine years. When I put my hand on his forehead I knew he had a fever.

"You go up to bed," I said, "you're sick."

"I'm all right," he said.

When the doctor came he took the boy's temperature.

"What is it" I asked him.

"One hundred and two."

Downstairs, the doctor left three different medicines in different colored capsules① with instructions for giving them. One was to bring down the fever, another a purgative②, the third to overcome an acid condition. The germs of influenza can only exist in an acid condition, he explained. He seemed to know all about influenza and said there was nothing to worry about if the fever did not go above one hundred and four degrees. This was a light epidemic③ of flu and there was no danger if you avoided pneumonia④.

Back in the room I wrote the boy's temperature down and made a note of the time to give the various capsules.

"Do you want me to read to you?"

"All right. If you want to," said the boy. His face was very white and there were dark areas under his eyes. He lay still in bed and seemed very detached⑤ from what was going on.

I read aloud from Howard Pyle's Book of *Pirates*⑥; but I could see he was not following what I was reading.

"How do you feel, Schatz?" I asked him.

"Just the same, so far," he said.

I sat at the foot of the bed and read to myself while I waited for it to be time to give another capsule. It would have been natural for him to go to sleep, but

---

① capsule：(医)胶囊

② purgative：泻药

③ epidemic：流行病

④ pneumonia：肺炎

⑤ detached：分离的,超然的

⑥ pirate：海盗

when I looked up he was looking at the foot of the bed, looking very strangely.

"Why don't you try to go to sleep? I'll wake you up for the medicine."

"I'd rather stay awake."

After a while he said to me, "You don't have to stay here with me, Papa, if it bothers you."

"It doesn't bother me."

"No, I mean you don't have to stay if it's going to bother you."

I thought perhaps he was a little light-headed and after giving him the prescribed① capsule at eleven o'clock I went out for a while.

It was a bright, cold day, the ground covered with a sleet② that had frozen so that it seemed as if all the bare trees, the bushes③, the cut brush and all the grass and the bare ground had been varnished④ with ice. I took the young Irish⑤ setter⑥ for a little walk up the road and along a frozen creek⑦ but it was difficult to stand or walk on the glassy⑧ surface and the red dog slipped and slithered⑨ and fell twice, hard, once dropping my gun and having it slide over the ice.

We flushed⑩ a covey⑪ of quail⑫ under a high clay bank with overhanging brush and killed two as they went out of sight over the top of the bank. Some of the covey lit the trees, but most of them scattered into brush piles and it was necessary to jump on the ice-coated mounds⑬ of brush several times before they would flush. Coming out while you were poised⑭ unsteadily on the icy, springy⑮ brush they made difficult shooting and killed two, missed five, and started back pleased to have found a covey close to the house and happy there were so many

---

① prescribe：开(药)
② sleet：冻雨, 雨夹雪
③ bushes：矮灌木丛；断落的树枝
④ varnished：涂上清漆, 使……发光的
⑤ Irish：爱尔兰的
⑥ setter：塞特狗
⑦ creek：小溪, 小河
⑧ glassy：不稳地滑动
⑨ slither：不稳地滑动, 使滑动
⑩ flush：使(鸟等)惊飞
⑪ covey：一小群(鸟), 鹌鹑；悬于……之上, 突出于……之上, 停落
⑫ quail：鹌鹑
⑬ mounds：土墩
⑭ poise：使平衡, 使保持均衡
⑮ springy：有弹性的

left to find on another day.

At the house they said the boy had refused to let anyone come into the room.

"You can't come in," he said. "You mustn't get what I have."

I went up to him and found him in exactly the position I had left him, white-faced, but with the tops of his cheeks flushed① by the fever, staring still, as he had stared, at the foot of the bed.

I took his temperature.

"What is it?"

"Something like a hundred," I said. It was one hundred and two and four tenth.

"It was a hundred and two," he said.

"Who said so?"

"The doctor."

"Your temperature is all right," I said. "It's nothing to worry about."

"I don't worry," he said, "but I can't keep from thinking."

"don't think," I said. "Just take it easy."

"I'm taking it easy," he said and looked straight ahead. He was evidently holding tight onto himself about something.

"Take this with water."

"Do you think it will do any good?"

"Of course it will."

I sat down and opened the *Pirate* book and commenced② start; begin to read, but I could see he was not following, so I stopped.

"About what time do you think I'm going to die?" he asked.

"What?"

"About how long will it be before I die?"

"You aren't going to die. What's the matter with you?"

"Oh, yes, I am. I heard him say a hundred and two."

"People don't die with a fever of one hundred and two. That's a silly way to talk."

"I know they do. At school in France the boys told me you can't live with forty-four degrees. I've got a hundred and two."

---

① flush: 使(鸟等)惊飞
② commence: start, begin

He had been waiting to die all day, ever since nine o'clock in the morning.

"You poor Schatz," I said. "Poor old Schatz. It's like miles and kilometers. You aren't going to die. That's a different thermometer①. On that thermometer thirty-seven is normal. On this kind It's ninety-eight."

"Are you sure?"

"Absolutely②," I said. "It's like miles and kilometers. You know, like how many kilometers we make when we do seventy in the car?"

"Oh," he said.

But his gaze at the foot of his bed relaxed slowly. The hold over himself relaxed too, finally, and the next day it was very slack③ and he cried very easily at little things that were of no importance.

Questions for Discussion

1. How does the selected reading illustrate The Hemingway Hero?
2. What is Hemingway's writing style?

Fill in the following blanks with appropriate answers.

1. The story is told from _____ point of view.
2. The boy's illness was _____.
3. The author's purpose in writing about the doctor's visit is _____.
4. The child kept tight control over himself throughout the day because _____.
5. The title of the story probably means that _____.
6. The next day the boy cried very easily at trifling matters. The reason for this probably is that _____.
7. The theme of the story is _____.

---

① thermometer: 温度计
② absolutely: completely; certainly
③ slack: 懒散的,没精打采的

Unit 10 Eugene O'Neill (1888 – 1953)

Appreciation

Tinkin' and dreamin', what'll that get yuh? What's tinkin' got to do wit it? We move, don't we? Speed, ain't it? Fog, dat's all you stand for. But we drive troudat, don't we? We split dat up and smash trou—twenty-five knots a hour! 想心事和做梦,那会给你带来什么好处？那和想心事有什么相干？我们前进,是不是？速度,是不是？雾,那就是你所代表的一切。但是我们要冲过它去,是不是？我们突破它猛冲过去———个钟头二十五海里！

Eugene O'Neill was a Nobel laureate and American playwright and in literature. His plays poetically were among the first to introduce into American drama techniques of realism. The drama *Long Day's Journey into Night* is often numbered on the short list of the finest American plays in the 20th century, alongside Tennessee Williams's *A Streetcar Named Desire* and Arthur Miller's *Death of a Salesman*.

Almost all of O'Neill's tragedy plays involve some degree of tragedy and personal pessimism. His plays were among the first to include speeches in American vernacular and involve characters on the fringes of society. They struggle to maintain their hopes and aspirations, but ultimately slide into disillusionment and despair.

Brief Introduction

The Hairy Ape (1922) is an expressionist play by about a brutish, unthinking laborer known as Yank as he searches for a sense of belonging in a world controlled by the rich. At first Yank feels secure as he stokes the engines of an oceanliner, and is highly confident in his physical power over the ship's engines.

However, when the weak but rich daughter of an industrialist in the steel business refers to him as a "filthy beast," Yank undergoes a crisis of identity. He leaves the ship and wanders into Manhattan, only to find he does not belong anywhere—neither with the socialites on Fifth Avenue, nor with the labor organizers on the waterfront.

Chapter 6 American Modernism Literature

Selected Reading

The Hairy Ape

A COMEDY OF ANCIENT AND MODERN LIFE IN EIGHT SCENES

CHARACTERS

ROBERT SMITH, "YANK"	PADDY	LONG	MILDRED DOUGLAS
SECOND ENGINEER	HER AUNT	A GUARD	A SECRETARY OF AN ORGANIZATION

Stokers, Ladies, Gentlemen, etc...

SCENE Ⅰ: The fireman's forecastle of an ocean liner—an hour after sailing from New York

SCENE Ⅱ: Section of promenade deck, two days out—morning.

SCENE Ⅲ: The stokeholc. A few minutes later.

SCENE Ⅳ: Same as Scene I. Half an hour later.

SCENE Ⅴ: Fifth Avenue, New York. Three weeks later.

SCENE Ⅵ: An island near the city. The next night.

SCENE Ⅶ: In the city. About a month later.

SCENE Ⅷ: In the city. Twilight of the next day.

SCENE ONE

[THE firemen's forecastle of a transatlantic liner① an hour after sailing from New York for the voyage across. Tiers of narrow, steel bunkers②, three deep, on all sides. An entrance in rear. Benches on the floor before the bunks. The room is crowded with men, shouting, cursing, laughing, singing—a confused, inchoate③ uproar swelling into a sort of unity, a meaning—the bewildered④, furious⑤, baffled defiance of a beast in a cage. Nearly all the men are drunk. Many bottles are passed from hand to hand. All are dressed in dungaree pants⑥,

---

① a transatlantic liner：远洋邮轮,客轮
② steel bunker：铁架子
③ inchoate：才开始的；未完成的；不发达的
④ bewildered：困惑的，眩晕的；混乱的，不知所措的
⑤ furious：狂怒的；激烈的
⑥ dungaree pants：粗蓝布裤子

heavy ugly shoes. Some wear singlets①, but the majority are stripped to the waist.

The treatment of this scene, or of any other scene in the play, should by no means be naturalistic. The effect sought after is a cramped space in the bowels of a ship, imprisoned by white steel. The lines of bunks, the uprights supporting them, cross each other like the steel framework of a cage. The ceiling crushes down upon the men's heads. They cannot stand upright. This accentuates the natural stooping posture which shoveling coal and the resultant over-development of back and shoulder muscles have given them. The men themselves should resemble those pictures in which the appearance of Neanderthal Man is guessed at. All are hairy-chested, with long arms of tremendous power, and low, receding brows above their small, fierce, resentful eyes. All the civilized white races are represented, but except for the slight differentiation in color of hair, skin, eyes, all these men are alike.

The curtain rises on a tumult② of sound. YANK is seated in the foreground. He seems broader, fiercer, more truculent③, more powerful, more sure of himself than the rest. They respect his superior strength—the grudging respect of fear. Then, too, he represents to them a self-expression, the very last word in what they are, their most highly developed individual.]

VOICES: Gif me trinkdere, you!
'Ave a wet!
Salute!
Gesundheit!
Skoal!
Drunk as a lord, God stiffen you!
Here's how!
Luck!
Pass back that bottle, damn you!
Pourin' (pouring) it down his neck!
Ho, Froggy! Where the devil have you been?
La Touraine.

---

① singlets: 汗衫, 单衬衣
② tumult: 喧哗; 吵闹; 心烦意乱
③ truculent: 好斗的; 凶狠的; 致命的; 尖刻的

I hit him smash in yaw, pyGott!
Jenkins—the First—he's a rotten swine—
And the coppers nabbed him—and I run—
I like peer better. It don't pig head gif you.
A slut, I'm saying'! She robbed me aslape—
To hell with'em(them) all!
you're a bloody liar!
Say dot again! [Commotion. Two men about to fight are pulled apart.]
No scrappin' (scrapping) now!
Tonight—
See who's the best man!
Bloody Dutchman!
Tonight on the for'ard square.
I'll bet on Dutchy.
He packa da wallop, I tella you!
Shut up, Wop!
No fightin' (fighting), maties. We're all chums, aint(aren't) we?
(A voice starts bawling a song.)

"Beer, beer, glorious beer!
Fill yourselves up right up to here."
YANK: (for the first time seeming to take notice of the uproar about him, turns around threateningly—in a tone of contemptuous① authority) Choke off dat (that) noise! Where d'yuh(did you) get dat beer stuff? Beer, hell! Beer's for goils—and Dutchmen. Me for some wit(with) a kick to it! Gimme a drink, one of youse (yours) guys. (Several bottles are eagerly offered. He takes a tremendous gulp at one of them; then, keeping the bottle in his hand, glares belligerently at the owner, who hastens to acquiesce in this robbery by saying) All righto, Yank. Keep it and have another. (YANK contemptuously turns his back on the crowd again. For a second there is an embarrassed silence. Then—)
VOICES: We must be passing the Hook.
She's beginning to roll to it.

---

① contemptuous：蔑视的，鄙视的

Six days in hell—and then Southampton.
PyYesus, I vish(wish) somepody take my first vatch for me!
Gittin'(getting) seasick, Square-head?
Drink up and forget it!
What's in your bottle?
Gin.
Dot's(Does) nigger trink(drink).
Absinthe? It's doped. you'll go off your chump, Froggy!
Cochon!
Whisky, That's the ticket!
Where's Paddy?
Going asleep.
Sing us that whisky song, Paddy. (They all turn to an old, wizened Irishman who is dozing, very drunk, on the benches forward. His face is extremely monkey-like with all the sad, patient pathos of that animal in his small eyes.)
Sing da song, Caruso Pat!
He's gettin'(getting) old. The drink is too much for him.
He's too drunk.
PADDY: (blinking about him, starts to his feet resentfully, swaying, holding on to the edge of a bunk) I'm never too drunk to sing. 'Tis(this is) only when I'm dead to the world I'd be wishful to sing at all. (With a sort of sad contempt.) "Whisky Johnny," ye want? A chanty[①], ye want? Now That's a queer wish from the ugly like of you, God help you. But no matther(matter). (He starts to sing in a thin, nasal, doleful tone):
Oh, whisky is the life of man!
Whisky! O Johnny! (They all join in on this.)
Oh, whisky is the life of man!
Whisky for my Johnny! (Again chorus.)
Oh, whisky drove my old man mad!
Whisky! O Johnny!
Oh, whisky drove my old man mad!

---

① chanty: 船歌

Whisky for my Johnny!

YANK: (again turning around scornfully) Aw hell! Nix on dat(that) old sailing ship stuff! All dat bull's dead, see? And you're dead, too, yuh(you) damned old Harp, on'y yuh don't know it. Take it easy, see. Give us a rest. Nix on de loud noise. (With a cynical grin) Can't youse see I'm tryin' to t'ink (think)?

ALL: (repeating the word after him as one with the same cynical amused mockery) Think! (The chorused word has a brazen metallic quality as if their throats were phonograph horns. It is followed by a general uproar of hard, barking laughter.)

VOICES: don't be cracking① your head witut(with it), Yank.

You gat headache, pyyingo!

One thing about it—it rhymes with drink!

Ha, ha, ha!

Drink, don't think!

Drink, don't think!

Drink, don't think! (A whole chorus of voices has taken up this refrain, stamping on the floor, pounding on the benches with fists.)

YANK: (taking a gulp② from his bottle—good-naturedly) Aw right. Can de noise. I got yuh de foist time. (The uproar subsides. A very drunken sentimental tenor begins to sing):

"Far away in Canada,

Far across the sea,

There's a lass who fondly waits

Making a home for me—"

YANK: (fiercely contemptuous) Shut up, yuh lousy boob! Where d'yuh get dat tripe? Home? Home, hell! I'll make a home for yuh! I'll knock yuh dead. Home! T'hellwit(The hell is) home! Where d'yuh(did you) get dat (that) tripe? Dis is home, see? What d'yuh want wit home? (Proudly) I runned away from mine when I was a kid. On'y(you are) too glad to beat it, dat was me. Home was lickings for me, dat's all. But yuh can bet your shoit no

---

① cracking:优美的;美妙的;分裂的;极快的
② gulp:狼吞虎咽地吃,吞咽;大口吸气;哽住

one ain't never licked me since! Wanter try it, any of youse(yours)? Huh! I guess not. (In a more placated but still contemptuous tone) Goils waitin' for yuh, huh? Aw, hell! Dat's all tripe. Dey(They) don't wait for no one. Dey'd double-cross yuh for a nickle. Dey're all tarts, get me? Treat 'em rough, dat's me. To hell wit 'em. Tarts, dat's what, de whole bunch of 'em.

LONG: (very drunk, jumps up on a bench excitedly, gesticulating[①] with a bottle in his hand) Listen 'ere, Comrades! Yank 'ere is right. 'E says this 'ere stinkin' ship is our 'ome(home). And 'e says as 'ome is 'ell. And 'e's right! This is 'ell. We lives in 'ell, Comrades—and right enough We'll die in it. (Raging) And who's ter blame, I arsksyer? We ain't. We wasn't born this rotten way. All men is born free and ekal(equal). That's in the bleedin' (bleeding) Bible, maties. But what d'they care for the Bible—them lazy, bloated swine what travels first cabin? Them's the ones. They dragged us down 'til We're on'y(only) wage slaves in the bowels of a bloody ship, sweatin', burnin' up, eatin' coal dust! HIt's them 'ster blame—the damned Capitalist clarss! (There had been a gradual murmur of contemptuous resentment rising among the men until now he is interrupted by a storm of catcalls[②], hisses, boos, hard laughter.)

VOICES: Turn it off!
Shut up!
Sit down!
Closa da face!
Tamn fool! (Etc...)

YANK: (standing up and glaring at LONG) Sit down before I knock yuh down! (LONG makes haste to efface himself. YANK goes on contemptuously) De Bible, huh? De Cap'tlist(Capitalist) class, huh? Aw nix on dat Salvation Army-Socialist bull. Git a soapbox! Hire a hall! Come and be saved, huh? Jerk us to Jesus, huh? Aw g'wan! I've listened to lots of guys like you, see? you're all wrong. Wanter know what I t'ink? Yuhain'tno good for no one. Yuh're de bunk. Yuhain't got nonoive, get me? Yuh're yellow, dat's what. Yellow, dat's you. Say! What's dem slobs in de foist cabin got to do wit us? We're

---

① gesticulate:指指点点;做手势示意或强调
② catcall:嘘声

better men dandey are, ain't we? Sure! One of us guys could clean up de whole mob wit one mit. Put one of 'em down here for one watch in de stokehole, what'd happen? Day'd carry him off on a stretcher. Dem boids don't amount to nothin'. Dey're just baggage. Who makes dis old tub run? Ain't it us guys? Well den, we belong, don't we? We belong and dey don't. Dat's all. (A loud chorus of approval. YANK goes on.) As for dis bein' hell—aw, nuts! Yuh lost your noive, dat's what. Dis is a man's job, get me? It belongs. It runs dis tub. No stiffs need apply. But yuh're a stiff, see? Yuh're yellow, dat's you.

VOICES: (with a great hard pride in them)
Righto!
A man's job!
Talk is cheap, Long.
He never could hold up his end.
Divil take him!
Yank's right. We make it go.
PyGott, Yank say right ting!
We don't need no one cryin' over us.
Makin' speeches.
Throw him out!
Yellow!
Chuck him overboard!
I'll break his jaw for him!
(They crowd around LONG threateningly.)

YANK: (half good-natured again—contemptuously) Aw, take it easy. Leave him alone. He ain' twoith a punch. Drink up. Here's how, whoever owns dis. (He takes a long swallow from his bottle. All drink with him. In a flash all is hilarious amiability again, back-slapping, loud talk, etc...)

PADDY: (who has been sitting in a blinking, melancholy[①] daze—suddenly cries out in a voice full of old sorrow) We belong to this, you're saying? We make this ship go, you're saying? Yerra then, that Almighty God have pity on us! (His voice runs into the wail of a keen, he rocks back and forth on his bench. The men stare at him, startled and impressed in spite of themselves)

---

① melancholy: 忧郁的;悲哀的

Oh, to be back in the fine days of my youth, ochone! Oh, there was fine beautiful ships them days—clippers wid tall masts touching the sky—fine strong men in them—men that was sons of the sea as if 'twas the mother that bore them. Oh, the clean skins of them, and the clear eyes, the straight backs and full chests of them! Brave men they was, and bold men surely! We'd be sailing out, bound down round the Horn maybe. We'd be making sail in the dawn, with a fair breeze, singing a chanty song wid no care to it. And astern the land would be sinking low and dying out, but We'd give it no heed but a laugh, and never a look behind. For the day that was, was enough, for we was free men—and I'm thinking 'tis only slaves do be giving heed to the day. That's gone or the day to come—until they're old like me. (With a sort of religious exaltation①) Oh, to be scudding south again wid the power of the Trade Wind driving her on steady through the nights and days! Full sail on her! Nights and Days! Nights when the foam of the wake would be flaming wid fire, when the sky'd be blazing and winking wid stars. Or the full of the moon maybe. Then you'd see her driving through the gray night, her sails stretching aloft all silver and white, not a sound on the deck, the lot of us dreaming dreams, till you'd believe 't was no real ship at all you was on but a ghost ship like the Flying Dutchman they say does be roaming the seas forevermore widout touching a port. And there was the days, too. A warm sun on the clean decks. Sun warming the blood of you, and wind over the miles of shiny green ocean like strong drink to your lungs. Work—aye, hard work—but who'd mind that at all? Sure, you worked under the sky and 't was work wid skill and daring to it. And wid the day done, in the dog watch, smoking me pipe at ease, the lookout would be raising land maybe, and We'd see the mountains of South America wid the red fire of the setting sun painting their white tops and the clouds floating by them! (His tone of exaltation ceases. He goes on mournfully.) Yerra, what's the use of talking? 'Tis a dead man's whisper. (To YANK resentfully) 'Twas them days men belonged to ships, not now. 'T was them days a ship was part of the sea, and a man was part of a ship, and the sea joined all together and made it one. (Scornfully) Is it one wid this you'd be, Yank—black smoke from the funnels smudging the sea, smudging the decks—the bloody

---

① exaltation:兴奋,得意扬扬

engines pounding and throbbing and shaking—widdivil a sight of sun or a breath of clean air—choking our lungs wid coal dust—breaking our backs and hearts in the hell of the stokehole—feeding the bloody furnace—feeding our lives along wid the coal, I'm thinking—caged in by steel from a sight of the sky like bloody apes in the Zoo! (With a harsh laugh.) Ho-ho, divil mend you! Is it to belong to that you're wishing? Is it a flesh and blood wheel of the engines you'd be?

YANK: (who has been listening with a contemptuous sneer, barks out the answer.) Sure ting! Dat's me. What about it?

PADDY: (as if to himself—with great sorrow) Me time is past due. That a great wave wid sun in the heart of it may sweep me over the side sometime I'd be dreaming of the day's That's gone!

YANK: Aw, yuh crazy Mick! (He springs to his feet and advances on PADDY threateningly—then stops, fighting some queer struggle within himself—lets his hands fall to his sides—contemptuously) Aw, take it easy. Yuh're aw right, at dat. Yuh're bugs, dat's all—nutty as a cuckoo. All dat tripe yuh been pullin'—Aw, dat's all right. On' yIt's dead, get me? Yuh don't belong no more, see. Yuh don't get de stuff. Yuh're too old. (Disgustedly) But aw say, come up for air onct(once) in a while can't yuh? See what's happened since yuh croaked. (He suddenly bursts forth vehemently, growing more and more excited) Say! Sure! Sure I meant it! What de hell—Say, lemme talk! Hey! Hey, you old Harp! Hey, youse guys! Say, listen to me—wait a moment—I gotter talk, see. I belong and he don't. He's dead but I'm livin'. Listen to me! Sure I'm part of de engines! Why de hell not! Dey move, don't dey? Dey're speed, ain'tdey? Dey smash trou, don't dey? Twenty-five knots a hour! Dat'sgoin'some! Dat's new stuff! Dat belongs! But him, he's too old. He gets dizzy. Say, listen. All dat crazy tripe about nights and days; all dat crazy tripe about stars and moons; all dat crazy tripe about suns and winds, fresh air and de rest of it—Aw, hell, dat's all a dope dream! Hittin' (Hitting) de pipe of de past, dat's what he's doin' (doing). He's old and don't belong no more. But me, I'm young! I'm in de pink! I move wit it! It, get me! I mean de ting dat's de guts of all dis. It ploughs trou all de tripe he's been sayin'. It blows dat up! It knocks dat dead! It slams dat offen(often) de face of de oith! It, get me! De engines and de coal and de smoke and all de rest of it! He can't breathe and swallow coal dust, but I kin, see? Dat's fresh air for me!

Dat's food for me! I'm new, get me? Hell in de stokehole? Sure! It takes a man to work in hell. Hell, sure, dat's my fav'rite (favorite) climate. I eat it up! I get fat on it! It's me makes it hot! It's me makes it roar! It's me makes it move! Sure, on'y for me everyting stops. It all goes dead, get me? De noise and smoke and all de engines movin' (moving) de woild, dey stop. Dere ain't nothin' (nothing) no more! Dat's what I'm sayin' (saying). Everyting else dat makes de woild move, somep'n makes makes it move. It can't move witout somep'n (something) else, see? Den yuh get down to me. I'm at de bottom, get me? Dereain'tnothin'foither. I'm de end! I'm de start! I start somep'n and de woild moves! It—dat's me!—de new dat'smoiderin' de old! I'm de ting in coal dat makes it boin; I'm steam and oil for de engines; I'm de ting in noise dat makes yuh hear it; I'm smoke and express trains and steamers and factory whistles; I'm de ting in gold dat makes it money! And I'm what makes iron into steel! Steel, dat stands for de whole ting (thing)! And I'm steel—steel—steel! I'm de muscles in steel, de punch behind it! (As he says this he pounds with his fist against the steel bunks. All the men, roused to a pitch of frenzied self-glorification by his speech, do likewise. There is a deafening metallic roar, through which YANK's voice can be heard bellowing) Slaves, hell! We run de whole woiks. All de rich guys dattinkdey'resomep'n, deyain'tnothin'! Dey don't belong. But us guys, We're in de move, We're at de bottom, de whole ting is us! (PADDY from the start of YANK's speech has been taking one gulp after another from his bottle, at first frightenedly, as if he were afraid to listen, then desperately, as if to drown his senses, but finally has achieved complete indifferent, even amused, drunkenness. YANK sees his lips moving. He quells the uproar with a shout.) Hey, youse guys, take it easy! Wait a minute! De nutty Harp is sayin' somep'n.

  PADDY: (is heard now—throws back his head with a mocking burst of laughter) Ho-ho-ho-ho-ho——

  YANK: (drawing back his fist with a snarl) Aw! Look out who yuh're givin' (giving) the bark!

  PADDY: (begins to sing the "Miller of Dee" with enormous good nature):

  "I care for nobody, no, not I,

  And nobody cares for me."

  YANK: (good-natured himself in a flash, interrupts PADDY with a slap on the bare back like a report) Dat's de stuff! Now yuh 'regettin' wise to somep'n. Care for nobody, dat's de dope! To hell wit' (with) em all! And nix (next) on nobody else carin' (caring). I kin care for myself, get me! (Eight bells sound, muffled, vibrating through the steel walls as if some enormous brazen gong were imbedded in① the heart of the ship. All the men jump up mechanically, file through the door silently close upon each other's heels in what is very like a prisoners' lockstep. YANK slaps PADDY on the back) Our watch, yuh old Harp! (Mockingly) Come on down in hell. Eat up de coal dust. Drink in de heat. It's it, see! Act like yuh liked it, yuh better—or croak yuhself (yourself).

PADDY: (With jovial defiance) To the divilwid it! I'll not report this watch. Let thim log me and be damned. I'm no slave the like of you. I'll be sittin' here at me ease, and drinking, and thinking, and dreaming dreams.

YANK: (Contemptuously) Tinkin "and dreamin", what'll that get yuh? What's tinkin' got to do wit it? We move, don't we? Speed, ain't it? Fog, dat's all you stand for. But we drive troudat, don't we? We split dat up and smash trou—twenty-five knots a hour! (Turns his back on PADDY scornfully) Aw, yuh make me sick! Yuh don't belong! (He strides out the door in rear. PADDY hums to himself, blinking drowsily②.)

Questions for Discussion

1. How did O'Neill use metaphor in this scene?
2. Discuss about the repetition and mockery of Yank's language.

Terms

1. Lost Generation
2. Imagism

---

① imbed in: 嵌入
② drowsily: 懒洋洋地,昏昏欲睡地

Chapter 7

American Literature Post-World War II

I. Historical Background

1. The Second World War (1939–1945)

World War II was a global war, although related conflicts began earlier. The vast majority of the world's countries—including all of the great powers—eventually formed two opposing military alliances: the Allies and the Axis.

(1) War breaks out in the Pacific

On 7 December 1941, Japan attacked British and American holdings with near-simultaneous offensives against the United States and European colonies in the Pacific Ocean, and quickly conquered much of the Western Pacific, which included an attack on the American fleet at Pearl Harbor, the Philippines, landings in Thailand and Malaya and the battle of Hong Kong. The United States entered WW II and financed the Allied war effort and helped defeat Nazi Germany in the European theater. Its involvement culminated in using newly invented nuclear weapons on two Japanese cities to defeat Imperial Japan in the Pacific theater.

WW II was the deadliest conflict in human history, marked by 50 to 85 million fatalities, most of which were civilians in the Soviet Union and China. It included massacres, the genocide of the Holocaust, strategic bombing, premeditated death from starvation and disease and the only use of nuclear weapons in war.

(2) Impact of WW II

In the decades after WW II, the United States emerged as one of the two dominant superpowers. The U.S. Senate on a bipartisan vote approved U.S. participation in the United Nations (UN), which marked a turn away from the traditional isolationism of the U.S. and toward increased international involvement. The primary American goal of

1945 – 48 was to rescue Europe from the devastation of the war, whose industries had been damaged moved towards economic recovery. Political integration, especially in Europe, emerged as an effort to end pre-war enmities and to create a common identity.

The United States became a global influence in economic, political, military, cultural, and technological affairs. Beginning in the 1950s, middle-class culture became obsessed with consumer goods. White Americans made up nearly 90% of the population in 1950.

2. Cold War and the Civil Rights Movement

The United States and the Soviet Union emerged as rival superpowers in the aftermath of WW II. During the Cold War, the two countries confronted each other indirectly in the arms race, the Space Race, proxy wars, and propaganda campaigns. In the 1960s, in large part due to the strength of the Civil Rights Movement, another wave of social reforms was enacted by enforcing the constitutional rights of voting and freedom of movement to African-Americans and other racial minorities. The Cold War ended when the Soviet Union was officially dissolved in 1991, leaving the United States as the world's only superpower.

A new consciousness of the inequality of American women began sweeping the nation, starting with the 1963 publication of Betty Friedan's best-seller, The Feminine Mystique, which explained how many housewives felt trapped and unfulfilled, assaulted American culture for its creation of the notion that women could only find fulfillment through their roles as wives, mothers, and keepers of the home, and argued that women were just as able as men to do every type of job. State ERAs established women's equal status under the law, and social custom and consciousness began to change, accepting women's equality.

3. The 21st century America

After the Cold War, the United States began focusing on modern conflicts in the Middle East and nuclear programs in North Korea. The beginning of the 21st century saw the September 11 attacks by Al-Qaeda in 2001, which was later followed by the U.S.-led wars in Iraq and Afghanistan. In 2008, the United States had its worst economic crisis since the Great Depression, which was followed by slower-than-usual rates of economic growth during the 2010s.

II. Literary Background

About 50-year period after the war, it is a period of multicultural literature or culturally diversified literature, and postmodern literature. American literature took on the characteristic of globalization

1. The Post-War American Theater and Major Playwrights

Theater in the United States is part of the European theatrical tradition that dates back to ancient Greek theatre and is heavily influenced by the British theatre. The central hub of the US theater scene is New York City, with its divisions of Broadway Off-Broadway, and Off-Off-Broadway. Many movie and television stars got their big break working in New York productions.

Two post-WWII playwrights established reputations comparable to Eugene O'Neill's. In the 1950s and 1960s, experimentation in the Arts spread into theater as well, and American theater came into its own. Several American playwrights, such as Arthur Miller and Tennessee Williams, became world-renowned. Arthur Miller wrote eloquent essays defending his modern, democratic concept of tragedy; despite its abstract, allegorical quality and portentous language, *Death of a Salesman* (1949) came close to vindicating his views.

In the middle of the 20th century, American drama was dominated by the work of playwrights Tennessee Williams and Arthur Miller, as well as by the maturation of the American musical. Tennessee Williams at his best was a more powerful and effective playwright than Miller. Creating stellar roles for actors, especially women, Williams brought a passionate lyricism and a tragic Southern vision to such plays as The Glass Menagerie (1944), *A Streetcar Named Desire* (1947), *Cat on a Hot Tin Roof* (1955), and *The Night of the Iguana* (1961). He empathized with his characters' dreams and illusions and with the frustrations and defeats of their lives, and he wrote about his own dreams and disappointments in his beautifully etched short fiction, from which his plays were often adapted. Miller and Williams dominated the post-WWII theatre until the 1960s, and few other playwrights emerged to challenge them.

In 1962, Edward Albee's reputation, based on short plays such as *The Zoo Story* (1959) and *The American Dream* (1960), was secured by the stunning power of *Who's Afraid of Virginia Woolf* He established himself as a major figure in American drama. O'Neill eventually returned to favor with a complex autobiographical drama, *Three Tall Women* (1994).

2. The post-war fiction

The period in time from the end of WWII up until, roughly, the late 1960s and early 1970s saw the publication of some of the most popular works in American history such as *To Kill a Mockingbird* by Harper Lee. Regarding the war novel specifically, there was a literary explosion in America during the post-War era.

From J. D. Salinger's *The Catcher in the Rye* to Sylvia Plath's *The Bell Jar*, the perceived madness of the state of affairs in America was brought to the forefront of the nation's literary expression.

War novels become an important genre after WWII, represented by Norman Mailer, whose *The Naked and the Dead* has been held as the masterpiece of its category. James Jones' best novel *From Here to Eternity* is a powerful story of army life in Hawaii just before the attack on the Pearl Harbour.

3. Post-modernism

Post-modernism is regarded as a term encompassing all the new critical theories since the late 1960s. It is a literary experimentation focused largely on fiction and poetry in the United States from the middle 1960s till about 1975, which became aligned with Post-structuralism and deconstruction. Post-modernism literature is literature characterized by reliance on narrative techniques such as fragmentation, paradox, and the unreliable narrator; and is often (though not exclusively) defined as a style or a trend which emerged in the post-War era.

(1) Beat Generation

The fiction and poetry of the "Beat Generation", largely born of a circle of intellects formed in New York City around Columbia University and established more officially some time later in San Francisco, came of age. The term Beat referred, all at the same time, to the countercultural rhythm of the Jazz scene, to a sense of rebellion regarding the conservative stress of post-war society, and to an interest in new forms of spiritual experience through drugs, alcohol, philosophy, and religion, and specifically through Zen Buddhism.

Allen Ginsberg set the tone of the movement in his poem "Howl", among the most representative achievements of the Beats are Jack Kerouac's *On the Road* (1957), the chronicle of a soul-searching travel through the continent, and William S. Burroughs's *Naked Lunch* (1959), a more experimental work structured as a series of vignettes relating, among other things, the narrator's travels and experiments with hard drugs

(2) Black humor

Black humor is a term applied to a large group of American novels beginning in the 1950s. Although the writers of black humor did not intentionally form a school of literary movement, there is in their novels a common core of satire which is directed against hypocrisy, materialism, racial prejudice, and above all, the dehumanization of the individual by a modern society.

Black humor, in literature, drama, and film, grotesque or morbid humor used to express the absurdity, insensitivity, paradox, and cruelty of the modern world. Ordinary characters or situations are usually exaggerated far beyond the limits of normal satire or irony. Black humor uses devices often associated with tragedy and is sometimes equated with tragic farce. For example, Stanley Kubrick's *film* Dr. Strangelove; or, *How I Learned to Stop Worrying and Love the Bomb* (1963) is a terrifying comic treatment of the circumstances surrounding the dropping of an atom bomb, while Jules Feiffer's comedy *Little Murders* (1965) is a delineation of the horrors of modern urban life, focusing particularly on random assassinations. The novels of such writers as Norman Mailer's *The Naked and the Dead* (1948), Kurt Vonnegut's *Slaughterhouse-Five* (1969), Thomas Pynchon's *Gravity's Rainbow*, *V.* (1963), John Barth, Joseph Heller's *Catch*-22 (1961), and Philip Roth contain elements of black humor.

In their opinion, their society is full of institutionalized absurdity. Therefore, all of them hold a cynical attitude toward society and the conventional moral values which support that society.

(3) Metafiction

Metafiction is a form of literature that emphasizes its own constructedness that reminds the reader to be aware that they are reading or viewing a fictional work. Metafiction is self-conscious about language, literary form, storytelling, and directly or indirectly draw attention to their status as artefacts. Metafiction is frequently used as a form of parody or a tool to undermine literary conventions and explore the relationship between literature and reality, life, and art.

A notable modern example is John Fowles' *The French Lieutenant's Woman*, Barthelme's *Snow White*, etc. Southern, and John Hawkes were also major practitioners of black humour and the absurdist fable. Though writers such as Barthelme rejected the novel's traditional function as a mirror reflecting society, a significant number of contemporary novelists were reluctant to abandon Social Realism, which they pursued in much more personal terms.

Although metafiction is most commonly associated with postmodern literature, its use can be traced back to much earlier works of fiction, such as Geoffrey Chaucer's *Canterbury Tales* (1387), as well as more recent works such as J. R. R. Tolkien's *The Lord of the Rings* (1954 – 1955), or Douglas Adams' *The Hitchhiker's Guide to the Galaxy* (1979).

Metafiction, however, became particularly prominent in the 1960s, with authors and works such as John Barth's *Lost in the Funhouse*, Robert Coover's "The Babysitter" and "The Magic Poker", Kurt Vonnegut's *Slaughterhouse-Five*, John Fowles' *The French Lieutenant's Woman*, Thomas Pynchon's *The Crying of Lot 49* and William H. Gass's Willie Master's *Lonesome Wife*.

4. Poetry

A. Black Mountain Poet

Black Mountain poet, any of a loosely associated group of poets that formed an important part of the avant-garde of American poetry in the 1950s, publishing innovative yet disciplined verse in the Black Mountain Review (1954 – 57), which became a leading forum of experimental verse.

The group grew up around the poets Robert Creeley, Robert Duncan, and Charles Olson while they were teaching at Black Mountain College in North Carolina. Turning away from the poetic tradition espoused by T. S. Eliot, these poets emulated the freer style of William Carlos Williams. Olson emphasized the creative process, in which the poet's energy is transferred through the poem to the reader. Inherent in this new poetry was the reliance upon decidedly American conversational language.

B. Confessional Poetry or "Confessionalism"

It is a style of poetry that emerged in the United States during the 1950s, which has been described as poetry of the personal or "I", focusing on extreme moments of individual experience, the psyche, and personal trauma, including previously and occasionally still taboo matters such as mental illness, sexuality, and suicide, often set in relation to broader social themes. It is sometimes also classified as Postmodernism.

The school of "Confessional poetry" was associated with several poets who redefined American poetry in the 1950s and 1960s, including Robert Lowell, Sylvia Plath, John Berryman, Anne Sexton, Allen Ginsberg, and W. D. Snodgrass.

Beginning in the late 1950s, however, there were a variety of poets and schools who rebelled against these constraints and experimented with more-open forms and more-colloquial styles.

C. New York School

The New York School was an informal group of American poets, painters, dancers, and musicians active in the 1950s and 1960s in New York City. They often drew inspiration from surrealism and the contemporary avant-garde art movements, in particular action painting, abstract expressionism, jazz, improvisational theater, experimental music, and the interaction of friends in the New York City art world's vanguard circle.

Concerning the New York School poets, critics argued that their work was a reaction to the Confessionalist movement in Contemporary Poetry. Their poetic subject matter was often light, violent, or observational, while their writing style was often described as cosmopolitan and world-traveled.

The poets often wrote in an immediate and spontaneous manner reminiscent of stream of consciousness writing, often using vivid imagery. They drew on inspiration from Surrealism and the contemporary avant-garde art movements, in particular the action painting of their friends in the New York City art world circle such as Jackson Pollock and Willem de Kooning.

The leading figure of the late 1940s was Robert Lowell, who, influenced by Eliot and such Metaphysical poets as John Donne and Gerard Manley Hopkins, explored his spiritual torments and family history in Lord Weary's Castle (1946). Other impressive formal poets included Theodore Roethke, who, influenced by William Butler Yeats, revealed a genius for ironic lyricism and a profound empathy for the processes of nature in *The Lost Son*.

Poets often associated with the New York School include John Ashbery, Frank O' Hara, Kenneth Koch, James Schuyler, Barbara Guest.

5. Contemporary American literature

Other notable writers at the turn of the century include Michael Chabon, whose Pulitzer Prize-winning *The Amazing Adventures of Kavalier & Clay* (2000) tells the story of two friends, Joe Kavalier and Sam Clay, as they rise through the ranks of the comics industry in its heyday; Denis Johnson, whose 2007 novel *Tree of Smoke* about falsified intelligence during Vietnam both won the National Book Award and was a finalist for the Pulitzer Prize for Fiction and was called by critic Michiko Kakutani "one of the classic works of literature produced by [the Vietnam War]"; and Louise, whose 2008 novel *The Plague of Doves*, a distinctly Faulknerian, polyphonic examination of the tribal experience set against the backdrop of murder in the fictional *town of Pluto, North Dakota*, was nominated for the Pulitzer Prize, and her 2012 novel *The Round House*, which builds on the same themes, was awarded the 2012 National Book Award.

Unit 1 John Cheever (1912 – 1982)

Appreciation

Science and art are the obverse and reverse of Nature's medal; the one expressing the eternal order of things, in terms of feeling, the other in terms of thought. When men no longer love nor hate; when suffering causes no pity, and the tale of great deeds ceases to thrill, when the lily of the field shall seem no longer more beautifully arrayed than Solomon in all his glory, and the awe has vanished from the snow-capped peak and deep ravine, then indeed science may have the world to itself, but it will not be because the monster has devoured art, but because one side of human nature is dead, and because men have lost the half of their ancient and present attributes. ("SCIENCE AND ART", Thomas Henry Huxley, May 5, 1883)

科学和艺术乃是自然这枚圣牌的正反面。一个是用感情来表达事物的永恒秩序,另一个则是用思想。当人们不再有爱恨之心;当苦难不再引起同情,伟大的英雄业绩的故事不再动人地传唱;当田野里的百合花不能再与身披盛装荣耀已极的所罗门媲美,雪峰和深渊不再使人惊叹,到那时,科学确实有可能占据世界,但这不是因为怪物吞噬了艺术,而是因为人类天性的一个方面已经死亡,因为人类丢掉了古往今来所拥有的那一半天性。(秦文勇 译)

John William Cheever was an American novelist and short story writer. He is sometimes called "the Chekhov of the suburbs." He is now recognized as one of the most important short fiction writers of the 20th century. While Cheever is perhaps best remembered for his short stories including "The Enormous Radio", "Goodbye, My Brother", "The Five-Forty-Eight", "The Country Husband", and "The Swimmer". His fiction is mostly set in the Upper East Side of Manhattan, the Westchester suburbs, old New England villages based on various South Shore towns around Quincy, Massachusetts, where he was born, and Italy, especially Rome. He also wrote five novels, *The Wapshot Chronicle* (National Book Award, 1958), *The Wapshot Scandal* (William Dean Howells Medal, 1965), *Bullet Park* (1969), *Falconer* (1977) and a novella *Oh What a Paradise It Seems* (1982).

Brief Introduction

The Enormous Radio is a fascinating short story about a wife and a husband who own a radio that lets them overhear other people's lives. John Cheever's story shows our thirst to know other people's intimacies and how that desire has both good and bad consequences. The most intriguing part is the division between hearing people's woes and taking action to address them, as well as the slight gender themes in Cheever's piece. It's a great short story to represent magical realism.

Selected Reading

The Enormous Radio

  Jim and Irene Westcott were the kind of people who seem to strike that satisfactory average of income, endeavor①, and respectability that is reached by the statistical reports in college alumni bulletins. They were the parents of two young children, they had been married nine years, they lived on the twelfth floor of an apartment house near Sutton Place②, they went to the theatre on an average of 10.3 times a year, and they hoped some day to live in Westchester③. Irene Westcott was a pleasant, rather plain girl with soft brown hair and a wide, fine forehead upon which nothing at all had been written and in the cold weather she wore a coat of fitch skins dyed to resemble mink④. You could not say that Jim Westcott looked younger than he was, but you could at least say of him that he seemed to feel younger. He wore his graying hair cut very short, he dressed in the kind of clothes his class had worn at Andover⑤ and his manner was earnest, vehement⑥, and intentionally naive. The Westcotts differed from their friends, their classmates, and their neighbors only in an interest they shared in serious music. They went to a great many concerts—although they seldom mentioned this to anyone—and they spent a good deal of time listening to music on the radio.

  Their radio was an old instrument, sensitive, unpredictable, and beyond repair. Neither of them understood the mechanics of radio—or of any of the other appliances that surrounded them—and when the instrument faltered⑦, Jim

---

① endeavor：努力
② Sutton Place：Fashionable area on New York City's East Side. 萨顿区
③ Westchester：Affluent suburban country outside New York City. 韦斯特切斯特
④ mink：貂皮衣
⑤ Andover：Elite boarding school. 安杜佛学院
⑥ vehement：热情的
⑦ falter：颤抖,支吾

would strike the side of the cabinet① with his hand. This sometimes helped. One Sunday afternoon, in the middle of a Schubert quartet, the music faded away altogether. Jim struck the cabinet repeatedly, but there was no response; the Schubert was lost to them forever. He promised to buy Irene a new radio, and on Monday when he came home from work he told her that he had got one. He refused to describe it, and said it would be a surprise for her when it came.

The radio was delivered at the kitchen door the following afternoon, and with the assistance of her maid and the handyman② Irene uncrated③ it and brought it into the living room. She was struck at once with the physical ugliness of the large gumwood cabinet. Irene was proud of her living room, she had chosen its furnishings and colors as carefully as she chose her clothes, and now it seemed to her that the new radio stood among her intimate possessions like an aggressive intruder. She was confounded④ by the number of dials and switches on the instrument panel, and she studied them thoroughly before she put the plug into a wall socket and turned the radio on. The dials flooded with a malevolent⑤ green light, and in the distance she heard the music of a piano quintet. The quintet was in the distance for only an instant; it bore down upon her with a speed greater than light and filled the apartment with the noise of music amplified so mightily that it knocked a china ornament from a table to the floor. She rushed to the instrument and reduced the volume. The violent forces that were snared⑥ in the ugly gumwood cabinet made her uneasy. Her children came home from school then, and she took them to the Park. It was not until later in the afternoon that she was able to return to the radio.

The maid had given the children their suppers and was supervising their baths when Irene turned on the radio, reduced the volume, and sat down to listen to a Mozart quintet that she knew and enjoyed. The music came through clearly. The new instrument had a much purer tone, she thought, than the old one. She decided that tone was most important and that she could conceal the cabinet behind a sofa. But as soon as she had made her peace with the radio, the interference began. A crackling sound like the noise of a burning powder fuse⑦ began to accompany the singing of the strings. Beyond the music, there

---

① cabinet: 收音机的机盒
② handyman: 做零工的人
③ uncrate: 把……拿出箱子
④ confounded: 困惑的,讨厌的
⑤ malevolent: 恶毒的,幸灾乐祸的
⑥ snare: 捕捉
⑦ fuse: 保险丝

was a rustling that reminded Irene unpleasantly of the sea, and as the quintet progressed, these noises were joined by many others. She tried all the dials and switches but nothing dimmed the interference, and she sat down, disappointed and bewildered, and tried to trace the flight of the melody. The elevator shaft in her building ran beside the living room wall, and it was the noise of the elevator that gave her a clue to the character of the static①. The rattling of the elevator cables and the opening and closing of the elevator doors were reproduced in her loudspeaker, and realizing that the radio was sensitive to electrical currents of all sort, she began to discern② through the Mozart the ringing of telephone bells, the dialing of phones, and the lamentation③ of a vacuum cleaner. By listening more carefully, she was able to distinguish doorbells, elevator bells, electric razors, and Waring mixers, whose sounds had been picked up from the apartments that surrounded hers and transmitted through her loudspeaker. The powerful and ugly instrument, with its mistaken sensitivity to discord④, was more than she could hope to master, so she turned the thing off and went into the nursery to see her children.

When Jim Westcott came home that night, he went to the radio confidently and worked the controls. He had the same sort of experience Irene had had. A man was speaking on the station Jim had chosen, and his voice swung instantly from the distance into a force so powerful that it shook the apartment. Jim turned the volume control and reduced the voice. Then, a minute or two later, the interference began. The ringing of telephones and doorbells set in, joined by the rasp⑤ of the elevator doors and the whir⑥ of cooking appliances. The character of the noise had changed since Irene had tried the radio earlier; the last of the electric razors was being unplugged, the vacuum cleaners had all been returned to their closets, and the static reflected that change in pace that overtakes the city after the sun goes down. He fiddled with the knobs but couldn't get rid of the noises, so he turned the radio off and told Irene that in the morning he'd call the people who had sold it to him and give them hell.

The following afternoon, when Irene returned to the apartment from a luncheon date, the maid told her that a man had come and fixed the radio. Irene went into the living room before she took off her hat or her furs and tried

---

① static: 静止的
② discern: 看出,理解
③ lamentation: 悲叹,哀悼
④ discord: 不和,嘈噪声
⑤ rasp: 刺耳的刮擦声
⑥ whir: 呼呼声

the instrument. From the loudspeaker came a recording of the "Missouri Waltz." It reminded her of the thin, scratchy music from an old-fashioned phonograph① that she sometimes heard across the lake where she spent her summers. She waited until the waltz had finished, expecting an explanation of the recording, but there was none. The music was followed by silence, and then the plaintive② and scratchy record was repeated. She turned the dial and got a satisfactory burst of Caucasian music—the thump of bare feet in the dust and the rattle of coin jewelry—but in the background she could hear the ringing bells and a confusion of voices. Her children came home from school then, and she turned off the radio and went to the nursery. When Jim came home that night, he was tired, and he took a bath and changed his clothes. Then he joined Irene in the living room. He had just turned on the radio when the maid announced dinner, so he left it on, and he and Irene went to the table.

Jim was too tired to make even a pretense of sociability, and there was nothing about the dinner to hold Irene's interest, so her attention wandered from the food to the deposits of silver polish on the candlesticks and from there to the music in the other room. She listened for a few moments to a Chopin prelude③ and then was surprised to hear a man's voice break in. "For Christ's sake, Kathy," he said, "do you always have to play the piano when I get home?" The music stopped abruptly. "It's the only chance I have," a woman said. "I'm at the office all day." "So am I," the man said. He added something obscene④ about an upright piano, and slammed a door. The passionate and melancholy⑤ music began again.

"Did you hear that?" Irene asked.

"What?" Jim was eating his dessert.

"The radio. A man said something while the music was still going on something dirty."

"It's probably a play."

"I don't think it is a play," Irene said.

They left the table and took their coffee into the living room. Irene asked Jim to try another station. He turned the knob. Have you seen my garters⑥?

"A man my garters?" the man said again.

---

① phonograph：留声机
② plaintive：悲哀的
③ prelude：序曲，前奏曲
④ obscene：淫秽的，下流的
⑤ melancholy：忧郁的，悲哀的
⑥ garter：吊带袜

"Just button me up and I'll find your garters," the woman said. Jim shifted to another station.

"I wish you wouldn't leave apple cores in the ash-trays," a man said. "I hate the smell."

"This is strange," Jim said.

"Isn't it?" Irene said.

Jim turned the knob again. "On the coast of Coromandel where the early pumpkins blow," a woman with a pronounced English accent said, "in the middle of the woods lived the Yonghy – Bonghy – Bo: Two old chairs, and half a candle, one old jug without a handle..."

"My God!" Irene cried. "That's the Sweeneys' nurse."

"These were all his worldly goods," the British voice continued.

"Turn that thing off," Irene said. "Maybe they can hear us."

Jim switched the radio off. "That was Miss Armstrong, the Sweeneys' nurse," Irene said. "She must be reading to the little girl. They live in 17-B. I've talked with Miss Armstrong in the Park. I know her voice very well. We must be getting other people's apartments." "That's impossible," Jim said.

"Well, that was the Sweeneys' nurse," Irene said hotly. "I know her voice. I know it very well. I'm wondering if they can hear us."

Jim turned the switch. First from a distance and then nearer, nearer, as if borne on the wind, came the pure accents of the Sweeneys' nurse again: "Lady Jingly! Lady Jingly!" she said, "Sitting where the pumpkins blow, will you come and be my wife, said the Yonghy – Bonghy – Bo..."

Jim went over to the radio and said "Hello" loudly into the speaker.

"I am tired of living singly," the nurse went on, "On this coast so wild and shingly, I'm aweary of my life; if you'll come and be my wife, quite serene would be my life..."

"I guess she can't hear us," Irene said. "Try something else."

Jim turned to another station, and the living room was filled with the uproar of a cocktail party that had overshot its mark. Someone was playing the piano and singing the Whiffenpoof Song, and the voices that surrounded the piano were vehement and happy. "Eat some more sandwiches," a woman shrieked. There were screams of laughter and a dish of some sort crashed to the floor.

"Those must be the Fullers, in 11-E," Irene said. "I knew they were giving a party this afternoon. I saw her in the liquor store. isn't this too divine[①]? Try something else. See if you can get those people in 18-C."

The Westcotts overheard that evening a monologue on salmon fishing in

---

① divine：神的，天赐的

Canada, a bridge game, running comments on home movies of what had apparently been a fortnight at Sea Island, and a bitter family quarrel about an overdraft at the bank. They turned off their radio at midnight and went to bed, weak with laughter. Sometimes in the night, their son began to call for a glass of water and Irene got one and took it to his room. It was very early. All the lights in the neighborhood were extinguished, and from the boy's window she could see the empty street. She went into the living room and tried the radio. There was some faint coughing, a moan, and then a man spoke. "Are you all right, darling?" he asked. "Yes," a woman said wearily. "Yes, I'm all right, I guess," and then she added with great feeling, "but, you know, Charlie, I don't feel like myself any more. Sometimes there are about fifteen or twenty minutes in the week when I feel like myself. I don't like to go to another doctor, because the doctor's bills are so awful already, but I just don't feel like myself, Charlie. I just never feel like myself." They were not young, Irene thought. She guessed from the timbre① of their voices that they were middle-aged. The restrained melancholy of the dialogue and the draft from the bedroom window made her shiver, and she went back to bed.

The following morning, Irene cooked breakfast for the family—the maid didn't come up from her room in the basement—until she braided② her daughter's hair, and waited at the door until her children and her husband had been carried away in the elevator. Then she went into the living room and tried the radio. "I don't want to go to school," a child screamed. "I hate school. I won't go to school. I hate school." "You will go to school," an enraged woman said. "We paid eight hundred dollars to get you into that school and you'll go if it kills you." The next number on the dial produced the worn record of the "Missouri Waltz." Irene shifted the control and invaded the privacy of several breakfast tables. She overheard demonstrations of indigestion, carnal love, abysmal③ vanity, faith, and despair. Irene's life was nearly as simple and sheltered as it appeared to be, and the forthright④ and sometimes brutal language that came from the loudspeaker that morning astonished and troubled her. She continued to listen until her maid came in. Then she turned off the radio quickly, since this insight, she realized, was a furtive⑤ one. Irene had a luncheon date with a friend that day, and she left her apartment at a little after

---

① timbre：音色，音品
② braid：编辫子
③ abysmal：深不可测的，完全的
④ forthright：直率的
⑤ furtive：鬼鬼祟祟的

twelve. There were a number of women in the elevator when it stopped at her floor. She stared at their handsome and impassive① faces, their furs, and the cloth flowers in their hats. Which one of them had been to Sea Island, she wondered. Which one had overdrawn her bank account? The elevator stopped at the tenth floor and a woman with a pair of Skye terriers② joined them. Her hair was rigged high on her head and she wore a mink cape. She was humming the "Missouri Waltz." Irene had two Martinis at lunch, and she looked searchingly at her friend and wondered what her secrets were. They had intended to go shopping after lunch, but Irene excused herself and went home. She told the maid that she was not to be disturbed; then she went into the living room, closed the doors, and switched on the radio. She heard, in the course of the afternoon, the halting conversation of a woman entertaining her aunt, the hysterical conclusion of a luncheon party, and a hostess briefing her maid about some cocktail guests. "Don't give the best Scotch to anyone who hasn't white hair," the hostess said. "See if you can get rid of that liver paste before you pass those hot things, and could you lend me five dollars? I want to tip the elevator man."

As the afternoon waned, the conversation increased in intensity. From where Irene sat, she could see the open sky above the East River. There were hundreds of clouds in the sky, as though the south wind had broken the winter into pieces and were blowing it north, and on her radio she could hear the arrival of cocktail guests and the return of children and businessmen from their schools and offices. "I found a good-sized diamond on the bathroom floor this morning," a woman said. "It must have fallen out of that bracelet Mrs Dunston was wearing last night." "We'll sell it," a man said.

"Take it down to the jeweler on Madison Avenue and sell it. Mrs Dunston won't know the difference, and we could use a couple of hundred bucks..."

"Oranges and lemons, say the bells of St. Clement's," the Sweeneys' nurse sang.

"Half-pence and farthings, say the bells of St. Martin's. When will you pay me? Say the bells at Old Bailey..."

"It's not a hat," a woman cried, and at her back roared a cocktail party.

"It's not a hat, It's a love affair. That's what Walter Florell said. He said It's not a hat, It's a love affair," and then, in a lower voice, the same woman added, "Talk to somebody, for Christ's sake, honey, talk to somebody. If she catches you standing here not talking to anybody, she'll take us off her

---

① impassive: 冷漠的

② terrier: 小猎狗

invitation list, and I love these parties."

The Westcotts were going out for dinner that night, and when Jim came home, Irene was dressing. She seemed sad and vague, and he brought her a drink. They were dining with friends in the neighborhood, and they walked to where they were going. The sky was broad and filled with light. It was one of those splendid spring evenings that excite memory and desire, and the air that touched their hands and faces felt very soft. A Salvation Army band was on the corner playing "Jesus Is Sweeter" Irene drew on her husband's arm and held him there for a minute, to hear the music. "They're really such nice people, aren't they?" she said. "They have such nice faces. Actually, they're so much nicer than a lot of the people we know." She took a bill from her purse and walked over and dropped it into the tambourine①. There was in her face, when she returned to her husband, a look of radiant melancholy that he was not familiar with. And her conduct at the dinner party that night seemed strange to him, too. She interrupted her hostess rudely and stared at the people across the table from her with an intensity for which she would have punished her children.

It was still mild when they walked home from the party, and Irene looked up at the spring stars. "How far that little candle throws its beams," she exclaimed. "So shines a good deed in a naughty world." She waited that night until Jim had fallen asleep, and then went into the living room and turned on the radio.

Jim came home at about six the next night. Emma, the maid, let him in, and he had taken off his hat and was taking off his coat when Irene ran into the hall. Her face was shining with tears and her hair was disordered. "Go up to 16-C, Jim." she screamed. "don't take off your coat. Go up to 16-C. Mr Osborn's beating his wife. They've been quarrelling since four o'clock, and now he's hitting her. Go up and stop him."

From the radio in the living room, Jim heard screams, obscenities②, and thuds. "You know you don't have to listen to this sort of thing," he said. He strode into the living room and turned the switch. "It's indecent," he said. "It's like looking in windows. You know you don't have to listen to this sort of thing. You can turn it off."

"Oh, It's so horrible, It's so dreadful," Irene was sobbing. "I've been listening all day, and It's so depressing."

"Weil, if It's so depressing, why do you listen to it? I bought this damned radio to give you some pleasure," he said. "I paid a great deal of money for it.

---

① tambourine: 铃鼓,手鼓

② obscenity: 淫秽,下流

I thought it might make you happy. I wanted to make you happy."

"Don't, don't, don't, don't quarrel with me," she moaned, and laid her head on his shoulder. "All the others have been quarrelling all day. Everybody's been quarrelling. They're all worried about money. Mrs Hutchinson's mother is dying of cancer in Florida and they don't have enough money to send her to the Mayo Clinic. At least, Mr Hutchinson says they don't have enough money. And some woman in this building is having an affair with the handyman—with that hideous① handyman. It's too disgusting. And Mrs Melville has heart trouble and Mr Hendricks is going to lose his job in April and Mrs Hendricks is horrid about the whole thing and that girl who plays the "Missouri Waltz" is a whore, a common whore, and the elevator man has tuberculosis and Mr Osborn has been beating Mrs Osborn." She wailed②. She trembled with grief and checked the stream of tears down her face with the heel of her palm.

"Well, why do you have to listen?" Jim asked again. "Why do you have to listen to this stuff if it makes you so miserable?"

"Oh, don't, don't, don't," she cried. "Life is too terrible, too sordid③ and awful. But We've never been like that, have we, darling? Have we? I mean We've always been good and decent and loving to one another, haven't we? And we have two children, two beautiful children. Our lives aren't sordid, are they, darling? Are they?" She flung her arms around his neck and drew his face down to hers. "We're happy, aren't we, darling? We are happy, aren't we?"

"Of course We're happy," he said tiredly. He began to surrender his resentment. "Of course We're happy. I'll have that damned radio fixed or taken away tomorrow." He stroked her soft hair. "My poor girl," he said.

"You love me, don't you?" she asked. "And We're not hypocritical④ or worried about money or dishonest, are we?"

"No, darling," he said.

A man came in the morning and fixed the radio. Irene turned it on cautiously and was happy to hear a California-wine commercial and a recording of Beethoven's Ninth Symphony, including Schiller's "Ode to Joy." She kept the radio on all day and nothing untoward⑤ came from the speaker.

A Spanish suite was being played when Jim came home. "Is everything all

---

① hideous：可怕的

② wail：哭叫，哀号

③ sordid：肮脏的，污秽的

④ hypercritical：吹毛求疵的

⑤ untoward：意外的

right?" he asked. His face was pale, she thought. They had some cocktails and went in to dinner to the "Anvil Chorus" from "Il Trovatore." This was followed by Debussy's "La Mer."

"I paid the bill for the radio today," Jim said. "It cost four hundred dollars. I hope you'll get some enjoyment out of it."

"Oh, I'm sure I will," Irene said.

"Four hundred dollars is a good deal more than I can afford," he went on. "I wanted to get something that you'd enjoy. It's the last extravagance We'll be able to indulge in this year. I see that you haven't paid your clothing bills yet. I saw them on your dressing table." He looked directly at her. "Why did you tell me you'd paid them? Why did you lie to me?"

"I just didn't want you to worry, Jim," she said. She drank some water. "I'll be able to pay my bills out of this month's allowance. There were the slipcovers last month, and that party."

"You've got to learn to handle the money I give you a little more intelligently, Irene," he said. "You've got to understand that we won't have as much money this year as we had last. I had a very sobering talk with Mitchell today. No one is buying anything. We are spending all our time promoting new issues, and you know how long that takes. I'm not getting any younger, you know. I'm thirty-seven. My hair will be gray next year. I haven't done as well as I'd hoped to do. And I don't suppose things will get any better."

"Yes, dear," she said.

"We've got to start cutting down," Jim said. "We've got to think of the children. To be perfectly frank with you, I worry about money a great deal. I'm not at all sure of the future. No one is. If anything should happen to me, there's the insurance, but that wouldn't go very far today. I've worked awfully hard to give you and the children a comfortable life," he said bitterly. "I don't like to see all of my energies, all of my youth, wasted on fur coats and radios and slipcovers and—"

"Please, Jim," she said. "Please. They'll hear us."

"Who'll hear us? Emma can't hear us."

"The radio."

"Oh, I'm sick!" he shouted. "I'm sick to death of your apprehensiveness. The radio can't hear us. Nobody can hear us. And what if they can hear us? Who cares?"

Irene got up from the table and went into the living room. Jim went to the door and shouted at her from there. "Why are you so Christly all of a sudden?

What's turned you overnight into a convent① girl? You stole your mother's jewelry before they probated② her will. You never gave your sister a cent of that money that was intended for her—not even when she needed it. You made Grace Howland's life miserable, and where were all your piety③ and your virtue when you went to that abortionist? I'll never forget how cool you were. You packed your bag and went off to have that child murdered as if you were going to Nassau. If you'd had any reasons, if you'd had any good reasons—"

　　Irene stood for a minute before the hideous cabinet, disgraced and sickened, but she held her hand on the switch before she extinguished the music and the voices, hoping that the instrument might speak to her kindly, that she might hear the Sweeneys' nurse. Jim continued to shout at her from the door. The voice on the radio was suave④ and noncommittal⑤. "An early morning railroad disaster in Tokyo," the loudspeaker said, "killed twenty-nine people. A fire in a Catholic hospital near Buffalo for the care of blind children was extinguished early this morning by nuns. The temperature is forty-seven. The humidity is eighty-nine."

Questions for Discussion

1. Are there any people analyzing others based on their social media presence? How and why? For example, people post their portraits on Facebook or Wechat. Will you analyze them according to the posted files?
2. Do you agree to sell that enormous radio or keep it? Why or why not?
3. How do people remain happy in their life, knowing more or know less about yourselves, your neighbors, and your society?

---

① convent：女修道院
② probate：检验遗嘱
③ piety：虔诚
④ suave：平滑的
⑤ noncommittal：不表态的

Unit 2　Arthur Miller (1915 – 2005)

Appreciation

　　I was even observing the scenery. You can imagine, me looking at the scenery, on the road every week of my life. But it's so beautiful up there, Linda, the trees are so thick, and the sun is warm. I opened the windshield and just let the warm air bathe over me. And then all of a sudden I'm goin' off the road! I'm tellin' ya, I absolutely forgot I was driving. If gone the other way over the white line I might've killed somebody. So I went on again—and five minutes later I'm dreamin' again, and I nearly... (He presses two fingers against his eyes.) I have such thoughts. I have such strange thoughts. 我一路开过来,你明白吗? 我很好。我居然还欣赏风景呢。你想想看,我一生中每星期都在路上看风景。不过那一带地方的确很美,琳达,树木真密,太阳又温暖。我打开挡风玻璃,就让温暖的空气给我洗个澡。不料一下子我竟离开了车道! 说真的,我完全忘了自己在开车。要是我超出了白线开到对面的道上,不定会压死什么人呢。所以我就再开下去——过了五分钟我又做梦啦,我差点——(他用两个指头贴住眼睛)我有那么种想法,我有那么种奇怪的想法。

　　Arthur Asher Miller was a prominent figure in 20th century American theatre. His most popular plays are *All My Sons* (1947), *Death of a Salesman* (1949), *The Crucible* (1953) and *A View from the Bridge* (1955, revised 1956). He also wrote several *screenplays* and was most famous for his work on *The Misfits*. The drama *Death of a Salesman* is often numbered on the short list of finest American plays in the 20th century alongside *Long Day's Journey into Night* and *A Streetcar Named Desire*.

　　During the late 1940s, 1950s and early 1960s, Miller was often in the public eyes. During this time, he was awarded the Pulitzer Prize for Drama; testified before the House Un-American Activities Committee; and was married to Marilyn Monroe. He received the Prince of Asturias Award and the Praemium Imperiale Prize in 2002 and the Jerusalem Prize in 2003, as well as the Dorothy and Lillian Gish Lifetime Achievement Award.

Brief Introduction

　　Death of a Salesman is a play written by American playwright Arthur Miller in

1949. It was the recipient of the 1949 Pulitzer Prize for Drama and Tony Award for Best Play. The play premiered on Broadway in February 1949, running for 742 performances, and has been revived on Broadway four times, winning three Tony Awards for Best Revival. It is widely considered to be one of the greatest plays of the 20th century.

The main character Willy Loman returns home exhausted after a cancelled business trip. Worried over Willy's state of mind and recent car accident, his wife Linda suggests that he ask his boss Howard Wagner to allow him to work in his home city so he will not have to travel. Willy complains to Linda that their son, Biff, has yet to make good on his life. Despite Biff's promising showing as an athlete in his high school, he flunked senior-year math and never went to college.

Next day, Willy goes to ask his boss, Howard, for a job in town while Biff goes to make a business proposition, but both fail. Willy gets angry and ends up getting fired when the boss tells him he needs a rest and can no longer represent the company. Biff waits hours to see a former employer who does not remember him and turns him down. Biff impulsively steals a fountain pen. Willy then goes to the office of his neighbor Charley, where he runs into Charley's son Bernard (now a successful lawyer); Bernard tells him that Biff originally wanted to do well in summer school, but something happened in Boston when Biff went to visit his father that changed his mind.

Happy, Biff and Willy meet for dinner at a restaurant, but Willy refuses to hear bad news from Biff. Happy tries to get Biff to lie to their father. Biff tries to tell him what happened as Willy gets angry and slips into a flashback of what happened in Boston the day Biff came to see him. Willy had been having an affair with a receptionist on one of his sales trips when Biff unexpectedly arrived at Willy's hotel room. A shocked Biff angrily confronted his father, calling him a liar and a fraud. From that moment, Biff's views of his father changed and set Biff adrift.

The final scene takes place at Willy's funeral, which is attended only by his family, Bernard and Charley. The ambiguities at the funeral of mixed and unaddressed emotions persist, particularly over whether Willy's choices or circumstances were obsolete. At the funeral, Biff retains his belief that he does not want to become a businessman like his father. Happy, on the other hand, chooses to follow in his father's footsteps, while Linda laments her husband's decision just before her final payment on the house...

"...and there'll be nobody home. We're free and clear, Willy... We're free... We're free..."

Selected Reading

Death of a Salesman

THE CHARACTERS

WILLY LOMAN	THE WOMAN	JENNY
LINDA	CHARLEY	STANLEY
BIFF	UNCLE BEN	MISS FORSYTHE
HAPPY	HOWARD WAGNER	LETTA
BERNARD		

The action takes place in Willy Loman's house and yard and in various places he visits in New York and Boston of today. New York premiere February 10, 1949.

ACT ONE

A melody is heard, played upon a flute. It is small and fine, telling of grass and trees and the horizon. The curtain rises. Before us is the salesman's house. We are aware of towering, angular① shapes behind it, surrounding it on all sides. Only the blue light of the sky falls upon the house and forestage②; the surrounding area shows an angry glow of orange. As more light appears, we see a solid vault of apartment houses around the small, fragile-seeming home. An air of the dream dings to the place, a dream rising out of reality. The kitchen at center seems actual enough, for there is a kitchen table with three chairs, and a refrigerator. But no other fixtures are seen. At the back of the kitchen there is a draped entrance, which leads to the living room. To the right of the kitchen, on a level raised two feet, is a bedroom furnished only with a brass bedstead and a straight chair. On a shelf over the bed a silver athletic trophy stands. A window opens onto the apartment house at the side. Behind the kitchen, on a level raised six and a half feet, is the boys' bedroom, at present barely visible. Two beds are dimly seen, and at the back of the room a dormer window. (This

---

① angular: 有角的；用角测量的
② forestage: 舞台幕布以前的部分

bedroom is above the unseen living room.) At the left a stairway curves up to it from the kitchen. The entire setting is wholly or, in some places, partially① transparent. The roof-line of the house is one-dimensional; under and over it we see the apartment buildings. Before the house lies an apron, curving beyond the forestage into the orchestra. This forward area serves as the back yard as well as the locale of all Willy's imaginings and of his city scenes. Whenever the action is in the present the actors observe the imaginary wall-lines, entering the house only through its door at the left. But in the scenes of the past these boundaries are broken, and characters enter or leave a room by stepping through a wall onto the forestage. From the right, Willy Loman, the salesman, enters, carrying two large sample cases. The flute plays on. He hears but is not aware of it. He is past sixty years of age, dressed quietly. Even as he crosses the stage to the doorway of the house, his exhaustion is apparent②. He unlocks the door, comes into the kitchen, and thank fully lets his burden down, feeling the soreness of his palms. A word-sigh escapes his lips—it might be "Oh, boy, oh, boy."

He closes the door, then carries his cases out into the living room, through the draped kitchen doorway. Linda, his wife, has stirred in her bed at the right. She gets out and puts on a robe, listening. Most often jovial, she has developed an iron repression of her exceptions to Willy's behavior—she more than loves him, she admires him, as though his mercurial③ nature, his temper, his massive dreams and little cruelties, served her only as sharp reminders of the turbulent longings within him, longings which she shares but lacks the temperament to utter and follow to their end.

LINDA (hearing Willy outside the bedroom, calls with some trepidation): Willy!

WILLY: It's all right. I came back.

LINDA: Why What happened? (Slight pause.) Did something happen, Willy?

WILLY: No, nothing happened.

LINDA: You didn't smash the car, did you?

---

① partially: 部分地
② apparent: 可看见的；显然的
③ mercurial: 反复无常的；灵活的，易变的

WILLY (with casual irritation①): I said nothing happened. Didn't you hear me?

LINDA: Don't you feel well?

WILLY: I'm tired to the death. (The flute has faded away. He sits on the bed beside her, a little numb.) I couldn't make it. I just couldn't make it, Linda.

LINDA (very carefully, delicately): Where were you all day? You look terrible.

WILLY: I got as far as a little above Yonkers. I stopped for a cup of coffee. Maybe it was the coffee.

LINDA: What?

WILLY (after a pause): I suddenly couldn't drive any more. The car kept going off onto the shoulder, y'know?

LINDA (helpfully): Oh. Maybe it was the steering again. I don't think Angelo knows the Studebaker.

WILLY: No, it's me, it's me. Suddenly I realize I'm goin' sixty miles an hour and I don't remember the last five minutes. I'm—I can't seem to—keep my mind to it.

LINDA: Maybe it's your glasses. You never went for your new glasses.

WILLY: No, I see everything. I came back ten miles an hour. It took me nearly four hours from Yonkers.

LINDA (resigned): Well, you'll just have to take a rest, Willy, you can't continue this way.

WILLY: I just got back from Florida.

LINDA: But you didn't rest your mind. Your mind is overactive, and the mind is what counts, dear.

WILLY: I'll start out in the morning. Maybe I'll feel better in the morning. (She is taking off his shoes.) These goddam arch supports are killing me.

LINDA: Take an aspirin. Should I get you an aspirin? It'll soothe you.

WILLY (with wonder): I was driving along, you understand? And I was fine. I was even observing the scenery. You can imagine, me looking at the scenery, on the road every week of my life. But it's so beautiful up there,

---

① irritation：刺激；激怒；兴奋

Linda, the trees are so thick, and the sun is warm. I opened the windshield and just let the warm air bathe over me. And then all of a sudden I'm goin' off the road! I'm tellin' ya, I absolutely forgot I was driving. If I'd've gone the other way over the white line I might've killed somebody. So I went on again—and five minutes later I'm dreamin' again, and I nearly... (He presses two fingers against his eyes.) I have such thoughts; I have such strange thoughts.

LINDA: Willy, dear. Talk to them again. There's no reason why you can't work in New York.

WILLY: They don't need me in New York. I'm the New England man. I'm vital in New England.

LINDA: But you're sixty years old. They can't expect you to keep travelling every week.

WILLY: I'll have to send a wire to Portland. I'm supposed to see Brown and Morrison tomorrow morning at ten o'clock to show the line. Goddammit, I could sell them! (He starts putting on his jacket.)

LINDA (taking the jacket from him): Why don't you go down to the place tomorrow and tell Howard you've simply got to work in New York? You're too accommodating, dear.

WILLY: If old man Wagner was alive I'd a been in charge of New York now! That man was a prince, he was a masterful man. But that boy of his, that Howard, he don't appreciate. When I went north the first time, the Wagner Company didn't know where New England was!

LINDA: Why don't you tell those things to Howard, dear?

WILLY (encouraged): I will, I definitely will. Is there any cheese?

LINDA: I'll make you a sandwich.

WILLY: No, go to sleep. I'll take some milk. I'll be up right away. The boys in?

LINDA: They're sleeping. Happy took Biff on a date tonight.

WILLY (interested): That so?

LINDA: It was so nice to see them shaving together, one behind the other, in the bathroom. And going out together. You notice? The whole house smells of shaving lotion.

WILLY: Figure it out. Work a lifetime to pay off a house. You finally own it, and there's nobody to live in it.

LINDA: Well, dear, life is a casting off①. It's always that way.

WILLY: No, no, some people—some people accomplish something. Did Biff say anything after I went this morning?

LINDA: You shouldn't have criticised him, Willy, especially after he just got off the train. You mustn't lose your temper with him.

WILLY: When the hell did I lose my temper? I simply asked him if he was making any money. Is that a criticism?

LINDA: But, dear, how could he make any money?

WILLY (worried and angered): There's such an undercurrent in him. He became a moody man. Did he apologize when I left this morning?

LINDA: He was crestfallen, Willy. You know how he admires you. I think if he finds himself, then you'll both be happier and not fight any more.

WILLY: How can he find himself on a farm? Is that a life? A farm-hand? In the beginning, when he was young, I thought, well, a young man, it's good for him to tramp around, take a lot of different jobs. But it's more than ten years now and he has yet to make thirty-five dollars a week!

LINDA: He's finding himself, Willy.

WILLY: Not finding yourself at the age of thirty-four is a disgrace②!

LINDA: Shh!

WILLY: The trouble is he's lazy, goddammit!

LINDA: Willy, please!

WILLY: Biff is a lazy bum!

LINDA: They're sleeping. Get something to eat. Go on down.

WILLY: Why did he come home? I would like to know what brought him home.

LINDA: I don't know. I think he's still ost(clost), Willy. I think he's very lost.

WILLY: Biff Loman is lost. In the greatest country in the world a young man with such—personal attractiveness, gets lost. And such a hard worker. There's one thing about Biff—he's not lazy.

LINDA: Never.

---

① a casting off:摆脱,抛弃
② disgrace:丢脸,耻辱,不光彩

WILLY (with pity and resolve): I'll see him in the morning; I'll have a nice talk with him. I'll get him a job selling. He could be big in no time. My God! Remember how they used to follow him around in high school? When he smiled at one of them their faces lit up. When he walked down the street... (He loses himself in reminiscences.)

LINDA (trying to bring him out of it): Willy, dear, I got a new kind of American-type cheese today. It's whipped.

WILLY: Why do you get American when I like Swiss?

LINDA: I just thought you'd like a change...

WILLY: I don't want a change! I want Swiss cheese. Why am I always being contradicted?

LINDA (with a covering laugh): I thought it would be a surprise.

WILLY: Why don't you open a window in here, for God's sake?

LINDA (with infinite patience): They're all open, dear.

WILLY: The way they boxed us in here. Bricks and windows, windows and bricks.

LINDA: We should've bought the land next door.

WILLY: The street is lined with cars. There's not a breath of fresh air in the neighborhood. The grass don't grow any more, you can't raise a carrot in the back yard. They should've had a law against apartment houses. Remember those two beautiful elm trees out there? When I and Biff hung the swing between them?

LINDA: Yeah, like being a million miles from the city.

WILLY: They should'vearrested the builder for cutting those down. They massacred the neighbourhood. (Lost.) More and more I think of those days, Linda. This time of year it was lilac and wisteria. And then the peonies would come out, and the daffodils. What fragrance in this room!

LINDA: Well, after all, people had to move somewhere.

WILLY: No, there's more people now.

LINDA: I don't think there's more people. I think

WILLY: There's more people! That's what's ruining this country! Population is getting out of control. The competition is maddening! Smell the stink from that apartment house! And another one on the other side... How can they whip cheese?

(On Willy's last line, Biff and Happy raise themselves up in their beds, listening.)

LINDA: Go down, try it. And be quiet.

WILLY (turning to Linda, guiltily): You're not worried about me, are you, sweetheart?

BIFF: What's the matter?

HAPPY: Listen!

LINDA: You've got too much on the ball to worry about.

WILLY: You're my foundation and my support, Linda.

LINDA: Just try to relax, dear. You make mountains out of mole hills.

WILLY: I won't fight with him anymore. If he wants to go back to Texas, let him go.

LINDA: He'll find his way.

WILLY: Sure. Certain men just don't get started till later in life. Like Thomas Edison, I think. Or B. F. Goodrich. One of them was deaf. (He starts for the bedroom doorway.) I'll put my money on Biff.

LINDA: And Willy—if it's warm Sunday we'll drive in the country. And we'll open the windshield, and take lunch.

WILLY: No, the windshields don't open on the new cars.

LINDA: But you opened it today.

WILLY: Me? I didn't. (He stops.) Now isn't that peculiar! Isn't that a remarkable... (He breaks off in amazement and fright as the flute is heard distantly.)

LINDA: What, darling?

WILLY: That is the most remarkable thing.

LINDA: What, dear?

WILLY: I was thinking of the Chevvy. (Slight pause.) Nineteen twenty-eight... when I had that red Chevvy... (Breaks off.) That funny? I could a sworn I was driving that Chevvy today.

LINDA: Well, that's nothing. Something must've reminded you.

WILLY: Remarkable. Ts. Remember those days? The way Biff used to simonize that car? The dealer refused to believe there was eighty thousand miles on it. (He shakes his head.) Heh! (To Linda.) Close your eyes, I'll be right up. (He walks out of the bedroom.)

HAPPY (to Biff): Jesus, maybe he smashed up the car again!

LINDA (calling after Willy): Be careful on the stairs, dear! The cheese is on the middle shelf. (She turns, goes over to the bed, takes his jacket, and goes out of the bedroom.) (Light has risen on the boys' room. Unseen, Willy is heard talking to himself, "eighty thousand miles," and a little laugh. Biff gets out of bed, comes downstage a bit, and stands attentively. Biff is two years older than his brother Happy, well built, but in these days bears a worn air and seems less self-assured. He has succeeded less, and his dreams are stronger and less acceptable than Happy's. Happy is tall, powerfully made. Sexuality is like a visible color on him, or a scent that many women have discovered. He, like his brother, is lost, but in a different way, for he has never allowed himself to turn his face toward defeat and is thus more confused and hard-skinned, although seemingly more content.)

HAPPY (getting out of bed): He's going to get his license taken away if he keeps that up. I'm getting nervous about him, y'know, Biff?

BIFF: His eyes are going.

HAPPY: I've driven with him. He sees all right. He just doesn't keep his mind on it. I drove into the city with him last week.

Questions for Discussion

1. Could you give a brief analysis of Willy's home which are introduced many times in this part?
2. How does Willy's reality profoundly conflict with his hope?

Unit 3 Robert Traill Spence Lowell (1917 – 1977)

Robert Traill Spence Lowell IV was an American poet, considered the founder of the confessional poetry movement. He was appointed the sixth Poet Laureate Consultant in Poetry to the Library of Congress where he served from 1947 until 1948. He won the Pulitzer Prize in both 1947 and 1974, the National Book Award in 1960, and the National Book Critics Circle Award in 1977.

Lowell was born in Boston, Massachusetts, on March 1, 1917, and was kin to poet Amy Lowell. After elementary studies at the Brimmer Street School, he studied at St. Mark's School to prepare for entrance into Harvard. In his second year of college, he eluded his father's control by transferring to Kenyon College and boarding with Allen Tate and Caroline Gordon. He studied literary criticism under poet John Crowe Ransom and graduated summa cum laude in 1940.

Distinguished in family and literary career, Robert Traill Spence Lowell, Jr., flourished as a teacher, poet, translator, and playwright. His flight from an aristocratic background, numerous emotional breakdowns, and three failed marriages contrasts the bond he shared with the stars of modern American poetry—Randall Jarrell, John Berryman, William Carlos Williams, and Anne Sexton, all supportive friends who called him "Cal." To the literary world, he was the American prophet of a new poetic freedom, a structurally uninhibited lyricism that was true to self, speech, and history.

Lowell brought assorted baggage from his New England background to his personal and professional life. For his rigid piety, critics called him the "Catholic poet." At the height of WWII, Lowell spent five months in jail for refusing to register for the draft. He gained parole in March 1944 and undertook janitorial duties at the nurses' quarters of St. Vincent's hospital. He recounts the experience through "In the Cage" in *Lord Weary's Castle* (1946), an antiauthoritarian volume that won him the 1947 Pulitzer Prize for poetry.

In 1951, Lowell suffered full-blown manic depression, which burdened him until his death. After marrying critic Elizabeth Hardwick, he settled on Marlborough Street near his childhood home, entered psychoanalysis, and enjoyed a period of stability. While teaching and lecturing at Iowa State University, Kenyon School of Letters, Boston University, and Harvard, he produced his best known free verse in *Life Studies* (1959). The collection, which won a National Book Award, tapped the energy and audacity of Beat poetry and recorded Lowell's break with Catholicism, soul-bearing confessions, and revelations of dishonor and scandal among some of Boston's most revered families.

Following Lowell's marriage to his third wife, British author Lady Caroline Blackwood, and the birth of a son, he found hope in lithium treatment. He began detailing the emotional crisis and renewal in a deeply allusive sonnet series entitled *The Dolphin* (1973), winner of a second Pulitzer Prize.

To his detriment, Lowell explored personal events in indiscreet verse, which he performed at public readings. A final collection, *Day by Day* (1977), a pensive series weakened by obscurity and repetition, won a National Book Critics Circle award. Imitations, containing modernizations of Homer, Sappho, Rilke, Villon, Mallarme, and Baudelaire, won the 1962 Bollingen Prize; Poetry (1963) received a Helen Haire Levinson Prize. Shortly after abandoning England and his wife to return to Elizabeth Hardwick, on September 12, 1977, Lowell died unexpectedly of congestive heart failure in a New York City taxi. He was eulogized at Boston's Episcopal Church of the Advent and buried among his ancestors. Collected Poems was issued in 1997.

Brief Introduction

In a more contemplative mood, "Memories of West Street and Lepke," a bold first-person tour of jail, relates the poet's incarceration among extremists ranging from the radical vegetarian Abramowitz and an antiwar Jehovah's Witness to the balding Lepke Buchalter, syndicate chief of "Murder Incorporated."

'hanging like an oasis in his air/ of lost connections' Every syllable in this poem is perfect. It is a milestone in 20th Century American lit. Sad that the benighted readers.

Selected Reading

Memories of West Street and Lepke

Only teaching on Tuesdays, book-worming
in pajamas fresh from the washer each morning,
I hog a whole house on Boston's
"hardly passionate Marlborough Street,"
where even the man
scavenging filth in the back alley trash cans,
has two children, a beach wagon, a helpmate,
and is "a young Republican."
I have a nine months' daughter,
young enough to be my granddaughter.
Like the sun she rises in her flame-flamingo infants' wear.

These are the tranquilized Fifties,
and I am forty. Ought I to regret my seedtime?
I was a fire-breathing Catholic C.O.,

and made my manic statement,
telling off the state and president, and then
sat waiting sentence in the bull pen
beside a negro boy with curlicues
of marijuana in his hair.

Given a year,
I walked on the roof of the West Street Jail, a short
enclosure like my school soccer court,
and saw the Hudson River once a day
through sooty clothesline entanglements
and bleaching khaki tenements.
Strolling, I yammered metaphysics with Abramowitz,
a jaundice-yellow ("it's really tan")
and fly-weight pacifist,
so vegetarian,
he wore rope shoes and preferred fallen fruit.
He tried to convert Bioff and Brown,
the Hollywood pimps, to his diet.
Hairy, muscular, suburban,
wearing chocolate double-breasted suits,
they blew their tops and beat him black and blue.

I was so out of things, I'd never heard
of the Jehovah's Witnesses.
"Are you a C. O. ?" I asked a fellow jailbird.
"No," he answered, "I'm a J. W."
He taught me the "hospital tuck,"
and pointed out the T-shirted back
of Murder Incorporated's Czar Lepke,
there piling towels on a rack,
or dawdling off to his little segregated cell full
of things forbidden to the common man:
a portable radio, a dresser, two toy American

flags tied together with a ribbon of Easter palm.
Flabby, bald, lobotomized,
he drifted in a sheepish calm,
where no agonizing reappraisal
jarred his concentration on the electric chair
hanging like an oasis in his air
of lost connections. . . .

Notes:

当时美国轰动一时的大诈骗犯,1941 年被判谋杀罪

Question for Discussion

Discuss the various human relationships in "Memories of West Street and Lepke." What is Lowell's opinion of people considered as "fringe elements" of society?

Unit 4　Jerome David Salinger (1919 – 2010)

Appreciation

　　Anyway, I keep picturing all these little kids playing some game in this big field of rye and all. Thousands of little kids, and nobody's around-nobody big, I mean—except me.

　　And I'm standing on the edge of some crazy cliff. What I have to do, I have to catch everybody if they start to go over the cliff—I mean if they're running and they don't look where they're going I have to come out from somewhere and catch them.

　　That's all I do all day. I'd just be the catcher in the rye and all. I know it's crazy, but that's the only thing I'd really like to be.

—Salinger, The Cather in the Rye

　　我将来要当一名麦田里的守望者,有那么一群孩子在一大块麦田里玩。几千几万的小孩子,附近没有一个大人,我是说除了我。我呢,就在那混账的悬崖边我的职务就是在那守望,要是有哪个孩子往悬崖边来,我就把他捉住——我是说孩子们都是在狂奔,也不知道自己是在往哪儿跑—我得从什么地方出来,把他们捉住。我整天就干这样的事,我只想做个麦田里的守望者。

——塞林格《麦田里的守望者》

　　David Salinger was an iconic American author especially when it comes to the post-war realistic literature. His works inspired youth quake in the 1950s and 1960s, but he might be the most celebrated and enigmatic literary recluse in the world.

J. D. Salinger started writing while in secondary school. He spent very short time in New York University before he dropped out to work on a cruise ship. In 1939, he attended a Columbia University evening writing class, where his writing talent was found by Whit Burnett, longtime editor of *Story Magazine*. In 1951, Salinger released the novel *The Catcher in the Rye*. That masterpiece was an instant best-seller. However, his antisocial and reclusive personality soon took the upper hand. He went to great lengths to escape the subsequent publicity despite the publication of more short stories and novellas. In 2010, 91-year-old Salinger died in New Hampshire where he had lived in seclusion for over 50 years.

J. D. Salinger was born and raised in Manhattan. His father was a Jewish businessman, which points at his own Jewish background. Salinger had perceptive insights into the adolescent loss of innocence and identity. He was also sensitive to their sense of profound depression and alienation. Therefore, the spiritual quest of teenagers becomes a dominant subject matter in his literary career. In exchange his writing resonates especially with post-war young generation.

Apart from the theme, Salinger's language was critically acclaimed as "the most distinguishing thing" about his works. Most of his novels are pure voice pieces. He was so skilled in employing courageous truth-telling dialogs, cynical and sarcasitic dialects and slangs that some people even related this style to Mark Twain's in *Adventures of Huckleberry Finn*. His short stories are concise, colloquial and surprisingly ended in a manner of O'Henry.

Brief Introduction

Once published, *The Catcher in the Rye* achieved immediate and lasting success. Though never confirmed by Salinger himself, the novel is acknowledged as semi-autobiographical. Written in the first-person, *The Catcher in the Rye* relates Holden Caulfield's three-day misadventures in NY City in December 1949. The novel depicts in eloquent language his teenage disillusion with the phony world of adults.

Holden is a 16-year-old student in Pencey Prep, an elite boarding school. His terrible academic records put him in trouble of being expelled. To avert the earlier meeting with his parents, Holden decides to roam around. He runs into quarrelling, beating, cheating, and drinking in a hotel, a nightclub and the Rockfeller Center only to find days crawl on, boring and spiritless; he encounters taxi drivers, a pimp, a prostitute, three tourist girls from Seattle only to find the world superficial and hypocritical; he gets in contact with a friend, an old acquaintance, and a former teacher only to feel alienated and lonesome. Trapped in such a corrupt society, he thinks about taking a refuge in the west. The idea of committing suicide even flashes by. He decides to take the last look at Phoebe, his younger sister, just from whom he finds affection and salvation. To make her cheer up, Holden gives up his plan. The story ends up with his seeing a psychiatric. It is in this three-day nightmare that adolescent Holden begins to lose his own innocence and to go through a painful phase of growing into maturity. Generally speaking, those who illuminate the frustrating gloom in the story are children. Only children are loving, innocent and confidant. In this sense, our protagonist Holden dreams of becoming the single guardian of children.

Holden Caulfield has become an icon for teenage rebellion, too. But, criticism always goes hand in hand with compliments. Due to its colloquial cursing and profanity, the novel was banned in some countries and even some U. S. locales.

The following selection relates Holden's visit to Mr. Spencer, his former history teacher, before he drops out of school.

Selected Reading

The Catcher in the Rye

Chapter 2

They each had their own room and all. They were both around seventy years old, or even more than that. They got a bang out of[①] things, though—in a half-assed[②] way, of course. I know that sounds mean to say, but I don't mean it means. I just mean that I used to think about old Spencer quite a lot, and if you thought about him too much, you wondered what the heck he was still living for. I mean he was all stooped over, and he had very terrible posture, and in class, whenever he dropped a piece of chalk at the blackboard, some guy in the first row always had to get up and pick it up and hand it to him. That's awful, in my opinion. But if you thought about him just enough and not too

---

① get a bang out of: 从……中得到乐趣
② half-assed: 愚蠢的,考虑不周的

much, you could figure it out that he wasn't doing too bad for himself. For instance, one Sunday when some other guys and I were over there for hot chocolate, he showed us this old beat-up Navajo blanket that he and Mrs. Spencer'd bought off some Indian in Yellowstone Park. You could tell old Spencer'd got a big bang out of buying it. That's what I mean. You take somebody old as hell, like old Spencer, and they can get a big bang out of buying a blanket.

His door was open, but I sort of knocked on it anyway, just to be polite and all. I could see where he was sitting. He was sitting in a big leather chair, all wrapped up in that blanket I just told you about. He looked over at me when I knocked.

"Who's that?" he yelled. "Caulfield? Come in, boy." He was always yelling, outside class. It got on your nerves sometimes.

The minute I went in, I was sort of sorry I'd come. He was reading *The Atlantic Monthly*, and there were pills and medicine all over the place, and everything smelled like Vicks Nose Drops[①]. It was pretty depressing. I'm not too crazy about sick people, anyway. What made it even more depressing, old Spencer had on this very sad, ratty old bathrobe that he was probably born in or something. I don't much like to see old guys in their pajamas and bathrobes anyway. Their bumpy old chests are always showing. And their legs. Old guys' legs, at beaches and places, always look so white and unhairy. "Hello, sir," I said. "I got your note. Thanks a lot." He'd written me this note asking me to stop by and say goodbye before vacation started, on account of I wasn't coming back. "You didn't have to do all that. I'd have come over to say goodbye anyway."

"Have a seat there, boy," old Spencer said. He meant the bed.

I sat down on it. "How's your grippe[②], sir?"

"M'boy, if I felt any better I'd have to send for the doctor," old Spencer said. That knocked him out. He started chuckling like a madman. Then he finally straightened himself out and said, "Why aren't you down at the game? I thought this was the day of the big game."

---

① Vicks Nose Drops：维克斯滴鼻药水
② grippe：流感

"It is. I was. Only, I just got back from New York with the fencing① team," I said. Boy, his bed was like a rock.

He started getting serious as hell. I knew he would. "So you're leaving us, eh?" he said.

"Yes, sir. I guess I am."

He started going into this nodding routine. You never saw anybody nod as much in your life as old Spencer did. You never knew if he was nodding a lot because he was thinking and all, or just because he was a nice old guy that didn't know his ass from his elbow.

"What did Dr. Thurmer say to you, boy? I understand you had quite a little chat."

"Yes, we did. We really did. I was in his office for around two hours, I guess."

"What'd he say to you?"

"Oh... well, about Life being a game and all. And how you should play it according to the rules. He was pretty nice about it. I mean he didn't hit the ceiling or anything. He just kept talking about Life being a game and all. You know."

"Life is a game, boy. Life is a game that one plays according to the rules."

"Yes, sir. I know it is. I know it."

Game, my ass. Some game. If you get on the side where all the hot-shots② are, then It's a game, all right—I'll admit that. But if you get on the other side, where there aren't any hot-shots, then what's a game about it? Nothing. No game. "Has Dr. Thurmer written to your parents yet?" old Spencer asked me.

"He said he was going to write them Monday."

"Have you yourself communicated with them?"

"No, sir, I haven't communicated with them, because I'll probably see them Wednesday night when I get home."

"And how do you think they'll take the news?"

"Well... they'll be pretty irritated about it," I said. "They really will.

---

① fencing: 击剑
② hot-shot: 高手

This is about the fourth school I've gone to." I shook my head. I shake my head quite a lot. "Boy!" I said. I also say "Boy!" quite a lot. Partly because I have a lousy① vocabulary and partly because I act quite young for my age sometimes. I was sixteen then, and I'm seventeen now, and sometimes I act like I'm about thirteen. It's really ironical, because I'm six foot two and a half and I have gray hair. I really do. The one side of my head—the right side—is full of millions of gray hairs. I've had them ever since I was a kid. And yet I still act sometimes like I was only about twelve. Everybody says that, especially my father. It's partly true, too, but it isn't all true. People always think something's all true. I don't give a damn, except that I get bored sometimes when people tell me to act my age. Sometimes I act a lot older than I am—I really do—but people never notice it. People never notice anything.

Old Spencer started nodding again. He also started picking his nose. He made out like he was only pinching it, but he was really getting the old thumb right in there. I guess he thought it was all right to do so because it was only me that was in the room. I didn't care, except that It's pretty disgusting to watch somebody pick their nose.

Then he said, "I had the privilege of meeting your mother and dad when they had their little chat with Dr. Thurmer some weeks ago. They're grand people."

"Yes, they are. They're very nice."

Grand. There's a word I really hate. It's a phony②. I could puke③ every time I hear it.

Then all of a sudden old Spencer looked like he had something very good, something sharp as a tack④, to say to me. He sat up more in his chair and sort of moved around. It was a false alarm, though. All he did was lift *The Atlantic Monthly* off his lap and try to chuck it on the bed, next to me. He missed. It was only about two inches away, but he missed anyway. I got up and picked it up and put it down on the bed. All of a sudden then, I wanted to get the hell out of the room. I could feel a terrific lecture coming on. I didn't mind the idea

---

① lousy：糟糕的,蹩脚的
② phony：骗子,骗人的
③ puke：呕吐
④ tack：平头钉

so much, but I didn't feel like being lectured to and smell Vicks Nose Drops and look at old Spencer in his pajamas and bathrobe all at the same time. I really didn't.

It started, all right. "What's the matter with you, boy?" old Spencer said. He said it pretty tough, too, for him. "How many subjects did you carry this term?"

"Five, sir."

"Five. And how many are you failing in?"

"Four." I moved my ass a little bit on the bed. It was the hardest bed I ever sat on. "I passed English all right," I said, "because I had all that *Beowulf*①, and *Lord Randal*② *My Son* stuff when I was at the Whooton School. I mean I didn't have to do any work in English at all hardly, except write compositions once in a while."

He wasn't even listening. He hardly ever listened to you when you said something.

"I flunked③ you in history because you knew absolutely nothing."

"I know that, sir. Boy④, I know it. You couldn't help it."

"Absolutely nothing," he said over again. That's something that drives me crazy. When people say something twice that way, after you admit it the first time. Then he said it three times. "But absolutely nothing. I doubt very much if you opened your textbook even once the whole term. Did you? Tell the truth, boy."

"Well, I sort of glanced through it a couple of times," I told him. I didn't want to hurt his feelings. He was mad about history.

"You glanced through it, eh?" he said—very sarcastic⑤. "Your, ah, exam paper is over there on top of my chiffonier⑥. On top of the pile. Bring it here, please."

It was a very dirty trick, but I went over and brought it over to him—I

---

① *Beowulf*:《贝奥武甫》,英国最古老的史诗
② *Lord Randal*:《伦德尔勋爵》,英国中世纪晚期民谣
③ flunk: 使……不及格
④ Boy: 好家伙(表示激动、羡慕等情感)
⑤ sarcastic: 讽刺的,挖苦的
⑥ chiffonier: 小衣橱

Chapter 7 American Literature Post-World War II

didn't have any alternative or anything. Then I sat down on his cement bed again. Boy, you can't imagine how sorry I was getting that I'd stopped by to say goodbye to him.

He started handling my exam paper like it was a turd① or something. "We studied the Egyptians from November 4th to December 2nd," he said. "You chose to write about them for the optional essay question. Would you care to hear what you had to say?"

"No, sir, not very much," I said.

He read it anyway, though. You can't stop a teacher when they want to do something. They just do it.

The Egyptians were an ancient race of Caucasians② residing in one of the northern sections of Africa. The latter as we all know is the largest continent in the Eastern Hemisphere. I had to sit there and listen to that crap③. It certainly was a dirty trick.

The Egyptians are extremely interesting to us today for various reasons. Modern science would still like to know what the secret ingredients were that the Egyptians used when they wrapped up dead people so that their faces would not rot for innumerable centuries. This interesting riddle is still quite a challenge to modern science in the twentieth century.

He stopped reading and put my paper down. I was beginning to sort of hate him. "Your essay, shall we say, ends there," he said in this very sarcastic voice. You wouldn't think such an old guy would be so sarcastic and all. "However, you dropped me a little note, at the bottom of the page," he said.

"I know I did," I said. I said it very fast because I wanted to stop him before he started reading that out loud. But you couldn't stop him. He was hot as a firecracker.

>DEAR MR. SPENCER [he read out loud]. That is all I know about the Egyptians. I can't seem to get very interested in them although your lectures are very interesting. It is all right with me if you flunk me though as I am flunking everything else except English anyway.

---

① turd：可鄙之人
② Caucasian：高加索人
③ crap：废话，排泄物

Respectfully yours, HOLDEN CAULFIELD.

He put my goddam paper down then and looked at me like he'd just beaten hell out of① me in ping-pong or something. I don't think I'll ever forgive him for reading me that crap out loud. I wouldn't've read it out loud to him if he'd written it—I really wouldn't. In the first place, I'd only written that damn note so that he wouldn't feel too bad about flunking me.

"Do you blame me for flunking you, boy?" he said.

"No, sir! I certainly don't," I said. I wished to hell he'd stop calling me "boy" all the time.

He tried chucking my exam paper on the bed when he was through with it. Only, he missed again, naturally. I had to get up again and pick it up and put it on top of *The Atlantic Monthly*. It's boring to do that every two minutes.

"What would you have done in my place?" he said. "Tell the truth, boy."

Well, you could see he really felt pretty lousy about flunking me. So I shot the bull② for a while. I told him I was a real moron③, and all that stuff. I told him how I would've done exactly the same thing if I'd been in his place, and how most people didn't appreciate how tough it is being a teacher. That kind of stuff. The old bull④.

The funny thing is, though, I was sort of thinking of something else while I shot the bull. I live in New York, and I was thinking about the lagoon⑤ in Central Park, down near Central Park South. I was wondering if it would be frozen over when I got home, and if it was, where did the ducks go. I was wondering where the ducks went when the lagoon got all icy and frozen over. I wondered if some guy came in a truck and took them away to a zoo or something. Or if they just flew away.

I'm lucky, though. I mean I could shoot the old bull to old Spencer and think about those ducks at the same time. It's funny. You don't have to think too hard when you talk to a teacher. All of a sudden, though, he interrupted me

---

① beat hell out of: 痛打
② shoot the bull: 吹牛，侃大山
③ moron: 傻瓜
④ bull: 胡说，废话
⑤ lagoon: 泻湖，环礁湖

while I was shooting the bull. He was always interrupting you.

"How do you feel about all this, boy? I'd be very interested to know. Very interested."

"You mean about my flunking out of Pencey and all?" I said. I sort of wished he'd cover up his bumpy chest. It wasn't such a beautiful view.

"If I'm not mistaken, I believe you also had some difficulty at the Whooton School and at Elkton Hills." He didn't say it just sarcastic, but sort of nasty, too.

"I didn't have too much difficulty at Elkton Hills," I told him. "I didn't exactly flunk out or anything. I just quit, sort of."

"Why, may I ask?"

"Why? Oh, well It's a long story, sir. I mean It's pretty complicated." I didn't feel like going into the whole thing with him. He wouldn't have understood it anyway. It wasn't up his alley at all. One of the biggest reasons I left Elkton Hills was because I was surrounded by phonies. That's all. They were coming in the goddam window. For instance, they had this headmaster, Mr. Haas, that was the phoniest bastard① I ever met in my life. Ten times worse than old Thurmer. On Sundays, for instance, old Haas went around shaking hands with everybody's parents when they drove up to school. He'd be charming as hell and all. Except if some boy had little old funny-looking parents. You should've seen the way he did with my roommate's parents. I mean if a boy's mother was sort of fat or corny-looking or something, and if somebody's father was one of those guys that wear those suits with very big shoulders and corny black-and-white shoes, then old Haas would just shake hands with them and give them a phony smile and then he'd go talk, for maybe half an hour, with somebody else's parents. I can't stand that stuff. It drives me crazy. It makes me so depressed I go crazy. I hated that goddam Elkton Hills.

Old Spencer asked me something then, but I didn't hear him. I was thinking about old Haas. "What, sir?" I said.

"Do you have any particular qualms② about leaving Pencey?"

"Oh, I have a few qualms, all right. Sure. . . but not too many. Not yet, anyway. I guess it hasn't really hit me yet. It takes things a while to hit me. All

① bastard：杂种

② qualms：顾虑，不安

I'm doing right now is thinking about going home Wednesday. I'm a moron."

"Do you feel absolutely no concern for your future, boy?"

"Oh, I feel some concern for my future, all right. Sure. Sure, I do." I thought about it for a minute. "But not too much, I guess. Not too much, I guess."

"You will," old Spencer said. "You will, boy. You will when It's too late."

I didn't like hearing him say that. It made me sound dead or something. It was very depressing. "I guess I will," I said.

"I'd like to put some sense in that head of yours, boy. I'm trying to help you. I'm trying to help you, if I can."

He really was, too. You could see that. But it was just that we were too much on opposite sides of the pole, That's all.

"I know you are, sir," I said. "Thanks a lot. No kidding. I appreciate it. I really do." I got up from the bed then. Boy, I couldn't've sat there another ten minutes to save my life.

"The thing is, though, I have to get going now. I have quite a bit of equipment at the gym I have to get to take home with me. I really do."

He looked up at me and started nodding again, with this very serious look on his face. I felt sorry as hell for him, all of a sudden. But I just couldn't hang around there any longer, the way we were on opposite sides of the pole, and the way he kept missing the bed whenever he chucked something at it, and his sad old bathrobe with his chest showing, and that grippy smell of Vicks Nose Drops all over the place.

"Look, sir. don't worry about me," I said. "I mean it. I'll be all right. I'm just going through a phase right now. Everybody goes through phases and all, don't they?"

"I don't know, boy. I don't know."

I hate it when somebody answers that way. "Sure. Sure, they do," I said. "I mean it, sir. Please don't worry about me." I sort of put my hand on his shoulder. "Okay?" I said.

"Wouldn't you like a cup of hot chocolate before you go? Mrs. Spencer would be—"

"I would, I really would, but the thing is, I have to get going. I have to go right to the gym. Thanks, though. Thanks a lot, sir."

Then we shook hands. And all that crap. It made me feel sad as hell, though.

"I'll drop you a line, sir. Take care of your grippe, now."

"Goodbye, boy."

After I shut the door and started back to the living room, he yelled something at me, but I couldn't exactly hear him. I'm pretty sure he yelled "Good luck!" at me.

I hope to hell not. I'd never yell "Good luck!" at anybody. It sounds terrible, when you think about it.

Questions for Discussion

1. Both Dr. Thurman and Spencer speak about "Life is a game that one plays according to the rules." Does Holden agree? Why or Why not?
2. List the words Holden frequently uses in his speech and mental activities. What kind of words are they? Why does the author adopt such a language style when the protagonist comes from an elite school?

Unit 5 Kurt Vonnegut (1922—2007)

Appreciation

And not many words come now, either, when I have become an old fart with his memories and his Pall Malls, with his sons full grown. I think of how useless the Dresden—part of my memory has been, and yet how tempting Dresden has been to write about, and I am reminded of the famous limerick. 不过当时我脑子里关于德累斯顿并没有多少话要讲——横竖不够写一本书。就是现在，儿子已经成人，我已是一个饱经风霜、萦怀往事、爱抽帕玛牌香烟的老头儿了，却依然没有多少话要讲。虽然我感到回忆德累斯顿的往事毫无用处，但它却引诱着我非把它写出来不可。

Kurt Vonnegut Jr. was an American author. Vonnegut published fourteen novels, three short-story collections, five plays, and five works of non-fiction. He is most famous for his darkly satirical, best-selling novel *Slaughterhouse-Five* (1969).

The first novel Vonnegut published, *Player Piano*, in 1952. The novel was reviewed positively, but was not commercially successful. Vonnegut published several novels that were only marginally successful, such as *Cat's Cradle* (1963) and *God Bless You, Mr. Rosewater* (1964). Vonnegut's magnum opus, however, was his immediately successful sixth novel, *Slaughterhouse-Five*. The book's antiwar sentiment resounded with its readers among the ongoing Vietnam War. After its release, *Slaughterhouse-Five* went to the top of *The New York Times* Best Seller list, thrusting Vonnegut into fame. He was invited to give speeches, lectures, and commencement addresses around the country and received many awards and honors.

Later, he published several autobiographical essays and short-story collections, including *Fates Worse Than Death* (1991), and *A Man Without a Country* (2005). After his death, he was hailed as a morbidly comical commentator on the society, and as one of the most important contemporary writers. His son Mark published a compilation of his father's unpublished compositions, titled *Armageddon in Retrospect* (2008). Numerous scholarly works have examined Vonnegut's writing and humor.

Brief Introduction

Slaughterhouse-Five, or The Children's Crusade: A Duty-Dance with Death (1969) is a satirical novel. It is generally recognized as Vonnegut's most influential and popular work. Kurt Vonnegut described WWII experiences and journeys through time of Billy Pilgrim from his time as an American soldier and chaplain's assistant, to postwar and early years. A central event is Pilgrim's surviving the Allies' firebombing of Dresden as a prisoner-of-war, which was an event in Vonnegut's own life, and the novel is considered semi-autobiographical.

The first chapter of *Slaughterhouse-Five* is written in the style of an author's preface about how he came to write the novel. Vonnegut frequently uses the phrase, "So it goes," as a refrain when events of death, dying and mortality occur, as a narrative transition to another subject, as a *memento mori*, as comic relief, and to explain the unexplained. It appears 106 times. This has been classified as a postmodern, metafictional novel. He apologizes for the novel being "so short and jumbled and jangled", but says "there is nothing intelligent to say about a massacre."

Selected Reading

Slaughterhouse-Five

One

All this happened, more or less. The war parts, anyway, are pretty much true. One guy I knew really was shot in Dresden for taking a teapot that wasn't his. Another guy I knew really did threaten to have his personal enemies killed by hired gunmen after the war. And so on. I've changed all the names. I really did go back to Dresden with Guggenheim money (God love it) in 1967. It looked a lot like Dayton, Ohio, more open spaces than Dayton has. There must be tons of human bone meal in the ground.

I went back there with an old war buddy, Bernard V. O'Hare, and we made friends with a taxi driver, who took us to the slaughterhouse where we had been locked up at night as prisoner-of-war. His name was Gerhard Müller. He told us that he was a prisoner of the Americans for a while. We asked him how it was to live under Communism, and he said that it was terrible at first, because everybody had to work so hard, and because there wasn't much shelter or food or clothing. But things were much better now. He had a pleasant little apartment, and his daughter was getting an excellent education. His mother was incinerated in the Dresden fire-storm.

So it goes.

He sent O'Hare a postcard at Christmastime, and here is what it said: "I wish you and your family also as to your friend Merry Christmas and a Happy New Year and I hope that We'll meet again in a world of peace and freedom in the taxi cab if the accident will."

I like that very much: "If the accident will." I would hate to tell you what this lousy little book cost me in money and anxiety and time. When I got home from the Second World War twenty-three years ago, I thought it would be easy for me to write about the destruction of Dresden[①], since all I would have to do would be to report what I had seen. And I thought, too, that it would be a master piece or at least make me a lot of money, since the subject was so big.

---

① the destruction of Dresden: 德雷斯顿的毁灭

But not many words about Dresden came from my mind then—not enough of them to make a book, anyway. And not many words come now, either, when I have become an old fart with his memories and his Pall Malls, with his sons full grown. I think of how useless the Dresden—part of my memory has been, and yet how tempting Dresden has been to write about, and I am reminded of the famous limerick[①]:

There was a young man from Stamboul, Who soliloquized thus to his tool, "You took all my wealth And you ruined my health, And now you won't pee, you old fool." And I'm reminded, too, of the song that goes My name is Yon Yonson, I work in Wisconsin, I work in a lumber[②] mill there. The people I meet when I walk down the street, They say, "What's your name?" "And I say," "My name is Yon Yonson, I work in Wisconsin."... And so on to infinity.

Over the years, people I've met have often asked me what I'm working on, and I've usually replied that the main thing was a book about Dresden. I said that to Harrison Starr, the movie-maker, one time, and he raised his eyebrows and inquired, "Is it an anti-war book?"

"Yes," I said. "I guess."

"You know what I say to people when I hear they're writing anti-war books?"

"No. What do you say, Harrison Starr?"

I say, "Why don't you write an anti-glacier book instead?"

What he meant, of course, was that there would always be wars, that they were as easy to stop as glaciers[③]. I believe that too. And, even if wars didn't keep coming like glaciers, there would still be plain old death. When I was somewhat younger, working on my famous Dresden book, I asked an old war buddy named Bernard V. O'Hare if I could come to see him. He was a district attorney[④] in Pennsylvania. I was a writer on Cape Cod. We had been privates in the war, infantry scouts. We had never expected to make any money after the war, but we were doing quite well. I had the Bell Telephone Company find him for me. They are wonderful that way. I have this, disease late at night

---

① limerick：五行打油诗
② lumber：木料
③ glacier：冰川
④ attorney：律师

sometimes, involving alcohol and the telephone. I get drunk, and I drive my wife away with a breath like mustard gas and roses. And then, speaking gravely and elegantly into the telephone, I ask the telephone operators to connect me with this friend or that one, from whom I have not heard in years.

I got O'Hare on the line in this way. He is short and I am tall. We were Mutt and Jeff in the war. We were captured together in the war. I told him who I was on the telephone. He had no trouble believing it. He was up. He was reading. Everybody else in his house was asleep. "Listen," I said, "I'm writing this book about Dresden. I'd like some help remembering stuff. I wonder if I could come down and see you, and we could drink and talk and remember."

He was unenthusiastic. He said he couldn't remember much. He told me, though, to come ahead.

"I think the climax of the book will be the execution① of poor old Edgar Derby," I said.

"The irony is so great. A whole city gets burned down, and thousands and thousands of people are killed. And then this one American foot soldier is arrested in the ruins for taking a teapot. And he's given a regular trial, and then he's shot by a firing squad②."

"Um," said O'Hare.

"don't you think That's really where the climax should come?"

"I don't know anything about it," he said. "That's your trade, not mine."

As a trafficker in climaxes and thrills and characterization and wonderful dialogue and suspense and confrontations, I had outlined the Dresden story many times. The best outline I ever made, or anyway the prettiest one, was on the back of a roll of wall paper. I used my daughter's crayons, a different color for each main character. One end of the wall paper was the beginning of the story, and the other end was the end, and then there was all that middle part, which was the middle. And the blue line met the red line and then the yellow line, and the yellow line stopped because the character represented by the yellow line was dead. And so on. The destruction of Dresden was represented

---

① execution:处决
② a firing squad:行刑队

by a vertical band of orange cross-hatching, and all the lines that were still alive passed through it, came out the other side.

The end, where all the lines stopped, was a beetfield① on the Elbe, outside of Halle. The rain was coming down. The war in Europe had been over for a couple of weeks. We were formed in ranks, with Russian soldiers guarding us—Englishmen, Americans, Dutchmen, Belgians, Frenchmen, Canadians, South Africans, New Zealanders, Australians, thousands of us about to stop being prisoners-of-war.

And on the other side of the field were thousands of Russians and Poles and Yugoslavians and so on guarded by American soldiers. An exchange was made there in the rain—one for one. O'Hare and I climbed into the back of an American truck with a lot of others. O'Hare didn't have any souvenirs. Almost everybody else did. I had a ceremonial Luftwaffe saber, still do. The rabid little American I call Paul Lazzaro in this book had about a quart of diamonds and emeralds and rubies and so on. "He had taken these from dead people in the cellars of Dresden." So it goes.

An idiotic Englishman, who had lost all his teeth somewhere had his souvenir in a canvas bag. The bag was resting on my insteps. He would peek into the bag every now and then, and he would roll his eyes and swivel② his scrawny neck, trying to catch people looking covetously③ at his bag. And he would bounce the bag on my insteps. I thought this bouncing was accidental. But I was mistaken. He had to show somebody what was in the bag, and he had decided he could trust me. He caught my eye, winked, opened the bag. There was a plaster model of the Eiffel Tower in there. It was painted gold. It had a clock in it.

"There's a smash in' thing," he said.

And we were flown to a rest camp in France, where we were fed chocolate malted milkshakes and other rich foods until we were all covered with baby fat. Then we were sent home, and I married a pretty girl who was covered with baby fat, too.

And we had babies.

---

① beetfield:甜菜地
② swivel:旋转
③ covetously:虎视眈眈

And they're all grown up now, and I'm an old fart with his memories and his Pall Malls. My name is Yon Yonson, I work in Wisconsin. I work in a lumber mill there. Sometimes I try to call up old girl friends on the telephone late at night, after my wife has gone to bed. "Operator, I wonder if you could give me the number of a Mrs. So-and-So. I think she lives at such-and-such."

"I'm sorry, sir. There is no such listing."

"Thanks, Operator. Thanks just the same."

And I let the dog out or I let him in, and we talk some. I let him know I like him, and he lets me know he likes me. He doesn't mind the smell of mustard gas and roses. You're all right, Sandy, I'll say to the dog. "You know that, Sandy? you're O. K." Sometimes I'll turn on the radio and listen to a talk program from Boston or New York. I can't stand recorded music if I've been drinking a good deal. Sooner or later I go to bed, and my wife asks me what time it is. She always has to know the time. Sometimes I don't know, and I say, "Search me."

I think about my education sometimes. I went to the University of Chicago for a while after the Second World War. I was a student in the Department of Anthropology. At that time, they were teaching that there was absolutely no difference between anybody. They may be teaching that still.

Another thing they taught was that nobody was ridiculous or bad or disgusting. Shortly before my father died, he said to me, "You know—you never wrote a story with a villain in it."

I told him that was one of the things I learned in college after the war. While I was studying to be an anthropologist①, I was also working as a police reporter for the famous Chicago City News Bureau for twenty-eight dollars a week. One time they switched me from the night shift to the day shift, so I worked sixteen hours straight. We were supported by all the newspapers in town, and the AP and the UP and all that. And we would cover the courts and the police stations and the Fire Department and the Coastguard out on Lake Michigan and all that. We were connected to the institutions that supported us by means of pneumatic② tubes which ran under the streets of Chicago.

---

① anthropologist：人类学家
② pneumatic：气动的，充气的

Reporters would telephone in stories to writers wearing headphones, and the writers would stencil the stories on mimeograph sheets. The stories were mimeographed① and stuffed into the brass and velvet cartridges which the pneumatic tubes ate. The very toughest reporters and writers were women who had taken over the jobs of men who'd gone to war.

And the first story I covered I had to dictate over the telephone to one of those beastly girls. It was about a young veteran② who had taken a job running an old-fashioned elevator in an office building. The elevator door on the first floor was ornamental③ iron lace. Iron ivy snaked in and out of the holes. There was an iron twig with two iron lovebirds perched upon it.

This veteran decided to take his car into the basement, and he closed the door and started down, but his wedding ring Was caught in all the ornaments. So he was hoisted into the air and the floor of the car went down, dropped out from under him, and the top of the car squashed him. So it goes.

So I phoned this in, and the woman who was going to cut the stencil asked me.

"What did his wife say?"

"She doesn't know yet," I said. "It just happened."

"Call her up and get a statement."

"What?"

"Tell her you're Captain Finn of the Police Department. Say you have some sad news."

"Give her the news, and see what she says."

So I did. She said about what you would expect her to say. There was a baby. And soon. When I got back to the office, the woman writer asked me, just for her own information, what the squashed guy had looked Eke when he was squashed. I told her.

"Did it bother you?" she said. She was eating a Three Musketeers Candy Bar.

"Heck no, Nancy," I said. "I've seen lots worse than that in the war."

Even then I was supposedly writing a book about Dresden. It wasn't a

---

① mimeograph: 油印

② veteran: 老将

③ ornamental: 装饰的

famous air raid back then in America. Not many Americans knew how much worse it had been than Hiroshima, for instance. I didn't know that, either. There hadn't been much publicity. I happened to tell a University of Chicago professor at a cocktail party about the raid as I had seen it, about the book I would write. He was a member of a thing called The Committee on Social Thought. And he told me about the concentration camps, and about how the Germans had made soap and candles out of the fat of dead Jews and so on.

All could say was, "I know, I know. I know." The Second World War had certainly made everybody very tough. And I became a public relations man for General Electric in Schenectady①, New York, and a volunteer fireman in the Village of Alplaus, where I bought my first home. My boss there was one of the toughest guys I ever hope to meet. He had been a lieutenant colonel in public relations in Baltimore. While I was in Schenectady he joined the Dutch Reformed Church, which is a very tough church, indeed. He used to ask me sneeringly sometimes why I hadn't been an officer, as though I'd done something wrong.

My wife and I had lost our baby fat. Those were our scrawny years. We had a lot of scrawny veterans and their scrawny wives for friends. The nicest veterans in Schenectady, I thought, the kindest and funniest ones, the ones who hated war the most, were the ones who'd really fought. I wrote the Air Force back then, asking for details about the raid on Dresden, who ordered it, how many planes did it, why they did it, what desirable results there had been and so on. I was answered by a man who, like myself, was in public relations. He said that he was sorry, but that the information was top secret still. I read the letter out loud to my wife, and I said, "Secret? My God—from whom?"

We were United World Federalists back then. I don't know what we are now. Telephoners, I guess. We telephone a lot—or I do, anyway, late at night. A couple of weeks after I telephoned my old war buddy, Bernard V. O'Hare, I really did go to see him. That must have been in 1964 or so—whatever the last year was for the New York World's Fair. Eheu, fugaceslabunturanni. My name is Yon Yonson. There was a young man from Stamboul.

I took two little girls with me, my daughter, Nanny, and her best friend,

---

① Schenectady: 美国斯克内克塔迪

Allison Mitchell. They had never been off Cape Cod before. When we saw a river, we had to stop so they could stand by it and think about it for a while. They had never seen water in that long and narrow, unsalted form before. The river was the Hudson. There were carp in there and we saw them. They were as big as atomic submarines[①].

We saw waterfalls, too, streams jumping off cliffs into the valley of the Delaware. There were lots of things to stop and see—and then it was time to go, always time to go. The little girls were wearing white party dresses and black party shoes, so strangers would know at once how nice they were. "Time to go, girls," I'd say. And we would go. And the sun went down, and we had supper in an Italian place, and then I knocked on the front door of the beautiful stone house of Bernard V. O'Hare. I was carrying a bottle of Irish whiskey like a dinner bell.

I met his nice wife, Mary, to whom I dedicate this book. I dedicate it to Gerhard Müller, the Dresden taxi driver, too. Mary O'Hare is a trained nurse, which is a lovely thing for a woman to be. Mary admired the two little girls I'd brought, mixed them in with her own children, sent them all upstairs to play games and watch television. It was only after the children were gone that I sensed that Mary didn't like me or didn't like something about the night. She was polite but chilly.

"It's a nice cozy house you have here," I said, and it really was.

"I've fixed up a place where you can talk and not be bothered," she said.

"Good," I said, and I imagined two leather chairs near a fire in a paneled room, where two old soldiers could drink and talk. But she took us into the kitchen. She had put two straight-backed chairs at a kitchen table with a white porcelain top. That table top was screaming with reflected light from a two-hundred-watt bulb overhead. Mary had prepared an operating room. She put only one glass on it, which was for me. She explained that O'Hare couldn't drink the hard stuff since the war.

So we sat down. O'Hare was embarrassed, but he wouldn't tell me what was wrong. I couldn't imagine what it was about me that could bum up Mary so. I was a family man. I'd been married only once. I wasn't a drunk. I

---

① atomic submarine:原子潜艇

hadn't done her husband any dirt in the war.

She fixed herself a Coca-Cola, made a lot of noise banging the ice-cube tray in the stainless steel sink. Then she went into another part of the house. But she wouldn't sit still. She was moving all over the house, opening and shutting doors, even moving furniture around to work off anger. I asked O'Hare what I'd said or done to make her act that way.

"It's all right," he said. "don't worry about it. It doesn't have anything to do with you."

That was kind of him. He was lying. It had everything to do with me. So we tried to ignore Mary and remember the war. I took a couple of belts of the booze I'd brought. We would chuckle or grin sometimes, as though war stories were coming back, but neither one of us could remember anything good. O'Hare remembered one guy who got into a lot of wine in Dresden, before it was bombed, and we had to take him home in a wheelbarrow①.

It wasn't much to write a book about. I remembered two Russian soldiers who had looted a clock factory. They had a horse-drawn wagon full of clocks. They were happy and drunk. They were smoking huge cigarettes they had rolled in newspaper. That was about it for memories, and Mary was still making noise. She finally came out in the kitchen again for another Coke. She took another tray of ice cubes from the refrigerator, banged it in the sink, even though there was already plenty of ice out.

Then she turned to me, let me see how angry she was, and that the anger was for me. She had been talking to herself, so what she said was a fragment of a much larger conversation. "You were just babies then!" she said.

"What?" I said.

"You were just babies in the war-like the ones upstairs!"

I nodded that this was true. We had been foolish virgins in the war, right at the end of childhood. "But you're not going to write it that way, are you?" This wasn't a question. It was an accusation.

"I—I don't know," I said.

"Well, I know," she said. "you'll pretend you were men instead of babies, and you'll be played in the movies by Frank Sinatra and John Wayne or

---

① wheelbarrow:独轮车

some of those other glamorous, war-loving, dirty old men. And war will look just wonderful, so We'll have a lot more of them. And they'll be fought by babies like the babies upstairs."

So then I understood. It was war that made her so angry. She didn't want her babies or anybody else's babies killed in wars. And she thought wars were partly encouraged by books and movies.

So I held up my right hand and I made her a promise "Mary," I said, "I don't think this book is ever going to be finished. I must have written five thousand pages by now, and thrown them all away. If I ever do finish it, though, I give you my word of honor: there won't be a part for Frank Sinatra or John Wayne." "I tell you what," I said, "I'll call it *The Children's Crusade*." She was my friend after that. O'Hare and I gave up on remembering, went into the living room, talked about other things. We became curious about the real *Children's Crusade*, so O'Hare looked it up in a book he had, *Extraordinary Popular Delusions*① and *the Madness of Crowds*, by Charles Mackay, LL. D. It was first published in London in 1841.

Mackay had a low opinion of all Crusades. *The Children's Crusade* struck him as only slightly more sordid② than the Ten Crusades for grown-ups. O'Hare read this handsome passage out loud: History in her solemn page informs us that the Crusaders were but ignorant and savage men, that their motives were those of bigotry unmitigated③, and that their pathway was one of blood and rears. Romance, on the other hand, dilates upon their piety and heroism, and portrays, in her most glowing and impassioned hues, their virtue and magnanimity④, the imperishable⑤ honor they acquired for themselves, and the great services they rendered to Christianity.

And then O'Hare read this: Now what was the grand result of all these struggles? Europe expended millions of her treasures, and the blood of two million of her people; and a handful of quarrelsome knights retained possession of Palestine for about one hundred years!

---

① delusion: 错觉
② sordid: 污秽的
③ unmitigated: 十足的, 未缓和的, 未减轻的
④ magnanimity: 海量
⑤ imperishable: 不朽的

Chapter 7 American Literature Post-World War II

Mackay told us that *the Children's Crusade* started in 1213, when two monks got the idea of raising armies of children in Germany and France, and selling them in North Africa as slaves. Thirty thousand children volunteered, thinking they were going to Palestine. They were no doubt idle and deserted children who generally swarm in great cities, nurtured on vice and daring, said Mackay, and ready for anything. Pope Innocent the Third thought they were going to Palestine, too, and he was thrilled. "These children are awake while we are asleep!" he said. Most of the children were shipped out of Marseilles, and about half of them drownedin shipwrecks①. The other half got to North Africa where they were sold. Through a misunderstanding, some children reported for duty at Genoa, where no slave ships were waiting. They were fed and sheltered and questioned kindly by good people there—then given a little money and a lot of advice and sent back home. "Hooray for the good people of Genoa," said Mary O'Hare.

I slept that night in one of the children's bedrooms. O'Hare had put a book for me on the bedside table. It was *Dresden, History, Stage and Gallery*, by Mary Endell. It was published in 1908, and its introduction began. It is hoped that this little book will make itself useful. It attempts to give to an English—reading public a bird's—eye view of how Dresden came to look as it does, architecturally; of how it expanded musically, through the genius of a few men, to its present bloom; and it calls attention to certain permanent landmarks in art that make its Gallery the resort of those seeking lasting impressions.

I read some history further on Now, in 1760, Dresden underwent siege by the Prussians. On the fifteenth of July began the cannonade. The Picture—Gallery took fire. Many of the paintings had been transported to—the Konigstein, but some were seriously injured by splinters of bombshells-notably Francia's "Baptism of Christ." Furthermore, the stately Kreuzkirchetower, from which the enemy's movements had been watched day and night, stood in flames. It later succumbed. In sturdy contrast with the pitiful fate of the Kreuzkirche, stood the Frauenkirche, from the curves of whose stone dome the Prussian bombs-rebounded like rain. Friederich was obliged finally to give up the siege, because he learned of the fall of Glatz, the critical point of his new

---

① shipwreck:沉船

conquests. "We must be off to Silesia, so that we do not lose everything."

The devastation of Dresden was boundless. When Goethe as a young student visited the city, he still found sad ruins "Von der Kuppel der Frauenkirchesahich these leidigen Trümmerzwischen die schonestddtische Ordnunghineinges? da rühmtemir der Kiisterdie Kunst des Baumeisters, welcher Kirche und Kuppel auf einen so unerüinschten Fallschoneingeyichtet und bombenfesterbauthatte. Der gute Sakristandeutetemiralsdannauf Ruinennachallen Seiten und sagtebedenklichlakonisch: Das hat her Feind Gethan!"

The two little girls and I crossed the Delaware River where George Washington had crossed it, the next morning. We went to the New York World's Fair, saw what the past had been like, according to the Ford Motor Car Company and Walt Disney, saw what the future would be like, according to General Motors. And I asked myself about the present: how wide it was, how deep it was, how much was mine to keep. I taught creative writing in the famous Writers Workshop at the University of Iowa for a couple of years after that. I got into some perfectly beautiful trouble, got out of it again. I taught in the afternoons. In the mornings I wrote. I was not be disturbed. I was working on my famous book about Dresden.

And somewhere in there a nice man named Seymour Lawrence gave me a three-book contract, and I said, "O. K., the first of the three will be my famous book about Dresden." The friends of Seymour Lawrence call him "Sam." And I say to Sam now: "Sam—here's the book."

It is so short and jumbled and jangled, Sam, because there is nothing intelligent to say about a massacre. Everybody is supposed to be dead, so never say anything or want anything ever again. Everything is supposed to be very quiet after a massacre, and it always is, except for the birds. And what do the birds say? All there is to say about a massacre, things like "Poo-teeweet?" I have told my sons that they are not under any circumstances to take part in massacres, and that the news of massacres of enemies is not to fill them with satisfaction or glee.

I have also told them not to work for companies which make massacre machinery, and to express contempt for people who think we need machinery like that. As I've said I recently went back to Dresden with my friend O'Hare. We had a million laughs in Hamburg and West Berlin and East Berlin and Vienna and Salzburg and Helsinki, and in Leningrad, too. It was very good for me, because I saw a lot of authentic backgrounds for made-up stories which I will write later on. One of them will be Russian Baroque and another will be No Kissing and another will be Dollar Bar and another will be If the Accident Will, and so on. And so on.

There was a Lufthansa plane that was supposed to fly from Philadelphia to Boston to Frankfurt. O'Hare was supposed to get on in Philadelphia and I was supposed to get on in Boston, and off We'd go. But Boston was socked in, so the plane flew straight to Frankfurt from Philadelphia. And I became a non-person in the Boston Fog, and Lufthansa put me in a limousine with some other non-persons and sent us to a motel for anon-night.

The time would not pass. Somebody was playing with the clocks, and not only with the electric clocks, but the wind-up kind, too. The second hand on my watch would twitch once, and a year would pass, and then it would twitch again. There was nothing I could do about it. As an Earthling, I had to believe whatever clocks said—and calendars.

I had two books with me, which I'd meant to read on the plane. One was *Words for the Wind*, by Theodore Roethke, and this is what I found in there: I wake to steep 由浅入深, and take my waking slow. I feet my late in what I cannot fear. I learn by going where I have to go.

My other book was Erika Ostrovsky's *Céline and His Vision*. Céline was a brave French soldier in the First World War—until his skull was cracked. After that he couldn't sleep, and there were noises in his head. He became a doctor, and he treated poor people in the daytime, and he wrote grotesque① novels all night. No art is possible without a dance with death, he wrote.

The truth is death, he wrote. I've fought nicely against it as long as I could... danced with it, festooned it, waltzed it around... decorated it with streamers, titillated② it... Time obsessed him. Miss Ostrovsky reminded me of the amazing scene in Death on the Installment Plan where Céline wants to stop the bustling of a street crowd. He screams on paper, Make them stop... don't let them move anymore at all... There, make them freeze... once and for

---

① grotesque：奇怪的
② titillate：激发，逗引，使高兴

all! ... So that they won't disappear anymore!

I looked through the Gideon Bible in my motel room for tales of great destruction. The sun was risen upon the Earth when Lot entered into Zoar, I read. Then the Lord rained upon Sodom and upon Gomorrah brimstone and fire from the Lord out of Heaven; and He overthrew those cities, and all the plain, and all the inhabitants of the cities, and that which grew upon the ground.

So it goes.

Those were vile people in both those cities, as is well known. The world was better off without them. And Lot's wife, of course, was told not to look back where all those people and their homes had been. But she did look back, and I love her for that, because it was so human. She was turned to a pillar of salt.

So it goes.

People aren't supposed to look back. I'm certainly not going to do it anymore. I've finished my war book now. The next one I write is going to be fun. This one is a failure, and had to be, since it was written by a pillar of salt. It begins like this:

Listen:
Billy Pilgrim has come unstuck in time.
It ends like this:
Poo – tee – weet?

Questions for Discussion

1. What do you think the functions of the first chapter in this novel?
2. Please analyze the phrase "so it goes" in this chapter.

Unit 6   Joseph Heller (1923 – 1999)

Appreciation

If he flew them he was crazy and didn't have to; but if he didn't want to he was sane and had to. Yossarian was moved very deeply by the simplicity of this clause of *catch*-22 and let out a respectful whistle. 假如他去飞,他就是疯子,就无需飞;但假如他不想

飞,他就是正常的,就不得不飞。约萨里安被这22条军规的绝对深深地感动了,不由得充满敬意地吹了口哨。

海勒在一次接受采访时说过:"我要让人们先开怀大笑,然后回过头去以恐惧的心理回顾他们所笑过的一切。"看来,这是《第二十二条军规》的一个很好的注脚。

Joseph Heller was an American satirical novelist, short-story writer, and playwright. The title of one of his works, *Catch-22*, entered the English lexicon to refer to a vicious circle wherein an absurd, no-win choice, particularly in situations in which the desired outcome of the choice is an impossibility, and regardless of choice, a same negative outcome is a certainty. Although he is remembered primarily for *Catch-22*, his other works center on the lives of various members of the middle class and remain examples of modern satire.

Brief Introduction

Catch-22 is a satirical novel by the American author Joseph Heller. He began writing it in 1953; the novel was first published in 1961. It is frequently cited as one of the greatest literary works of the 20th century. It uses a distinctive non-chronological third-person omniscient narration, describing events from the points of view of different characters. The separate storylines are out of sequence so that the timeline develops along with the plot.

The novel is set during WWII, from 1942 to 1944, which mainly follows the life of Captain John Yossarian, a U.S. Army Air Forces B-25 bombardier. Most of the events in the book occur while the fictional 256th Squadron is based on the island of Pianosa, in the Mediterranean Sea, west of Italy. The novel looks into the experiences of Yossarian and the other airmen in the camp, who attempt to maintain their sanity while fulfilling their service requirements so that they may return home.

The novel's title refers to a plot device that is repeatedly invoked in the story. *Catch-22* starts as a set of paradoxical requirements whereby airmen mentally unfit to fly did not have to do so, but could not actually be excused. By the end of the novel it is invoked as the explanation for many unreasonable restrictions. The phrase "*Catch-22*" has since entered the English language, referring to a type of unsolvable logic puzzle sometimes called a double bind. According to the novel, people who were crazy were not obliged to fly missions; but anyone who applied to stop flying was showing a rational concern for his safety and, therefore, was sane.

Selected Reading

Catch-22

Chapter 40

There was, of course, a catch.

"Catch-22?" inquired Yossarian.

"Of course," Colonel Korn answered pleasantly, after he had chased the mighty guard of massive M. P. s out with an insouciant① flick of his hand and a slightly contemptuous nod—most relaxed, as always, when he could be most cynical. His rimless square eyeglasses glinted with sly amusement as he gazed at Yossarian. "After all, we can't simply send you home for refusing to fly more missions and keep the rest of the men here, can we? That would hardly be fair to them."

"You're goddam right!" Colonel Cathcart blurted out, lumbering② back and forth gracelessly like a winded bull, puffing and pouting angrily. "I'd like to tie him up hand and foot and throw him aboard a plane on every mission. That's what I'd like to do."

Colonel Korn motioned Colonel Cathcart to be silent and smiled at Yossarian. "You know, you really have been making things terribly difficult for Colonel Cathcart," he observed with flip good humor, as though the fact did not displease him at all. "The men are unhappy and morale is beginning to deteriorate③. And it's all your fault."

"It's your fault," Yossarian argued, "for raising the number of missions."

"No, it's your fault for refusing to fly them," Colonel Korn retorted. "The men were perfectly content to fly as many missions as we asked as long as they thought they had no alternative. Now you've given them hope, and they're unhappy. So the blame is all yours."

"Doesn't he know there's a war going on?" Colonel Cathcart, still stamping back and forth, demanded morosely without looking at Yossarian.

---

① insouciant:无忧无虑的,漠不关心的
② lumbering:笨重的
③ deteriorate:恶化

"I'm quite sure he does," Colonel Korn answered. "That's probably why he refuses to fly them."

"Doesn't it make any difference to him?"

"Will the knowledge that there's a war going on weaken your decision to refuse to participate in it?" Colonel Korn inquired with sarcastic seriousness, mocking Colonel Cathcart.

"No, sir," Yossarian replied, almost returning Colonel Korn's smile.

"I was afraid of that," Colonel Korn remarked with an elaborate sigh, locking his fingers together comfortably on top of his smooth, bald, broad, shiny brown head. "You know, in all fairness, we really haven't treated you too badly, have we? We've fed you and paid you on time. We gave you a medal and even made you a captain."

"I never should have made him a captain," Colonel Cathcart exclaimed bitterly. "I should have given him a court-martial after he loused up① that Ferrara mission and went around twice."

"I told you not to promote him," said Colonel Korn, "but you wouldn't listen to me."

"No you didn't. You told me to promote him, didn't you?"

"I told you not to promote him. But you just wouldn't listen."

"I should have listened."

"You never listen to me," Colonel Korn persisted with relish. "That's the reason we're in this spot."

"All right, gee whiz. Stop rubbing it in, will you?"

Colonel Cathcart burrowed his fists down deep inside his pockets and turned away in a slouch. "Instead of picking on me, why don't you figure out what we're going to do about him?"

"We're going to send him home, I'm afraid." Colonel Korn was chuckling triumphantly② when he turned away from Colonel Cathcart to face Yossarian. "Yossarian, the war is over for you. We're going to send you home. You really don't deserve it, you know, which is one of the reasons I don't mind doing it. Since there's nothing else we can risk doing to you at this time, we've decided

---

① louse up:打乱

② chuckle triumphantly:得意扬扬地笑

to return you to the States. We've worked out this little deal to—"

"What kind of deal?" Yossarian demanded with defiant mistrust.

Colonel Korn tossed his head back and laughed. "Oh, a thoroughly despicable deal, make no mistake about that. It's absolutely revolting. But you'll accept it quickly enough."

"Don't be too sure."

"I haven't the slightest doubt you will, even though it stinks to high heaven. Oh, by the way, you haven't told any of the men you've refused to fly more missions, have you?"

"No, sir," Yossarian answered promptly.

Colonel Korn nodded approvingly. "That's good. I like the way you lie. You'll go far in this world if you ever acquire some decent ambition."

"Doesn't he know there's a war going on?" Colonel Cathcart yelled out suddenly, and blew with vigorous disbelief into the open end of his cigarette holder.

"I'm quite sure he does," Colonel Korn replied acidly, "since you brought that identical point to his attention just a moment ago." Colonel Korn frowned wearily for Yossarian's benefit, his eyes twinkling swarthily[①] with sly and daring scorn. Gripping the edge of Colonel Cathcart's desk with both hands, he lifted his flaccid haunches far back on the corner to sit with both short legs dangling freely. His shoes kicked lightly against the yellow oak wood, his sludge-brown[②] socks, garterless, collapsed in sagging circles below ankles that were surprisingly small and white. "You know, Yossarian," he mused affably in a manner of casual reflection that seemed both derisive and sincere, "I really do admire you a bit. You're an intelligent person of great moral character who has taken a very courageous stand. I'm an intelligent person with no moral character at all, so I'm in an ideal position to appreciate it."

"These are very critical times," Colonel Cathcart asserted petulantly from a far corner of the office, paying no attention to Colonel Korn.

"Very critical times indeed," Colonel Korn agreed with a placid[③] nod. "We've just had a change of command above, and we can't afford a situation

---

① swarthily:黑黝黝地
② sludge-brown:泥棕色
③ placid:平和的,宁静的

that might put us in a bad light with either General Scheisskopf or General Peckem. Isn't that what you mean, Colonel?"

"Hasn't he got any patriotism?"

"Won't you fight for your country?" Colonel Korn demanded, emulating Colonel Cathcart's harsh, self-righteous tone. "Won't you give up your life for Colonel Cathcart and me?"

Yossarian tensed with alert astonishment when he heard Colonel Korn's concluding words. "What's that?" he exclaimed. "What have you and Colonel Cathcart got to do with my country? You're not the same."

"How can you separate us?" Colonel Korn inquired with ironical tranquility①.

"That's right," Colonel Cathcart cried emphatically②. "You're either for us or against us. There's no two ways about it."

"I'm afraid he's got you," added Colonel Korn. "You're either for us or against your country. It's as simple as that."

"Oh, no, Colonel. I don't buy that."

Colonel Korn was unrufed. "Neither do I, frankly, but everyone else will. So there you are."

"You're a disgrace to your uniform!" Colonel Cathcart declared with blustering wrath, whirling to confront Yossarian for the first time. "I'd like to know how you ever got to be a captain, anyway."

"You promoted him," Colonel Korn reminded sweetly, stifling a snicker. "Don't you remember?"

"Well, I never should have done it."

"I told you not to do it," Colonel Korn said. "But you just wouldn't listen to me."

"Gee whiz, will you stop rubbing it in?" Colonel Cathcart cried. He furrowed his brow and glowered at Colonel Korn through eyes narrow with suspicion, his fists clenched on his hips. "Say, whose side are you on, anyway?"

"Your side, Colonel. What other side could I be on?"

---

① tranquility:平静,安静
② emphatically:强调地,断然地,明显地

"Then stop picking on me, will you? Get off my back, will you?"

"I'm on your side, Colonel. I'm just loaded with patriotism."

"Well, just make sure you don't forget that." Colonel Cathcart turned away grudgingly① after another moment, incompletely reassured, and began striding the floor, his hands kneading② his long cigarette holder. He jerked a thumb toward Yossarian. "Let's settle with him. I know what I'd like to do with him. I'd like to take him outside and shoot him. That's what I'd like to do with him. That's what General Dreedle would do with him."

"But General Dreedle isn't with us any more," said Colonel Korn, "so we can't take him outside and shoot him."

Now that his moment of tension with Colonel Cathcart had passed, Colonel Korn relaxed again and resumed kicking softly against Colonel Cathcart's desk. He returned to Yossarian. "So we're going to send you home instead. It took a bit of thinking, but we finally worked out this horrible little plan for sending you home without causing too much dissatisfaction among the friends you'll leave behind. Doesn't that make you happy?"

"What kind of plan? I'm not sure I'm going to like it."

"I know you're not going to like it." Colonel Korn laughed, locking his hands contentedly on top of his head again. "You're going to loathe③ it. It really is odious and certainly will offend your conscience. But you'll agree to it quickly enough. You'll agree to it because it will send you home safe and sound in two weeks, and because you have no choice. It's that or a court-martial④. Take it or leave it."

Yossarian snorted. "Stop bluffing, Colonel. You can't court-martial me for desertion⑤ in the face of the enemy. It would make you look bad and you probably couldn't get a conviction."

"But we can court-martial you now for desertion from duty, since you went to Rome without a pass. And we could make it stick. If you think about it a minute, you'll see that you'd leave us no alternative. We can't simply let you

---

① grudgingly:勉强地
② knead:捏合
③ loathe:憎恨,厌恶
④ court-martial:军事法庭审判
⑤ desertion:擅离职守

keep walking around in open insubordination① without punishing you. All the other men would stop flying missions, too. No, you have my word for it. We will court-martial you if you turn our deal down, even though it would raise a lot of questions and be a terrible black eye for Colonel Cathcart."

Colonel Cathcart winced at the words "black eye" and, without any apparent premeditation②, hurled his slender onyx-and-ivory③ cigarette holder down viciously on the wooden surface on his desk. "Jesus Christ!" he shouted unexpectedly. "I hate this goddam cigarette holder!" The cigarette holder bounced off the desk to the wall, ricocheted④ across the window sill to the floor and came to a stop almost where he was standing. Colonel Cathcart stared down at it with an irascible scowl. "I wonder if it's really doing me any good."

"It's a feather in your cap with General Peckem, but a black eye for you with General Scheisskopf," Colonel Korn informed him with a mischievous⑤ look of innocence.

"Well, which one am I supposed to please?"

"Both."

"How can I please them both? They hate each other. How am I ever going to get a feather in my cap from General Scheisskopf without getting a black eye from General Peckem?"

"March."

"Yeah, March. That's the only way to please him. March. March." Colonel Cathcart grimaced⑥ sullenly. "Some generals! They're a disgrace to their uniforms. If people like those two can make general, I don't see how I can miss."

"You're going to go far." Colonel Korn assured him with a flat lack of conviction, and turned back chuckling to Yossarian, his disdainful merriment increasing at the sight of Yossarian's unyielding expression of antagonism and distrust. "And there you have the crux of the situation. Colonel Cathcart wants

---

① insubordination:不顺从,反抗
② premeditation:预谋,预先策划
③ onyx-and-ivory:玛瑙象牙
④ ricochet:指接触地面后的跳飞和反弹
⑤ mischievous:淘气的,恶作剧的
⑥ grimace:扮鬼脸

to be a general and I want to be a colonel, and that's why we have to send you home."

"Why does he want to be a general?"

"Why? For the same reason that I want to be a colonel. What else have we got to do? Everyone teaches us to aspire to higher things. A general is higher than a colonel, and a colonel is higher than a lieutenant colonel. So we're both aspiring. And you know, Yossarian, it's a lucky thing for you that we are. Your timing on this is absolutely perfect, but I suppose you took that factor into account in your calculations."

"I haven't been doing any calculating," Yossarian retorted.

"Yes, I really do enjoy the way you lie," Colonel Korn answered. "Won't it make you proud to have your commanding officer promoted to general—to know you served in an outfit that averaged more combat missions per person than any other? Don't you want to earn more unit citations and more oak leaf clusters for your Air Medal? Where's your 'sprit de corps?' Don't you want to contribute further to this great record by flying more combat missions? It's your last chance to answer yes."

"No."

"In that case, you have us over a barrel—" said Colonel Korn without rancor[①].

"He ought to be ashamed of himself!"

"—and we have to send you home. Just do a few little things for us, and—"

"What sort of things?" Yossarian interrupted with belligerent[②] misgiving.

"Oh, tiny, insignificant things. Really, this is a very generous deal we're making with you. We will issue orders returning you to the States—really, we will—and all you have to do in return is..."

"What? What must I do?"

Colonel Korn laughed curtly. "Like us."

Yossarian blinked. "Like you?"

"Like us."

---

① rancor:深仇,积怨,怨恨
② belligerent:交战的,卷入冲突的

"Like you?"

"That's right," said Colonel Korn, nodding, gratified immeasurably by Yossarian's guileless surprise and bewilderment. "Like us. Join us. Be our pal. Say nice things about us here and back in the States. Become one of the boys. Now, that isn't asking too much, is it?"

"You just want me to like you? Is that all?"

"That's all."

"That's all?"

"Just find it in your heart to like us."

Yossarian wanted to laugh confidently when he saw with amazement that Colonel Korn was telling the truth.

"That isn't going to be too easy," he sneered.

"Oh, it will be a lot easier than you think," Colonel Korn taunted in return, undismayed by Yossarian's barb.

"You'll be surprised at how easy you'll find it to like us once you begin." Colonel Korn hitched up the waist of his loose, voluminous trousers. The deep black grooves isolating his square chin from his jowls were bent again in a kind of jeering and reprehensible mirth. "You see, Yossarian, we're going to put you on easy street. We're going to promote you to major and even give you another medal. Captain Flume is already working on glowing press releases describing your valor over Ferrara, your deep and abiding loyalty to your outfit and your consummate dedication to duty. Those phrases are all actual quotations, by the way. We're going to glorify you and send you home a hero, recalled by the Pentagon[①] for morale and public-relations purposes. You'll live like a millionaire. Everyone will lionize you. You'll have parades in your honor and make speeches to raise money for war bonds. A whole new world of luxury awaits you once you become our pal. Isn't it lovely?"

Yossarian found himself listening intently to the fascinating elucidation[②] of details. "I'm not sure I want to make speeches."

"Then we'll forget the speeches. The important thing is what you say to people here." Colonel Korn leaned forward earnestly, no longer smiling. "We

---

① the Pentagon: 五角大楼
② elucidation: 说明,阐明

don't want any of the men in the group to know that we're sending you home as a result of your refusal to fly more missions. And we don't want General Peckem or General Scheisskopf to get wind of any friction between us, either. That's why we're going to become such good pals."

"What will I say to the men who asked me why I refused to fly more missions?"

"Tell them you had been informed in confidence that you were being returned to the States and that you were unwilling to risk your life for another mission or two. Just a minor disagreement between pals, that's all."

"Will they believe it?"

"Of course they'll believe it, once they see what great friends we've become and when they see the press releases and read the flattering things you have to say about me and Colonel Cathcart. Don't worry about the men. They'll be easy enough to discipline and control when you've gone. It's only while you're still here that they may prove troublesome. You know, one good apple can spoil the rest," Colonel Korn concluded with conscious irony. "You know—this would really be wonderful—you might even serve as an inspiration to them to fly more missions."

"Suppose I denounce you when I get back to the States?"

"After you've accepted our medal and promotion and all the fanfare[①]? No one would believe you, the Army wouldn't let you, and why in the world should you want to? You're going to be one of the boys, remember? You'll enjoy a rich, rewarding, luxurious, privileged existence. You'd have to be a fool to throw it all away just for a moral principle, and you're not a fool. Is it a deal?"

"I don't know."

"It's that or a court-martial."

"That's a pretty scummy trick I'd be playing on the men in the squadron[②], isn't it?"

"Odious," Colonel Korn agreed amiably, and waited, watching Yossarian patiently with a glimmer of private delight.

---

① fanfare:喧耀;号角齐鸣
② squadron:飞行中队

"But what the hell!" Yossarian exclaimed. "If they don't want to fly more missions, let them stand up and do something about it the way I did. Right?"

"Of course," said Colonel Korn.

"There's no reason I have to risk my life for them, is there?"

"Of course not."

Yossarian arrived at his decision with a swift grin. "It's a deal!" he announced jubilantly①.

"Great," said Colonel Korn with somewhat less cordiality② than Yossarian had expected, and he slid himself off Colonel Cathcart's desk to stand on the floor. He tugged the folds of cloth of his pants and undershorts free from his crotch and gave Yossarian a limp hand to shake. "Welcome aboard."

"Thanks, Colonel. I—"

"Call me Blackie, John. We're pals now."

"Sure, Blackie. My friends call me Yo-Yo. Blackie, I—"

"His friends call him Yo—Yo," Colonel Korn sang out to Colonel Cathcart. "Why don't you congratulate Yo—Yoon what a sensible move he's making?"

"That's a real sensible move you're making, Yo—Yo," Colonel Cathcart said, pumping Yossarian's hand with clumsy zeal③.

"Thank you, Colonel, I—"

"Call him Chuck," said Colonel Korn.

"Sure, call me Chuck," said Colonel Cathcart with a laugh that was hearty and awkward. "We're all pals now."

"Sure, Chuck."

"Exit smiling," said Colonel Korn, his hands on both their shoulders as the three of them moved to the door.

"Come on over for dinner with us some night, Yo—Yo," Colonel Cathcart invited hospitably. "How about tonight? In the group dining room."

"I'd love to, sir."

"Chuck," Colonel Korn corrected reprovingly.

"I'm sorry, Blackie. Chuck. I can't get used to it."

"That's all right, pal."

---

① jubilantly:喜庆地,欢呼地
② cordiality:热诚,诚挚
③ zeal:热心,热情

"Sure, pal."

"Thanks, pal."

"Don't mention it, pal."

"So long, pal."

Yossarian waved goodbye fondly to his new pals and sauntered out onto the balcony corridor, almost bursting into song the instant he was alone. He was home free: he had pulled it off; his act of rebellion had succeeded; he was safe, and he had nothing to be ashamed of to anyone. He started toward the staircase with a jaunty and exhilarated air. A private in green fatigues saluted him. Yossarian returned the salute happily, staring at the private with curiosity. He looked strangely familiar. When Yossarian returned the salute, the private in green fatigues turned suddenly into Nately's whore and lunged at him murderously with a bone-handled kitchen knife that caught him in the side below his upraised arm. Yossarian sank to the floor with a shriek, shutting his eyes in overwhelming terror as he saw the girl lift the knife to strike at him again. He was already unconscious when Colonel Korn and Colonel Cathcart dashed out of the office and saved his life by frightening her away.

Questions for Discussion

1. Throughout the novel, the idea of *Catch-22* is explained in a number of ways. What are some of them? Does any of them represent the real *Catch-22*, or are they all simple examples of a larger abstract idea? If *Catch-22* is an abstract concept, which explanation comes closest to it?
2. What do you think of the literary concept of the word "Catch-22"?

Unit 7　John Ashbery(1927 – 2017)

John Lawrence Ashbery was an American poet. Among the most respected of the postwar American poets are John Ashbery, the key figure of the surrealistic New York School of poetry. Renowned for its postmodern complexity and opacity, Ashbery's work still proves controversial. Ashbery stated that he wished his work to be accessible to as many people as possible, and not to be a private dialogue with himself. At the same time, he once joked that some critics still view him as "a harebrained, homegrown surrealist whose poetry defies even the rules and logic of Surrealism."

Langdon Hammer, chairman of the English Department at Yale University, wrote in 2008, "No figure looms so large in American poetry over the past 50 years as John Ashbery" and "No American poet has had a larger, more diverse vocabulary, not Whitman not Pound." Stephanie Burt, a poet and Harvard professor of English, has compared Ashbery to T. S. Eliot, calling Ashbery "the last figure whom half the English-language poets alive thought a great model, and the other half thought incomprehensible".

John Ashbery was the author of more than twenty-five collections of poetry, including "Self-Portrait in a Convex Mirror," which won the Pulitzer Prize, the National Book Award, and the National Book Critics Circle Award; *Selected Poems* (1985); and *Selected Later Poems* (2007), which was awarded the 2008 International Griffin Poetry Prize. Ashbery's honors included a MacArthur Fellowship and a Lifetime Achievement Award from the National Book Foundation in 2011.

The Pulitzer-prize winning work of poet John Ashbery who died in September of 2017. Its distinctive circular shape echoes the poem's inspiration—a round self-portrait by Italian painter Parmigianino (1503–1540).

Brief Introduction

John Ashberry won the Pulitzer Prize, the National Book Award, and the National Book Critics Circle Award for "Self-Portrait in a Convex Mirror". Ashbery reaffirms the poetic powers that have made him such an outstanding figure in contemporary literature. He continues his astonishing explorations of places where no one has ever been.

First released in 1975, "Self-Portrait in a Convex Mirror" is today regarded as one of the most important collections of poetry published in the last fifty years. These are poems "of breathtaking freshness and adventure in which dazzling orchestrations of language open up whole areas of consciousness no other American poet as ever begun to explore" (The New York Times).

Selected Reading

Self-Portrait in a Convex Mirror

As Parmigianino did it, the right hand
Bigger than the head, thrust at the viewer
And swerving easily away, as though to protect
What it advertises. A few leaded panes, old beams,
Fur, pleated muslin, a coral ring run together
In a movement supporting the face, which swims
Toward and away like the hand
Except that it is in repose. It is what is
Sequestered. Vasari says, "Francesco one day set himself
To take his own portrait, looking at himself from that purpose
In a convex mirror, such as is used by barbers . . .
He accordingly caused a ball of wood to be made
By a turner, and having divided it in half and
Brought it to the size of the mirror, he set himself
With great art to copy all that he saw in the glass,"
Chiefly his reflection, of which the portrait
Is the reflection, of which the portrait
Is the reflection once removed.

The glass chose to reflect only what he saw
Which was enough for his purpose: his image
Glazed, embalmed, projected at a 180-degree angle.
The time of day or the density of the light
Adhering to the face keeps it
Lively and intact in a recurring wave
Of arrival. The soul establishes itself.
But how far can it swim out through the eyes
And still return safely to its nest The surface
Of the mirror being convex, the distance increases

Significantly; that is, enough to make the point
That the soul is a captive, treated humanely, kept
In suspension, unable to advance much farther
Than your look as it intercepts the picture.

Pope Clement and his court were "stupefied"
By it, according to Vasari, and promised a commission
That never materialized. The soul has to stay where it is,
Even though restless, hearing raindrops at the pane,
The sighing of autumn leaves thrashed by the wind,
Longing to be free, outside, but it must stay
Posing in this place. It must move
As little as possible. This is what the portrait says.

But there is in that gaze a combination
Of tenderness, amusement and regret, so powerful
In its restraint that one cannot look for long.
The secret is too plain. The pity of it smarts,
Makes hot tears spurt: that the soul is not a soul,
Has no secret, is small, and it fits
Its hollow perfectly: its room, our moment of attention.
That is the tune but there are no words.
The words are only speculation
(From the Latin speculum, mirror):
They seek and cannot find the meaning of the music.

We see only postures of the dream,
Riders of the motion that swings the face
Into view under evening skies, with no
False disarray as proof of authenticity.
But it is life englobed.
One would like to stick one's hand
Out of the globe, but its dimension,
What carries it, will not allow it.

No doubt it is this, not the reflex
To hide something, which makes the hand loom large
As it retreats slightly. There is no way
To build it flat like a section of wall:
It must join the segment of a circle,
Roving back to the body of which it seems
So unlikely a part, to fence in and shore up the face
On which the effort of this condition reads
Like a pinpoint of a smile, a spark
Or star one is not sure of having seen
As darkness resumes. A perverse light whose
Imperative of subtlety dooms in advance its
Conceit to light up: unimportant but meant.

Francesco, your hand is big enough
To wreck the sphere, and too big,
One would think, to weave delicate meshes
That only argue its further detention.
(Big, but not coarse, merely on another scale,
Like a dozing whale on the sea bottom
In relation to the tiny, self-important ship
On the surface.) But your eyes proclaim
That everything is surface. The surface is what's there
And nothing can exist except what's there.
There are no recesses in the room, only alcoves,
And the window doesn't matter much, or that
Sliver of window or mirror on the right, even
As a gauge of the weather, which in French is
Le temps, the word for time, and which
Follows a course wherein changes are merely
Features of the whole. The whole is stable within
Instability, a globe like ours, resting
On a pedestal of vacuum, a ping-pong ball
Secure on its jet of water.

    And just as there are no words for the surface, that is,
    No words to say what it really is, that it is not
    Superficial but a visible core, then there is
    No way out of the problem of pathos vs. experience.
    You will stay on, restive, serene in
    Your gesture which is neither embrace nor warning
    But which holds something of both in pure
    Affirmation that doesn't affirm anything.

Questions for discussion

Analyze the title of Self – Portrait in a Convex Mirror.

Unit 8 Bob Dylan(May 24, 1941 –)

    Bob Dylan born Robert Allen Zimmerman is an American singer-songwriter, author, and painter, who has been an influential figure in popular music and culture for more than five decades. Much of his most celebrated work dates from the 1960s, when he became a reluctant "voice of a generation" with songs such as "Blowin' in the Wind" and "The Times They Are a-Changin" that became anthems for the Civil Rights Movement and anti-war movement. In 1965, he controversially abandoned his early fan-base in the American folk music revival, recording a six-minute single, "Like a Rolling Stone", which enlarged the scope of popular music.

    Dylan's lyrics incorporate a wide range of political, social, philosophical, and literary influences. They defied existing pop-music conventions and appealed to the burgeoning counterculture. His accomplishments as a recording artist and performer have been central to his career, but his songwriting is considered his greatest contribution.

    The Nobel Prize committee announced on October 13, 2016, that it would be awarding Dylan the Nobel Prize in Literature "for having created new poetic expressions within the great American song tradition". The New York Times reported: "Mr. Dylan, 75, is the first musician to win the award, and his selection on Thursday is perhaps the most radical choice in a history stretching back to 1901." Dylan is the only person in history apart from George Bernard Shaw to be a recipient of both an Academy Award and a Nobel prize.

Dylan has been described as one of the most influential figures of the 20th century, musically and culturally. He was included in the Time 100: The Most Important People of the Century where he was called "master poet, caustic social critic and intrepid, guiding spirit of the counterculture generation". In 2008, The Pulitzer Prize jury awarded him a special citation for "his profound impact on popular music and American culture, marked by lyrical compositions of extraordinary poetic power." President Barack Obama said of Dylan in 2012, "There is not a bigger giant in the history of American music." For 20 years, academics lobbied the Swedish Academy to give Dylan the Nobel Prize in Literature, which awarded it to him in 2016, making Dylan the first musician to be awarded the Literature Prize. Horace Engdahl, a member of the Nobel Committee, described Dylan's place in literary history.

Brief Introduction

"Blowin' in the Wind" is a song written by Bob Dylan in 1962 and released as a single and on his albumThe Freewheelin' Bob Dylan in 1963. Although it has been described as a protest song, it poses a series of rhetorical questions about peace, war, and freedom. The refrain "The answer, my friend, is blowin' in the wind" has been described as "impenetrably ambiguous: either the answer is so obvious it is right in your face, or the answer is as intangible as the wind". In 1994, the song was inducted into the Grammy Hall of Fame. In 2004, it was ranked number 14 on Rolling Stone magazine's list of the "500 Greatest Songs of All Time".

The song is also known as the "father of American folk rock" and one of the best and most famous of all his songs. In 1957, the Vietnam war broke out, the United States put a lot of manpower and material resources to the Vietnam war, resulting in heavy casualties. So there was an anti-war craze in American society. At the same time, folk songs are also popular in schools across the United States, many young people use the creation of folk songs to express the voice of the people. This song because cater to the social trend of thought at that time, so quickly swept the world.

Selected Reading

Blowing in the Wind

How many roads must a man walk down
Before you call him a man?
Yes, 'n' how many seas must a white dove sail
Before she sleeps in the sand
Yes, 'n' how many times must the cannon balls fly
Before they're forever banned
The answer, my friend, is blowin' in the wind,
The answer is blowin' in the wind.

How many times must a man look up
Before he can see the sky
Yes, 'n' how many ears must one man have
Before he can hear people cry
Yes, 'n' how many deaths will it take till he knows
That too many people have died
The answer, my friend, is blowin' in the wind,
The answer is blowin' in the wind.

How many years can a mountain exist
Before it's washed to the sea
Yes, 'n' how many years can some people exist
Before they're allowed to be free
Yes, 'n' how many times can a man turn his head,
Pretending he just doesn't see
The answer, my friend, is blowin' in the wind,
The answer is blowin' in the wind.

Questions for Discussion

Make an analysis of blowin' in the wind.

Unit 9 John Denver (1943 – 1997)

John Denver was an American singer-songwriter, record producer, actor, activist, and humanitarian, whose greatest commercial success was as a solo singer. Starting in the 1970s, Denver was one of the most popular acoustic artists of the decade and one of its best-selling artists. By 1974, he was firmly established as one of America's best-selling performers, and All Music has described Denver as "among the most beloved entertainers of his era".

Selected Reading

"Take Me Home, Country Road" has a prominent status as an iconic symbol of West Virginia, which it describes as "almost Heaven". In March 2014, it became one of several official state anthems of West Virginia. Similarly, the Blue Ridge Mountains are only peripherally associated with West Virgina, but do form the boundary between West Virginia and the State of Virginia for a few miles at Jefferson County.

"Take Me Home, Country Roads" received an enthusiastic response from West Virginians. The song is the theme song of West Virginia University and it has been performed during every home football pregame show since 1972.

Selected Reading

Take Me Home, Country Road

Almost heaven, West Virginia,
Blue ridge mountain, Shenandoah river,
Life is old there, older than the trees,
Younger than the mountains, growing like a breeze

Country roads, take me home
To the place I belong,
West Virginia,
Mountain mamma, take me home
Country roads

All my memories, gather round her
Miner's lady, stranger to blue water
Dark and dusty, painted on the sky

※ Chapter 7 American Literature Post-World War II ※

Misty taste of moonshine, teardrops in my eye

Country roads, take me home
To the place I belong,
West Virginia,
Mountain mamma, take me home
Country roads

I hear her voice in the morning hour she calls me
Radio reminds me of my home far away
Driving down the road I get a feeling
That I should have been home yesterday, yesterday

Country roads, take me home
To the place I belong,
West virginia,
Mountain mamma, take me home
Country roads

I hear her voice in the morning hour she calls me
Radio reminds me of my home far away
Driving down the road I get a feeling
That I should have been home yesterday, yesterday

Country roads, take me home
To the place I belong,
West Virginia,
Mountain mamma, take me home
Country roads
Take me home, country roads
Take me home, country roads

Questions for Discussion

Make an Analysis of "Take me home, country road".

Chapter 8

Canadian Literature

I. Historical Background

While various theories have been postulated for the origins of Canada, the name is now accepted from the St. Lawrence Iroquoian word kanata, meaning "village" or "settlement". In 1867, Canada was adopted as the legal name for the new country and was conferred as the country's title.

The history of Canada covers the period from the arrival of Paleo—Indians thousands of years ago to the present day. Canada has been inhabited for millennia by Aboriginal peoples.

In the late 15th century, French and British expeditions explored, and later settled along the Atlantic Coast. In 1867, Canada was formed as a federal dominion of four provinces and legal dependence on the British Parliament.

Over centuries, elements of Aboriginal, French, British and more recent immigrant customs have combined to form Canadian culture. Since the end of the WWⅡ, Canadians have supported multilateralism abroad and socioeconomic development domestically. Canada now consists of ten provinces and three territories and is governed as a parliamentary democracy and a constitutional monarchy with Queen Elizabeth Ⅱ as its head of state.

II. Literary Background

Canadian literature has a rather short history, a history of about 200years. Literary critics generally agree that the development of Canadian literature can be dividede into four periods or stages. From Aboriginal writing to Margaret Atwood, this is a complete English-language history of Canadian writing in English and French from its beginnings. Canadian literature is often divided into French-and English-language literatures, which are rooted in the literary traditions of France and Britain, respectively. Reflecting the country's dual origin and its official bilingualism, the literature of Canada can be split into two major divisions: English and French.

1. Major Periods in the history of British Literature

1.1 Colonial Period

The first period, "Colonial Period" began in the mid-16th century with the arrival of White settlers in the eastern part of Canada and ended in 1867, when Canada became the Dominion of Canada, or the Canadian Confederation. Literary works gave vivid descriptions of the hardships new immigrants encountered in their new environment. They also recorded the way of life and the customs of both the settlers and the North American Indians. Some of the works also described the sceneries and features of the newly established towns and villages in Canada, generally with the British readers in mind.

Mrs. Frances Brooke (1723 – 1789) can be considered as one of the eminent literary figures. She is remembered for her book, *The History of Emily Montague* consisting of 228 letters, the book gives detailed descriptions of the various aspects of Canada, including the manners and customs of the then Quebecois and Indians and the paradise-like scenery of places in Quebec.

1.2 Embryonic Period

The second period, which began with the founding of the Dominion in 1867 and ended around 1900, can be called the "Embryonic Period". The intellectuals among Canadians came to realize the importance of a national identity and have a sense of political and cultural independence. And some of them even raised the slogan "Canada First". Such patriotism was reflected in a lot of poems, the major form of literature in this period.

During that period, a number of published their patriotic poems, calling on the people to realize their obligations to their own newly emerging country. Among them was Sir Charles G. D. Roberts(1860 – 1943), who has been called the father of Canadian literature because of the patriotic nature of his poems, such as Canada and An Ode for the Canadian Confederacy. He is also remembered for his invention of the modern animal story, which relies heavily on observation of animal life.

1.3 Fledglingzo Period

The third period, "Fledglingzo Period" spanned the first half of the 20th century, up to the end of WW II, and a number of Canadian novelists emerged.

More and more Canadian poets came to the fore and held a distinguished place in Canadian literature were A. J. M. Smit (1902 – 1980), Francis Reginald Smith (1899 – 1985) A. M. Klein (1909 – 1972), Leo Kennedy (1907 – ?), E. J. Pratt (1882 – 1964) and Robert Finch (1900 – ?). The first four is known as the Montreal Group as they lived and wrote poetry there. The last two were from Toronto. They have been held in esteem because of the publication in 1936 of a collection of poems entitled New Provinces. Its publication has been regarded as a landmark in Canada's modern poetry.

The Fledgling Period also witnessed the initial prosperity of fiction writing. A number of Canadian novelists won worldwide recognition, the Canadian humorist Stephen Leacock (1869 – 1944), novelist (and play wright) Morley Callaghan (1903 – 1990) and Hugh MacLennan (1907 – 1990). As a humorist, Stephen Leacock achieved fame not only in Canada but also in other English speaking countries. The two best sellers by him are Sunshine Skerches of a Little Town (1912) and Acadian Adventures with the Idle Rich (1914).

1.4 Stage of Maturity

The fourth period, which were ushered in by the end of WWI and reached its height in the 60's, and has extended to present, can be described as a "Stage of Maturity." This maturity is reflected in the recognition of Canadian literature by the English speaking world first, and then by many other countries. It is also reflected in the appearance of courses on Canadian literature in Canadian universities, and in universities all over the world.

At present, Canadian literature is a variety of literature in its own right. It is neither a branch of British literature nor an affiliated part of the American literature.

2. Major themes of Canadian literature

Canada's literature often reflects the Canadian perspective on nature, frontier life, and Canada's position in the world. Canada's ethnic and cultural diversity are reflected in its literature, with many of its most prominent writers focusing on ethnic life minority identity, duality and cultural differences; themes are in contrast to environmental readings.

3. Contemporary Canadian literature: late 20th to 21st century

By the 1990s, Canadian literature was viewed as some of the world's best. Arguably, the best-known living Canadian writer internationally is Margaret Atwood, a prolific novelist, poet, and literary critic. Numerous other Canadian authors have accumulated international literary awards; including Nobel Laureate Alice Munro, who has been called the best living writer of short stories in English; and Booker Prize recipient Michael Ondaatje, who is perhaps best known for the novel The English Patient, which was adapted as a film of the same name that won the Academy Award for Best Picture.

4. Notable figures

One of the earliest "Canadian" writers is Thomas Chandler Haliburton (1796 – 1865), who is remembered for his comic character. The best-known living Canadian writer internationally is Margaret Atwood, a prolific novelist, poet, and literary critic, and her major works: *The Blind Assassin* 盲刺客, *Oryx and Crake* 末世男女, *The Year of the Flood* 水灾之年. This group, along with Alice Munro, who has been called the best living writer of short stories in English, was the first to elevate Canadian Literature to the world stage.

Canadian poet Leonard Cohen is perhaps best known as a folk singer and songwriter, with an international following. Canadian Author Farley Mowat was best known for his work "Never Cry Wolf", also author of "Lost in the Barrens" (1956), Governor General's Award-winning children's book. By the 1990s, Canadian literature was viewed as some of the world's best.

Unit 1　Red River Valley

Brief Introduction

"Red River Valley" is a folk song and cowboy music standard of uncertain origins that has gone by different names. It spreads in the northern red river area, it mainly shows the immigrants in the northern red river area residents here reclamation farming, construction of homes, the development of the city, and eventually the bison infested wasteland into the home of people's lives. It reviews the history of people's hard work and their yearning for a better life. It expresses the sorrow of a local woman (possibly a Métis) as her soldier lover prepares to return to the east.

The earliest known written manuscript of the lyrics, titled "The Red River Valley", bears the notations "Nemaha 1879" and "Harlan 1885." Nemaha and Harlan are the names of counties in Nebraska, and are also the names of towns in Iowa. Members of the Western Writers of America chose it as one of the Top 100 Western songs of all time.

Selected Reading

> From this valley they say you're going,
> I will miss your bright eyes and sweet smile,
> For they say you're taking the sunshine,
> That has brightened our path-way a while.
> I've been thinking a long time my darling,
> Of the sweet words you never would say.
> Now at last must my fond hopes all vanished.
> For they say you are going away.
> Come and sit by my side if you love me,
> Do not hasten to bid me adieu,
> But remember the Red River Valley,
> And the one who has loved you so true.

Unit 2 Margaret Laurence (1926 – 1987)

Appreciation

At night the lake was like black glass with a streak of amber which was the path of the moon. All around, the spruce trees grew tall and close-set, branches blackly sharp against the sky, which was lightened by a cold flickering of stars. Then the loons began their calling. They rose like phantom birds from the nests on the shore, and flew out onto the dark still surface of the water. 夜间的湖面看起来像一块黑色玻璃，只有一线水面因映照着月光才呈现出琥珀色，湖的周围到处密密丛丛地生长着高大的云杉树，在寒光闪烁的星空映衬下，云杉树的枝丫呈现出清晰的黑色剪影。过了一会儿，潜水鸟开始鸣叫。它们像幽灵般地从岸边的窝巢中腾起，飞往平静幽暗的湖面上。

Margaret Laurence is one of Canada's most well-known female writers of the 20th century, often referred to as "godmother" of contemporary Canadian literature. During her lifetime, she has written numerous fictions, children books, book reviews and essays. She has been awarded the Governor General's Award twice and nominated for the Nobel Prize in Literature in 1982.

Margaret Laurence was born in a small prairie town of Neepawa, Manitoba in 1926. Her father was a local lawyer and her mother a music teacher. When she was four, her mother died and she was brought up by her aunt—an intelligent woman who founded the Neepawa Public Library and who had encouraged Margaret to write.

Margaret Laurence had been an assistant editor and a reporter writing for prestigious newspapers when she was in college. In 1947, she married Jack Laurence, a civil engineer and three years later the couple moved to Somali in East Africa. The experience in Africa offers her rich materials for her writing career. She wrote short stories and travel books about Africa. In 1954 the Somali government published *A Tree of Poverty*《贫穷树》, her translation of Somali folktales and poetry, the first such collection ever published in English. In 1952, the couple went to the Gold Coast (now known as Ghana); there she began her first novel, *This Side Jordan*《约旦河比岸》, which was published in 1960. Her other well-known novels include *The Stone Angel*《石头天使》, *A Jest of God*《上帝的玩笑》, *The Fire-Dwellers*《火中人》, and *The Diviners*《占卜者》.

Brief Introduction

"The Loons" (1970) is a story about the plight of Piquette Tonnerre, a girl from a native Indian family. Impoverished and marginalized, her people were unable to live independently in a respectable and dignified way. Piquette's family is falling apart. Her mother has left them and her father is jobless and always gets drunk and involved in fights. Concerned with her health condition, the narrator's family invites Piquette, then 13 with a bone disease, to stay with them for a while near Diamond Lake. Piquette stays aloof and remains a mystery to the narrator. Four years later, when the narrator sees her again in a town pub, she is a girl of 17, cynical about the place and the people. She is looking forward to a new start, a prospective marriage with a white man. However, later from the narrator's conversation with her mother, the narrator learns that she is discarded and killed in a fire accident.

The loon is a common name for five species of diving birds having heavy, straight, sharp-edged bills; heavy and elongated bodies; short, slender, pointed wings; and short, stiff tails. Their legs are short, and the three front toes are webbed. Because their legs are placed far back on the body, loons cannot walk on land. They therefore place their nests along the shores of lakes or in marshes and swamps, where they can slide directly into the water. The nests are usually loose structures made of aquatic vegetation, in which the female lays two dark brownish eggs.

The story compels the reader to see the connection between the aboriginal bird and the native girl and shows deep concerns for the pathetic fate of both.

Selected Reading

The Loons

Just below Manawaka①, where the Wachakwa River ran brown and noisy over the pebbles, the scrub oak and grey-green willow and chokecherry bushes grew in a dense thicket. In a clearing② at the centre of the thicket stood the Tonnerre family's shack③. The basis of this dwelling was a small square cabin made of poplar poles and chinked④ with mud, which had been built by Jules Tonnerre some fifty years before, when he came back from Batoche with a bullet in his thigh, the year that Louis Riel⑤ was hung and the voices of the Metis entered their long silence. Jules had only intended to stay the winter in the Wachakwa Valley, but the family was still there in the thirties, when I was a child. As the Tonnerres had increased, their settlement had been added to, until the clearing at the foot of the town hill was a chaos of lean-tos⑥, wooden packing cases, warped lumber⑦, discarded car types, ramshackle⑧ chicken coops⑨, tangled strands of barbed⑩ wire and rusty tin cans.

The Tonnerres were French halfbreeds⑪, and among themselves they spoke

---

① Manawaka: 加拿大中西部曼尼托巴省(Manitoba)的一个小镇,马纳瓦卡
② clearing: an area of land cleared of trees,林中无树木的空地
③ shack: 棚屋
④ chinked: 裂缝的
⑤ Louis Riel (1844 – 1885): 路易斯·瑞尔,加拿大高原草原梅蒂人(Metis,印第安人和法国人的混血)领袖,分别于 1869 – 1870 和 1884 – 1885 领导了两次针对加拿大政府的抵抗运动。后在 Batoche 战役中被政府军队镇压,受审并被宣判死刑
⑥ lean-to: 单坡顶的小屋
⑦ warped lumber: 变形的木材
⑧ ramshackle: 东倒西歪的
⑨ coop: 鸡笼
⑩ barbed: 带刺的
⑪ halfbreed: 混血儿

a patois① that was neither Cree② nor French. Their English was broken and full of obscenities③. They did not belong among *the Cree of the Galloping Mountain reservation*④, further north, and they did not belong among the Scots-Irish and Ukrainians of Manawaka, either. They were, as my Grandmother MacLeod would have put it, neither flesh, fowl, nor good salt herring⑤. When their men were not working at odd jobs or as section hands⑥ on the C. P. R. ⑦ they lived on relief. In the summers, one of the Tonnerre youngsters, with a face that seemed totally unfamiliar with laughter, would knock at the doors of the town's brick houses and offer for sale a lard-pail full of bruised wild strawberries, and if he got as much as a quarter he would grab the coin and run before the customer had time to change her mind. Sometimes old Jules, or his son Lazarus, would get mixed up in a Saturday-night brawl⑧, and would hit out at whoever was nearest or howl drunkenly among the offended shoppers on Main Street, and then the Mountie⑨ would put them for the night in the barred cell⑩ underneath the Court House, and the next morning they would be quiet again.

Piquette Tonnerre, the daughter of Lazarus, was in my class at school. She was older than I, but she had failed several grades⑪, perhaps because her attendance had always been sporadic⑫ and her interest in schoolwork negligible⑬. Part of the reason she had missed a lot of school was that she had

---

① patois：方言，土语
② Cree：北美印第安人得克里族
③ obscenities：淫秽
④ reservation：保留地
⑤ Neither flesh, fowl, nor good salt herring：also "neither fish, flesh, nor fowl" meaning not anything definite or recognizable 不伦不类
⑥ section hands：(section gang) a crew of persons who do maintenance work on a railroad section. 铁路护路工
⑦ C. P. R.：Canadian Pacific Railroad
⑧ brawl：打斗，争吵
⑨ Mountie：a member of the Royal Canadian Mounted Police，加拿大骑警
⑩ barred cell：栓上门的牢房
⑪ failed several grades：failed in schoolwork and had to repeat the same grade
⑫ sporadic：零星的，偶尔的
⑬ negligible：可忽略不计的

had tuberculosis① of the bone, and had once spent many months in hospital. I knew this because my father was the doctor who had looked after her. Her sickness was almost the only thing I knew about her, however. Otherwise, she existed for me only as a vaguely embarrassing presence, with her hoarse voice and her clumsy limping② walk and her grimy cotton dresses that were always miles too long. I was neither friendly nor unfriendly towards her. She dwelt and moved somewhere within my scope of vision, but I did not actually notice her very much until that peculiar summer when I was eleven.

"I don't know what to do about that kid," my father said at dinner one evening. "Piquette Tonnerre, I mean. The damn③ bone's flared up④ again. I've had her in hospital for quite a while now, and it's under control all right, but I hate like the dickens to send her home again."

"Couldn't you explain to her mother that she has to rest a lot?" my mother said.

"The mother's not there," my father replied. "She took off a few years back. Can't say I blame her. Piquette cooks for them, and she says Lazarus would never do anything for himself as long as she's there. Anyway, I don't think she'd take much care of herself, once she got back. She's only thirteen, after all. Beth, I was thinking—What about taking her up to Diamond Lake with us this summer? A couple of months rest would give that bone a much better chance."

My mother looked stunned.

"But Ewen—what about Roddie and Vanessa?"

"She's not contagious⑤," my father said. "And it would be company for Vanessa."

"Oh dear," my mother said in distress, "I'll bet anything she has nits⑥ in her hair."

"For Pete's sake," my father said crossly, "do you think Matron would let

---

① tuberculosis: 肺结核
② limping: 无力的
③ damn: 该死
④ flare up: 发炎
⑤ contagious: 传染的
⑥ nits: 虱子

her stay in the hospital for all this time like that? Don't be silly, Beth."

Grandmother MacLeod, her delicately featured face as rigid as a cameo①, now brought her mauve-veined hands together as though she were about to begin prayer.

"Ewen, if that half breed youngster comes along to Diamond Lake, I'm not going," she announced. "I'll go to Morag's for the summer."

I had trouble in stifling② my urge to laugh, for my mother brightened visibly and quickly tried to hide it. If it came to a choice between Grandmother MacLeod and Piquette, Piquette would win hands down, nits or not.

"It might be quite nice for you, at that," she mused③. "You haven't seen Morag for over a year, and you might enjoy being in the city for a while. Well, Ewen dear, you do what you think best. If you think it would do Piquette some good, then we'll be glad to have her, as long as she behaves herself."

So it happened that several weeks later, when we all piled into④ my father's old Nash⑤, surrounded by suitcases and boxes of provisions and toys for my ten-month-old brother, Piquette was with us and Grandmother MacLeod, miraculously, was not. My father would only be staying at the cottage for a couple of weeks, for he had to get back to his practice⑥, but the rest of us would stay at Diamond Lake until the end of August.

Our cottage was not named, as many were, "Dew Drop Inn" or "Bide-a-Wee," or "Bonnie Doon". The sign on the roadway bore in austere⑦ letters only our name, MacLeod. It was not a large cottage, but it was on the lakefront. You could look out the windows and see, through the filigree⑧ of the spruce⑨ trees, the water glistening greenly as the sun caught it. All around the cottage

---

① cameo：浮雕
② stifle：克制
③ muse：若有所思地说
④ pile into：把……摞起来
⑤ Nash：former make of automobiles
⑥ practice：行医工作
⑦ austere：简陋的
⑧ filigree：银丝细工饰品
⑨ spruce：云杉

were ferns①, and sharp-branched raspberry② bushes, and moss that had grown over fallen tree trunks. If you looked carefully among the weeds and grass, you could find wild strawberry plants which were in white flower now and in another month would bear fruit, the fragrant globes hanging like miniature③ scarlet lanterns④ on the thin hairy stems. The two grey squirrels were still there, gossiping at us from the tall spruce beside the cottage, and by the end of the summer they would again be tame enough to take pieces of crust from my hands. The broad moose antlers that hung above the back door were a little more bleached⑤ and fissured⑥ after the winter, but otherwise everything was the same. I raced joyfully around my kingdom, greeting all the places I had not seen for a year. My brother, Roderick, who had not been born when we were here last summer, sat on the car rug in the sunshine and examined a brown spruce cone⑦, meticulously⑧ turning it round and round in his small and curious hands. My mother and father toted the luggage from car to cottage, exclaiming over how well the place had wintered⑨, no broken windows, thank goodness, no apparent damage from storm-felled branches or snow.

Only after I had finished looking around did I notice Piquette. She was sitting on the swing her lame leg held stiffly out, and her other foot scuffing⑩ the ground as she swung slowly back and forth. Her long hair hung black and straight around her shoulders, and her broad coarse-featured face bore no expression—it was blank, as though she no longer dwelt within her own skull, as though she had gone elsewhere.

I approached her very hesitantly.

"Want to come and play?"

---

① fern：蕨类植物
② raspberry：覆盆子，树莓
③ miniature：小型的
④ lantern：灯笼
⑤ bleach：染白
⑥ fissure：裂缝
⑦ cone：锥形球果
⑧ meticulously：注意细节地，非常仔细地
⑨ winter：不及物动词 pass the winter
⑩ scuff：摩擦

Piquette looked at me with a sudden flash of scorn.

"I ain't a kid①," she said.

Wounded, I stamped angrily away, swearing I would not speak to her for the rest of the summer. In the days that followed, however, Piquette began to interest me, and I began to want to interest her. My reasons did not appear bizarre to me. Unlikely as it may seem, I had only just realised that the Tonnerre family, whom I had always heard called half breeds, were actually Indians, or as near as made no difference. My acquaintance with Indians was not extensive. I did not remember ever having seen a real Indian, and my new awareness that Piquette sprang from the people of Big Bear and Poundmaker, of Tecumseh, of the Iroquois who had eaten Father Brébeuf's② heart—all this gave her an instant attraction in my eyes. I was devoted reader of Pauline Johnson at this age, and sometimes would orate③ aloud and in an exalted④ voice, *West Wind, blow from your prairie nest; Blow from the mountains, blow from the west*⑤—and so on. It seemed to me that Piquette must be in some way a daughter of the forest, a kind of junior prophetess⑥ of the wilds, who might impart⑦ to me, if I took the right approach, some of the secrets which she undoubtedly knew—where the whippoorwill⑧ made her nest, how the coyote reared her young, or whatever it was that it said in Hiawatha⑨.

I set about gaining Piquette's trust. She was not allowed to go swimming, with her bad leg, but I managed to lure her down to the beach—or rather, she came because there was nothing else to do. The water was always icy, for the

---

① I ain't a kid：(口语) I am not a kid (like you)

② Father Brébeuf (1593 – 1649)：Jesuit missionary to the Hurons; Tecumseh (1768 – 1813), chief of the Shawnee; Big Bear and Poundmake (1842 – 1886), leader of the Cree. 北美洲印第安土著民族，休伦部落、肖尼族、克里族

③ orate：长篇大论地演讲

④ exalt：提升

⑤ West Wind, blow from your prairie nest; Blow from the mountains, blow from the west：the first two lines from "The Song My Paddle Sings" by Pauline Johnson (1861 – 1913), Canadian poet who was the daughter of an English woman and a Mohawk chief

⑥ prophetess：女预言家

⑦ impart：传授

⑧ whippoorwill：北美洲夜鹰

⑨ Hiawatha：Romantic poem about Indians by Henry Wadsworth Longfellow (1807 – 1882)

lake was fed by springs, but I swam like a dog, thrashing① my arms and legs around at such speed and with such an output of energy that I never grew cold. Finally, when I had enough, I came out and sat beside Piquette on the sand. When she saw me approaching, her hands squashed② flat the sand castle she had been building, and she looked at me sullenly③, without speaking.

"Do you like this place?" I asked, after a while, intending to lead on from there into the question of forest lore.

Piquette shrugged. "It's okay. Good as anywhere."

"I love it," I said. "We come here every summer."

"So what?" Her voice was distant, and I glanced at her uncertainly, wondering what I could have said wrong.

"Do you want to come for a walk?" I asked her. "We wouldn't need to go far. If you walk just around the point there, you come to a bay where great big reeds grow in the water, and all kinds of fish hang around there. Want to? Come on."

She shook her head.

"Your dad said I ain't supposed to do no more walking than I got to." I tried another line.

"I bet you know a lot about the woods and all that, eh?" I began respectfully.

Piquette looked at me from her large dark unsmiling eyes.

"I don't know what in hell you're talkin' about," she replied. "You nuts④ or somethin'? If you mean where my old man, and me, and all them live, you better shut up, by Jesus, you hear?"

I was startled and my feelings were hurt, but I had a kind of dogged perseverance⑤. I ignored her rebuff⑥.

"You know something, Piquette? There's loons here, on this lake. You can see their nests just up the shore there, behind those logs. At night, you can hear

---

① thrash：使劲晃动
② squash：把……压扁
③ sullenly：闷闷不乐地
④ You nuts：俚语 Are you crazy? 的意思。somethin 是 something 不标准发音的写法
⑤ perseverance：坚持不懈
⑥ rebuff：断然拒绝

them even from the cottage, but It's better to listen from the beach. My dad says we should listen and try to remember how they sound, because in a few years when more cottages are built at Diamond Lake and more people come in, the loons will go away."

Piquette was picking up stones and snail shells and then dropping them again.

"Who gives a good goddamn?" she said.

It became increasingly obvious that, as an Indian, Piquette was a dead loss. That evening I went out by myself, scrambling① through the bushes that overhung② the steep path, my feet slipping on the fallen spruce needles that covered the ground. When I reached the shore, I walked along the firm damp sand to the small pier that my father had built, and sat down there. I heard someone else crashing through the undergrowth and the bracken③, and for a moment I thought Piquette had changed her mind, but it turned out to be my father. He sat beside me on the pier and we waited, without speaking.

At night the lake was like black glass with a streak of amber which was the path of the moon. All around, the spruce trees grew tall and close—set, branches blackly sharp against the sky, which was lightened by a cold flickering④ of stars. Then the loons began their calling. They rose like phantom⑤ birds from the nests on the shore, and flew out onto the dark still surface of the water.

No one can ever describe that ululating⑥ sound, the crying of the loons, and no one who has heard it can ever forget it. Plaintive⑦, and yet with a quality of chilling mockery⑧, those voices belonged to a world separated by aeon⑨ from our neat world of summer cottages and the lighted lamps of home.

"They must have sounded just like that," my father remarked, "before any

---

① scramble: 爬
② overhung: 悬垂于……之上
③ bracken: 欧洲蕨
④ flickering: 闪烁
⑤ phantom: 幽灵
⑥ ululatie: 悲泣
⑦ plaintive: 悲伤的
⑧ mockery: 嘲讽
⑨ aeon: 极漫长的时期

person ever set foot here." Then he laughed. "You could say the same, of course, about sparrows① or chipmunk②, but somehow it only strikes you that way with the loons."

"I know," I said.

Neither of us suspected that this would be the last time we would ever sit here together on the shore, listening. We stayed for perhaps half an hour, and then we went back to the cottage. My mother was reading beside the fireplace. Piquette was looking at the burning birch log, and not doing anything.

"You should have come along," I said, although in fact I was glad she had not.

"Not me," Piquette said. "You wouldn'catch me walkin'way down there jus' for a bunch of squawkin' birds."

Piquette and I remained ill at ease with one another. I felt I had somehow failed my father, but I did not know what was the matter, nor why she would not or could not respond when I suggested exploring the woods or playing house. I thought it was probably her slow and difficult walking that held her back. She stayed most of the time in the cottage with my mother, helping her with the dishes or with Roddie, but hardly ever talking. Then the Duncans arrived at their cottage, and I spent my days with Mavis, who was my best friend. I could not reach Piquette at all, and I soon lost interest in trying. But all that summer she remained as both a reproach and a mystery to me.③

That winter my father died of pneumonia, after less than a week's illness. For some time I saw nothing around me, being completely immersed in my own pain and my mother's. When I looked outward once more, I scarcely noticed that Piquette Tonnerre was no longer at school. I do not remember seeing her at all until four years later, one Saturday night when Mavis and I were having Cokes in the Regal Café④. The jukebox⑤ was booming like tuneful⑥ thunder, and

---

① sparrow: 麻雀
② chipmunk: 金花鼠
③ she remained as both a reproach and a mystery to me: I blamed myself for being unable to make Piquette's response warmer and at the same time found her mysterious
④ Regal Café: 咖啡店的名字
⑤ jukebox: 投币式自动点唱机
⑥ tuneful: 音调优美的

beside it, leaning lightly on its chrome① and its rainbow glass, was a girl.

  Piquette must have been seventeen then, although she looked about twenty. I stared at her, astounded② that anyone could have changed so much. Her face, so stolid and expressionless before, was animated③ now with a gaiety④ that was almost violent. She laughed and talked very loudly with the boys around her. Her lipstick was bright carmine⑤, and her hair was cut short and frizzily⑥ permed⑦. She had not been pretty as a child, and she was not pretty now, for her features were still heavy and blunt⑧. But her dark and slightly slanted⑨ eyes were beautiful, and her skin-tight skirt and orange sweater displayed to enviable advantage a soft and slender⑩ body.

  She saw me, and walked over. She teetered a little, but it was not due to her once-tubercular⑪ leg, for her limp was almost gone.

  "Hi, Vanessa," Her voice still had the same hoarseness. "Long time no see, eh?"

  "Hi," I said "Where've you been keeping yourself, Piquette?"

  "Oh, I been around," she said. "I been away almost two years now. Been all over the place—Winnipeg, Regina, Saskatoon⑫. Jesus, what I could tell you! I come back this summer, but I ain't stayin'. You kids go in to the dance?"

  "No," I said abruptly⑬, for this was a sore⑭ point with me. I was fifteen, and thought I was old enough to go to the Saturday-night dances at the

---

① chrome：镀铬层
② astounded：震惊的
③ animated：活跃的,欢乐的
④ gaiety：快乐
⑤ carmine：深红色的
⑥ frizzily：满是小卷地
⑦ permed：烫出卷发的
⑧ blunt：钝的
⑨ slanted：歪斜的
⑩ slender：细长的
⑪ tubercular：患结核的
⑫ Winnipeg, Regina, Saskatoon：(加拿大城市)温尼伯,里贾纳市,萨斯卡通市
⑬ abruptly：突然
⑭ sore：痛的

Flamingo①. My mother, however, thought otherwise.

"Y' oughta come," Piquette said. "I never miss one. It's just about the on'y thing in this jerkwater② town that's any fun. Boy, you couldn' catch me stayin' here. I don' give a shit③ about this place. It stinks④."

She sat down beside me, and I caught the harsh over-sweetness of her perfume.

"Listen, you wanna know something, Vanessa?" she confided, her voice only slightly blurred. "Your dad was the only person in Manawaka that ever done anything good to me."

I nodded speechlessly. I was certain she was speaking the truth. I knew a little more than I had that summer at Diamond Lake, but I could not reach her now any more than I had then. I was ashamed, ashamed of my own timidity⑤, the frightened tendency to look the other way⑥. Yet I felt no real warmth towards her—I only felt that I ought to, because of that distant summer and because my father had hoped she would be company for me, or perhaps that I would be for her, but it had not happened that way. At this moment, meeting her again, I had to admit that she repelled and embarrassed me, and I could not help despising the self-pity⑦ in her voice. I wished she would go away. I did not want to see her did not know what to say to her. It seemed that we had nothing to say to one another.

"I'll tell you something else," Piquette went on. "All the old bitches an' biddies⑧ in this town will sure be surprised. I'm getting' married this fall—my boy friend, he's an English fella, works in the stockyards in the city there, a

---

① Flamingo: 酒吧名字"火烈鸟"
② jerkwater: it refers to a train on an early branch railroad. When used as an adjective it means small, unimportant
③ I don't give a shit: once a taboo but now a colloquial sang, meaning "I don't care a bit."
④ stink: 发臭
⑤ timidity: 怯懦
⑥ to look the other way: to avoid the real issue
⑦ self-pity: By stating that Vanessa's father was the only person that had ever done anything good to her, Piquette was saying that almost everybody treated her badly
⑧ All the old bitches an' biddies: 俚语 all the old malicious, bad-tempered, gossiping women.

very tall guy, got blond wavy hair. Gee, is he ever handsome. Got this real classy① name. Alvin Gerald Cummings—some handle②, eh? They call him Al."

For the merest instant, then I saw her③. I really did see her, for the first and only time in all the years we had both lived in the same town. Her defiant face, momentarily, became unguarded and unmasked, and in her eyes there was a terrifying hope.

"Gee, Piquette—" I burst out awkwardly, "that's swell④. That's really wonderful. Congratulations—good luck—I hope you'll be happy—"

As I mouthed⑤ the conventional phrases, I could only guess how great her need must have been, that she had been forced to seek the very things she so bitterly rejected.

When I was eighteen, I left Manawaka and went away to college. At the end of my first year, I came back home for the summer. I spent the first few days in talking non-stop with my mother, as we exchanged all the news that somehow had not found its way into letters—what had happened in my life and what had happened here in Manawaka while I was away. My mother searched her memory for events that concerned people I knew.

"Did I ever write you about Piquette Tonnerre, Vanessa?" she asked one morning.

"No, I don't think so," I replied. "Last I heard of her, she was going to marry some guy in the city. Is she still there?"

My mother looked perturbed⑥, and it was a moment before she spoke, as though she did not know how to express what she had to tell and wished she did not need to try.

"She's dead," she said at last. Then, as I stared at her, "Oh, Vanessa, when it happened, I couldn't help thinking of her as she was that summer—so sullen and gauche⑦ and badly dressed. I couldn't help wondering if we could

---

① classy: 俚语 first class, elegant, fine
② some handle: a special name. handle: (colloquial) a person's name, nickname or title
③ I saw her: I saw her as what she really was without her usual pretence
④ swell: 俚语 excellent
⑤ mouth: to say, especially, in an affected, oratorical, insincere manner
⑥ perturbed: 不安的
⑦ gauche: 不擅交际的

have done something more at that time—but what could we do? She used to be around in the cottage there with me all day, and honestly it was all I could do to get a word out of her. She didn't even talk to your father very much, although I think she liked him in her way."

"What happened?" I asked.

"Either her husband left her, or she left him," my mother said. "I don't know which. Anyway, she came back here with two youngsters, both only babies—they must have been born very close together. She kept house, I guess, for Lazarus and her brothers, down in the valley there, in the old Tonnerre place. I used to see her on the street sometimes, but she never spoke to me. She'd put on an awful lot of weight, and she looked a mess, to tell you the truth, a real slattern①, dressed any old how. She was up in court a couple of times—drunk and disorderly, of course. One Saturday night last winter, during the coldest weather, Piquette was alone in the shack with the children. The Tonnerres made home brew② all the time, so I've heard, and Lazarus said later she'd been drinking most of the day when he and the boys went out that evening. They had an old woodstove there—you know the kind, with exposed pipes. The shack caught fire. Piquette didn't get out, and neither did the children."

I did not say anything. As so often with Piquette, there did not seem to be anything to say. There was a kind of silence around the image in my mind of the fire and the snow, and I wished I could put from my memory the look that I had seen once in Piquette's eyes.

I went up to Diamond Lake for a few days that summer, with Mavis and her family. The MacLeod cottage had been sold after my father's death, and I did not even go to look at it, not wanting to witness my long-ago kingdom possessed now by strangers. But one evening I went clown to the shore by myself.

The small pier③ which my father had built was gone, and in its place there was a large and solid pier built by the government, for Galloping Mountain was now a national park, and Diamond Lake had been re-named Lake Wapakata, for it was felt that an Indian name would have a greater appeal to tourists. The one

---

① slattern：邋遢的女人
② brew：啤酒
③ pier：凸式码头

store had become several dozen, and the settlement had all the attributes① of a flourishing resort—hotels, a dance-hall, cafes with neon signs, the penetrating odours of potato chips and hot dogs.

I sat on the government pier and looked out across the water. At night the lake at least was the same as it had always been, darkly shining and bearing within its black glass the streak of amber that was the path of the moon. There was no wind that evening, and everything was quiet all around me. It seemed too quiet, and then I realized that the loons were no longer here. I listened for some time, to make sure, but never once did I hear that long-drawn call, half mocking and half plaintive, spearing through the stillness across the lake.

I did not know what had happened to the birds. Perhaps they had gone away to some far place of belonging. Perhaps they had been unable to find such a place, and had simply died out, having ceased to care any longer whether they lived or not. I remembered how Piquette had scorned to come along, when my father and I sat there and listened to the lake birds. It seemed to me now that in some unconscious and totally unrecognized way, Piquette might have been the only one, after all, who had heard the crying of the loons.

Questions for Discussion

1. What kind of character is Piquette?
2. What did the narrator's father propose doing with Piquette and why?
3. What was the reactions to the narrator's mother to the proposal and why?
4. What did the narrator ask Piquette when they were together? Why did she think that Piquette knew a lot about the woods?
5. The narrator says that all that summer Piquette remained as both "a reproach and a mystery" to her. Why does she say so?
6. When the narrator says, "For the merest instant, then, I saw her." What does she mean?
7. How is the disappearance of the loons related to Piquette's death?
8. What is the symbolic value of the loons to Vanessa, the narrator?

---

① attribute: 属性,标志

Unit 3   Alice Munro (1931 –)

Appreciation

While she was running away from him—now—Clark still kept his place in her life. But when she was finished running away, when she just went on, what would she put in his place? What else—who else—could ever be so vivid a challenge? 在她正在逃离他的时候——也就是此刻——克拉克仍然在她的生活里占据着一个位置。可是等逃离一结束,她自顾自往前走自己的路时,她又用什么来取代他的位置呢? 又能有什么别的东西——别的人——能成为如此清晰鲜明的一个挑战呢?

Alice Munro, the Canadian female short story writer and the winner of 2013 Nobel Prize in Literature for her lifetime body of work, is universally regarded as "master of the contemporary short story" and also dubbed "Canadian Chekhov".

Alice Munro was born in Wingham, Ontario in July, 1931. When she was a teenager, she started writing and published her first story *The Dimensions of a Shadow*. During her fruitful writing career, she has published eleven collections of stories, a volume of selected stories and a novel. She also gained other awards and prizes including Canada's Governor General's Award in 1968, 1978, and 1986 respectively for *Dance of the Happy Shades*, *Who Do You Think You Are?* and *The Progress of Love*, Canadian Booksellers Award in 1971 for *Lives of Girls and Women*, Man Booker Prize in 1980 for *The Beggar Maid*, Man Booker International Prize for her lifetime body of work in 2009, and Rogers Writers Trust Fiction Prize for *Runaway* in 2004.

Alice Munro puts most of her stories in the setting of small town and narrates the life of people who live there, esp. the life of females. She excels in narrative and it is through this strategy that she displays the dilemma, confusion, bafflement and struggle of girls and married women.

Munro writes about the human condition and relationships seen through the lens of daily life, generally regarded as one of the world's foremost writers of fiction,

Brief Introduction

Runaway tells a story about a young woman who wants to leave her husband but ends up coming back to him. Carla, an 18-year-old girl, had a strong dislike for her parents and despised everything that they had and they did. In order to get rid of her parents, she chose to elope with her boyfriend Clark, hoping to live a new and free life. They lived in a remote town in Ontario, making a living by providing trail rides lessons to people nearby and helping take care of their neighbors' horses, but their business was not good and they could only live by. As a result, Carla had to help Mrs. Jamieson do some household chores in order to provide some subsides for their life. When Mr. Clark learned from the newspaper that Mrs. Jamieson's deceased husband had been a famous poet and had ever been awarded a handsome sum of money, he began to persuade Carla to blackmail Mrs. Jamieson by saying that her husband had sexually harassed her before he died. Carla didn't want to do that. Once at Mrs. Jamieson's home, Carla complained to her that how painful she felt living with Clark and she wanted to leave him. On hearing that, Mrs. Jamieson would like to give her some money and help her to start a new life in Toronto. Carla then took the bus and left the town, making her mind to pursue a new life and find a real herself. However, she finally lost courage to leave and came back to Clark.

Selected Reading

Runaway

Carla had kept her head down until the bus was clear of town. The windows were tinted, nobody could see in, but she had to guard herself against seeing out. Lest Clark appear. Coming out of a store or waiting to cross the street, all ignorant of her abandoning him, thinking this an ordinary afternoon. No, thinking it the afternoon when their scheme—his scheme—was put in motion, eager to know how far she had got with it.

Once they were out in the country she looked up, breathed deeply, took account of the fields, which were slightly violet-tinted through the glass. Mrs. Jamieson's presence had surrounded her with some kind of remarkable safety and sanity[①] and had made her escape seem the most rational thing you could imagine, in fact the only self-respecting thing that a person in Carla's shoes could do. Carla had felt herself capable of an unaccustomed confidence, even of a mature sense of humor, revealing her life to Mrs. Jamieson in a way that seemed bound to gain sympathy and yet to be ironic and truthful. And adapted

---

① sanity: 心智健全

to live up to what, as far as she could see, were Mrs. Jamieson's—Sylvia's—expectations. She did have a feeling that it would be possible to disappoint Mrs. Jamieson, who struck her as a most sensitive and rigorous person, but she thought that she was in no danger of doing that.

If she didn't have to be around her for too long.

The sun was shining, as it had been for some time. When they sat at lunch it had made the wineglasses sparkle. No rain had fallen since early morning. There was enough of a wind blowing to lift the roadside grass, the flowering weeds, out of their drenched[①] clumps. Summer clouds, not rain clouds, were scudding[②] across the sky. The whole countryside was changing, shaking itself loose, into the true brightness of a July day. And as they sped along she was able to see not much trace at all of the recent past—no big puddles[③] in the fields, showing where the seed had washed out, no miserable spindly[④] cornstalks or lodged grain.

It occurred to her that she must tell Clark about this—that perhaps they had chosen what was for some freakish reason a very wet and dreary corner of the country, and there were other places where they could have been successful.

Or could be yet?

Then it came to her of course that she would not be telling Clark anything. Never again. She would not be concerned about what happened to him, or to Grace or Mike or Juniper or Blackberry or Lizzie Borden. If by any chance Flora came back, she would not hear of it.

This was her second time to leave everything behind. The first time was just like the old Beatles song—her putting the note on the table and slipping out of the house at five o'clock in the morning, meeting Clark in the church parking lot down the street. She was actually humming that song as they rattled away. *She's leaving home*, *bye-bye*. She recalled now how the sun was coming up behind them, how she looked at Clark's hands on the wheel, the dark hairs on his competent forearms, and breathed in the smell of the inside of the truck, a smell of oil and metal, tools and horse barns. The cold air of the fall morning blew in through the truck's rusted seams[⑤]. It was the sort of vehicle that

---

① drench: 使湿透
② scud: 疾行, 掠过
③ puddle: 水坑
④ spindly: 纤弱的, 细长的
⑤ seam: 裂缝

nobody in her family ever rode in, that scarcely ever appeared on the streets where they lived.

Clark's preoccupation on that morning with the traffic (they had reached Highway 401), his concern about the truck's behavior, his curt answers, his narrowed eyes, even his slight irritation at her giddy① delight—all of that thrilled her. As did the disorder of his past life, his avowed② loneliness, the tender way he could have with a horse, and with her. She saw him as the architect of the life ahead of them, herself as captive, her submission both proper and exquisite③.

"You don't know what you're leaving behind," her mother wrote to her, in that one letter that she received, and never answered. But in those shivering moments of early-morning flight she certainly did know what she was leaving behind, even if she had rather a hazy idea of what she was going to. She despised her parents, their house, their backyard, their photo albums, their vacations, their Cuisinart, their *powder room*, their walk-in closets, their underground lawn-sprinkling system. In the brief note she had written she had used the word authentic. *I have always felt the need of a more authentic kind of life. I know I cannot expect you to understand this.*

The bus had stopped now at the first town on the way. The depot④ was a gas station. It was the very station she and Clark used to drive to, in their early days, to buy cheap gas. In those days their world had included several towns in the surrounding countryside and they had sometimes behaved like tourists, sampling the specialties in grimy hotel bars. Pigs' feet, sauerkraut⑤, potato pancakes, beer. And they would sing all the way home like crazy hillbillies⑥.

But after a while all outings came to be seen as a waste of time and money. They were what people did before they understood the realities of their lives.

She was crying now, her eyes had filled up without her realizing it. She set herself to thinking about Toronto, the first steps ahead. The taxi, the house she had never seen, the strange bed she would sleep in alone. Looking in the phone book tomorrow for the addresses of riding stables, then getting to wherever they

---

① giddy: 轻狂的, 轻浮的
② avow: 公开承认, 声明
③ exquisite: 细腻的, 精致的
④ depot: 火车站或汽车站
⑤ sauerkraut: 德国泡菜
⑥ hillbilly: 乡巴佬

were, asking for a job.

She could not picture it. Herself riding on the subway or streetcar, caring for new horses, talking to new people, living among hordes of people every day who were not Clark.

A life, a place, chosen for that specific reason—that it would not contain Clark.

The strange and terrible thing coming clear to her about that world of the future, as she now pictured it, was that she would not exist there. She would only walk around, and open her mouth and speak, and do this and do that. She would not really be there. And what was strange about it was that she was doing all this, she was riding on this bus in the hope of recovering herself. As Mrs. Jamieson might say—and as she herself might with satisfaction have said—*taking charge of her own life*. With nobody glowering① over her, nobody's mood infecting her with misery.

But what would she care about? How would she know that she was alive?

While she was running away from him—now—Clark still kept his place in her life. But when she was finished running away, when she just went on, what would she put in his place? What else—who else—could ever be so vivid a challenge?

She had managed to stop crying, but she had started to shake. She was in a bad way and would have to take hold, get a grip on herself. "Get a grip on yourself," Clark had sometimes told her, passing through a room where she was scrunched② up, trying not to weep, and that indeed was what she must do.

They had stopped in another town. This was the third town away from the one where she had got on the bus, which meant that they had passed through the second town without her even noticing. The bus must have stopped, the driver must have called out the name, and she had not heard or seen anything in her fog of fright. Soon enough they would reach the major highway, they would be tearing along towards Toronto.

And she would be lost.

She would be lost. What would be the point of getting into a taxi and giving the new address, of getting up in the morning and brushing her teeth and going into the world? Why should she get a job, put food in her mouth, be carried by public transportation from place to place?

---

① glower：怒视
② scrunch：蜷缩

Her feet seemed now to be at some enormous distance from her body. Her knees, in the unfamiliar crisp pants, were weighted with irons. She was sinking to the ground like a stricken horse who will never get up.

Already the bus had loaded on the few passengers and the parcels that had been waiting in this town. A woman and a baby in its stroller were waving somebody good-bye. The building behind them, the cafe that served as a bus stop, was also in motion. A liquefying① wave passed through the bricks and windows as if they were about to dissolve. In peril of② her life, Carla pulled her huge body, her iron limbs, forward. She stumbled, she cried out, "Let me off."

The driver braked, he called out irritably, "I thought you were going to Toronto?" People gave her casually curious looks, nobody seemed to understand that she was in anguish.

"I have to get off here."

"There's a washroom in the back."

"No. No. I have to get off."

"I'm not waiting. You understand that? You got luggage underneath?"

"No. Yes. No."

"No luggage?"

A voice in the bus said, "Claustrophobia③. That's what's the matter with her."

"You sick?" said the driver.

"No. No. I just want off."

"Okay. Okay. Fine by me."

"*Come and get me. Please. Come and get me.*"

"*I will.*"

Question for Discussion

How do you understand Carla's two runaways?

---

① liquefy:液化,溶解
② in peril of:有……的危险
③ claustrophobia:幽闭恐惧症

References

[1] 张伯香. 英美文学选读[M]. 北京:外语教学与研究出版社,1999.
[2] 李正栓. 美国文学学习指南[M]. 北京:清华大学出版,2006.
[3] 张伯香. 英美文学教程学习指南[M]. 武汉:武汉大学出版社,2006.
[4] 来安方. 新编英美概况[M]. 郑州:河南人民出版社,2010.
[5] 刘守兰. 英美名诗解读[M]. 上海:上海外语教育出版社,2006.
[6] 杨仁. 20世纪美国文学史[M]. 青岛:青岛出版社,2000.
[7] 刁克利. 英美文学欣赏[M]. 北京:中国人民大学出版社,2003.
[8] 刘洊波. 英美文学史及作品选读[M]. 北京:高等教育出版社,2006.
[9] 福克纳. 喧嚣与骚动. [M]. 李文俊,译. 上海:上海译文出版社,1996.
[10] 杨仁敬. 20世纪美国文学史[M]. 青岛:青岛出版社,2000.
[11] 陶洁. 美国文学选[M]. 北京:高等教育出版社,2001.
[12] 吴伟仁. 美国文学史及选读[M]. 北京:外语教学与研究出版社,2002.
[13] 王守仁. 美国文学选读[M]. 北京:高等教育出版社,2002.
[13] 童明. 美国文学史[M]. 南京:译林出版社,2002.
[14] 杨岂深,龙文佩. 美国文学选读[M]. 上海:译文出版社,1985.
[15] 常耀信. 美国文学简史(修订版)[M]. 天津:南开大学出版社,2003.